More Than Magick

Rick Taubold

GOLD IMPRINT

PRESS

Dedication,
For my wife

September 2004
Published by Medallion Press, Inc.
225 Seabreeze Ave.
Palm Beach, FL 33480

Cover Illustration by Adam Mock

ISBN 0-9743639-8-7

Printed in the United States of America

For more great books visit www.medallionpress.com.

Acknowledgments

My brother, Lance, has for years encouraged my writing, given me his thoughts, and pushed me to get my novel published.

I thank Scott Bater, Jeff Packard, and Marilyn Hawryliak for reading the manuscript. Your nod of approval meant a lot.

From the time he began reading it, David Marton believed that this novel was worthy of publication. His suggestions made it better, and the many hours he spent helping me edit and fine tune the final draft were appreciated.

Many fine writers and friends at Zoetrope.com—too numerous to mention individually—offered insightful comments and sound advice.

Thanks to all the Medallion staff for their support. Pam Ficarella, my editor, nitpicked this to perfection.

GLOSSARY OF NAMES AND TERMS

Pronunciations are shown phonetically in brackets [ ]. The accented syllable is capitalized. The vowel pronunciation conventions are as follows:

ay = day	a = cat	ah = clock
e = let, air	ee = feet	
i = it	iy = eye	
oh = gold	oo = fool	
u = up		

ADANA [ah-DAH-nah]: A female vampire

ADOR [AY-dohr]: Homeworld (Magick) of the Elfaeden race

ALEX KESTEN: Jake Kesten's brother, not seen in the novel

ALIR [ah-LEER]: Daughter of Kart and close friend of Kedda in Rysten

ANDRIK [AN-drik]: A Town Guard of Rysten

AREL [AIR-el]: Older brother of Dayon

ARION [A-ree-ahn]: Main character, Elfaeden Mage living on Stracos

BAHRAT [bah-RAHT]: A person capable of using the Bahratic Power

BAHRATIC POWER: The power of creation enabled when the three Parton forces are combined

BEKKAH [BEK-kah]: A drug-yielding plant

BLACK ARTIFACTS: Any of several artifacts made by the ancient Yorben and which combine two or more of the Magick, Psi, or Pneuma powers, sometimes incorporating a circuit chip, to concentrate and enhance the Forces, such as the Tri-Lith and Staff of Chaos

BRYCE DUNCAN: Archaeologist friend of Jake

CARON WOOD [KE- rahn]: A dense wood; the doors of Arion's keep are made from it

COLONEL MADISON: (Jackson Andrew Madison) Scott's father

DANDRAY [dan-DRAY]: Home city of Enelle

DAYON [DAY-ahn]: Elf Mage born on Tava

DEV ANTOS [AN-tohs]: Mayor of Freetown, minor Mage, and friend of Arion.

DROGO [DROH-goh]: A thief in the town of Rysten

EARTH: Homeworld (Pneuma) of Jake, Scott, and the readers of this novel

ELFAEDEN [el-FAY-den]: True racial name of the Elves

ENELLE [e-NEL]: Daughter of Lord Hane from the world of Yandall

EREBOR [E-re-bohr]: Homeworld (Psi) of Kedda and the Yorben race

ESAK [EE-sak]: Runaway youth on Ranor and retrieved by Jen-Varth

FEHLEN [FAY-len]: Strong but dim-witted youth and charge of Arion

FEZECCAH [FE-ze-ka]: A female crystal dragon

FREETOWN: Town founded by Arion on world of Stracos

HAJEN [HAY-jen]: A Protector from Jen-Varth's dream

HASTAIN [hah-STAYN]: A settlement on Ranor

HOLOSTOS [hoh-LOHS-tohs]: Neighboring world (Psi) of Stracos, the next one out from its sun and homeworld of Ot-Vorell

ILKAF [IL-kahf]: A card player friend of Trax

JAKE KESTEN: (Dr. Jeremiah Avery Kesten) Main character; mathematician, and computer scientist from Earth

JEN-VARTH: A Protector currently residing on Ranor

JOCATHAN [joh-KAH-thahn]: Home city of Trax on the world of Thalar

JUN: A card game in the Kedda chapter

KARAYDEON [kah-RAY-dee-ahn]: Deceased Mage who originally imprisoned Orfo in a complex set of pocket universes

KART: Mage and proprietor of the Silver Spectre Inn in Rysten

KEDDA [KE-dah]: The mystery character

LORD HANE [hayn]: Enelle's father; ruler of Dandray

LYNN: Scott Madison's girlfriend, a biochemistry grad student, in Colorado, not seen in the novel

MAGICK: One of the three Parton forces, broadly the "magical" force

MARHESSE [mar-HESS]: A male crystal dragon

MOKA [MOH-ka]: An apprentice Mage/Apothecary, resident of Rysten, and friend of Trax

MONROE ADAM MADISON: Scott Madison's brother, not seen in the novel

MORTHEN [MOHR-thin]: A male vampire

MYLANE [my-LAYN]: Trax's female guardian

NIKKI QUIST: Proprietor of "The Vampire's Den" Inn in Freetown

NISTENNA [nis-TEN-ah]: Trax's first love

NYALLOS [ny-AH-lohs]: Neighboring world (Magick) of Stracos and the next one closer to its sun

ORFO [OHR-foh]: A malevolent S'pharn, currently imprisoned

OT-VORELL [AHT-vohr-EL]: A leader and councilman on planet Holostos

PARTON (PAHR-tahn) **FORCE**: The generic term (not used in the novel) for the three properties or forces of matter: Magick, Psi, Pneuma. It is as a fifth fundamental force in matter, not yet discovered by Earth scientists, to complement the strong, weak, electromagnetic, and gravitational forces already known

PIRRO [PEER-oh]: Young Protector cadet on Ranor

PNEUMA [NOO-mah]: One of the three Parton forces, the spiritual or psychic sensing force

PROTECTORS: An interplanetary organization, sort of a National Guard, providing protective and law-enforcement services for smaller worlds lacking the resources to do so themselves

PSI [sigh]: One of the three Parton forces, the force of mind projection and telepathy

QUASTOR [KWAS-tohr]: A town near Rysten

RANOR [rah-NOHR]: Current residence world (Pneuma) of Jen-Varth

RIADON [RY-ah-dahn]: A deceased Mage who invented the Spell Spheres bearing his name; these spheres can capture a single Magick spell and "replay" it later one time only

RYSTEN: Town in Thalar, current residence of Kedda and Kart

SCOTT MADISON (Jefferson Scott Madison): Main character from Earth, narrator of the story

SHADOW MASTER: A Mage/Necromancer and foe of Dayon on Tava

SILVER SPECTRE INN: An establishment owned by Kart in the town of Rysten

S'PHARN [sfahrn]: Homeworld (Psi) and racial name of the powerful Psi beings to which Orfo and Vraasz belong

STAFF OF CHAOS: Black Artifact given to Trax

STRACOS [STRAY-kohs]: World (Magick), which Arion now calls home

TARSK: A thief in the town of Rysten

TAVA [TAH-vah]: Homeworld (Magick) of Dayon

THALAR [thah-LAHR]: Homeworld (Magick) of Trax; current home of Kart

TRAX [tracks]: A young thief-become-Mage born in the town of Jocathan

TRI-LITH [TRY-lith]: A Yorben Black Artifact that combines the three Parton powers into the Bahratic Power

VRAASZ [vrahz]: Psi being who finds the Tri-Lith of the Yorben

WEYDA [WAY-dah]: Kart's wife and Alir's mother; she is deceased

XENNA [ZE-nah]: Homeworld (Pneuma) of Jen-Varth

YANDALL [yahn-DAHL]: Homeworld (Psi) of Enelle

YORBEN [YOHR-ben]: An ancient race of Psi Beings who made the Black Artifacts and are from the world of Erebor

ZIM: A friend of Arion and Fehlen, not seen in the novel

PROLOGUE

Four Years Ago: Monday, July 15, 1996

Jake hadn't expected the phone call from Bryce Duncan.

"Hiya, Jake."

He recognized the slight Australian accent. "Bryce?"

"Your one and only grad school roommate."

"It's good to hear from you. What've you been up to?"

"Still digging up the past, except I have a small problem that requires your kind of genius. Can you hop a flight tomorrow morning to scenic Upstate New York?"

Granted, Jake hadn't seen him in over two years because they'd both been busy, but this was a bit too impulsive, even for capricious Bryce. Still, a short vacation from this hot, humid Illinois summer sounded good. But . . .

"Can't do it. I'm in the middle of a project. How about next weekend?"

"That'll be too late."

Jake heard a nervous edge in Bryce's voice. "Bryce, what's this about?"

"I can't discuss it over the phone. Bring old clothes. Your ticket's waiting for you at the airport."

"Are you in some kind of trouble?"

"No, not yet. I'm relying on you to keep me out of it.

I know you're never out of bed before ten, but a 6:30 a.m. flight was the best I could arrange. You'll have to switch planes a couple of times, and there're no in-flight meals. Best I could do. Sorry. I'll meet you at the Plattsburgh airport late tomorrow afternoon."

✳ ✳ ✳

Bryce met him at Clinton County Airport wearing a khaki shirt and shorts. He wasn't quite as lean as Jake remembered. His sun-bleached brown hair now touched his shoulders, and he'd learned how to use a comb. It was good to see him, but . . . "What the hell's going on, Bryce?"

"Did you eat anything?"

"Only from the vending machines. Why am I here?"

"Well, I guarantee you a dinner to make up for it."

During the fifteen-minute drive to Ausable Chasm, at the southern tip of Lake Champlain, Bryce refused to talk about why he'd asked Jake to come here. He wanted to know all about Jake's research at Illinois.

They drove up to an RV nestled in the woods. "Whatever happened to roughing it?" Jake asked.

"It's out of fashion."

Bryce unloaded Jake's overnight bag from the trunk and pointed to a woman standing next to a gas grill. "Diane and I live in Plattsburgh."

"You got married and didn't tell me?"

"Not yet. Next June. Will you be my best man?" They walked over to the grill.

"Bryce, I'd be honored to be your best man, and I'm glad to see you again, but what's so urgent you had to bring me here?"

"Patience. We'll get to that. Diane, this is Jake Kesten."

She turned around, full dark hair, wonderfully prominent cheekbones on a tanned face, captivating brown eyes. "Bryce told me all about your times as roommates," she said, tongs in hand, "and the wild parties."

"We two geeks never got invited to any wild parties," Jake said.

Bryce grinned. "Right. I met Diane a year ago. She was a journalism major and wanted to interview an archaeologist. As I recall, the interview lasted all night. How's your situation at Illinois? Any serious relationships?"

"Just tension relief and sanity maintenance. That's about all I can handle for now. Most of the unmarried women at U. of I. are either too studious to be interested in anything serious or were cursed with cruel genes."

Bryce nodded. "Let's get you settled." He opened the door of the RV, and Jake stepped up inside.

"God, do I smell peppers and onions? I'm salivating."

"Oh, yeah. I remembered how much you like them. Throw your stuff on the bed in back. Bathroom's here."

Jake washed up and joined Bryce and Diane at the foldout table up front. Before Jake could ask him the question, Bryce said, "Eat and enjoy. We'll take a walk afterward."

Why was Bryce so calm today when he had sounded so nervous on the phone yesterday?

After they each ate a pound of medium-rare sirloin, Bryce took him outside—an hour or two of daylight was still left—to talk. "My boss, the esteemed Dr. Ferraro, has been pissed lately at his grad students who—through no fault of theirs—have not produced anything he can publish. He expected me, his postdoc, to remedy that situation. He knew my attention for detail, so he sent me here to re-survey this old Indian site for something useful. I didn't argue. With his foul mood, I was glad for the time away. Even though he's tenured, he takes 'publish or perish' too seriously."

"Bryce, *I'm* getting pissed off. You yank me here for something that can't wait another few days, then make it sound like it can."

"I just wanted you to relax first."

"I haven't been able to relax since I got your call. Explain. Now. What does this have to do with me?"

"Language translation." He looked at Jake. "I think I forgot to mention that on the phone."

Jake shook his head.

"I'd been digging here a few weeks, finding nothing. Then I got lucky. I'm not sure yet if it's good luck or bad luck. In any case, I doubt that we'll be able to publish my findings."

They walked down a slope. A pair of lanterns hung next to a cliffside entrance. Bryce lit both and handed one to Jake. "I spotted a crack in the hillside behind the over-growth. It took me two days to clear the debris and rocks. Duck, there's a nasty protrusion." Bryce rubbed the top of his head and faked a wince.

They entered a small cave about eight feet high and twenty feet in diameter. A uniformed body lay on the floor near the center. Jake saw it was a skeleton under the uniform once Bryce brought his lantern close to it. "His skull was cracked. I cleared away a lot of loose rocks around him. I suspect a cave-in killed him and buried the entrance," Bryce said.

"You flew me here to see a dead body?"

"Note the uniform is perfectly intact despite the flesh

having completely decayed away."

Jake looked at the coal black shirt, tight-weave pants with an Oriental-looking insignia on the leg, and dark green boots.

Bryce squatted and undid a press seal on the shirt. "Not Velcro. It's something I've never seen. The pants have a fly front with the same press seal. Except for a bit of mustiness in the cave, there was no odor when I opened it. This fellow's been here a long time. Tomorrow I expect the military to be all over this place like fleas on the family pet. That's why I needed you here today."

"*Military*? You find a body and you call the military instead of the police?"

"Trust me, this isn't a police matter, and I wasn't the one who called the military. A few inches from the skeleton's hand was a smooth, black stone. I work out of Stony Brook, which is too far from here for a quick trip, so I took it to the SUNY college in Plattsburgh, to a discreet technician I've worked with before. We measured the stone's density at two point seven, same as granite. The fluorescence analysis equipment—to determine mineral composition— was down for maintenance, so we x-rayed it. Here, take a look."

Bryce pulled out of his pocket an object the size and shape of a charcoal briquette. Jake ran his fingers over the surface, feeling them drag slightly against its matte finish. He handed it back.

"We would have been fine if his boss—an asshole who we thought had left for the day—hadn't walked in and gotten a look over our shoulders before we could stop him. We knew we were screwed. He called his friends at the Plattsburgh Air Force Base."

"Why would he notify the military?" Jake asked.

"Besides being an asshole, he got a nice research grant from the Air Force, so he sucks up to them every chance he gets."

"So, what did he see?"

Bryce grinned evilly. "The x-ray showed what we think is a microchip embedded in it. There's another twist. I sent a bone sample for carbon dating. It came back with a carbon-14 content one point three times *greater* than what a living specimen should contain."

"I don't understand."

"While an organism is alive, the carbon-14 ratio in its body maintains an equilibrium with the environment. After it dies, the radioactive decay takes over. Every 5700 years, half of the C-14 decays."

"I think I remember some of that from a freshman chem course, but what do you mean that the carbon-14 content was too high?"

"Any organic material should have a C-14 content equal to or less than what's in the carbon dioxide in the atmosphere. If it's greater, then either the lab screwed up—but they said they ran it three times to be sure they hadn't—or the sample was exposed to radiation. The black stone was not radioactive, and my Geiger counter picked up no radiation around the area."

"There's no other explanation?"

"Just one. After the C-14 results, I took a second bone sample to a biochemist at Stony Brook who works with ancient DNA. To cover my ass, I told him I thought it might belong to a Pleistocene mammal. He said it was more human than anything, but it matched nothing in the databases. He was curious about where I'd gotten it. I said I'd get back to him. Meanwhile, I had given a small piece of the uniform and the scroll to a forensic chemist I know."

"What scroll?"

Bryce reached into a crevice and pulled out a cylinder six inches long. "Feel."

Jake rubbed his fingers over it. "Plastic?"

"Protein. Similar in composition to spider silk, but with a couple of unusual amino acids. It's highly stable, which explains why it didn't decay. The chemist said it was similar to stuff he knew the military's working on. He's still analyzing the uniform. It's a polymer he's not familiar with."

"So exactly what are you suggesting?"

"This skeleton—guy—is not from Earth. And this is where you come in." Bryce unrolled the scroll. "I need you to decipher these."

Jake examined the scrawls. "They almost look Oriental."

"They're nothing I recognize, and my research came up negative. I called you because you're the expert in this area."

"I don't know anything about ancient languages."

"That paper you wrote on language decoding algorithms from your PhD research was brilliant. This is a new language. Here's where you test your work in the real world."

"I wouldn't know where to start."

"Remember, I know what your grad school GPA was, genius. You'll figure out something. Meanwhile, I'll try to keep your name out of it. Here's how I see it happening: I lie and tell them I found the black stone outside the cave. Then, I say this may be an Indian burial site—even though

I'm sure it's not—and that they'll need permission from Indian Affairs to move the skeleton or anything inside the cave. They'll cordon off the area, and no one will get in or out. An Indian Affairs rep will come out and, seeing the uniform, agree that it's not an Indian skeleton and let them take it away. At that point, they will strap me to a chair, aim nasty bright lights at me, inject me with turn-your-brain-to-mush drugs, and threaten to dissect my nuts for good measure if I don't spill my guts."

"That'd dampen your wedding plans too."

"I'm glad one of us finds this amusing."

"You're exaggerating, Bryce."

"Yeah. There are stories about what happens to archaeologists who find certain stuff and fail to report it to the proper authorities in a timely manner. I made photo enlargements of the scroll for you. I'll put it back and pretend surprise when they find it." He gave Jake a serious look. "Diane is the only other person who knows you're here. I paid for your plane ticket with cash. I won't mention you until I have no other choice. You should be safe for a few days."

Jake picked up his lantern. "Safe from what?"

"A government incursion into your private life."

"Shit, Bryce. There goes my government grant."

"If you can decipher that writing, we'll be heroes. They might offer us cushy government jobs."

"Or your imagined interrogation session might become a reality. Why didn't you report it right away?"

"Because last year I made an important find near an Indian burial ground. I reported it, waited for permission to proceed, and got it. Know what happened? Someone along the way, who knew for sure it was not on a burial ground, got there first, and took the credit! That skeleton isn't Indian, and this cave is not on Indian land. It's public land, no permission needed. But I guess we still get screwed."

"Maybe not."

The next day, Bryce took him to the airport, after a much shorter vacation than Jake had counted on. He got on the commuter plane not sure what Bryce had really discovered, but determined as hell to find out.

✳ ✳ ✳

Jake got back to his apartment around nine that night. He dropped his overnight bag on the floor and flopped onto the couch facing a black TV screen. Two days ago he'd been comfortably entrenched in near academic anonymity. What the hell was he supposed to do now? Sure, his language translation program worked. His thesis proved how it could break down a language into its basic linguistic elements, but he'd only tried it on known Earth languages. Bryce's mystery language wasn't from Earth. It defied description, despite him saying it looked Oriental. If Jake was certain that no way could he decipher even the smallest part of it in a few days, he was more certain that, as beat as he was from the last two days, no way could he sleep now. He closed his eyes anyway.

He was slowly convincing his body to relax when he felt a buzzing inside him and a slight shiver. When his body suddenly struck the floor, he opened his eyes.

"Please forgive the abrupt transference."

Where the hell was he? The room was lit by candles evenly spaced in sconces around the dark wood paneling. The air was lightly fragrant with spice. In front of him stood a . . . humanoid in a dark red robe. Behind this person were a desk and bookcase.

"Who the hell are you, and where the hell am I?"

"I am Arion, an Elfaeden Mage. You are in my keep because I need you to prepare a young man named Scott Madison for his future."

"I don't know anyone by that name."

"I will show you where to find him."

1

JAKE

Two Years Ago, Spring 1998: Planet Earth

My senior year in college had ended. It was Thursday morning, the day after finals. Two things kept me on campus: a graduation ceremony on Sunday and my job. I was dorm resident advisor and had to stay until the dorm was empty. I received free room and board in exchange for babysitting undergraduates. In the past year I had learned to be tolerant; I had learned to counsel; I had learned when to shut my door—all valuable, real-world skills.

The RA's room had a coveted location near the door, although making it easy to sneak women in and out of the room undetected surely was not the designer's original intent. However, this coming Sunday I, J. Scott Madison, was graduating at my virginal best, having been scared spermless by the do-it-and-watch-it-rot Army training films thrust upon an impressionable, pubescent child of twelve. At least, that's where I had convinced myself the blame lay.

UCSD sits above a gorgeous beach along North Torrey Pines Road in San Diego, where the students surf at lunch. I didn't surf, and I didn't worship the Great Yellow Ball in the sky. Scholarships aside, at those tuition prices I was there to study, as the Colonel frequently reminded me.

With nothing else to do until graduation, I caught up on my TV viewing. During the commercials I alternately considered grad school in marine biology and a real job. The Colonel still hoped I'd choose career military, as my brother had.

I'd gone on a few job interviews, mostly for the experience, and had papered my dorm door with the rejection letters. For sure I wanted to get away from La Jolla, second only to Beverly Hills with its pretentious inhabitants.

When TV soap opera time arrived, I grabbed my wallet, locked my door, and went hunting for lunch. An ad on the dorm bulletin board outside my room caught my eye:

> *WANTED*: College graduate with no outstanding obligations interested in fieldwork in a war-like atmosphere. If you are a marine biologist looking for that last hurrah before undertaking grad school, this job is for you. No experience necessary. Must like to travel. Excellent pay. No résumé required. Leave message at the number below.

A phone number followed.

No résumé required? Was this a prank, aimed at me, a last dig from those under my care? The monetary reference piqued my interest, though. I needed money for the summer, and I didn't want to live at home.

During lunch at the all-you-can-eat-buffet at Pizza Hut, the ad played games with my mind. If I went to grad school, I was still fair game for my father's career suggestions. What if the ad wasn't a prank? What if it was my chance at autonomous, Colonel-free living? When I got back to the dorm, I wrote down the number and went into my room to call.

A machine identified itself as Jake. It asked for my name, phone number, and the date and time I was calling. It thanked me and promised to get back to me. I gave my dorm phone number, not my cell. If he was legit, he'd call right away. If not, my phone would be disconnected Monday with no forwarding number. I'd already exchanged email addresses with any friends I wanted to stay in touch with.

Why had I called? The ad said, "Travel." I hated to travel. Life as an Army brat had dragged me through six different grade schools and five different high schools.

"Field work in a war-like atmosphere." That chimed military, and reinforced the prank aspect.

And how many job applications are made by leaving a message on an answering machine?

* * *

Nine a.m. the following Monday morning, with a B.S. officially appended to my name, I packed the last of my college memorabilia, a senescent toothbrush, and my beloved, face-scouring razor that had faithfully brought me to attention for numerous early-morning exams.

Only two other students were still in the dorm, a sophomore who had stayed to see his brother graduate—he was leaving shortly—and a junior who had taken an on-campus summer job and was moving into off-campus housing today. Where was *I* going?

Someone knocked on my door. "It's open." Probably one of the two dorm stragglers coming to wish me luck with my life, although I couldn't imagine them up this early.

"Do you normally invite men into your room this early in the morning?"

I came to attention—force of habit—and stared at the body behind the unfamiliar voice. "Excuse me?"

"You wanted a job." He made it a statement.

How did he know? "The bulletin board ad? I figured that was a prank."

"So why did you call?"

"Then you're Jake?"

"Yep. I've been called a prick, but never a prank. Is that modern college slang for the same thing?" He stepped forward and proffered his hand over the bed.

I shrugged and shook his hand. He was six feet tall and well acquainted with the gym. Short, kinky, black hair came to a point on his forehead, and inch-long sideburns framed a square jaw with a shaved-last-night stubble. I guessed him late twenties.

"Ready for the interview?" he said.

"I'm not exactly dressed for an interview."

He smiled. "Neither am I." His barely ironed, button-down white shirt, jeans, and deck shoes were still better than my denim shorts and tan, pocket T-shirt. And he was wearing a nouveau formal, black leather tie.

"I have a flight at twelve forty-five," I said.

"We'll be done long before that."

This had to be a joke, but since I'd finished packing and had nothing better to do for the moment, it might prove amusing. I offered him my chair and sat on the bed. "Sorry, my résumés are packed away."

"My ad said none required." He pointed to my suitcase. "I appreciate my employees being ready to go on a moment's notice." He pulled a tattered, spiral notebook from his shirt pocket and flipped it open. He read, "Name: Jefferson Scott Madison."

"Scott. I don't use my first name."

But he continued. "Place of residence: Fort Bragg, North Carolina. Age: Twenty-two. Height: Six-four. Weight: One-ninety. Major: Biology, marine concentration. Minors: Art and Literature. Marital status: . . . Single." He looked up. "Any kids?"

"You said I was single."

His eyes drilled into mine. "Marriage is not a prerequisite to procreation, as I'm sure your biology classes adequately taught you." He grinned, displaying perfect, white teeth. "You're still a virgin."

I felt the warmth rising in my neck. "That's a rather personal question." But it wasn't a question.

He dropped the smile. "This is a personal interview."

"I think the question is considered discriminatory."

"That's only for EOEs."

I tilted my head at him.

"Equal Opportunity Employer. I'm not, so I don't give a shit."

Keep cool, Scott. "Unless you're recruiting male prostitutes, what would my sexual activity have to do with this job?"

Above his blue eyes, thick eyebrows came within a quarter inch of joining. He raised one. "What I don't need is someone whose first priority in life is getting laid. You're the Colonel's boy, all right. Evasive."

"You know my father? Did he send you?"

"Yes, I do, and no, he didn't." He pushed back the chair and stood up. "Let's go get some breakfast."

"I have a plane to catch."

"Plenty of time. I'm hungry, I'm buying, and I guarantee you won't miss your flight because I'm leaving at the same time. I'll drive you to the airport to save you cab fare. Besides, you must have questions about the job."

"I'm not interested."

"Not even in free food? College students—"

"Ex-student."

"—never turn down free food. It's a law of the universe."

He drove us in his rental car to a nearby café frequented by the college crowd. Today most of the tables were empty. After we sat and ordered, he asked, "Questions about the job?"

"Was that ad meant for me?"

"Yes."

"What if I hadn't called?"

"I'd have come anyway."

"You must have had other inquiries."

"Two. I told them the job was already filled."

"Even military recruiters aren't that cocky," I said. "It must be nice."

"What is?"

"Living in fantasyland. Do you work for my father?"

"Not directly. I'm a civilian consultant at Fort Bragg."

"Finally, a straight answer?"

"I told him I was headed this way and asked if he wanted me to say hi to you."

"What did he say to that?"

" 'Keep the hell away from my son!' " He did a good imitation of the Colonel's resonant, authoritative voice.

"That makes sense. He tries to keep unsavory, civilian influences out of my life."

"I don't consider myself unsavory."

Our food arrived. "Okay, what's the job involve?" I finally asked.

"Do you like computer hackers?"

"It depends on whether they're my friends."

He cut a piece of sausage and put it in his mouth. He chewed and swallowed. "The first prerequisite is willingness to do the job."

"You haven't told me what the job is yet."

"Classified. I can't tell you until you accept."

This guy seemed to be doing his best to make me *not* want the job. He knew who I was and knew my father, but this wasn't my father's style, unless my father had gotten more desperate than I thought.

I looked at my watch, then at him. "Yes, sir. No, sir. Anything you say, sir. No fucking way, sir. Military is not my favorite color. Clear enough? Thank you for breakfast. Now, if that offer of a ride to the airport is still open, I would appreciate it. If not, please drive me back to the dorm and I'll call a cab."

He raised an eyebrow. " 'Military is not my favorite color?' I like that."

* * *

Back at the dorm I was going to change into a short-sleeved shirt and long pants, but he said, "Just the shirt, keep the shorts. It's a long flight, be comfortable. Who's going to care what you look like on the plane?"

I made sure I hadn't forgotten anything before we loaded my bags into the car. I sat quietly during the drive and wondered when he'd bring up the job again.

At the airport he drove past where he should have dropped me off.

"Um, you should have let me off back there."

"No." He stopped at a pedestrian crossing. "I canceled your reservation yesterday. Your credit card will be refunded."

"What the *fuck* is going on?"

His jaw muscles tightened. "Saving you money. Commercial airlines are such a rip-off, and I really don't like my employees using the f-word."

"I'm not your employee!" A muffled thunk greeted my attempt to open the car door.

A roguish smile crept out of the side of his mouth. "I wouldn't want you falling out of a moving vehicle and hurting yourself."

The vehicle wasn't moving.

"But, if want to leave—"

The lock thunked again.

"Remember that I'm holding your luggage hostage."

"And *I'm* not a hostage?"

"No." He pressed the accelerator. A few minutes later we drove up to where small, private planes were parked. He got out, unloaded my three bags plus his overnight one, and set them next to the car. Then he courteously opened my door and gestured for me to get out. He pointed to a dual prop plane. "Ever fly in one of those?"

I folded my arms. "No."

"Well, it's what's taking you home as soon as you get your ass out of the car."

I got out.

"Watch the luggage, and don't wander off while I return this to the rental folks."

"You trust me not to leave?"

"Yep."

He got back in and drove away. The only place I could have gone was to the commercial terminals to try to get on the flight I was supposed to be on. I sat on one of my suitcases and stared at the small plane. What was this guy all about, and why was *I* trusting *him*?

So far he hadn't given me any reason *not* to trust him. He'd never threatened me. Locking the car door on me was no threat because I could have unlocked it myself. He'd done it to get my attention. As a kid, I remembered once asking my father if I could go for a ride in a small plane, but there was no way this man could know that. Even if he'd spoken at length with my father about me, the Colonel always brushed aside frivolous wishes that had no direct bearing on the future he saw for his sons. Although I'd had a logical-decision and cold-hard-facts upbringing—tempered by a sympathetic mother—and never believed in things like intuition, something told me to trust this guy.

I felt that if I had pressed the issue on my original plan for getting home, he would have respected my wish.

Less than ten minutes later he reappeared. "Ready to fly cross-country?"

"Where's the pilot?"

That roguish smile again. "And you get the copilot's seat."

He picked up his bag and my heaviest suitcase. "Why do students keep all their books and notes? Sell your books and get some return on your investment. They'll be outdated in a couple of years anyway. As for notebooks, ninety percent of what the professors say is in those overpriced textbooks, and the other ten percent is irrelevant or intuitively obvious. You carry a notebook to class for two reasons: so the professors won't think you're cocky, and to record significant phone numbers. Grab your bags."

He distributed our luggage among three of the plane's six seats. "Wait here while I go check in." He disappeared into one of the buildings, returning a few minutes later. "All set. I've registered a three-day flight plan."

"Three?"

"Scenic route. We fly over the Grand Canyon and buzz Pike's Peak. By then it'll be close to dark. I made overnight reservations in Colorado Springs. The next night we spend in Champaign-Urbana, Illinois. I want to say hi to some friends at U of I. I did my postdoctoral work there."

"You have a PhD?"

"I don't boast about it."

"So, I should call you Doctor?"

"If you like. We'll have you home by mid-afternoon on Wednesday."

"And I should trust you on this?"

"Why not?"

I could think of a dozen reasons, but in truth I was looking forward to the trip. Air Force brats got rides in high-tech planes, but Army brats got stuck in low-tech jeeps. "I need to call my parents about the change in plans."

"You already emailed your father."

"No, I didn't."

"Your email told him that a college buddy who has a pilot's license was flying your way to see some friends, log some hours, and wanted company."

Son of a bitch. I now understood his computer hacker remark in the San Diego cafe.

I got into the plane. He walked around it once then got in and went through his pre-flight checks, started the engines, did more checks, and radioed the tower for clearance. "Now, let's see the United States as they ought to be seen, not through clouds at thirty thousand feet."

He told me I had the pleasure of flying in a Piper Seneca PA34 with a cruising velocity of 160 miles per hour. From what I could tell, he was a good pilot. Mostly, the weather accommodated us. However, the rising thermals—his explanation—over the Rockies put my stomach out of sorts. He made sure I had an airsick bag in hand before demonstrating his bank-and-turn maneuvers around Pike's Peak.

"You bio majors can rip the guts out of dead animals in anatomy class with no problem, but you upchuck over a little plane ride. On the floor behind you is a cooler with some cans of Coke. Strike the can on the bottom before you open it. We're at reduced pressure, and we'll get showered if you don't. This plane's mine, so I don't want it messed up."

When I was feeling better, he asked, "How come your parents didn't attend your graduation?"

"No way I wanted my father there reminding me how I should take up a real man's profession and join the Army."

"I share your sentiments. What about your Mom? Mothers love to see their sons graduate."

"She has sinus problems and gets migraines when she flies. I had a friend video tape the ceremony for her."

* * *

The next day we stopped in Kansas City for gas and continued on to Illinois for our second overnight stay. We left there around noon and landed in Fayetteville just after four. He packed me into a cab, paying the driver in advance. "See ya later."

I looked back at him as the cab pulled away. Several things struck me. He'd never told me his last name. He hadn't brought up the job again during the trip—just as well, because I knew I didn't want it. Despite his lack of forthrightness, I was sure it was not biology related. And, "See ya later?"

Fort Bragg stretches for miles and miles and isn't high security. Having spent as little time here as possible, I didn't know my way around well enough to give the cab driver directions. The last place I wanted us to end up was on the Playground, what they called the artillery range, dodging live artillery. I had him drop me at one of the manned gates where I called Dad to send a driver.

The Colonel met me outside his office building as we pulled up. "Your email surprised me, Scott," he said with his usual military formality. "Your mother and I are glad you're home for the summer. Any plans yet for the fall?" The Colonel never minced words.

"Undecided, sir." He still expected my brother and me to address him that way.

"Take your time. We Madisons aren't known for making hasty decisions."

Take my time? Was an alien occupying his body?

"I have a staff meeting and some reports to go over. I won't be home until late." Late for him was eight o'clock. "I'm sure you'll be in bed." The condescending smile.

He'd been to college, but I think he'd forgotten the all-nighter concept.

"Be here tomorrow morning at nine. I've invited someone to meet you."

Never "please." But there it was. Colonel Madison hadn't been replaced by an alien. "Take your time" meant "sleep on it." I had hoped that he wouldn't bug me, this summer at least, as a graduation present. The driver took me and my luggage home where Mom would be waiting to see my graduation video.

∗ ∗ ∗

The honking jeep outside my window at eight-thirty a.m. quashed my planned sleep-in. I had not intended to attend my father's make-Scott-miserable party. I didn't bother shaving. What should I wear though? I considered scrungy jeans, but they all looked pretty sad, and deciding which pair was the scrungiest was just too tough this early in the morning. Inspiration struck. Cammies! I'd bought them as a personal protest this past year in San Diego so he didn't know about them. Sneakers completed the look.

At ten to nine, I got in the jeep. The driver, a corporal I knew, nodded his approval. I think he envied me.

Five minutes later, I entered Dad's office, identical to all the other offices. Remove the nameplates and family pictures, and you couldn't tell whose office was whose. Dad stood up behind the gray metal desk that had taken root there in World War II. His narrowed eyes affirmed my sartorial decision.

Off to the left I noticed a man with his back to me. His khaki uniform had camouflaged him among the dull and drab surroundings.

"Scott, I'd like you to meet Dr. Jeremiah Kesten."

The doctor turned around as I shuffled forward. *Jake? Shit! A setup after all!* I made an involuntary fist.

"I am very pleased to meet you, Scott," he said.

Something in my facial expression must have alerted him

23

because he subtly shook his head. Khaki slacks, white shirt, and blue tie. No uniform. No insignia or fruit salad. So, he hadn't lied about being non-military.

"Your father has told me about you. Having a son graduate with top honors gives him a lot to be proud of." He extended his hand with military courtesy and stiffness. I slowly extended mine, which he promptly grabbed and shook.

A moment of recovery and a throat clearing later, I acknowledged, "Doctor Kesten."

He nodded.

So, his real name was Jeremiah. How prophetic. But what was going on here?

"Dr. Kesten has some important contacts," the Colonel said. "He wants to talk with you about career choices." Dad had reluctantly accepted my biology major. He would have preferred my being an engineer like my older brother Adam, something the Army could use, but he considered *marine* biology a mortal sin. This was a setup, but who had set it up?

"Sir, I'd like to take your son to breakfast." Jake turned his head at me and said with sickening politeness, "If that's all right with Scott."

I cleared my throat again. "Fine with me."

"If you'll excuse us, sir?" He gave Dad a snappy salute, gave me a "let's go" look, about-faced, and headed for the door.

I followed. Over my shoulder I saw Dad's pleased-with-himself facial expression.

Jake slowed to let me catch up and said in a throaty whisper, "Not a word until we're out of the building." He looked askance. "Nice attire."

After we got into his jeep, he said, "You looked ready to punch me."

"In the shadows you looked like you had on a uniform. You're lucky you're not military."

"He treats me like I am and keeps trying to enlist me, and I keep telling him, 'Captain's bars would be nice.' "

"Little chance of that."

He sighed. "I know." He started the jeep and headed toward the main gate.

"I chose UCSD because it was on the opposite coast from him and constantly prayed that the Army didn't transfer him again. So, it's Doctor Jeremiah Kesten?"

"Yep. My job title is senior analyst."

"You lied that my Dad knew about your coming to see me."

"No, I didn't. I told you that I told him I was headed your way and did he want me to stop by to say hello."

"He'd dissect your nuts if he knew—"

He punched the brake and clutch. The jeep lurched to a halt, just short of a skid.

I thrust out a hand to brace myself barely in time. I snapped my head at him. "What the hell's wrong?"

He dropped his hand to the gearshift, eased it into neutral, and let out the clutch. Without looking up he said, " 'Dissect your nuts.' Where did you hear that expression?" His face was white.

"Nowhere. It just sort of popped into my head." Whoa. "Sorry. I was out of line."

He suddenly smiled. "Let's get breakfast." But I could tell that he hadn't dismissed it completely.

After we passed through the main gate, he asked, "How come you go by 'Scott'? A name like 'Jefferson' makes you sound important."

"Maybe for someone else. Our genealogy traces back to President James Madison. The Colonel never told you?"

"Never came up."

"By tradition the sons are named after presidents. He's Jackson Andrew Madison. His father was Lincoln Tyler Madison. I was supposed to be Jefferson Thomas Madison, but Mom told him it was a cruel name to bestow on a boy these days, and Thomas was her first boyfriend's name."

"Where did 'Scott' come from?"

"Her father's name. He's never let her forget that she broke a family tradition, and that breaking it was likely what took my life off its destined career military path."

"And you didn't use 'Jeff' because . . ."

"When your classmates find out it's short for 'Jefferson,' you get mocked like hell. I asked Mom to enroll me as J. Scott Madison in my second high school. My older brother, by two years, had it worse than me. Monroe Adam Madison. In his junior year he tried the first-initial, middle-name ploy. They called him Madam Madison, and he didn't have the tall genes that I got so he lost the fights he got into, and started working out. Once, he came home with bloody knuckles and a blood-smeared face. 'Lose another one, Adam?' I asked.

" 'That's his blood, not mine. He insulted our sister.'

" 'We don't have a sister.'

" 'Nobody's sister should have that said about her.' "

"While we're talking names, where did 'Jake' come from?"

"It's an acronym. J for Jeremiah, A for Avery, the K-E should be obvious."

"You don't like 'Jerry'?"

"Jerry isn't a rogue's name, but Jake is."

"What are you a doctor of?"

"Mathematics."

"So what's the government do with a mathematician?"

"Officially, I work on complexity theory applied to NP-complete problems. Did you take any computer science?"

"I avoided the geek classes."

"NP-complete problems don't have easy or structured solutions. Theory says you can only solve them by what amounts to brute force, like breaking complex codes, in large amounts of time. Of course, the Army doesn't believe in theoretical limitations. I'm sure you know they don't define portability by weight. If they can find enough lackeys to carry it, it's portable. On paper, they pay me to accomplish the impossible—Army Intelligence at its finest."

"What do they pay you to do *off* paper?"

"Do you have Top Secret clearance, young Mr. Madison?"

"Nope."

"Can I trust you?"

"I wouldn't."

"The job's not really classified, just kept under wraps. Unofficially, they pay me to hack into computers, usually private ones, and destroy information they believe falls under military jurisdiction. When hacking fails, I make an on-site visit, and I'm authorized to use deadly force against the offending PCs."

I looked for some reassurance that he was joking. "You're serious?"

"When I picked you up, I was supposedly attending a seminar in Los Angeles. Of course, I never attended."

"After you asked Dad about visiting me, he would have had someone check on you. I'm sure of that."

"Thanks to this wonderful age of computers, I can be two places at once. I checked in and out of the hotel's computer, right on schedule, all automated from back home. Besides, I already knew most of what was being presented. I can fake it if anyone challenges me."

He pulled into a shabby diner. "Breakfast beckons. This place looks like a hole, but I dare you to find better pancakes and waffles anywhere in North Carolina."

In college, breakfast was an occasion I rose for only when I absolutely had to, but I agreed with his assessment. He got off on every bite, a sight bordering on the obscene. Our conversation resumed after his pleasure centers returned to normal.

"How did you find time to finish grad school, learn to fly, and become a mercenary?" I asked him.

"Mercenary?"

"What would you call destroying innocent people's computers for profit?"

"They're not innocent. To answer your question, I was good. Finished grad school at twenty-five, met your Dad after you started UCSD, and four years later, here I am dragging his son into the depths of my depravity."

"You should consider teaching. It's the same thing."

"I've thought about it."

"Were you a disappointment to your research advisor?"

"That's cruel, but no, not really. I always was more of a computer scientist than a mathematician anyway. Since computers at the University of Illinois in 1976 helped solve a famous and previously unsolved problem known as the four-color map theorem, computer science has become a semi-respectable part of mathematics." He looked me straight in the eye. "Do you want to work with me? I can't promise you fame or a long life, but it'll be lucrative and occasionally dangerous."

I leaned forward. "Why not."

Maybe I should have questioned his motives, like why did he want someone like me? Mysteries aside, I saw him as my salvation.

* * *

The following fall, Boulder, Colorado, became my new home, heaven to all who worshiped the snow-covered slopes. I didn't ski. Neither did Jake, but we both derived sadistic pleasure from watching those fools who thought they could. And the snow bunnies enhanced the scenery. Jake said he had always wanted to live here.

He got a part-time faculty position at the University of Colorado to conceal his covert activities and to provide him with a legitimate means of inflicting mental anguish on students. He suggested that I apply to grad school to keep myself out of trouble. I was accepted in the biochemistry program for the following spring. He somehow managed a tuition waiver for me.

Although he started paying me right away as his partner, I wasn't doing that much. What he paid me more than covered living expenses, and he made sure I had health insurance. There was another puzzle though. My paycheck came from him, not from the government. If they were paying him enough for two, he could have lived high and fancy, yet he chose a modest, homey apartment. From what I could tell, he really didn't need me, so it wasn't much of a partnership. Mostly, he just taught me the finer points of computer hacking, techie stuff that I found I liked. I asked myself if Colonel Madison was behind any of this. Had he used Jake to hoodwink me into something I really enjoyed and let me continue my education? Then, he could later yank the Persian carpet from under my feet and leave me only two options: fending for myself or enlisting to keep the job. In all of my twenty-two years I'd never known the Colonel to be devious. Jake had agreed with me on that. Everything traced back to Jake and *his* agenda.

"Why me?" I asked him.

"To train you," he replied.

"For what?"

"For your future. Whatever it turns out to be." Then he said, "You're the brother I never got the time to appreciate."

* * *

Spring came fast, and grad school kept me pretty busy. I studied a lot. Jake's training of me consisted of now and then accompanying him on one of his on-site jobs. That summer, a year after meeting Jake, I discovered Lynn, a psychology graduate student. So far, she and I were just friends, maybe a little more than that—but I was still a virgin. She didn't seem averse to sex, but neither had she suggested it. And I still had that wait-until-it's-right thing going on inside me. For all I knew, I might have been part of her graduate research.

Jake found an attractive, computer science postdoc. His nightly romps in his bedroom distracted me from studying.

"The tenant next door is leaving at the end of October. Separate apartments will offer us more options," he suggested.

Nice guy that he was, he offered to move. I didn't argue.

In December he invited me to an on-campus karate

demonstration in which he was participating. I figured I'd enjoy seeing him get mangled. He failed to tell me that he was the demonstrator. He made it look so easy, and his finesse entranced me. If he could do it, so could I. I asked him for lessons.

"On two conditions," he said. "First, you agree to my exercise program, which will add muscle and help protect against broken bones. Second, you take my grad math class in the spring. Math will give you mental muscle."

"Deal!" A good physique wouldn't do me any harm, and I was good at math. How hard could *Number Theory* be?

$$* * *$$

Monday, first day of class: He greeted us, took attendance, picked up his chalk, and began, "Consider this problem. An Arab has seven camels and three sons. He dies. In his will he leaves one-half of the camels to the eldest son, one-fourth to the middle son, and one-eighth to the youngest. How can you divide the camels among the sons and avoid a confrontation with animal rights' advocates?"

One self-proclaimed genius thrust up his hand. "It can't be done, Dr. Kesten."

Jake arched his eyebrows. "Maybe you should drop the class." He turned to the chalkboard. "A wise man with one camel comes along and adds it to the herd, making eight. The sons each take their share and the wise man leaves with his original camel." On the board he annotated.

"It's a trick!" the genius protested.

Jake faced the class. "But it perfectly solves the problem. Now, what if the father had seventeen camels? Does there exist a set of simple fractions such that adding and then subtracting one camel would provide a solution? Yes, and they are 1/2, 1/3, 1/9. Your homework is to determine how many different herd sizes exist that satisfy these conditions, namely, all of the fractions must be in the form of 1/x; you have to add, then later subtract just one camel; no camels can be sacrificed in the solving of this problem; and a younger son must not receive more camels than an older son. Clear?" He dismissed the class early.

On Wednesday, the genius thrust up his hand before Jake even asked. "The answer is fourteen, Dr. Kesten."

"Ah, you found the June 1992 *Scientific American* article that discussed the problem." The genius slowly lowered his hand. "However, it asked how many different solutions, sets of fractions, existed. I asked how many different herd sizes there were. Besides, if you had checked the solutions in the article, you would have found two of them to be incorrect—camel deaths would occur. Even *Scientific American* makes mistakes. Anyone else?"

No one had the correct answer of nine.

The next week, Jake popped a quiz on us. After class, several students, including the faux genius, went up to him and said they were dropping the class. I wondered if I should have done the same.

The martial arts training was equally painful. He also made me learn the Japanese terms and quizzed me frequently. After one week of his mental and physical torture, my body ached, my brain throbbed, my hair hurt, and my brain cells were ready to strangle each other.

That evening we had dinner at my apartment. Jake did the cooking. Afterward and after listening to my complaints of the damage he'd done to my body, he assured me, "Working out will improve your sex life."

"I don't have a sex life."

"My point exactly."

The phone rang. I answered it.

"Jake?" the male voice said.

"This is Scott."

"I must have the wrong number."

"No, Jake's right here. May I tell him who's calling?"

"Bryce Duncan," the voice said.

I handed Jake the portable phone. "For you. Don't forget to lock the door when you leave. I'm gonna crash for the next two days."

Jake nodded as I headed for bed.

∗ ∗ ∗

"Jake Kesten."

"Jake, it's Bryce. I have some updates for you."

"Hang on a second." Phone in hand, Jake walked out into the hallway and shut the door to Scott's apartment. "Okay, Bryce, what's this about?"

"You never told me you'd moved. I called your old phone number, in Illinois, and that now belongs to someone else. Am I calling Colorado?"

"Boulder. I thought I told you to stick to email—for security."

"A phone call is more personal. Who answered the phone?"

"Did you call to tell me something important or to interrogate me? That was Scott Madison. He's my . . . trainee."

"Poor guy."

"Bryce, why the phone call?"

"They finally gave me the detailed DNA analysis of the

skeleton. God knows how long they've had it and never told me. Of course, we both know what slow movers these government guys are."

"The point?"

"It's human, very human. Except for one anomaly that has them stumped."

"Three years ago you said it was only close to human."

"That was a quick and dirty analysis. Besides, they've got newer technology now. Some of the genes are arranged differently, so at first it doesn't look human. The anomaly is the male Y-chromosome. It's longer in the alien, and they have no idea what those extra genes do." Bryce was silent after that.

"Bryce? You still there?"

"Yeah. Any more luck with the scroll?"

"Nothing new. I've checked and rechecked the translation so many times, I'm sick of it. I know what it says. I still can't figure out what it means, and I'm beginning to wonder if I ever will."

"You giving up?" Bryce asked.

"No. I'm just frustrated. Have they ever figured out what the briquette is or does?"

"Every time I ask, I hear, 'No need for you to know, Dr. Duncan.' They might've tried to crack it open and destroyed it. That's my life for now. Is Jake Kesten keeping his nose clean? Your emails never tell me about your personal life."

"I'm teaching a college math class."

"Good for you, bad for students."

"How's Diane?"

"Pregnant. We just found out; that's the other reason for the call."

"Congratulations!"

"Thanks. Don't give up on the scroll. Take out your frustrations on your students."

Jake put the phone back inside Scott's apartment and went to his own place. Their worst fears, after the Government had gotten hold of Bryce's find, had never surfaced—no drugs or torture. Neither were they heroes because there were still more questions than answers. After three years, about all they could confirm was that the skeleton didn't belong to anyone from Earth.

He'd never told Scott about Bryce. That might take him down a road he didn't want to travel, not yet. He still wasn't sure why he'd never told Bryce about Arion. Probably the same reason. He'd always suspected that Bryce's find and Arion's appearance were related.

He'd never told Scott about Arion, either. Jake knew better than to think he'd never have to.

2

THE PORTENT
The Present: Planet Stracos

Arion felt the unmistakable ripple, the interruption of a Mage's power, pass through him and knew at once that Marhesse's feared prediction had come true. A moment later he saw the Light spells that lit the library beyond his study go out. In the study, as if nothing had happened, the light of the ensconced candles continued to flicker off the red stenn wood that paneled the walls and low ceiling.

He expected what came next, the rhythmic, muffled thud of heavy, hard boots hitting the stone floor from the other side of the library doors. The doors groaned open, and the boots hammered the wooden library floor. A moment later, he heard a single polite knock on his study door. He gestured it open.

"Me see all lights go out." Fehlen carried a small lantern. Arion pushed back his carved chair, a present from one of Freetown's woodworkers, and stood as Fehlen entered. "Arion wear Fehlen's favorite color. I forget name."

Arion tilted his head back to meet Fehlen's eyes. "Crimson."

"Crim-sun . . . Why lights go out?" Fehlen smiled widely. "I un-der-stand. Arion make bad spell. Fehlen not tell Dev." Fehlen turned and left, pulling the massive, blue-gray, caron wood slabs shut behind him. Although they could be moved by verbal command, Fehlen had difficulty pronouncing the words.

Arion sat. The desk, the chair, and the single bookcase behind him provided the sole furnishings of the intimate study. He had barely had time to consider his next action when the flash of light and low hum of a Communication spell interrupted his thoughts. It was one of the few spells that he allowed to penetrate his keep's protections. Moments later the slender, sharp-featured image of Ot-Vorell stood before him. Vorell headed the Ruling Council on Holostos, the fourth world from the sun in the same star system as Stracos.

Vorell's intense, dark eyes regarded him. "Forgive the intrusion. I seek your counsel."

Arion hid his surprise. Vorell had never sought his advice before. "How may I assist you, Councillor?"

Vorell drew his gold-threaded, white robe together. "Moments ago our Psi Adepts experienced a period of void."

Arion noted the near-panic on Vorell's face and said, "I also felt an interruption."

"Do you know the cause?"

"I require a few days to investigate."

Vorell seemed to want more but said, "I can assuage the concerns of my people with your assurance that it will not happen again."

"We can hope that it won't." Yet he knew that it would repeat, stronger each time. Such a void could render a

Psi unconscious. "I will contact you when I have more information."

Vorell's image dissolved.

Arion stepped into the library and spoke a Word of Magick to open the doors. He withdrew a summoning sphere from his pocket and tossed it into the air. It hung there a moment, then moved out the doors. Shortly, he again heard Fehlen's heavy steps in the corridor.

"Arion want Fehlen?"

"I need to send you to Freetown."

Fehlen beamed. "Fehlen visit Zim. Not see Zim for . . ." He squinted, tightened his jaw muscles, and looked at his large hands. ". . . for eight days."

Zim had taught Fehlen to read, at least the rudiments.

"How long Fehlen visit?"

"Two days." Arion began the gestures. A circle of light appeared. Fehlen smiled, stepped into it, and vanished.

Arion did not smile. He had again felt the shudder, stronger and more focused, but brief enough not to misdirect the Gate spell.

He exited the library and pulled out a luminous wand to light his way as he strode toward his keep's exit. Outside, sunset was approaching. He reached around his neck, under his robe, and withdrew the medallion that enabled him to summon Marhesse.

After he recast the Shield around his keep, he patiently watched the setting sun deepen the colors of the trees surrounding the clearing. Just after it set, the Gate appeared and the dragon Marhesse came through. As great as Arion's own power was, Marhesse's humbled his.

"We expected a summons from our favorite Elfaeden Mage." Marhesse beckoned. "Come. Fezeccah will be pleased to see you again, and our children enjoy seeing their godfather."

How could Marhesse remain so calm? He and Fezeccah were in mortal danger. If Orfo got free, their deaths would soon follow. But Arion also knew the depth of Marhesse's wisdom. Despite the challenge that lay ahead of them, he felt privileged that this dragon regarded him as a friend.

* * *

The next morning Dev Antos dismounted from his pegasid outside Arion's keep. When Fehlen appeared in Freetown yesterday after that mysterious disturbance, Dev had thought little of it. Arion often sent Fehlen there, though he usually came with Fehlen. When the disturbances recurred without word from Arion, he realized that Fehlen's unaccompanied presence in Freetown meant something urgent had required Arion's attention.

After giving the pegasid leave to graze, Dev walked to the tall wooden doors. He spoke the Words Arion had given him to temporarily suspend the keep's Shield spell. The doors opened to admit him.

The corridors were quiet. And dark. What had happened to the Light spells Arion kept in place? Dev took a coin from his pocket, gestured. It began to glow brightly, enough to light his way. He strode toward the library.

He found the library doors open. He entered and crossed between the two heavy tables to the also-open study, ignoring the hundreds of histories and arcane volumes in the bookcases that paneled the twelve-foot-high walls. Arion had often invited him here to read and had taught him the Elfaeden language.

Dev stared at the empty chair behind the desk in the study. He knew Arion to be a fastidious keeper of records. His eyes fell on the lone, carved bookcase centered behind the desk.

Dev entered the room and halted. Out in the library he felt welcome. In this room he felt like a thief invading Arion's privacy, but he needed answers that the Elf was not here to provide. Arion owed him that for the years he had taken care of Freetown.

He approached the bookcase. Three of the six shelves were empty. Two held what he recognized as spell books. On the top shelf, just above his head, stood ten narrow volumes—journals. One for each of the past ten years Arion had spent on Stracos. Arion had not shared anything of his life before that. Dev knew only that Arion had come here with the intention of establishing Freetown.

Dev withdrew the last volume and browsed its pages. The script was unmistakably Arion's and recounted some events that Dev had experienced. He replaced it and pulled out the first volume. It began with Arion's arrival on Stracos. No answers there.

Then he noticed a volume on the desk. He lifted the cover with one finger. On the first page was inscribed, "Orfo." The script was Elfaeden. Dev recognized Arion's writing, although the author was not identified. Dev placed the book on the desk, sat, and began to read.

In the dream I saw a cave. Inside the cave a steep tunnel summoned me—compelled me—beneath the Elfaeden homeworld of Ador. The tunnel ended at what I thought was a door. The image sharpened. I saw not a door, but a barrier. The name of Karaydeon—a name at the edge of legend—

was inscribed above it. My dream ended there and I sought immediate counsel from the Elders.

The Elders talked around me. "It is not possible. Even novices have resistance to Compulsion."

"A stray spell accosted him," another suggested.

A third stated, "He has not yet lived two centuries, and he questions the wisdom of his tutors. We should defer his schooling in the Art until he masters discipline."

"Nevertheless, he has achieved his eighth degree of mastery in less time than any student in our recent history," a fourth Elder corrected.

They addressed me. "Our sensitivity to the Power sets us apart. Return to your studies if you wish to achieve your ninth degree. Don't concern yourself with distant history."

Over the next days the vision reasserted itself and defied my attempts to push it aside. I sought enlightenment from our library. After many days there, my questions remained unanswered and new ones had surfaced. The Great Mage Karaydeon had died seven centuries ago. Yet despite his recorded greatness, the precise date of his passing was nowhere written. While the records contained every detail of his early and middle years, those of his later years, the time of greatest achievement among Elfaeden, were missing. The details of his later years had been ignored. If Karaydeon had left behind an uncompleted task, surely other Elfaeden, those with higher skill levels, were more capable of accomplishing it.

Sitting in a cubicle in the library, I came out of my reflections when a scroll appeared on the desk before me. I was only mildly surprised, given recent events, and unrolled the brittle parchment. I recognized the ancient script and a language unused by Elfaeden for millennia. The name

41

signed at the bottom was Karaydeon.

In the cubicle I found a reference volume. I spent the next days, some without sleep, translating the difficult, ancient language. It began, "A millennium has passed. You, Arion, are my descendant. A grave task now falls upon you. Unless you succeed, the end of our race is at hand."

My father's lineage did not trace to Karaydeon. I went to the genealogical section. Because Elfaeden women did not have the Power, their role was child-rearing, but records were still kept. The one I sought was difficult to locate and consisted of two lines, as if they were an afterthought. Karaydeon had a daughter.

The scroll clarified a previous mystery. Karaydeon had spent his latter years on another world. No doubt his journals, recounting his later days, were there as well.

Following the explicit directions given, I came upon a portal unlike any I had ever seen. It stood on the peak of the mountain amid swirling snows. I knew this mountain as a proscribed place. The Elders never said why.

As I stood before this Gate, one inescapable truth troubled me. No spell of Magick is permanent—except those which lead to death. According to the scroll, this Gate had stood for centuries. What power held it here? Was this one made by the rumored ancient race who made permanent Gates between worlds?

I reasoned that this Gate could not have existed for centuries. Even if it were built from Mage-stone, that would not ensure permanency. Nulling Magick, stray spell energy, or natural forces could disrupt its stabilizing ability. Nevertheless, whatever had brought me to this Gate also made me believe that an answer lay through it.

On the other side, total darkness enveloped me. The

scroll warned against the use of Magick in here so I lit the lantern I had brought. I was in a bare, rough stone anteroom just wide enough and tall enough to contain the Gate. A few paces in front of me stood a door with Karaydeon's name engraved above it, the door in my dreams. Although I hadn't understood their significance at the time, the dreams had also provided the entry commands.

I stayed and studied here in Karaydeon's library, returning through the Gate twice for more provisions. My absence was of no consequence to my people. Three months after first passing through the Gate, I stood on a subterranean level far beneath the safehold, in front of a translucent, blue barrier. Beyond this lay a malignant revenge—imprisoned a millennium ago—with the decimation of all Elfaeden at its heart. Unless I took action, Orfo would be free tomorrow. If what I had read about Orfo was true, why had Karaydeon imprisoned him for only a millennium? Had the Great Mage possessed pity?

Orfo was S'pharn. The S'pharn race had turned rape, pillage, and plunder into an art form, but no S'pharn in recent memory possessed the level of power that Orfo had. Orfo was an agitator. He pressed the S'pharn leaders not to be content with subduing worlds in their part of the universe. He boasted that Psi was a greater power than Magick. With the Elfaeden as the acknowledged masters of Magick, he gathered followers against the Elfaeden, to challenge them. He preached that the Elfaeden were too passive to oppose them.

Orfo's plan was no secret, yet even before he reached Ador, the Elfaeden homeworld, Karaydeon had prepared himself to challenge Orfo. With his Magick he put the arrogant Orfo into a thousand-year stasis. He imprisoned

Orfo's body, but left his mind free to reflect upon his mistakes and humiliation.

I reached into the leather pouch on my belt and withdrew a small, silver sphere of Riadon from among those that I had prepared for this journey. I flung it at the barrier. The sphere hit and disintegrated in a white flash. The barrier stayed.

With this first challenge I already felt that my three months of preparation were inadequate. Elfaeden were taught that the universe had a consciousness and knew what it was doing. Perhaps it had chosen to rid itself of those who no longer contributed to it. Perhaps another race was due to replace us.

Elfaeden teaching in Magick says to counter like with unlike, but Karaydeon had written, "Like strengthens like and like weakens like." I cast a spell from his books, which formed a translucent sphere around me. When it and the barrier touched, they merged. I passed through to the other side. As I did so, the sphere dissipated.

Numbing cold engulfed me. I fought to reach again into my belt pouch and sense the different Magicks by touch. My hand had barely cleared the mouth of the pouch before my frostbitten fingers were no longer able to grasp the sphere I had selected. It fell to the ground and activated lifesaving warmth around me. The sting of the cold-hot suffused my hands and crept through me. In the dim, gray light with no apparent source, the layer of frost sublimed off my body.

Pocket universes are generally regarded to be useless, theoretical constructs. Karaydeon's use of them here would surprise my tutors.

I came to another barrier. After I penetrated it, swamp odors greeted me. Diffuse, pale pink light gave everything a surreal appearance. Somber, gray plants with scaled stems and no flowers poked through the light mist lying over the ground. In places I could see large roots protruding upward. But the ground was dry, and the humidity felt low. Both argued against the presence of mist and the odors of a swamp. From inside my robe I withdrew a wand.

At first the mist parted easily, swirling in brief eddies on the sides as I passed through it. I noticed its movement slowing. The swirls held and began to coalesce into a vague, humanoid form. A misshapen head molded itself atop a body three times my height while tentacles grew from its trunk. I heard movement nearby. Tentacles from behind grabbed me. My wand fell to the ground.

I uttered a Translocation. Instead of moving several paces to my right, I felt the power of my spell travel along the tentacles. Over my shoulder I saw the creature grow in size. I felt its strength likewise increase.

More wisdom of Karaydeon flashed into my mind, "Magick is a tool to be used wisely. Knowing when not to use it makes the true Mage." Below that admonition had been a strange meditation that altered physiological balances in a way no Elfaeden would have believed possible. Why would a Mage wish to void himself of his Magick? The tentacles squeezed me. I shut my eyes against the visual distraction, fighting to keep air in my lungs to prevent my ribs from breaking, and invoked the meditation. A moment after I could hold my breath no longer, the pressure against my sides vanished.

I opened my eyes. The swamp, a tangible illusion as deadly as reality, had disappeared along with my foe. But a worse sensation replaced the abating ache in my sides. I was void and preferred the physical pain to this new emptiness inside me.

Dev paused in his reading. For an Elf to die separated from his Magick would be an unspeakable humiliation. He wanted to close the book, but curiosity overcame his desire to do that.

I picked up my wand, sheathed it again inside my robe, and felt in my belt pouch to verify that the remaining six spheres were intact.

Next came an opaque barrier different from the two before it. This, I realized, enveloped a third, concentric pocket universe. Being void meant that I was cut off from Magick until my body's internal balance returned to normal, however long that might be. Yet Magick still existed around me. Was being void the key? I reached out to touch the barrier and found no resistance. I passed through it into a mountain range.

Stark angularities of immense size stabbed the sky. Soundless lightning flashed angry, white strokes that sheared off slabs of rock and formed craters. As I watched, the land healed itself. Bolts arose from the ground to collide with those from above, annihilating each other in red flashes both resplendent and terrifying at the same time. Such emotions had been foreign to my experience, but being void let me appreciate Karaydeon's artistry.

I had no protections against these bolts. I withdrew a yellow sphere. Knowing the precise distance to the next barrier would have been useful to direct the Teleportation. As I spoke the Word, a bolt of lightning struck where I had stood. The energy of the silent, ceraunic shock wave was caught in the spell and flung me through the next barrier into empty space.

The previous pocket universe had lacked smells. In this one hung an overpowering, warm smell of something living.

My momentum slowed. I began to fall through mist, although falling was an inaccurate term for what I experienced. I was being towed. A moment later I was abruptly pulled in a new direction. The same diffuse, pink light that had illuminated the swamp also lit this area, except that the thick mist obstructed my sight.

My motion ceased. I felt no support beneath me. The force that had towed me now suspended me in place.

A cavernous voice accosted me. "He has come to visit us."

I felt surprise at having reached Orfo this easily.

The voice laughed. "The intruder's fortune is not that good."

My wand appeared in my hand—

"A defenseless Mage is no challenge. Show us your powers."

I said nothing.

"Ah, but you have voided yourself. You are no longer Mage. Have you come to free our enemy? If so, we must destroy you, and if your soul is reincarnated, may you be less foolish in your next life." There was a pause. "On the other hand, after a millennium of boredom, you may have entertainment value for us."

In front of me the mists swirled aside to reveal the image of a fabled, crystal dragon. The image before me raised a taloned foot. In the next moment I was hurled backward.

Something stopped me. Talons closed over my body, imprisoning me. I brought up my wand. "I am void, but this is not."

"Your toys won't help you," the higher voice said.

The deeper voice returned, soft and provocative, *"You have another option. Have you the courage to use it?"*

I looked down at my wand. A sibilant "yes-ss" drifted through the air at the threshold of my hearing. I could use the wand as a lens and focus a spell through it, an act that would likely destroy the wand, terminate my life, and only possibly kill my foe. I had not come here to end any life.

"A wise choice, Mage," the lower voice said.

"You are Psi aware." The voice sounded almost respectful.

I felt forward motion. Soon, the mist thinned. We entered a large tunnel. The sound of heavy cloth flapping in the wind echoed off the walls. The tunnel ended at a huge cavern illuminated to near daylight. My captor released me and moved back for me to see him and the other.

Two magnificent crystal dragons rose before me at three-quarters the height of the cavern. The hide of their lithe bodies scintillated every imaginable color against the dull gray rock. They turned their slender heads at one another then back at me. The lower-voiced dragon spoke, *"You may call me Marhesse. My mate is Fezeccah. You could not pronounce our proper names."*

I arched my eyebrows.

"Nevertheless, a dragon does not reveal his true name to any but his own kind."

"We have provided nourishing vegetation for you. After you have dined, we will talk," Fezeccah said.

I regarded my surroundings. The bare stone of the cavern was too smooth to be natural. A table and chair, elegantly carved in an old Elfaeden design from a wood I did not recognize, provided the sole furnishings. On the table I saw a variety of fresh vegetables. I ate sparingly, not wishing to offend them, and awaited further enlightenment.

Dev looked up from the book. Dragons once existed, but in all accounts that he knew of they were now extinct. This must be an old tale, yet the parchment pages of the book were pliable and not yellowed.

After I finished my meal, Marhesse again spoke, "You have a thousand questions for us: Who are we? Why are we here? How did we know about you? Why was all this created? My dear Elf, we have known about you since your birth. You have not disappointed us."

"Karaydeon brought us. We were his pets," Fezeccah said.

"Or perhaps the other way around," Marhesse added. "We are the last of our kind. Crystal dragons were hunted for their hide, which is rich in Magick matter—Mage-stone as you call it. Karaydeon offered us the chance to bear off-spring in the safety of this place while we tended his prisoner. When our eggs hatch, our kind will again inhabit the universe of men."

"Have you been here for all of the thousand years?"

"What is a mere millennium? We have spent the time studying Karaydeon's Magick and have become quite adept at his spells. No other dragons could boast as much."

"You have copies of his spell books?"

"Those in his safehold are the copies, and only minor spells."

"I found potent ones."

"To you, perhaps, they seemed so. Did you discover among them how to create what you see here? Karaydeon's contemporaries lacked vision and imagination. He left behind those particular spells to prepare you.

We summoned you, in the visions, and observed your every move."

I asked them what happened to Karaydeon and why he made all this.

"He exiled himself because your people outcast him for his deed against Orfo, for having interfered with Destiny, they said. That is why no records of him were kept by the Elfaeden. They tried to forget him, but they did not know about us. All of this he made as his final creation, an intricate set of traps to keep out those who would free Orfo, even if they were able to find this place. We sent you the scroll in the library. Karaydeon wrote it long ago in preparation for this time. He created it for our pleasure and hoped that his descendant would also appreciate his artistry. Do you?"

I said that I did, although many Elfaeden would see this creation as a waste of the Power.

"We are not prisoners here," Marhesse said. "We stayed to guard Orfo. Karaydeon had a tinge of compassion in him, an unfortunate weakness. He left Orfo alive. Eight hundred years ago, an ambitious Mage found this place and hoped to secure a reward for freeing Orfo. The unfortunate Mage did not survive the swamp trap."

"Why can you not reactivate the Imprisonment on Orfo when the old one expires?"

"Don't underestimate Orfo's power," Marhesse said. "The spell worked once because Karaydeon caught him unawares. What spell have you chosen?"

"Encasement."

"A good spell, if you're competent to cast it."

I held up a small box and from it took a black cylinder a handspan tall. "This will focus and amplify my power."

"Where did you find that?"

"In the safehold."

Marhesse regarded me with a scowl, then looked at his mate. "Of course, he hid it from us." To me he said, "Please, set it on the table." He approached and spoke Words. White sparks from the tips of his claws encircled the cylinder. It flashed blue, green, and red. "Blue is Magick; green is Psi; the red is—" His eyes burned into mine. "You didn't know of the third power called Pneuma? You should respect and fear the three in conjunction, Elf." His voice took on an edge. "Even so, Orfo has the power to counter your spell unless you can persuade him to touch this cylinder."

Fezeccah said to me, "Karaydeon left Orfo one self-protection in case someone—including us—sought to kill him. Only Orfo can admit you to his presence. You will need to win his confidence. Perhaps guile, which you Elves are unacquainted with, can serve you."

"Even if you succeed, the Encasement will not be permanent," Marhesse said. He twisted his lower jaw. "The cylinder gives you the power to destroy Orfo." He sighed. "But you Elves have a sanctity-of-all-life code. We recommend that you not permit Orfo to live, or you will bring future woe upon yourself and others."

"Karaydeon wrote that a spell will hold while the cylinder remains in proximity to it," I told Marhesse.

"How will you ensure that it does, and where will you safely place him?" Fezeccah asked me.

"I had assumed that he could stay here."

The dragons accompanied me to the barrier encompassing Orfo's pocket universe. "One more barrier lies between you and Orfo," Marhesse said. "To seek his audience, touch it. Before you do, the cylinder must be in the shielded box so that he does not detect it." Marhesse grew solemn. "Once he touches it, you must act quickly or he can use it to amplify his own power and reverse your spell. He will kill you, then find and kill us."

Fezeccah said to Marhesse, "Until his meeting with Orfo, a pure Elf will encounter no further obstacles."

Marhesse regarded me. "Your purest state, do you know what that means, Elf?"

I nodded.

"Take this medallion." He extended his claw. "Use it to summon us whenever you require our aid."

As I accepted their gift, I felt its power. Though not metal, it was heavier than precious metal would have been. Set into its center was a hexagonally cut piece of dragon scale. The power aura around the medallion so distracted me that I scarcely saw them leave.

This barrier differed from the previous ones. Tan, jelly-like material filled the space before me. The substance gave no indication of Magick, and nothing in Karaydeon's records had mentioned it. The dragons' words about being pure returned to me. I pondered how I could enter without my needed items.

I disrobed and placed my possessions in one pile. With my knife I cut a thin slice of skin from my thigh and employed a spell to heal the wound.

Dev cringed.

I cast Reshape to form the piece of skin into a long, narrow sack and cast Pliancy to prevent it from bursting. Within it I carefully placed my rope belt, my leather pouch containing the spell spheres, my wand, the dragons' medallion, and the case with the black cylinder. I tied the opening shut with strands of my hair then cast two spells upon myself.

I held the sack in my left hand and the knife in my right and walked forward. The jelly offered no resistance. By the time I exited, the knife had disintegrated.

I faced the final barrier that Orfo would have to open for me. Untying the sack, I put my belt around my waist and placed my pouch and wand on the belt. Otherwise, I was naked. The box containing the cylinder I carried prominently in my right hand so it would seem important.

No immediate reply came. Then, a mental voice, "Enter. If you are friend and agree to serve me, I will let you live. If you are foe, Orfo the merciful will slay you quickly." The power behind that mental voice unsteadied me. The dragons told me that Orfo had once endured incredible pain to have a piece of Psi-stone implanted in his skull to give him power beyond any of his kind. Having felt that power, I knew that I could not allow his freedom.

An oval opening slightly taller than me appeared. I barely had time to recover from my surprise at being admitted before it began to close. I hurried through into a hemi-ellipsoidal chamber.

The ellipse's narrow end rose above Orfo, who was suspended, immobile, in the otherwise empty space at what would be one focus of the ellipse. I had seen S'pharn only in drawings. Most renderings depicted them with the slit eyes and the thick hide of a dragon. I knew that Psi powers could create any form desired in the beholder. I also knew that because of the stasis operating here I viewed his true form. None of the renderings were accurate. Beneath the pale cream glow of his prison, his slender and graceful—human—figure stood fully twice my own height. His naked, smooth skin was dark tan and devoid of hair except for a thin blond covering on his head and face. I felt the power of his mind straining against the forces that imprisoned him. Despite his placid appearance, Orfo embodied the evil and cruelty of his race.

The hatred of all life not of his own kind emanated from him, and I understood what had driven Karaydeon to act against him.

"If you come seeking death, I shall not disappoint you."

I felt a ripple of Magick. The glow surrounding Orfo shimmered and faded. The restraining forces terminated their existence. I extended my right hand, holding the box in mock warding of his impending attack.

He laughed. "An Object of Warding will not help you. It shall start the collection of mementos from my new conquests. Before you feel my power, I would know who has the courage to challenge me."

"You must gain that knowledge without my help."

"You spurn my generosity in not killing you immediately?"

My Magick let me see the invisible cone of energy discharge from him. I raised my left hand to deflect it.

"Perhaps you are not a waste of my time," he said.

I withdrew my wand.

Orfo threw his head back and laughed again. "Do not disappoint me with your insignificant Magick, Elf."

I loosed its blue bolts of Magick energy. Instead of striking him, they curved around him and formed into a whirlpool. The whirlpool compressed itself upward above his head and condensed into a tight spiral. He narrowed his deep eyes intently at the floor in front of me. The spiral shot out and landed harmlessly on the spot where he had focused it. "Have you nothing more?"

I gestured and spoke Words. The green light spray halted in front of him, suspended in the air. He molded it as if it were clay. The energy condensed into a ball, brightening as he added his own power. He drew the ball to himself, studied it a moment, then threw it back.

One of the spells I had cast upon myself protected me. The force shook me nonetheless. Counting on his momentary distraction, I issued a Probe spell at him.

"Such impudence! I might have been merciful! You will beg for death."

I felt the explosion inside my head. My body went numb and my consciousness wavered. Pain sliced through me. Blinding white light flashed around me. My legs collapsed. I heard his distant laughter. Before my body stiffened fully, I was able to place my hand inside my belt pouch and finger a sphere, hoping that a Psi user would not detect its restorative energy being released.

Orfo took three large strides and stood over me. "Behold, my dominion begins." I watched the barrier of this last pocket universe dissipate into nothingness. Bending, he picked up the box, which had fallen a few feet away. He opened the latch and smiled. I knew he felt its power.

When I saw him lift the cylinder from the case, I uttered a Word of Magick.

He jerked his head down at me. "What?"

As my spell formed a translucent covering around him, making him look like a statue, I said to him, "I am Arion, Karaydeon's descendant."

Dev closed the book. When he looked up, he saw Arion standing in the doorway of the study. "I left the book so that you might understand what is happening and the danger we face."

Dev did not understand. What he had read filled him with fear, but how was it related to the disturbances now? What had become of Orfo? Was he still imprisoned?

"I have just returned from speaking with Marhesse. Even before I battled Orfo those ten years ago, a chain of events stretching back centuries was already leading to the present circumstances. With the knowledge I had gained from Karaydeon's library, I thought I knew better. I did not heed Marhesse's warning about Orfo's power, and my decisions then have now endangered all of you as well. Four years ago, the dragons told me to set in motion another chain of events. Fortunately, that time I listened to them."

Dev didn't know what to say. He had always looked to Arion for wisdom and answers, and his mentor had just confessed a weakness in both of those areas. "Is there a way I can help?"

"While it is still safe for me to do so, I must leave again to bring here those who can help. I rely on you to show them our hospitality. Though Orfo remains imprisoned and unable to act in these times, another seeks to free him. If that happens, he will first destroy this world—your home and mine—and I lack the power to prevent it."

3

HALLOWEEN ARRIVES EARLY
Early Fall 2000, Day Zero: Planet Earth

Pain brought my groggy mind back to cruel reality. I remembered where I was, and the cause of my pain: Jake.

My ears rang. Every muscle and bone in my body screamed. Bouncing around in the back of Jake's van while speeding over a pothole-riddled back road didn't help.

Once the volume of the unmusical monotone in my ears had been turned down enough to admit the familiar sounds of the living world—upon whose knife-edge I balanced—I tried to lift my head and shoulders. This is a bad move when half the muscles in your torso don't feel like they're attached to the same places they used to be.

Gasping is another bad move. I was sure that my ribs had been shuffled and re-dealt into new positions. As I slowly rolled onto my side, more pain hugged me. I inched my head forward to examine the status of what it was attached to.

The twinkles of light in my eyes finally ran out of power. I squinted to discern the boundaries between my body and clothing, both artistically dotted with blood. I remembered Jake dragging me, then shouldering me.

The van hit a bump. The jolt shook me from reminiscing about my past. Jake yelled over his shoulder, "Hang in there, Scott. I'll have you home soon." The van, Jake's mission machine, shook as if it were in its death throes.

I didn't recall leaving the van; I didn't recall falling asleep. I awoke sprawled across my bed, in my underwear, the crumpled sheet most of the way off. I heard noises in the kitchen, like either Jake or someone else was stealing my pots and pans. A bit of sunlight slid through the curtains. The smell of smoke, burnt electronics, and pungent Essence de Scott swirled over me. I glanced at the floor. My blood-and-mud-stained jeans stared back. I had to take a leak, but my body rebelled at the threat of moving.

Jake poked his head into the room. "Good morning. How do you feel?"

I growled. "I'm battered, bruised, and in pain!"

"Computer sabotage is not an exact science. Besides, I put you in charge of safety. Breakfast is ready, and it will not be served in bed." He left. I heard cabinets open and close, water running, and the microwave beep a few times.

Yesterday's disaster pushed its way into my thoughts. Our mission had been to teach a group of hackers never again to tap into a secure military network.

A few minutes after seven p.m., we had entered a small office building that, in addition to housing doctors and dentists, also housed "Information Resources, Inc." Jake's proficiency with picking locks still raised questions in my mind about the extent of his government training.

Jake has in his backpack a twelve-volt motorcycle battery and a power inverter. To these he connects a large, magnetic tape eraser, the kind that TV studios use to wipe their videotapes. He sets the eraser on top of the PC and presses the button. The surge of magnetic power destroys the hard drive and susceptible memory chips, including the one that boots the computer. The backup battery in the PC often self-destructs as well. When the PC is next turned on, instead of a solitary, everything-is-okay beep, the poor little CPU multi-beeps—system failure.

This procedure will also toast a monitor, which is how I got damaged. I was supposed to be sure everything was powered off. I missed one monitor. I had my back to it when Jake pressed the eraser button. The monitor exploded all over me. During the summer, the undergrads go home, most of the grad students do research, and I play saboteur.

Now, this was not a common practice for us. When the PC or network had no firewall or insufficient protection, he could simply hack back. I once asked him, "Why not just disconnect them? It's safer than up close and personal."

"Disconnect them and they'll try again somewhere else. Maybe next time they're smarter. Maybe we don't detect them before they download. This way, they get the message that someone cares. This way it costs them money out of pocket to replace the lost equipment. Besides, I'm rather fond of the fragrance of silicon chip meltdown."

I wondered how he'd feel after having monitor glass sprayed all over him.

Still lying in bed, I felt a strange tingling in my body, above the aches and pains. Chills, but I wasn't cold. If anything, I was sweating.

I heard running footsteps, then Jake's raised voice. "What are *you* doing here?"

"Jake?" I said feebly. I tried to sit up, but I hurt too much. "Jake, is anything wrong," I said louder. I thought I heard another voice before everything got quiet.

Jake entered my bedroom carrying a tray with my breakfast.

"I thought you said—"

"Eat and get some rest. I'll be back later." He set the tray on my nightstand.

"Is someone here?"

"Just business."

He shut the door. I heard muffled voices in the living room. My clock radio said nine twenty-four. That was way too early on a Saturday for Scott Madison to be awake and out of bed, especially in his present condition. I closed my eyes for a few moments.

✳ ✳ ✳

Under a bright sun, two men approached a crumbling structure surrounded by nothing except harsh, rocky terrain. The smaller man wore a rose-colored, hoodless caftan. Rivulets of sweat crept down his forehead. His companion, a muscular figure a head taller and clad in thick, brown garments more appropriate for a cold climate, appeared comfortable.

What remained of the structure, barely the height of a man at its highest spots, was elliptical. Its original shape was impossible to ascertain. If something larger once enclosed it, no traces of that remained. There was a break in one side of the ellipse, possibly an entrance at one time. On closer inspection I saw that it might have once been a small amphitheater. The two passed through the opening and stopped at a pile of rubble near its center.

The larger man spoke first, "I sense it here, Necromancer. Before we proceed, you have earned the right to know my name and to see my true form."

The Necromancer's left hand shook as he wiped the back of it across his forehead. "Your t-true form?"

"You thought that we looked like you? That you consider the S'pharn human is an insult." His figure shimmered. The skin on his face and hands took on a coarse appearance. His fingernails elongated an inch on his slender fingers. Although his slanted eyes had a reptilian appearance, his final semblance was human.

The Necromancer began to shake.

"My name is Vraasz, soon to be important among my kind." His visage widened into what might be construed as a smile. He confronted the rubble, narrowed his eyes, and furrowed the thick skin of his brow. Soil and rock upwelled and moved aside—apparently by the power of his will—to reveal a rectangular, silver-blue chest just over a foot long. Three large strides brought him in front of it. He bent, dug his fingers along the sides of the chest, and lifted it out. He regarded it a moment then set it before the Necromancer. "*Open the lock.*" Vraasz had not spoken those words.

"I have paid you for this."

"Y-your power is greater than mine."

"What lies within amplifies my power. Too long have I sought it to risk its destruction. *Now open the lock*!"

The Necromancer staggered and blanched from what must have been a blast of mental power slamming into him. He took a deep breath and began chanting staccato syllables of an alien language. In rhythm with his chant, he slowly curved and straightened various fingers at the chest in random order. When he finished, he stepped back, trembling less.

Vraasz bent over the chest again. He lifted the lid and took out a velvet-black object, admiring it, turning it over and over. The object, scarcely larger than a tall drinking mug, was a triangular prism open at the ends. Rectangular, black slabs fused along the seams composed its faces. He stopped turning the object and grasped it firmly. Without looking up, he said, "Our business is concluded."

"You made a pact with us. Would you cheat us?"

Vraasz regarded him. "This object gives me the power to annul the Elfaeden Magick that imprisons him. He and I will exact revenge on the Elfaeden, as promised. We don't require you for that. I will demonstrate."

He shaped his fingers around the black object and held it between himself and the other man. As he focused on it, ribbons of dull color swept along its faces. The colors brightened.

The Necromancer's body vaporized . . .

✳ ✳ ✳

"Scott!"

My eyes popped open.

Jake stood in the bedroom doorway glaring at my limp figure. "You're wanted in the living room. Make yourself decent first."

What a weird dream. I didn't remember ever dreaming in science fiction before.

My bladder felt ready to explode. I persuaded my body to support itself while I grimaced my way to the bathroom. After peeing a gallon, I painfully pulled on a clean pair of jeans. I grabbed a shirt and glanced at the clock radio—ten fifty-eight—as I stumbled out the door.

I reached the living room, shirt still in hand, to see that Halloween had arrived a month early. Merlin the Magician, with pointed ears and a heavy crimson robe that nearly covered his feet, stood next to the couch. I gawked while I attempted to think up a suitable title for this piece of fiction confronting me.

"About time you showed up," Jake said. "This gentleman has a job for us."

"Sorry, but I don't do costume parties on Saturdays."

"Adventure calls."

"I'll pass." I did an awkward about-face and shuffled toward the bedroom.

"I hope you're going to pack."

I tilted my head up and raised my voice. "Not likely. I'm going to reheat my breakfast in the microwave."

Boom! I ran into a wall. An invisible wall! Even Jake couldn't manage a trick like that.

I turned around. "What the hell's going on?"

"We've been invited to take a trip."

"Where to?"

"Offplanet. I think that's the appropriate term."

"Right." Only the pain in my bruised ribs prevented me from laughing.

"Scott, meet Arion."

Merlin nodded.

"What, no 'Take me to your leader'?"

"Have a seat," Jake said.

Aliens indeed. I Cheshire-cat grinned and considered my seating options. This Arion had taken a seat on one end of my brand-new, black Naugahyde couch. If I sat on the floor I could savor the fragrance of the new carpet that the landlord installed before I moved in a few months ago. But I was hurting. Maneuvering onto the floor would not be pleasant.

Wait a minute. I remembered that it was around nine-thirty when Jake had unexpectedly brought me breakfast and I'd heard another voice out here, but it was ten fifty-eight when he woke me up again. Had he and this guy been talking all that while?

"Jake, can I see you for a moment, in private?" I smiled at our guest. Jake followed me into the kitchen.

"Is he some demented serial killer that you're humoring until the police arrive? Or did he hypnotic-stare you into submission? Or maybe I'm dreaming?"

"What makes you think you're dreaming?"

"Real life isn't this weird, not even around you."

"It's very real. You need to trust me on this. You're on the clock. We're going on a field trip. Go pack. Shower if you need to, and be ready in an hour."

I headed into my bedroom, and he went back to the living room. If this field trip was like his last one, my body wasn't looking forward to it.

After showering, into my backpack went a clean set of underwear—black, because it made a statement—a denim shirt, a denim jacket, the thigh-length athletic boxers that I sometimes slept in, plus deodorant and a disposable razor. On me I put the jeans I'd been wearing plus a dark red, long-sleeved shirt and white sneakers—I felt patriotic. On my way out of the bedroom I grabbed a notebook.

Arion had waited patiently for the past hour in the living room. Jake came back from his apartment in black jeans and a white, banded-collar shirt, his usual business attire.

"Can you die in a dream?" I asked Jake.

"You still think this is a dream?"

"What else could it be?"

He saw the notebook in my hand and pointed.

"For significant phone numbers," I said.

He smiled. "We're ready," he told Arion.

I was about to ask where he'd parked his spaceship when he made some hand gestures. A six-by-four oval of pale light appeared in my living room and floated two inches above the floor. Jake and Arion wasted no time stepping into it. They disappeared. I remembered that weird, sci-fi dream. Was this part of it? Or was I about to have a near-death experience?

I stepped into the lighthole. A prickling shiver darted through me, and for a heartbeat, I was nowhere.

4

JEN-VARTH
Two Days Ago: Planet Ranor

Jen-Varth shivered miserably. The night cold on this fringe-world called Ranor tore into him. He clenched his shoulder and chest muscles to squeeze the minute, residual warmth in his body to the surface and increased his already brisk stride. His skintight thermosuit wouldn't let him freeze to death. Small consolation.

He raised his head. In the dim light of Ranor's twin moons, uninviting barrenness—jagged landscapes with scant flora the same dull green as the soil—spread itself on both sides of the semi-road. A few distant hills broke the monotony. From above, the stars cast hostile light at him. He usually welcomed the night as a friend that heralded the end of his miserable days. This night was not his friend.

He retrieved his TL-5 Locator from its compartment at his waist and checked the numbers. He'd been walking in this cold for half an hour. His disabled surface skimmer lay 110 stads back, its older power cells frozen by the harsh Ranoran nights. The other Protectors had complained about them enough, but he'd allowed his preoccupation with the end of his ten-year contract to distract him from checking for upgraded cells.

His foot struck a rock, causing his water pack to bounce painfully against his hip. He slowed to adjust the strap that was brittle from the cold. The water pack had frozen an hour ago. While the medi-kit on his back provided a measure of insulation there, its normally soft shoulder straps responded abrasively to his every muscle movement. Only the DN-32 neural assault weapon holstered across his right shoulder had caused no problem, the one thing he didn't need out here. Ranor's predators had better sense than to venture out at night.

If the small planet ever had native humans, they were long gone. Those who now called themselves Ranorans had come from other worlds. Naïveté or desperation, he wasn't sure which, had driven settlers here. He wasn't entirely sure why they stayed.

The thirteen-year-old boy he'd been sent after was not the first to journey to the ancient site to prove his manhood. The legends claimed that the spirits who supposedly dwelt in it granted wisdom. Surely those who built this place, and their spirits, were long extinct. But the boy's caretaker had requested help. Legally, the Protectors had to provide it. This time the duty fell to Jen-Varth. Once, he had taken pride in his duties. Now, duty was a curse word to him.

On his homeworld of Xenna, when Jen-Varth was sixteen, his father had introduced him to a Protector who had come there to learn Xennan herbal medicine. Jen-Varth walked with him through the rich Xennan forests and taught him what he knew. The Protector offered to sponsor him when he came of age, in three years. Jen-Varth had looked forward to Protector service.

His breath came forth in puffs of frost and dissipated into the frigid air like the past ten, wasted years of his life. He had wanted to be an explorer and to use his skills to improve the lives of those he encountered. Perhaps those were someone else's dreams.

Dayon had joined the Protectors three years before Jen-Varth and was assigned to Mesca where Jen-Varth was first stationed. They assigned Dayon as Jen-Varth's partner. Dayon the Elfaeden.

Suspicions and rumors accompanied Dayon. Elfaeden were the reputed keepers of Magick. Why would an Elfaeden come to this region of space so far away from the rest of his kind? Why would an Elfaeden join the Protectors and chance serving on a non-Magick world? Weren't they also devout pacifists? One Protector had asked Jen-Varth if the Elfaeden had bisexual tastes. He and Dayon shared nothing more than a common spirit, something shallow minds could not understand. Their aspersions hadn't bothered him until that day in the bar, two days after Dayon's death.

It had been two hours past moonset. Apart from the Ranoran bartender only seven people occupied the room. An especially malicious Protector named Hajen had just finished his work cycle and was still wearing his blue uniform as he approached the table where his own partner sat. "I heard Golden Boy and pointy-ears couldn't handle a few slavers that I could've done single-handed." Hajen spoke loudly enough to be heard throughout the room, always mocking the color of Jen-Varth's bronze-tan skin.

"I heard twenty slavers attacked the settlement. Even you aren't that good, Hajen," the other, not in uniform, said.

Hajen sat. "It was only twelve, and we all have to learn disappointment sometime." He laughed unkindly.

Jen-Varth slid his left hand up his chest until his fingers touched the synth-hide of his DN-32 holster. His fingers moved along its edge to the handle. He squeezed it.

"Is he drunk?" Hajen asked.

"He hasn't touched whatever he ordered."

"Probably not ready to forget his playmate yet," Hajen said. "I heard the slavers vaporized the Elf. I bet it caused quite a stench."

Both laughed loudly and heartily.

Jen-Varth eased his DN-32 from its holster and fingered the setting to incapacitate. He didn't care that there were witnesses. He turned and fired. Hajen's muscles locked. Jen-Varth fired again. Despite violent spasms, Hajen choked out one scream. Jen-Varth watched with pleasure before resetting the DN-32 to sedate and firing a third time. While the observers had begun to react, Jen-Varth picked up his drink and downed it.

His service record showed an official reprimand for brawling blamed on the grief of losing a partner. Prejudice against Jen-Varth and Dayon went all the way up the ranks to the Mescan outpost commander whose decision it had been to send the pair alone against the slaver incursion. The Governing Committee didn't want one commander's bigotry and misconduct to smear Protector reputation. They quietly retired the commander and suggested reassignment for Jen-Varth.

They sent him to Ranor. An unofficial punishment, as was his lack of promotion.

A new wave of cold redirected his thoughts back to the present. His six-foot plus height caught the wind's icy blades. He thrust his slender, gloved hands into his suit pouches. Long black hair protruding from his hood added marginal extra protection for his ears.

His goal shimmered ahead. The black, needle-like towers were connected by an elevated tunnel. He'd flown over them once, but he'd never been inside them. Similar structures had been reported in other solar systems, the product of a long-extinct elder race.

Jen-Varth spotted an opening at the base of one tower and began to jog toward the promise of shelter. Several steps away, he stumbled and hit the rough ground. He gasped. The inrush of cold seared his lungs. He forced the air out.

Many slow, shallow breaths later he was able to crawl forward. As he crossed the ancient threshold, a cloak of warmth arose from the floor to enshroud him. He rolled onto his back and lay there listening to his heartbeats while the heat burrowed into his body. When his frozen olfactory nerves began to function again, instead of musty staleness, he thought he detected scents of vegetation. The air was circulating.

He sat up to scan the elliptical chamber, which he judged to be one stad across and greater than that in height. The pale gray floor was smooth, stone-like, but not stone. Fine dust, fresh with footprints, covered it. Ahead lay an aisle flanked by tiered rows of seats that followed the curve of the chamber. The walls glowed blue. The room reminded him of a small amphitheater. At the back, the highest tier of seats rose well above his head. He walked along the downward slope of the aisle to where it ended next to a rectangular dais. Behind it an opening led into a corridor lit with the same dim blue as the chamber walls. He followed the footprints.

His boots hitting the flooring echoed softly along the corridor. He heard a second echo, halted, and panned his head. A moment after he heard the twang, pain shot down his right leg. He tumbled forward and landed heavily on his knees. Gasping, he stared at the barbed Ranoran arrow protruding from his thigh. Down the corridor he glimpsed a moving shadow and cursed his carelessness. He should have drawn his DN-32 at first alert. While he hadn't expected the boy to come begging to be returned to his settlement, neither had he expected the boy to attack him.

He scooted himself toward the wall to use it for support. There he drew his DN-32 and peered into the distance, slowly bending his leg and wincing as the arrow's barbs bit into his thigh.

He set the DN-32 down next to him and leaned forward to unfasten the leg seals of his thermosuit already soaked with blood. He maneuvered the medi-kit off his shoulders. He first sprayed topical anesthetic around the wound, feeling the momentary sting before it took effect. He took out a small surgical laser, made the adjustments, placed it in his left hand, then curled the fingers of his right hand carefully around the arrow's wooden shaft. The vibrations of his shaking hand efficiently translated along the shaft into his thigh. The anesthetic wasn't strong enough for this deep a wound, but a systemic painkiller would impair his reflexes. He needed to remain alert.

Jen-Varth set his jaw, aimed the laser, and engaged it. He didn't feel its burn at first, not until the beam heated the arrow's barbs and the flesh around them. After the arrow came free, he let the blood flow before he sprayed anti-infective and sutured the wound. He cleaned around it, dressed it, and refastened his thermosuit over it.

Pressing his back against the wall he stared at the opposite one, fifteen feet distant, and took long, deliberate breaths.

He hated Ranor; he hated Ranorans; he hated the Protectors. He shut his eyes to relish the pain in his leg. Why should he help a boy who didn't want his help?

He heard a noise. He retrieved his DN-32, set it to wide dispersal, and fired down the corridor. Instinctively he yanked the injured limb beneath him and attempted to rise. Pain exploded in his leg. His head jerked backward and banged against the wall. He fell to the floor.

He was weak from lack of food and the loss of blood, but it wasn't safe here, in a long corridor, injured, with no cover. His medi-kit contained an extensible splint strong enough to serve as a crutch. With the wall and the crutch for support, he hobbled back into the entry chamber, stopping periodically to fire his DN-32 behind him as a deterrent.

Climbing the ramp to the outside exit proved a challenge. Daylight filled the horizon. In his disabled condition the skimmer was too distant to reach before night came again. He limped back down the aisle to the corridor entrance. No place was safe, but at least here the boy couldn't get behind him. Exhausted from his efforts, he slid down the wall and passed out.

* * *

When his awareness returned, the pain in his leg had abated to a dull ache. His throat was dry; his stomach was empty. He unfastened his water pack, glad to find its contents liquid again, and sipped a quarter of it.

From somewhere came a faint tapping. He drew his DN-32, checked the setting—sedate—and strained to see down the corridor. "Esak?" The sound came again, nearer. He fired a barrage. A shadow darted and vanished. An agile youth could easily outrun him now, and hiding in here would not be difficult. Then he realized that he'd left his medi-kit out in the corridor.

He should stay here. Esak couldn't approach him without being seen. He checked his charge status of the DN-32; eighty-percent remained. He had enough water for a day or two, and when he failed to report, his commander would send out two men. Standard procedure. They'd find the abandoned skimmer and follow his trail here.

He couldn't accept failing that way. The other Protectors on Ranor would use his failure as an excuse to mock him further, to remind him of his ten wasted years in Protector service.

Jen-Varth tried to visualize the layout of the buildings based on what he had seen on the outside. The two towers were eight or nine levels high. A tunnel connected them two-thirds of the way up. There must be an access to that tunnel. The entry chamber was too small to fill the base of a tower so there could be exterior rooms and transport mechanisms to provide access to the other levels. The heating and lighting still functioned. Perhaps those did also. Had the smell of vegetation been an illusion?

He found that he could stand and walk without external support. Good. The crutch would impair his reflexes. He collapsed it and wedged it out of the way into the DN-32 holster. With his DN-32 in hand, he limped cautiously forward. He returned to the spot where the boy had injured him. The arrow and his medi-kit were gone. Forty hobbled paces down the corridor—he counted them then checked the TL-5 to verify its accuracy in this building—a pair of side corridors joined the main one at right angles. Following the footprints, he chose the corridor on the left.

The footprints led him to a descending stairway. Its thirty-five painful steps ended at a wall. A section of the wall rose with a dull hiss as he approached it.

Scents of vegetation burst forth around him. He inhaled sharply, not from the scents but from the sight that accompanied them. A thriving, mature forest spread itself before and below him. The walls and dome radiated a light as pure as sunlight, and the vibrant green of the trees delighted his eyes. He stepped forward onto a walkway that circled the huge chamber near the tops of the tallest trees and leaned over the parapet fashioned for those shorter than him. And he marveled.

He recognized trees from his homeworld and from worlds that he had visited. Scores of fragrances floated past him in the circulating air. He inhaled deeply the scents of rich soil, herbs, flowers, and fruits. His empty stomach reacted to the latter.

The sound of trickling water issued from far below. A quarter of the way around the chamber a crosswalk spanned its diameter. He limped to it then aimed the TL-5 across it. It registered two-point-eight stads. Underneath this crosswalk were two more. Through the dense foliage he could barely see the distant forest floor.

He heard a distant rustling. Esak? Or did animal life inhabit the forest as well? "I am a Protector!" he shouted down into the forest. "I have come to help you!" No answer returned.

He followed the outside path back to the door, now closed, but it again opened at his approach. At the top of the stairway he turned left to continue his previous course, staying close to the forest chamber. A way to the bottom should be nearby.

Two more left turns brought him to a door that did not automatically open. In the thin dust on the floor he saw footprints leading in all directions and back and forth. The boy had come this way and had likewise been confused about where to go next. A circular panel to the door's left caught Jen-Varth's attention. When he placed his hand against it, he felt a slight vibration. Abruptly, the door slid right to reveal a cylindrical room six feet across. He stepped inside. To his left and just above his waist, he saw four differently colored indentations arranged in a diamond pattern with a fifth white one in the center. He suspected that this room was a conveyance. He pressed the lowest button in the diamond array, the rose-colored one, and felt brief motion. The door opened into a corridor that turned right.

When he stepped out, the walls lit up with a soft rose glow, the color of the button. He surmised that the blue button to the right in the pattern would return him to the level he had come from. In the dust he again saw footprints leading away and returning. This corridor curved to the right, the direction that seemed correct. He came to a door like the one on the main level. It slid upward to admit him.

He had come to the ground level of the forest. "Esak, I am a Protector come to return you to your settlement!"

"I kill ss-slavers-ss!"

A barbed arrow struck the ground at his feet. He recognized the sibilant Ranoran speech. He would not play this game. Let Esak come to him. He took careful steps, watching the trees. Why had the boy called him a slaver? The Protector presence on Ranor discouraged slave trader raids, and he didn't think they were desperate enough to foray in the challenging climate of Ranor. Also, Ranoran youth had a reputation for tenacity and unbreakable spirits.

Except for a few footprints in the loosely packed soil, he saw no other traces of Esak's presence. Flowing water was the only sound. The footprints disappeared in the low growth on the forest floor, weed-free as if cultivated.

He headed toward the water sound. Within a copse of trees he found a waterfall nearly twice his height flowing over the same gray material that he'd seen throughout the towers and which was the only evidence of artificiality in the forest. The water was pleasantly cool to his touch. With his medi-kit stolen, he couldn't test its purity.

Jen-Varth turned his head sharply at a sound behind him. His momentary distraction had allowed the boy to creep up. Before Jen-Varth could act, Esak jumped at him, tumbling him to the ground and causing him to drop the DN-32. "Filthy ss-slaver!" the boy hissed.

Strong fists hammered Jen-Varth's head. He tried to roll away, but the boy clung fast. They rolled over several times while the boy pummeled him. Their eyes met. Jen-Varth had never seen such wild hatred. He cuffed the boy to gain a brief respite. Esak hung on and yanked Jen-Varth's right arm as if trying to rip it off. But Jen-Varth was stronger, despite his injury, and left-handed.

With his left hand he grabbed the lanky boy around the waist, threw him aside, and drew a breath. The youth was on his feet and charging before Jen-Varth had exhaled completely. His right hand clutched a dagger. "Ss-slaver!"

Jen-Varth's reflexes took over. He dodged the sharp steel aimed at his chest, spotted his DN-32, rolled to grab it. In two heartbeats he was standing. A trigger click later Esak slumped to the ground.

He moved toward the motionless but conscious boy, ignoring the throbs in his own leg. The twisted viciousness on Esak's narrow face, framed by long, sand-colored hair, had been transformed into frightened innocence. Jen-Varth was hungry; his strength was gone. He needed sleep, but Esak would regain his muscle control shortly. Under a bush, a few feet away, he saw the sack. In it he found some tattered clothing, a heavy animal skin, and a length of rope. He secured Esak's legs and tied his bare arms behind his back. His sleeveless shirt was ripped under the left arm. The seams of his long, hide pants also needed repair.

Jen-Varth returned to the sack. Underneath the animal skin he found his medi-kit, an extra knife, a sling, two empty food canisters. The boy had been missing for eight days when Jen-Varth started after him, but he wasn't in as weakened a state as expected from so little food. The forest must have sustained him, but Jen-Varth doubted that it had fruits that Esak would recognize. Consuming unknown plants—

Esak moaned. At first Jen-Varth thought the boy was struggling to free himself. When Jen-Varth saw him start to retch, he rushed to untie the boy's arms. Jen-Varth turned him over while his stomach emptied. After five or six spasms, Esak calmed but was still shaking. Jen-Varth noted the purple-colored bits in the boy's stomach fluid and gently laid him on the ground. The enticing fruit of the bekkah tree had a wonderful flavor. It also contained potent drugs, among them a psychotomimetic and a hallucinogen. In proper and limited doses they were valuable drugs.

He recalled his own experience with the fruit at age fourteen. Some of his friends had told him about its euphoric properties. He'd consulted his father's books then decided that a first-hand experience would be more instructive. The bitter, green fruit was not dangerous in small amounts. If he had read further, he would have learned that the drug content of the fruit increased several fold as it ripened. His father found him barely in time. Jen-Varth remembered the disorientation, the violent retching, and the painful spasms as the drugs in the fruit exerted their effects. He remembered his father's words, "You have neglected your reading. Let this memory drive you to more diligent study."

Two years later, at sixteen, his knowledge of medicinals had exceeded that of his father. When Jen-Varth joined the Protectors, his father counseled, "I have always given you my best. Do no less for those you serve."

Brown eyes suddenly flew open. He lurched and Jen-Varth leaned on him. "I'm not here to harm you, Esak. The fruit has made you sick. Where did you find it?" The boy pushed against him. "Let me help you."

The boy's eyes glazed and the tremors returned. He rolled the boy onto his side. The boy was nearing critical condition. His medi-kit held nothing of use in this case. Uncharacteristically, the tree's roots contained an antidote for the most potent toxin in the fruit. He had to find the tree quickly. Although it had been a lifetime since he'd smelled bekkah flowers, they had a volatile fragrance resembling fresh human sweat that was not entirely unpleasant and which some found alluring. But the forest was large and held so many fragrances. The bekkah fragrance was not a strong one. Jen-Varth stood shakily and realized how much his fight with the boy had drained his strength.

A new concern presented itself. The light was dimming. If the lights shut down completely, as he suspected they would, locating the tree in time would be even less likely. He heard whirring sounds and saw movement nearby, which answered one question. Light cycles ensured the forest's survival, and robotic keepers cultivated it.

He briefly marveled at the enduring technology before he dug deep into his memories. Bekkah trees were symbionts and grew only in the presence of certain other plants. One of those plants bore luminescent flowers. The dwindling illumination might prove an advantage.

Another observation gave him hope. The boy's sack being here suggested that this was his camp. The tree might be nearby. He closed his eyes to let them adjust, breathing in the scents and slowly turning his body in case the one he sought presented itself and offered a promising direction.

Perhaps there. He opened his eyes and walked into the forest. His endeavor was soon rewarded by a cluster of yellow, luminescent flowers at the base of a bekkah tree. He reached into his boot sheath and pulled out his knife. Bekkah roots grew close to the surface. He dug away the soil and cut off a piece of root.

He returned to Esak. Under normal circumstances he would extract the antidote by boiling the root in a solution of salts. He suspected that that would be too late even if he had what he needed. After propping the barely conscious boy against a tree, he finely chopped the root, made a paste with water, then scooped the paste onto his fingertips and forced it into the boy's mouth. Saliva would have to suffice to extract the antidote. Jen-Varth manipulated the boy's jaw, gave him a sip of water, and rubbed his throat to make him swallow. He repeated this then gave him more water to rinse down the root particles, finally laying the boy down and putting the animal skin over him. A lightstick in hand, Jen-Varth sought edible fruits.

✳ ✳ ✳

Jen-Varth awoke next to Esak, who was still asleep from the sedative also contained in the root. The lights had cycled back on. The boy's color had improved. He went to the waterfall, tested the water, drank, and filled his water-pack. Then he removed his thermosuit and used a piece of tree bark to scrub out the blood. The suit's fabric repelled stains.

He had just put his suit back on and returned when Esak stirred and glanced sleepily at him. Jen-Varth offered him fresh water. The boy started to gulp it. "Easy." After Esak had quenched his thirst, Jen-Varth handed Esak the fruits he'd procured. "These are safe and will restore your strength. I must retrieve my skimmer." The warmth of the day and the solar recharger would have restored the power cells. "We will stay here another night while you recover, then I'll take you back to your settlement."

"No! They will outcast me because you helped me."

"I won't tell them."

He retraced his way back to the entry chamber. Outside, Ranor was changing color with the light of approaching day, still barren, but less harsh. He was about to step through the opening when a voice came from behind. "You are Jen-Varth."

Jen-Varth turned. There stood an Elfaeden wearing a long, berry-red robe. "Who are you?"

"I am Arion."

"How did you come here?"

"I require your skills."

Jen-Varth found himself suddenly irritable and defensive. "My contract with the Protectors terminates in a few days," he replied. "If you require help, contact my commander. I'll gladly direct you."

"Many worlds are in danger, your home among them. Your skills have healed the boy. I can return him to his village so that you may come with me."

"I don't appreciate your interference in affairs that don't concern you."

"Are you certain that they don't concern me?"

Jen-Varth turned and stepped through the portal to the outside. When he looked back, the Elfaeden was gone. Perhaps he had imagined him.

He trekked back to his skimmer, keyed his personal code into the side panel, entered, and coaxed it to start. By the time he returned, most of the short Ranoran day had passed. He made his way back to the forest and found Esak walking about. "Ss-sir, I am ss-sorry for the trouble I caused."

"The fruit caused it. Call me Jen-Varth."

"I was-ss hungry. It was-ss ss-o ss-sweet."

Jen-Varth obtained more fruit for them. After they ate, he asked, "Esak, did you see anyone in here while I was gone?"

"No."

Esak related his explorations in the buildings. "In the other tower I found ss-sealed places-ss. I can ss-show you."

"Perhaps tomorrow." Jen-Varth rubbed his injured leg.

"I am ss-sorry I hurt you."

"You have a good aim."

"The others-ss don't think ss-so. I am always-ss last in the ss-skill games-ss."

Esak was smaller and scrawnier than most Ranoran boys his age. Jen-Varth had observed some of their weaponry competitions and tests of strength and courage, occasionally imaginative and mostly harmless—except those that involved stalking a Ranoran predator and the one that had brought Esak out here.

"Will you leave Ranor after you reach Age?"

"No one will ss-sponsor me."

Without demonstrable skills Esak would have little hope of ever leaving Ranor. "What happened to your parents?"

"Ss-slavers-ss killed them."

"Slavers don't raid here."

"Before the Protectors-ss came."

The Protectors hadn't been on Ranor much longer than Jen-Varth had.

"Why did your parents come here?"

"My caretaker ss-said they wanted a better life. He is-ss old and will die ss-soon."

Life on Ranor was simple and hard. It was a place where one lived and died. How was that better?

Esak fell asleep immediately. Despite his lingering fatigue, Jen-Varth pondered his own future. With his education and training, he had options. He could return to Xenna, although he could never face his father again, not after his failure.

* * *

He awoke suddenly from his fitful sleep. The boy huddled next to him, shivering. "I ss-saw a . . . m-man . . . in dark clothes-ss . . . in the . . . f-forest."

Jen-Varth heard a noise among the trees. Moments later, Arion stepped into his view.

Jen-Varth's anger rose. "Leave us alone!"

"Come with me and learn."

"I don't care!"

"You once cared."

How did this Elf know his past? "That was a lifetime ago."

"Ten years is not a lifetime."

"Not for an Elf who lives ten times as long as I will!" Jen-Varth fought against the memory of the friend he had lost. He finally asked, "Did you know one called Dayon?"

"I seek his aid as well."

Perhaps this Elf wasn't as all-knowing as he seemed. Jen-Varth managed a stiff reply. "Dayon is dead."

"My information indicates otherwise."

"I watched him die!"

Arion mumbled words and made gestures. A circle of light enveloped Esak. The boy vanished.

"What have you done!" Jen-Varth grabbed his DN-32 from its holster, but before he could fire, Arion gestured and Jen-Varth found himself unable to move.

"I returned the boy to his settlement. Accompany me. You may find what you seek."

The Elf gestured and Jen-Varth was able to move again. He saw no answers in the Elf's impassive eyes, but he did see trust. Perhaps that was a place to start.

5

I MUST BE DREAMING
Day One: Planet Stracos, Morning

Dragons? Two extra-large saurians were debating whether I'd taste better raw or charbroiled.

Loud knocks on the door brought me out of that nightmare. I sat up and rubbed the crumbles out of my eyes as I looked around. No dragons, but this sure wasn't my apartment. Then I remembered that I was in my other dream, the one where Jake and this guy Arion had dragged me to another world.

I stretched myself on the dream feather bed I'd fallen asleep on and which had done wonders for my aching body. Interesting. Time had passed in my dream. The fire in the fireplace had gone out. Dawn had poked its light through two windows and was warming the straw-colored woolen blanket over me. The knock returned.

Stumbling out of bed, I went to the door and opened it. There stood a clone of Conan the Barbarian smiling back at me. "Break-fast," it said.

Jake came into view from behind him. "Sleep well?"

"Not particularly," I lied.

He stared at the boxer briefs I'd slept in. "Those aren't sleeping attire for mixed company."

"Arion didn't say this adventure was coed."

"Arion didn't say it wasn't. I'm hungry. Get dressed."

He and Conan waited outside while I did.

We walked down a hewn-stone hall wide enough for five people abreast. Artificial torches ensconced in the walls lit our way. The hunk of meat leading the way towered over me.

"This is an interesting dream," I said.

"You still think you're dreaming?"

I pointed ahead. "What would you call that?"

"Fehlen."

"And the ninja we met last night?"

"Dev isn't a ninja."

Well, I'd never seen ninjas with light brown hair. Maybe it was sun-bleached. His skin was dark enough to explain a lot of time outdoors. His black eyes made him look spooky enough to be a ninja, though.

We came to a pair of doors so high that I expected to see clouds at the top. "Time for me and new friends to eat," Fehlen said. His *basso profundo* boomed through the hall. He pulled open the three-inch-thick door with astonishing ease. I'd dislocate a shoulder if I tried it.

"He does that to show off." Dev Antos—maybe they were formal, black pajamas—came up behind us. "I'll show how the rest of us open them. Fehlen, please go in, then close the doors behind you." After Fehlen had complied, Dev nonchalantly said, "Shit." (Actually, it was *shtet*, the magical password, my dream's version of voice-activated technology.) The doors parted as if they were crepe paper strips in a delicate breeze. Dev beckoned us to enter the room.

We stepped into the Great Hall. The expected crystal

chandelier hung from the ceiling, with more artificial torches instead of candles. The warm illumination efficiently lit the twenty-by-forty-foot room. Each of the two longer walls was covered with a large tapestry. I stared at these somber-colored tapestries woven with scenes of dragons, unicorns, and fantasy creatures to which I couldn't put names.

"Many find them compelling," Dev said. "Please, excuse me while I summon breakfast."

Maybe I was lying in the trauma ward of a hospital, being pumped full of potent drugs. No way could my brain kick out this much fantasy on its own. That sounded right. I looked down at the pager-sized, translator device clipped to my belt. We were all wearing one. Why had I dreamed those up?

"Scott?" Jake's voice jolted me out of my ruminations.

"Him sick?" Fehlen asked Jake.

"Only in the psychiatric sense," Jake said.

Dev returned. Jen-Varth, in his shiny blue bodysuit, strode beside him. Behind them two male servant types in snug, sea-green tunics and forest-green slacks each pushed a large cart laden with covered, metal dishes.

Dev took a seat at the end of the walnut-colored table. Jake and I sat opposite each other two seats down. Jake said to me, "You probably won't like this." To Dev he said, "Scott isn't used to anything that doesn't come wrapped in plastic and seasoned with preservatives."

Let Jake have his fun in my dream. I'd get even when I figured out how to get inside of one of his.

While the servants transferred the contents of their carts to the table, I eyed Jen-Varth's bodysuit. Maybe because I wasn't accustomed to eating breakfast with an alien I asked,

"Is that warm enough?" The room was on the cool side, and it was a logical question, but why hadn't I just asked him how he was or how he'd slept?

"Embedded power cells maintain a constant temperature except in extreme conditions."

His blue bodysuit had the snug fit of ballet dancers' tights, and the hood was down. His long black hair hung over it.

When the servants removed the covers from the serving dishes, wonderful scents of bacon, sausage, fried potatoes, onions, cinnamon, and butter strolled up my nasal passages. That's what they smelled like. I didn't dare ask what they really were. Jake thrust a platter of carrot-colored scrambled eggs under my nose. *What species donated those*? Dream or not, I was hungry and I figured that blowing chunks in a dream wouldn't be as bad as doing it for real. I took generous helpings of everything he passed to me. Large ovals of toasted bread liberally embedded with fragrant, maroon berries came by last. I took two slices.

I pointed my fork, with its carved handle and sculptured tines, at my plate. "Pewter? Wonder how I dreamed this up. I thought I slept through Medieval History 201."

Jake said between mouthfuls of food, "Reality doesn't require imagination."

"I *know* reality, and this isn't it!"

Jake shook his head and continued eating.

Given Fehlen's size, I expected him to shovel down the grub. On the contrary, he ate politely, and after he finished he wiped his mouth with his linen napkin and asked Dev, "Fehlen go now?" Dev nodded. Fehlen scooted his chair back, got up, pushed it gently back into place, and hulked out.

"How strong is he?" I asked Dev.

"I've seen him lift a fully laden horse cart."

I could imagine him bench-pressing me without losing a drop of sweat. "Where did he come from?"

"Arion found him in a deserted village on another island." This world, Dev had told us, consisted mostly of various-sized islands with a few settlements on each. Arion, as the most powerful wizard on this world, received frequent requests for aid. He traveled a lot.

"Who else lives here?" I asked.

"In the keep? No one."

"Pretty big place for two people. Must be a challenge to keep this keep clean."

"Caretakers come every three days."

"Who cooks for him in the meantime?"

Dev flashed a look of surprise. "Arion prepares his own meals."

Who would have guessed?

"When he entertains visitors, he brings in servants from Freetown."

Freetown? Just before Arion left last night, I had over-heard him give Dev some instructions about Freetown.

"What's Freetown?"

"A nearby settlement that Arion founded."

I resisted the temptation to call Arion a scum lord.

Jake finished his last bite of toast and asked, "Where is Arion today?"

"Gathering the rest of your team. I expect him back tomorrow. Today, I will fly you to Freetown."

"Jake's also got a pilot's license," I said.

Dev squinted. "You'll need to change your clothing before we go. I've put suitable items in your rooms."

I lagged behind in the dining hall after the others left to talk to Dev. "I heard Arion tell you last night not to take us to Freetown. He mentioned me specifically."

"To protect you."

"From what?"

"Sometimes he believes that he's the only one here with Magick skills. Freetown presents no danger to any of you."

* * *

An hour later we rejoined in the main hallway. Jake had on olive-green, peasant garb. Jen-Varth had replaced his iridescent bodysuit with a cream, thigh-length tunic that complimented his bronze skin and black hair. Without the bodysuit his blue eyes really stood out. He'd kept his tall, black boots. I noted a small knife sheathed on the outside of his right one. Dev was attired in a medium-weight, charcoal robe trimmed in light gray.

I saw Jake smirking. "Ah, Friar Scott. What prompted the lifestyle change?"

"It's all that would fit me," I mumbled. Indigo didn't match my recollection of medieval monks' robes, but neither did the gaudy yellow one I had chosen not to wear.

Jake wrinkled his brow. "It might keep your mind where it belongs."

"My mind's not the problem."

Jake shook his head. "What happened to that legendary Scott Madison self control?"

"Legendary?"

He shook his head and snorted. "Twenty-four, and still a virgin? That's the stuff of legends." Then he said, "It'll be that much more special when you find the right person."

To complete my character's attire, they'd provided soft, dark-brown leather shoes that felt like gloves on my feet. The robe was the natural-fiber-catalogue variety and had the softness of a seasoned sweatshirt. I'd remembered hearing that monks wore scratchy burlap to keep themselves virtuous.

We came to the main entrance, monstrous wooden doors standing wide open, and I got my first look at this fantasy planet. Arion had popped us through his lighthole inside his place. Dev chanted something, then said, "Our transportation will arrive shortly."

Outside didn't look any different from a typical Earth woods: green trees, brown soil, blue sky. The temperature felt like low seventies. Arion's mini castle sat in a clearing and wasn't anything close to medieval. The dark stone structure was hexagonal, single-storied, and had a nearly flat roof. There were no windows on this side. I had to look hard to find the seams where the stone blocks joined. His house looked smaller outside than it seemed from the inside. Still, it was a modest mansion.

From behind me came the sound of heavy cloth flapping in the wind. Jake burst into laughter. "What's so funny?" I said, turning around. "Oh, shit! *Flying* horses?"

"These are Arion's pet pegasids," Dev said.

"No way!"

"Is Scott afraid of flying?" he asked Jake.

"His stomach doesn't like to fly."

I bared my teeth at Jake.

"Don't be a jellyfish. Besides, you're in a dream. You can't die in a dream."

"And if this isn't a dream?" I was having doubts.

"Then I'll tell your parents that you fell off a horse." He

deadpanned. "Mount up, buckaroo. No need for an airsick bag. Just lean over and spray whatever's below."

I looked at Dev. "Bareback? Wouldn't it be easier to pop through one of those lightholes like Arion uses?"

"Gates are far beyond my abilities. It took Arion more years than I have been alive to achieve their creation."

"How old is he?"

"Nearly two hundred years."

"What!"

"Elfaeden live for centuries," he said. Like we should know that.

The horses knelt so we could get on. We paired up. Jake and Dev got on the male. As I awkwardly got on the female behind Jen-Varth, Jake said, "This adventure's coed after all. You just mounted a female."

I snarled.

"Think monkly thoughts," Jake suggested.

The animals were pure white with a faint ferret aroma. The horses snorted, spread their wings, began to gallop, and we were airborne. Their wings didn't seem to be moving fast enough to keep them aloft and racing along. Was this magic? On the other hand, some people believe that airplanes fly by magic.

At first, looking down wasn't my choice of ways to pass the time, but I screwed up my courage to enjoy the view and the scenery that I was dreaming up.

The sun shone larger and with a touch more orange than good old Sol. We flew over lush forests, vegetation-covered hills, and a small river meandering its way along. I spied animal life, but we were too high for me to see any details. "Is Jen-Varth your full name?" I asked my riding partner.

"The people of Xenna don't have parts to their names,

Scott Madison." A cordial reply.

"Is Xenna your home planet?"

"Yes." A neutral tone.

"What's it like?"

"Our forests are thicker, and greener, and warmer." His tone said that he didn't want to discuss it further.

Had I offended him? "How many times have you flown on these horses?"

"This is my first time." Out of the blue he said, "Dev told me that we will encounter willing females in Freetown."

"I'm not sure what you mean."

"Women to satisfy your biological desires. From your words to Jake, I assume that you have not done so recently."

I noticed the slight bulge of the translator under the back of his tunic. I tapped it. "I'm not sure this is translating your language properly."

"I believe it is working efficiently. You require the same periodic sexual release that I do."

The fit of his bodysuit had suggested that his anatomy at least was identical to mine.

"Do you not engage with a female if you desire it?"

He must be a free-love advocate. I answered cautiously, "Not always."

"Why not?"

"We have to be careful," I said.

"Of what?"

"Unwanted babies and . . . diseases."

"I don't understand your problem."

Great. Talking sex with an alien. "Uh, how do you prevent unwanted offspring?" I asked.

"We have medications."

Aliens on the pill? "Our methods of preventing conception aren't always certain," I said.

"I will provide you with an effective herb."

Before I could comment, a wave of cold passed over me. The horses' wings quit flapping.

Dev shouted, "Jump!"

Is he crazy?

Jen-Varth grabbed my arm and pulled me off the horse with him.

Oh, shit! *Men overboard!*

6

MEDIEVAL HISTORY 101
Day One: Planet Stracos, Late Morning

I closed my eyes to fight the surge of panic. *It's a dream.*
A tingle coursed through my body. For a moment I thought
I'd stopped falling until the pressure buildup in my ears told
me otherwise. An alcohol daze overcame me.

Next, I was standing on my feet, and my brain felt like it
had been washed and dried and someone had forgotten to
take the Kleenex out of the pants' pockets. A Jake voice
said, "You okay, Scott?"

Through blurred vision I said, "I'm mellow."

The Jake voice spoke again. "He looks drunk."

My mud-brain registered the following: being grabbed
around the waist; horizontalized; lifted; legs spread apart;
planted on a soft, warm body; rhythmic up and down
bouncing like the pony ride I'd had as a kid. My head fell
onto the pony's mane. Nighty night.

* * *

Someone nudged me awake. My body attempted to
straighten itself and promptly fell sideways. Strong arms

caught me before I hit the ground. "Most people get off a horse feet first," Jake spoke softly in my ear.

I felt bladder pressure. Struggling to focus my eyes, I muttered, " 'scuse me," and stumbled toward the nearest grove of trees.

After several minutes, Jake shouted, "We're waiting, but not much longer."

Comfortable, and with most of the grog gone from my head, I ambled back, squinting at my trusty analog watch that Mom and Dad had given me as a graduation present. Eleven-fifty. We'd left Arion's place about ten-thirty. The sun looked a little earlier than eleven-fifty. "Where are we?"

"We're outside Freetown, and I see you've returned to normal," Jake said.

"I'm always normal." But I was doubting what "normal" meant in this dream.

We stood a couple hundred yards outside the town. Sentries wearing chain mail vests patrolled the top of its walls, which were over twice my height. One sentry perked up as we approached. Moments later, the front gates opened and the two came out to greet Dev. "Welcome back, Mayor Antos."

Mayor?

Dev pointed to each of us in turn. "These are guests of Arion: Jake, Scott, and Jen-Varth."

One sentry motioned us in. "Welcome to Freetown."

We entered an approximation of twelfth-century England. My mouth opened and gushed forth words . . . "Ah, the age of Robin Hood and his merry men. Actually, there is some debate as to when Robin Hood supposedly lived. The late twelfth and early thirteenth centuries would place him in the time of King Richard I—alias Richard the Lionhearted, Coeur de Lion—and King John."

Jake stared at me. Why had I suddenly remembered a dull history class with a monotonous professor?

I shook the lint out of my head. Freetown reminded me of Disneyland—abnormally clean. The air had a hint of heaviness and the fragrance of a summer morning when the last of the evaporating dew carries up the scents of the grass and ground. No car exhaust, no chemical fumes, no factory smoke. Just curing leather, and the pungency of live animals.

Two stables flanked the town entrance a hundred feet past the guardhouse. I pointed to a pair of wingless horses, one being brushed by a young stablehand and the other patiently waiting its turn. "*Equus caballus*, the common Earth horse. However, we'd need a DNA analysis to be certain." Everyone stared.

"Maybe we should leave Scott here. An ass will feel at home among horses," Jake said.

"I feel like someone else is inside me," I said.

Concern flickered in Dev's eyes. "After lunch we'll visit the apothecary for a remedy."

I envisioned a bloodletting quack placing slimy leeches over my bared chest then poking and prodding my body. I glared at Dev. "I don't think so!"

On our right the town blacksmith banged away on his anvil. When I caught the hot, metallic smell from his forge, I let loose Longfellow, loud and clear:

> *Under a spreading chestnut-tree*
> *The village smithy stands;*
> *The smith, a mighty man is he,*
> *With large and sinewy hands;*
> *And the muscles of his brawny arms*
> *Are strong as iron bands.*

The blacksmith paused his blacksmithing, raised his head, and nodded at Mayor Dev.

Jake told Dev, "That's a poem from our world," and ground his knuckles into my left arm.

"Ow!"

"Close your mouth and keep it that way." He turned to Dev. "I noticed farms outside but no farmhouses."

The crops looked like early summer to me.

"The farmers live inside for safety," Dev said.

Jake raised his eyebrows. "Who would bother them out here?"

"Stracos harbors many creatures who delight in attacking for pure pleasure."

We'd entered along the main drag. Just past the stables and smithy—the corner smithy, because Freetown had two—we hit a four-way intersection. From the left a horse-drawn cart clip-clopped across our path. The feculent redolence of manure stung my nostrils as it passed.

The Crystal Dragon Inn—What would a *crystal* dragon look like?—stood on the far right corner of the intersection. Beyond the inn small houses on neat patches of grass lined the road. Well-kept, conservative dwellings of tan brick, gray stone, and wood.

I sniffed the air, and Dev must have noticed what I did. "Freetown produces excellent wine and ale," he said.

The street surfaces varied. By the stables the road was packed dirt. Here it had become cobblestone. Just ahead it turned into tan brick. No potholes, no wagon ruts. Two carts passed us heading out of town.

"It's so clean," Jake said.

"Each resident is here because he wants to be. This is

our home. We take care of it."

Jake pointed. "Scott, please note clean and neat."

Despite my military upbringing, tidiness wasn't my forte.

Freetown came right out of a fairy tale—no ghettos, no slums, no winos, no garbage in the streets. If I wasn't dreaming, then this really was Disneyland or a Hollywood back lot. Except that those smelled fake. This place smelled real.

After another intersection, shops of every shape and variety lined the street. A street sign said, "White Pegasid Way." The shops were mostly two-storied, alternately red and gray stone, and butted against each other, a faded vertical checkerboard. From the appearance of the buildings, the owners lived above their businesses. Some of the shop doors were open, with the occasional proprietor clad in a tunic and breeches standing in the doorway, theme-park style, enjoying the pleasant day.

I panned my head from side to side and tried to peer into the shops. All of them had signs: Cartographer, Physician, Clothier, Perfumer, Jeweler, Salter—they must not have refrigerators. I had no idea what a Chandler and Posologist were. Did that one say *Courtesans*? In Disneyland? The abundance of anomalies confirmed that I was dreaming. I touched the translator on my belt. Not only did I understand what everyone said, but I could also read the signs. I didn't see how a clip-on gimmick could perform that feat. This was further confirmation of a dream. Unless Freetown spoke English. I said to no one in particular, "So, this is Arion's little domain. I'd like to own a town like this when I retire."

"You misunderstand," Dev said. "Arion founded

Freetown, but he doesn't own it."

He couldn't fool me. I'd been to college. I knew about landlords and how the world worked for them. A powerful guy like Arion sat back and raked in the revenue to finance his castle and frequent trips abroad, taxing peasants into poverty and casting nasty curses if they didn't pay. You didn't build and run a place like Freetown for free, whatever its name. I hoped that my dream would still be running when the peasants revolted against Arion's flagrant misuse of their tax dollars.

Dev took us around the left side of the Town Square with tiled sidewalks and no graffiti anywhere. I was seriously hungry. I figured we'd walked at least a quarter mile. My watch said twelve-twenty, but the sun hadn't reached overhead yet. Maybe it got up late today.

Vendors lined the Square in farmers' market fashion. The shapes and colors of the fruits and vegetables didn't match anything familiar. The lettuce stuff was green-gray. Many of the smells were familiar, but the shapes of the produce didn't match.

We came to the river, which was a couple of hundred feet wide at this point. Across the flowing, debris-free, mud-free water I saw docks. Beyond those were small factories. I asked Dev what they made.

"Furniture and brick. The wineries and breweries are to the left."

Dev pointed to the olive-green buildings with smoke stacks of like color tucked among them. A small amount of steam flowed out of the smoke stacks and angled toward us.

Upstream, to our left, was a wooden drawbridge—the type that splits in the middle—built from whole trees stripped of bark. Stout ropes connected the bridge halves to pulleys. A one-man gatehouse stood alongside. "Reading the local newspaper while waiting for boats to come by to lift the bridge must be a cushy job," I said.

No one answered.

The towpaths were logical since I wouldn't expect gasoline engines, but wouldn't they have magic-powered ones?

On the other side of the river, burly dockworkers unloaded crates from a small barge. "What's on the barge?" I asked Dev.

"Supplies from the towns upriver, and we're shipping out hogsheads of our wine and ale."

As we strolled, I was conscious of many stares in my direction. I thought we were supposed to blend in. From what I could see, we looked like everyone else, and I spied a couple of monks making purchases in the market. Missing, however, were the little urchins who should be running up to rip us off.

Jake asked first. "Where are your children?"

"In school. The few we have are mostly orphans and cast-outs from other islands of Stracos."

"But this looks like a great place for families."

"Not all of this world is as you see here. Families are rare in Freetown. Arion established it as a haven where one can make a new life for oneself."

"If you're all here for the same reason, I'd think families would be a natural outcome."

"When distrust has been your way of life, it is difficult to unlearn."

"Are you from this world?"

"No. I sought to reform a corrupt government. In return they sought my life."

Dev didn't look the fugitive type. "I saw a sign for

courtesans back there," I said. "What are *they* running from?"

"Slavery."

Dev led us behind the Square and next to the river.

Jake asked about Freetown's population.

"Just over nine hundred. Our town has been in existence for eight years."

Jake arched his caterpillar eyebrows. "No wonder it's so clean."

I turned my head at two lovely young women staring at me as they passed. My pulse began to race. I was grateful for wearing the robe because I could sense them mentally undressing me to access my lean, mean, love machine. I nodded at them. "Morning, ladies. A fine day in Freetown." My head followed them as they walked by. I sighed.

What the hell was that about? For a moment I'd felt as if I were outside my body.

We came to the middle of the Square. A huge birdbath fountain confronted us. To each side and behind it four chunks of carved white marble bared their teeth at me. I pointed. "What are those?"

"Creatures that inhabit our world," Dev said.

The large bat statue with simulated saliva-dripping fangs was perched on a stone. It didn't look like a vegetarian. I pointed to a fifth statue in front of the fountain. "Is that Arion?"

"That is Karaydeon, an Elf of great renown and power who lived centuries ago. His presence reminds us that Arion has sworn to protect Freetown. That's why he brought you."

Jake's eyes flared. "Do you know why we're here?"

Dev looked embarrassed. "That's for Arion to tell you when he returns."

As I stepped closer to the statue for a better look, a stench descended over me and made me feel sick to my stomach. I clamped my hand over my mouth and nose and stumbled back into Jake.

"Scott, what's wrong?"

I lowered my hand. "That *smell*."

"What smell?"

I inhaled again, but it was gone. "I caught a whiff of something nasty." I took a couple more breaths. The nausea vanished. "Must be low blood sugar. How about that lunch you suggested?" I asked Dev. While he led us onward, I glanced back and shivered. I wasn't sure why.

We came to a tavern. The sign above the door read, "The Vampire's Den." I halted on my heels and pointed at the sign. "I hope *we're* not lunch." I grabbed my throat with my left hand and stuck out my tongue.

Jake cracked a smile.

"The Crystal Dragon is also an excellent inn, but this one is my personal favorite," Dev said. "I've arranged for you to sleep here tonight. Nikki Quist will see to your comfort."

And we wake up in the morning a few pints low. On the other hand, this was my dream world. I was projecting my preconceptions into it. "What's the vampire population here?"

"We have a few vampiric species of animals, but no human vampires inhabit Stracos."

"What?" I said and pointed back at the fountain. "On this world of flying horses and nightmarish creatures, a simple vampire doesn't exist? I am deeply disappointed." Too bad. A svelte vampiress, dressed in sensual black velvet, sinking her incisors into my neck to taste my hormone-laden blood might be an interesting experience.

"Do human vampires exist on your world?" Dev asked Jake.

"Only in Scott's imagination."

Dev motioned us inside ahead of him.

Stout oak tables lined most of the wall space and filled a good portion of the tavern. Fragrances of spices and fried food hung in the air above a background of beer and wine. Sunlight streaming through the windows gave the place that alternating bright-dark look. It seemed harmless enough. I inspected the floor for bat guano, but found it as clean as the rest of the town.

We chose a booth along the wall, next to a window. Before I sat, I asked directions to the outhouse. Surprise, no outhouse. The place had indoor facilities with hot and cold running water, like Arion's castle.

When I returned, Dev and Jake were discussing me. Naturally. "Why is Scott attracting attention?" Jake asked Dev.

"I erred in my selection of garments."

"Explain."

"The Blue Robes are an elite order of monks who concentrate their efforts on intellectual pursuits. They rarely converse with anyone outside their order. I had not anticipated Scott's behavior, which has attracted attention to him."

"Are those monks celibate?" Jake asked.

"By no means. It's considered an honor to share their bed. They are not overt about it, but women rarely refuse their requests."

I listened intently as I scooted into the booth.

"What's to prevent someone without scruples from donning a blue robe?" Jake asked.

"I haven't heard of it happening. Punishment from the Order and local officials would be swift and severe."

"What about Yellow Robes?" I asked.

"The members of the Order of The Pure Sun are strict celibates. No woman will go near them for fear of reprisals from the Order."

"Why did you choose those two colors?"

"Both Orders visit Freetown."

"Scott is behaving this way because of a reaction to magic?"

"Yes."

"You mean my naturally bewitching charm," I said.

Jake ignored me. "Why did you bring us here?"

"To help you relax before your mission begins."

Jake gave him a hard look. "We'd appreciate enlightenment about our mission."

Dev hesitated. "As I told you before, that is Arion's responsibility."

"Do you know why Arion chose *us*?"

"He didn't."

Before we could ask any more questions, Nikki Quist personally waited on us. Dev introduced us. I thought Nikki was a girl's name. Well-muscled Nikki Quist looked like a bouncer. He was fortyish, wearing a leather apron, and stood taller than the average Freetownie. I decided not to challenge his parents' choice of names or his chosen occupation. For all I knew, he might double as the town executioner. On the other hand, Dev Antos wasn't behaving like what I expected a mayor to behave like. He seemed . . . Dev-ious, and he had admitted to having a clandestine past.

Lunch consisted of a meat pie packed with some of the vegetables that we'd seen raw in the market, all mixed in a superb gravy under a flaky crust. I told myself that the meat was beef though I'd seen no cows, pigs, or chickens. Only horses.

I ordered wine. The others ordered ale. Not bad. Deep red, with a woody flavor. Potent. I finished one glass and had two refills. Was I trying to get drunk? Yes. Was I achieving my goal? Not that I could tell.

I gorged myself like a pig, or whatever the porcine counterpart here was. Dev paid for the food with silver coins and gave each of us a pouch of spending money for the market.

"Do we get shopping carts?" They ignored me. Jen-Varth had been silent since entering Freetown, so I asked him, "Jen-Varth, why so quiet?"

"I'm observing. You should do more of it."

Dev said to Jake, "After we visit the apothecary, you can go wherever you wish. We'll meet here for supper."

Jen-Varth perked up when Dev mentioned the apothecary. Jen-Varth didn't strike me as a connoisseur of pharmacological agents. On the other hand, I wouldn't have thought him a sex-crazed alien, either.

I think Jake expected me to stumble out the door after I had dined and wined to excess. He asked me how I felt.

"Fine." I had a full stomach and a clearer head than I'd had all day. I was ready to see the sights. Jake whispered something to Dev and Jen-Varth on the way out.

We returned to the bright and warm outdoors. I smiled pleasantly at everyone, especially the ladies. After all, Blue Robes had an image to uphold.

Dev led us to the apothecary shop where he purchased some bottles of liquid. He shoved one at me. "This will counteract the effect that my Magick had on you."

"And probably make me puke my guts out. No thanks."

He gave that vial and the others to Jen-Varth, who was reverently hovering over the jars and canisters of herbs. We waited while he made some purchases.

We next went to a Magick shop. The sign outside spelled it with a "k" and cleared up another puzzle. Dev had pronounced it "MAH-jeeck" and emphasized the hard "k" sound. I pointed this out to Jake as we stepped inside. He pretended indifference, but I could see the intensity in his face that said he was absorbing his surroundings.

I felt as if I'd entered one of those old curio shops you see in the movies, complete with creaky wooden floors and lit by those same non-electric lights I'd seen in Arion's place. Cobwebs decorated the corners. This prop room for a Hollywood fantasy epic had jeweled daggers, amulets, pendants, medallions, and fancy bottles of every style and color. I wondered if any had genies in them. Glass cases held gimmicks and gizmos. Pack rat heaven.

As we walked toward the back of the shop, incense accosted my nostrils. Where were the psychedelic posters? I watched the counter for the hippie who ran this head shop to appear while Jake perused a rack of medieval weapons.

A voice from behind startled me. "Good day, gentlemen, and a special greeting to you, Mayor."

Jake and I pivoted simultaneously. Before us stood not the hunched-over little man with a cane, but a soap-opera face barely out of its teens topping a skinny, robed body. He immediately bowed to me in such a fawning fashion that I thought he was going to bend over and kiss my feet. "Welcome, Brother. Allow this lowly apprentice to fetch the Master to serve you."

The toady started to leave. Dev stopped him. "The Blue

Robe is my guest. He is not here as emptor."

The apprentice left anyway.

"When a Blue Robe enters a shop such as this, he is usually seeking rare items and substances for his research and is prepared to pay very well for them," Dev said.

The shop owner came out from in back and smiled at me. No gnarled walking stick or wire-rimmed glasses adorned this person either. He looked the part in every other way, though: beady eyes, balding, short, perhaps in his late fifties. His knee-length robe of putrid purple cut quite the fashion statement.

"What in our humble shop interests you today, Brother?"

How about a couple of scented candles and a sampler pack of Magick condoms?

Jen-Varth interrupted the little man's attempts to hawk his wares. "May I inquire about your herbs, sir?"

Without losing his focus on me, the owner signaled the apprentice to wait on Jen-Varth. *Greedy little runt.* "I'd like to browse," I told him. "I'll call you if I need you." I politely waved him away.

The apprentice had captured Jen-Varth's attention. I came up alongside him while the kid performed illusions with various objects in the cases, clearly ignoring Jen-Varth's herbal inquiries. The apprentice glanced in my direction and picked up four small, colored wooden balls. He held them in one hand, made gestures over them, and spoke some words I didn't understand. The balls began to levitate. He cupped his hands around them and poked them with his fingers, making them bounce off each other while his hands confined their movement. After displaying his skills, he pushed them together with his hands, spoke some more words, then set the balls on the counter. They stayed.

For his next trick, he placed his fingertips together and meditated for a moment. As he drew his hands apart, colored sparks flew out. He traced glowing letters in the air, fire runes he called them.

"What good is that?" I asked.

"Why, to fascinate attacking creatures." Like I should know. I didn't bother to ask what sort of attacking creature would stop in mid-munch to watch the performance.

The owner came up behind me. "Perhaps I could interest you in more substantial items?"

"Your apprentice is doing fine by me."

The kid reached into another case and took out a miniature vase. He spoke a single word then poured glowing dust from it. As soon as the dust touched the floor, flames shot forth. He ignored the floor being on fire. He spoke another word and poured out a liquid that extinguished the flames. The floor was undamaged.

"How much for that?" I asked.

"We sell it for two thousand gold coin."

I looked at Dev. "Is that a lot?"

"Approximately two years' salary," Dev said casually.

Okay. "But what good is fire that doesn't burn anything? The price is a bit steep for a parlor trick. Got any Magick wands?"

He replaced the jug in the case and pulled out a metal disk. "What type in particular interests you?"

"How about one that shoots fireworks?" I could use it on the Fourth of July.

The kid dropped the disk, and his eyes welled with tears. He excused himself. *Did I say something wrong?*

Dev motioned the owner over, conversed quietly with him for several moments, then turned to me. "The Blue

Robes are known for impatience and for getting what they seek. If one shop cannot immediately supply their needs, they may never return to it. The apprentice just made a wand of the type you requested, his first major accomplishment. Unfortunately, he sold it yesterday to someone of much less importance than a Blue Robe."

Dev went after the apprentice. A few moments later they returned together. The apprentice's face beamed like a little kid's at Christmas.

"Oh, thank you, Brother." He held out his hands and presented me with a ring, an earring to be precise. Dev discreetly motioned for me to accept it and to put it on. I don't wear earrings, but my conscience told me I'd better start. Fortunately, this was an ear cuff. No pierced ears on me. The apprentice bowed, smiling widely.

"How much do I owe him for this?" I quietly asked Dev, meaning the earring.

"Nothing. It's his gift to you."

We exited the shop and headed back to the market.

"All right, Dev, what was that all about?"

"I told him that your request for the wand was to decide his skill level so that you might commission an item. The earring is a token of his gratitude for your purchase."

"What did I order?"

"A medallion."

I held up my coin pouch. "Can I afford it?"

"Don't be concerned about the cost."

"What's the purpose of this medallion?"

"It will absorb certain Magick spells, my gift to aid you on your journey. They will have it ready tomorrow."

Peddlers abounded in the market, everything from clothing, jewelry, furniture, and art pieces, like an Antique and

Collectible Show at a shopping mall, but without wall-to-wall bodies pushing each other aside in mad fury. I eyed and mouthed some wonderful pastries.

Late in the afternoon we headed back to The Vampire's Den and were passing the fountain. I was about to ask Dev what the purpose of our shopping trip had been, since it was kind of impromptu, when the air around us began to ripple and turn colors, like someone had dropped gauze over us and filled the air with multicolored spray paint. Some peasants were dazed; others fainted. Dev paled and looked worse than a dog's dinner. Only Jake and Jen-Varth were unaffected.

Then it hit *me*. I began quaking worse than San Francisco in 1906. Every muscle in me went into spasms. Buildings swayed and inverted. The stone sculptures by the fountain writhed and twisted. The world turned black.

* * *

I awoke lying on my back, brain-fuzzed again. Jen-Varth knelt over me, propping my head up while he poured down my throat a liquid that tasted like moldy spinach. When I started coughing, he gave me a few sips of water. Whatever the stuff was, it vacuumed away the fuzz in my head.

He put my head down on the ground, and I saw an upside-down Dev looking into my eyes. "I'm sorry that your stay in Freetown has been tainted with unpleasantness."

From behind him, Jake asked, "What happened?"

"Another of the disturbances we have been experiencing recently, not significant enough to worry about."

Jake zeeked out. "It seemed pretty *significant* to me!" He shouted something about warping space-time. Jen-Varth tried to calm him while Dev helped me up.

Then, suspended above the center of the fountain, I saw a statue that hadn't been there before. It strongly resembled the character named Vraasz from that strange dream I'd had last Saturday morning about the time Arion showed up and before Jake got me out of bed to meet him. I pointed and asked Dev, "What's that up there?"

"Where do you mean?" He acted like he didn't see it.

"Above the fountain." When I looked again, it was gone. "Must have been my imagination. Maybe a bird." But I didn't believe that. I'd also smelled the same stench I'd caught earlier. What the hell was going on?

We continued back to the inn. Dev and I lagged behind Jake and Jen-Varth. "Tell me what you saw," Dev asked me quietly.

I'd only seen it for a few seconds, but the details were vivid in my mind. "Bipedal, taller than me I'm pretty sure, coarse skin, slanted eyes with slit-like pupils." I didn't tell him about my dream. Instead of heavy garments like the dream creature, this one had a sort of thick plastic bodysuit.

"A S'pharn."

That's what it had been called in my dream. "What exactly is a S'pharn?"

"One of the few nonhuman races."

"What do you mean?"

"Most races are human like you and Jake and Jen-Varth and the people here. Even the Elfaeden, Arion's people, are human, although they rarely admit it. The legends say that S'pharn were human until they genetically altered themselves. They see all humans as enemies."

"You didn't see that statue?"

"Nor does anyone else, except for Arion, I believe. One

more of his little secrets. He told us that he built Freetown as a haven for strays and fugitives. I have long suspected that it serves another purpose."

"You brought me here against Arion's wishes to confirm your suspicions."

"Yes."

"What's it mean? And why can I see it?"

"I'm not sure. I knew there was a Magick around the fountain that I was unable to penetrate, but *my* Magick skills are minor. That you can see it must be related to why you were chosen."

I didn't like his implication.

* * *

For supper I ate just enough to sate my hunger without inducing after-meal drowsiness. I considered drowning the day's bad memories with the wine, which for some reason was affecting me this time. The buzz started after the second glass. I was now halfway through my third. The window next to our table provided a view of the setting sun. I pushed back my chair and politely excused myself. "I'm going for a stroll to help digest my food. In case I get lucky tonight, don't wake me too early tomorrow morning."

"Will he be safe out alone?" Jake asked Dev.

"We lock the gates at dusk and our sentries patrol the town all night."

"No problem, I'm a martial artist," I said.

I stepped into the encroaching evening. Two lamp-lighters were turning on the streetlights. They paused at each lamp, waved their hands at it, and the light came on. Sweet.

The sidewalk vendors had thrown tarps over their carts. Street sweepers broomed away the day's debris. Like Disneyland. I kept clear of the fountain and found myself strolling along the outer edge of the Square where I spotted one of the locals.

"My name's Scott," I said.

She flashed me a puzzled smile. Right. No translator on her. My dream was far too logical for my taste. But the language of love was universal.

"Does the Blue Robe wish something?" she asked.

In this dream I was duty bound to uphold the reputation of the Order.

7

NOTCHES ON THE BEDPOST
Day Two: Planet Stracos, Morning

In a dark cave I saw two figures, both familiar in appearance. I'd seen their likenesses in my earlier dream and above the fountain in Freetown. S'pharn. They were talking.

"You summoned me, Lord Vraasz?"

"I have acquired information valuable to our cause."

"My lord?"

"I have learned of an artifact powerful enough to free Orfo, and to grant Orfo power many times beyond anything he had before once we free him. The information only cost me the blood of thirty humans."

"My Lord Vraasz, this news will inspire your followers."

"Morale and loyalty are your responsibility. I go now to enlist the aid of a necromancer who can lead me to it. I will then prepare for the final assault. During my absence, charge our followers to redouble their efforts to find where the Elfaeden have hidden Lord Orfo."

* * *

I came awake, but eyes still closed. Where were these

weird dreams coming from? I heard a tapping on my door and Jake's muffled voice calling my name. "Scott?"

"Come in." I heard the door open. "Can't a guy get some sleep? My body needs serious rack time after that torturous mission and your incredibly bad driving over the worst roads in Colorado."

"Get up," Jake's voice became less gentle, "or I'll find a serious rack that you won't relish spending time on."

Funny, Jake. I stretched my legs and extended my toes. My extra-long mattress assured me that the dream was over. Too bad, because the sex part, at least, was nice. After a long, deep sigh I popped one eye open. "Have you no pity? Waking up is bad enough. Seeing your ugly face the first thing in the morning ought to be a capital crime." I grunted. "I had this dream that you and I went to another world where magic was real—they called it 'Magick' there—and horses could fly. We were on some kind of mission to save the universe." I propped myself up on my elbows and inhaled deeply. "Smell that Colorado air."

"I think you're hung over."

"Not me. We went to this place called Freetown where I met a girl and we made real magic happen. Then I woke up and saw you and some of the magic went away." I grinned.

He arched his eyebrows. "I hope you enjoyed the long mattress we set up for you. We're downstairs and just ordered breakfast. Hurry up and get dressed. She's welcome to join us."

"Later, Jake." I flopped back down. Jake's footsteps faded and I heard the door close. I stretched my arms sideways on the bed—

I rolled my head left at the half of the bed I wasn't occupying. Just enough light came around what I had thought were the dark curtains in my apartment bedroom to show me a tightly curled body topped with long, blonde hair.

Ohhh, shit. I eased myself out of bed, walked to the window, and pushed the curtains apart. A stream of orange sunlight entered the room. The small window gave me a good view of the river. On the other bank, workers pushed and rolled crates and barrels.

I heard the girl stir, and I gazed over my shoulder. Jefferson Scott Madison had scoped out the streets of Freetown for women like a pathetic teenager trying to get laid. Except I didn't remember any of it. I remember getting undressed, getting into bed . . . And nothing after. Still, if I were Dev Antos, I'd kick me out of town. I wanted to check out of this inn, sneak out of town, get off this planet, and go someplace where I couldn't screw up—oops, bad choice of words. And I'd cheated on Lynn.

The girl rolled onto her back and rubbed her eyes with her fists. Her innocent smile didn't help. Standing naked at the window with a morning erection that didn't share my guilt made it worse. Maybe this was natural to her. I pictured the cover of a tabloid next to the supermarket checkout counter. "Man Sires Alien Baby" suddenly didn't seem farfetched.

I followed her eyes to the blue robe draped over the only chair in the room. I was ready to wring Dev's neck, and Jake Kesten was pond scum for letting this happen. *Right, Scott. Blame someone else because you didn't take this seriously. So, what happens next? Do we leave the room separately or together?*

She pushed off the blanket. She was naked. I turned my head. She said something I couldn't understand—since I wasn't wearing my translator. Probably good I wasn't. I looked down at my briefs, lying on the floor where I'd tossed them last night. I picked them up and put them on.

The Colonel had drilled self-control into me. I'd been drunk a few times in college. Once, during my sophomore year I'd attended a fraternity party where the women had flowed as freely as the beer. Two coeds coaxed me upstairs to a room apparently designated for this purpose and began undressing me. Lightly drunk, I was fully aware of my actions and their stimulating presence. One millimeter away from losing my virginity, I stopped myself, not that I didn't want to, but I knew it wasn't the right way. I was buttoning my jeans when they returned with a more willing prospect. I never regretted my decision.

The girl got out of the bed and put on her simple, one-piece, apricot dress. She was pretty, and I didn't even know her name.

I stood there, in my briefs, while she walked out and closed the door behind her. End of scene.

✳ ✳ ✳

With as blank an expression as I could summon, I took a seat at the table across from Jake and Dev. "What's for breakfast and where's Jen-Varth?"

"He went to the herbalist and the potion shop for some things he ordered yesterday," Jake said. "Rough night? Get any sleep or did you puppy out early?"

"She wanted me to stay," I said evenly, trying to make it sound like a simple truth.

"Of course she did. She was a courtesan."

Courtesan?

"By the way, Stracos runs on a twenty-five-hour day so you could have stayed in bed an extra hour."

"You're the one who woke me!" I met his gaze. "How will I explain this to Lynn?"

"No reason to mention it. It was simple tension relief. Besides, you and Lynn made no commitments to each other." I didn't appreciate his cool logic.

Food arrived. Their hot beverage, a hearty tea with a cola flavor, lacked the caffeine kick that I could have used.

"I've arranged for a wagon and one of our drivers to take you back to Arion's," Dev said.

"Why can't we fly?" I asked.

"The disruptions are getting more frequent. Because the pegasids are Magick creatures, flying would not be safe, since I'm not going with you."

"You never told me exactly what happened after we fell."

"The disturbance stunned the pegasids. You and Jen-Varth fell off. I cast a spell to levitate you safely to the ground. The Magick had an unexpected effect on you."

"Why didn't it affect Jake? Or Jen-Varth?"

"You should ask Arion." He handed me a silver medallion, about two inches in diameter and dangling from a chain. It had a crude rune scratched into its face. "This will protect you."

Before I could press for details, Jen-Varth returned with a bulging leather sack half the size of a grocery bag.

"What did you buy?" Jake asked him.

I forked Freetown pancakes into my mouth. Not bad. Crispy, like fritters.

"Some herbs and a potion to help our young friend."

I eyed Jake suspiciously. He anticipated the question I couldn't ask with my mouth full. "Dev thinks you're allergic to Magick."

I sipped the tea. "Magick can't trigger an allergic reaction," I said with scientific authority and popped another pancake bite while my brain processed.

"Dev consulted a specialist this morning. Allergy might be the wrong term for your adverse reaction," Jake continued.

"You're the only one I have an adverse reaction to. You always get me into trouble."

"I don't think that last night's debauchery was in any way my fault."

I stabbed a fat sausage and looked straight at Jake. "Perfect word choice. Debauchery connotes extreme indulgence in sensual pleasures. That about describes it."

Jake cracked a smile.

"Jen-Varth procured more of what we gave you yesterday when you collapsed by the fountain," Dev said.

"No, thanks! It tasted like rotten salad and made me want to puke." Feeling my anger growing, I took another bite of pancakes.

"He's trying to help you, Scott."

I met Jake's eyes. "You want to blame someone? Blame Dev and his *stinking* blue robe!"

"Pull in your horns."

I slammed my fork down, grabbed the napkin from my lap, and threw it onto my plate. Shoving my chair back, I got up and headed for the door. Outside, I located the river. My long, angry strides didn't stop until I was in the middle of the drawbridge, leaning over the railing and staring down into the rippling water of the river.

Jen-Varth came up beside me some time later. The pure water rippled beneath us. Freetown busied itself with its daily activities and paid us no heed.

"None of us knows why we were selected for this task," he said quietly.

I bowed my head back over the water. "We're forced labor," I mumbled.

"We are volunteers." I heard a pang in his voice.

"I don't remember volunteering."

"Arion believes in us."

Chills passed through me, and I started shaking. He reached into his sack and offered me a vial, but a couple of deep breaths made the dizziness pass. I looked at his bronze face and into his deep eyes. "What's happening to me?"

"I don't know."

"Did Arion assign you to be my babysitter?"

"I don't know what role I play here. We don't make our destinies, we merely follow them."

I took another slow, deep breath. "What could I possibly have that Jake doesn't? Why do I keep passing out, or feel like I'm going to? I don't belong here."

"I wish I could tell you that was true. You are connected to what's happening."

"Then you *would* be better off without me."

"No."

"You can say that because you're an *alien*." He sort of looked like one, and I knew he didn't speak English.

"I'm human like you."

"You're not from Earth," I reminded him.

"Why should that matter?"

"Your world has space travel, doesn't it?"

"Limited," he said.

"Well, we don't have space travel at all."

"You think that makes us wiser?"

"Yes—no, not wiser. On Earth, aliens are the stuff of

science fiction. Because we talk about them visiting us in space ships, we assume they're smarter than we are."

"Do the people on Earth all look the same?"

"No."

"Are your people all the same species?"

"As far as we know."

"What is your definition of a species?"

"Organisms that can interbreed."

He nodded. "You and I and the people of this planet are the same species. The Travel Gates have existed for centuries. We don't know how the various worlds were populated. There is strong evidence of a common origin. Do your scientists profess that theory?"

"Only the lunatic fringe and writers of science fiction, but I don't understand your point."

"Your sexual pleasure with the girl is what bothers you. You feel guilt because she was not of your kind."

"That's not the reason. I have a girl back on Earth. We call what I did cheating." Was it? Even though Lynn and I had never had sex? And did it even count if I couldn't remember it?

"You show too much concern over a natural biological function. I wasn't alone last night either. Whatever it may seem, we don't engage in the act carelessly, not my people, not those here. If you enjoyed the encounter, why should it bother you? It didn't bother her."

"She's a *courtesan*! It's what she does!"

"She shows hospitality. We're free creatures, Scott. The One who created us endowed us with free choice. If He didn't want us to make decisions, He would prevent us from doing so."

"Well, I acted like a jerk."

"Factors beyond your control are operating here."

"I disappointed Jake."

"The only one you have disappointed is yourself."

He was right, but it didn't make me feel any better.

"You're different from those around you only when you act that way." I saw the darkness in his eyes as he said that.

During our stroll back I realized that, while Freetown's architecture and customs and some of the lifeforms were different, if you eliminated the Magick, this could be somewhere on Earth.

We came near the fountain. The white statues glowed under the pre-noon sun. When I tried to hurry past them, Jen-Varth stopped me. "What did you see here yesterday, Scott?"

I approached the statue of Karaydeon the Elf and stroked my fingertips along one side of what I expected to feel like a smooth surface. My fingers prickled as if the statue were charged with static electricity. The evil smell came back.

I tilted my head up at the ghostly image I now saw shimmering above the fountain and said, "What the *hell* are you!" I pointed and looked at Jen-Varth. "You don't see that?"

He was shaking. "Y-yes, I d-do."

Someone hit the power switch. A jolt of energy propelled me backward into him. We fell together onto the pavement. I heard distant screams.

By the time Jen-Varth and I untangled ourselves and got to our feet, Jake was running toward us. "What happened?"

"Either lightning hit me or I just had a major religious experience."

Jake pointed around the Square. "Half of the town passed out!" He said it like it was my fault.

Dev rushed up. "You must leave Freetown at once."

Jake's nostrils flared. He aimed his rat-killer stare at Dev. "Exactly what happened here?"

"I don't know."

"There's too much of that going around." The glowing embers in Jake's eyes threatened to catch fire.

Jake's eyes weren't the only things glowing. The image over the fountain was pulsing, and a lighthole was opening a few yards away.

8

KEDDA

Day Two: Planet Thalar,
Town of Rysten, Evening

Everyone liked Kedda, or rather, everyone liked Kedda's money. Each night Kedda the gambler came here to play cards. Each night his purse was full. Each night he lost.

How could this man, who carried his own deck of cards, who used them in the game—the other players let him because he couldn't possibly be cheating—always lose? This puzzled Kart as well.

From behind the bar, Kart surveyed the Common Room of his inn, the Silver Spectre, illuminated by lanterns and waning daylight coming through the three front windows. In the corner, across from the entrance, sat two chain-jacketed mercenaries enjoying Kart's famous ale. The longshoremen, who were usually well into a drunken stupor by now, had been delayed by two late-arriving ships. Rysten's innkeepers, Kart in particular, knew what went on in the town.

At a table near the middle of the room, five laborers sat discussing long hours, backbreaking work, and meager pay. The popular center table held a strange mix of what had come to be regular patrons in the past month. Seated clockwise were the following people: the town blacksmith and his new apprentice; Andrik, one of the Town Guards; and two gentlemen of questionable character, Tarsk and Drogo. All awaited the arrival of Kedda, their unlucky gambling partner.

The Smith, a quiet man who had rarely socialized until recently, had biceps the size of most men's thighs. If his brawny body left any doubt about his profession, the singed tips of his thick beard and his leathery skin cured by years at the forges did not. His abnormally flattened nose suggested his life had at some past time been less peaceful.

Kart turned his attention to the two thieves, Tarsk and Drogo. They were good-looking when cleaned up. Dressed differently, either one could pass for a reputable citizen, a tactic they frequently used to their advantage. Both wore an earring in each ear. An outsider might wonder why they let Andrik associate with them, given their reputations and that he was a law enforcer. The thieves of Rysten—they called themselves the working class—adopted the nicknames of animals as a boast of their prowess. Tarsk and Drogo, whose real names had been forgotten by everyone except Tarsk and Drogo, followed the tradition. The tarsk was a large, slippery rodent; the drogo was a hawk-like bird, now extinct. Drogo's competition claimed that he would shortly join his namesake.

As an inn, the Silver Spectre had no equal in Rysten. So said Kart's patrons. Kart himself made no boasts. While its name discouraged some travelers from staying the night, he had no intention of changing it. "There's a long history in it." He never elaborated. And he preferred local clientele—even the ones who didn't pay—to what wandered in from the roads. "Occasional charity never hurts, and with the locals you know what you're getting, like Tarsk and Drogo. They're interesting company, and they always pay their bills, usually with someone else's money."

Kart freely shared his business philosophies. "Take the mercenaries. They come in every few days looking for employment. Sometimes they find it and leave sober. I know when I need to drug their drinks to prevent a brawl." Kart saw more than most folks realized.

Rysten had been quiet lately, with the winter season not far off. The seers predicted a hard one. No one believed the seers, but everyone was preparing anyway. Rysten's four thousand inhabitants were mostly artisans, merchants, and laborers. Having the only harbor along two hundred miles of coast made Rysten a prosperous trading center. Tarsk and Drogo never complained about business being slow.

Although it was a coastal town, the hilly and rocky land surrounding it made agriculture difficult. Many people found Rysten peaceful, unlike Quastor, a day's journey away on horseback. While the source of one's income was never asked in Quastor, Tarsk and Drogo said it had too much competition for their tastes.

At the bar, Kart's three hostlers discussed the Smith's new apprentice. "He's a scrawny street urchin. Why the Smith took him on mystifies me. Maybe the forge fires have cooked his brain." A second hostler raised his voice. "I don't think the Smith feeds him enough. He won't last another month."

The Smith eyed them disapprovingly.

The third hostler cautioned, "I wouldn't speak so loud. He nearly killed three mercs the other day. They commissioned broadswords, agreed to his price, and left. Four days later they returned, approved the work, and tossed him a pouch of silver worth half the agreement. I saw it all from across the street. When the Smith pointed out their error, they turned to leave. By the time the Town Guards got there, he'd bloodied all three. The guards returned their money, gave the swords back to the Smith, and told them to get out of town or they'd let the Smith finish what he'd started."

Kart didn't hear the rest of their conversation. He saw a figure enter and quietly move to a dark booth in the farthest corner. He felt himself shiver, then busied himself washing mugs and wiping up behind the bar.

Two mercenaries that he hadn't seen before entered and walked up to the center table. He focused on them to redirect his thoughts.

"Can you direct us to the best inn in town?" Kart heard trouble in the man's voice.

Drogo looked up. "You've found it."

"This is your *best*? I've seen better stables."

"Try Hilfar's place two streets north, three east."

Tarsk laughed. "We call it 'The Lice and Mice.' You'll fit right in."

The mercenary drew a dagger and waved it in front of Drogo.

Andrik rose from his chair. "May I help you?" Kart treated all the Town Guards well.

"This is none of your affair."

"It is now." Staring the mercenary down, Andrik crossed his gloved right hand to the sword sheathed on his left side.

Kart shifted his attention to the dark corner. He saw the man's lips move, his hands gesture lightly above the oak tabletop.

The scene with the mercenaries changed abruptly. The one calmly replaced his dagger. A puzzled-looking Andrik escorted them both outside.

Kart made his rounds to refill drinks. Drogo stroked his

scant, sandy goatee. "Mighty peculiar. His kind gives us reputable folk a bad name."

As Kart finished up, Andrik returned. Since he was off duty, he would have turned his prisoners over to the current watch. Behind him came the awaited arrival.

Drogo smiled widely. "Kedda! Purse full? I feel lucky."

With a sideways glance at his partner, Tarsk said, "Luck has nothing to do with it. You know he always loses." He looked up at Kedda. "Why do you play with us? You always lose all your coin, yet come back to lose more?"

Kart knew that Tarsk and Drogo wondered where Kedda got a purse full of gold and silver each night. They secretly feared him as competition.

Kedda grinned, spreading his arms. "For the enjoyment, gentlemen. What good is having money if one does not enjoy life? Do I seem malcontent?" Drogo started to speak, but Kedda continued, "After good Innkeeper Kart has supplied me with a bit of the savory stew that I smell, I shall be ready to trounce you." He regarded Kart. "More ale for each of my friends."

All laughed heartily. Andrik took his seat on Tarsk's right. Kedda pulled a chair from another table and wedged it between Tarsk and Drogo. "I expect you to keep an eye on me from both sides to be sure that I don't cheat."

Kedda's fair-skinned, unbearded face, and modest length, brown hair made him look young. His manner bespoke experience. His five-foot-four height made him unremarkable. Except for his violet eyes.

Kart stepped into the kitchen to give Alir, his daughter, the order for the food. He knew that Kedda often vanished during the day and that Drogo had made discreet inquiries to see if more purses than usual came up missing.

Kart returned with bread and cheese. Kedda flipped him four pieces of gold. Drogo's eyes widened. "*One* would be overpayment."

"Kart deserves something extra to make his life more comfortable," Kedda replied.

"He's jealous because that's four he won't get his hands on tonight," Andrik said.

Kedda sipped his ale and took a bite of bread. While he chewed, he dumped the contents of his pouch onto the table. Drogo's eyes widened. He reached for the gems that tumbled out. The Smith caught his hand. "I believe those are for tonight's play and not a gift to you, my friend."

"Just wanted a closer look," Drogo grumbled.

"Win them, and you can look all you want." He released Drogo's wrist.

"Are you ever going to bet that ring?" Tarsk asked Kedda.

Kart had seen the thieves eye Kedda's silver ring and its deep black stone numerous times.

"It's my past, present, and future. To give it up would be to lose what I am. It takes me where I wish to go and enables me to do what I must."

Kart noted their puzzled expressions as his daughter came from the kitchen to serve the food. Alir was comely, taller than most women, and still unspoken for at twenty years of age. A number of young men had tried, and failed, to gain her attention. Kart had heard her proclaim, "I'm not ready to marry. When I am, I'll select my own husband." She was headstrong enough to mean it and single-minded enough to get the man she wanted. She was currently taking nightly walks with Kedda.

After she left, the Smith asked Kart, "Is this a new brew? It's especially hearty."

"An experiment."

One of the mercenaries, who was barely awake at the other table, said, "He probably let the rats piss in it."

With a dramatic gesture, Kedda added, "Ah, but surely the most noble of rodents, for none of low breeding would dare visit Kart's fine establishment." Snickers and chuckles came from all around the table.

Kedda had arrived several months ago, at the beginning of the summer season. Hair matted with dirt and sweat, dressed in worse rags than street beggars, and looking like an escaped prisoner, the Town Guards arrested him when he left the shop of Rysten's finest clothier wearing garments that few lords could afford. They were sure he had stolen them and killed the proprietor. They said that Kedda cooperated peacefully, never raising his voice or protesting while they investigated.

Recently, a merchant asked him what he had done before coming to Rysten. Kedda answered, "A man's present and past are his own. If he loses those, he is no longer himself." Kedda smiled politely and walked away after overpaying for his purchase.

Kart heard all the stories. No one in Rysten, except Kedda, knew who or what Kedda really was. Of that Kart was certain. Nothing about him revealed his place of origin. One rumor suggested that he might be a powerful Mage in disguise. Kedda was not a Mage. That Kart also knew.

Stranger people than Kedda lived in Rysten. Like the Potion Maker, the scrawny little man who always had boiling pots and vats of liquids smelling up his shop on the edge of town. Some smells were deliciously alluring; others could ward off carrion beasts. "Potions, lotions, and sundry notions," he called out when anyone entered the shop. His top-selling items were love potions and vermin repellents. The Thieves' Guild provided some of his best clients.

After Kedda finished his meal, he began the ritual that prefaced their card game. "I don't suppose you gentlemen would care to engage me in cards?"

Feigning disinterest, Andrik replied first, "Perhaps another night."

Tarsk followed with, "I might play for an hour."

Tonight, Drogo broke form. "Why don't we forget the game and just split his money among us? We're going to win it all anyway." The others glared at him.

Kart washed more mugs while the card players continued.

"It's a slow night," Alir said behind him.

"I thought I noticed the lights brighten. They always do when my daughter enters a room."

She laughed. "They do not, Father."

"For me they do. Would you ask the gentleman in the far corner if he wishes something?" He was testing his suspicions.

"I see no one there."

Not wanting to alarm her, he lied, "I didn't notice him leave." After Alir went back into the kitchen, he cast an uneasy glance into the corner. He saw what she didn't. The stranger was still there. Why would a Mage of such power visit his inn?

Kart saw Kedda look toward the stranger. Did Kedda see him as well? How could that be? Kart gasped as the possibility struck him. *They sent Kedda to spy on me!* He looked over at the card players.

"Friend Andrik, it's your turn tonight to deal the cards first." Kedda handed him his Tarot deck.

I would know if Kedda were spying on me, Kart assured himself. He returned to his work.

Their game was Jun. As Andrik separated the Major and Minor Arcana and shuffled them separately, the Smith's apprentice, who had shown prior disinterest, perked up.

"It appears your apprentice has played before." Drogo said it to annoy the Blacksmith.

"Have you?" the Smith asked the boy.

The boy shook his head rapidly.

"He should learn." Drogo fingered his left earring.

The Smith frowned. "He can watch until his bedtime. I will trust Andrik to keep him away from your kind."

Tarsk snickered.

"So all that will soil him is the soot from your forge? The boy's life will be dull indeed," Drogo said.

The Smith flexed his biceps for the thief to see and said in his raspy voice, "Continue the game."

Kart saw in the expression that flashed across the boy's face that he didn't intend to lead a dull life.

"Why do you stir up trouble? Was today unkind to you?" Andrik asked.

Kedda took a long drink. "A fine meal tonight, Kart. My compliments to your daughter." He turned to Drogo. "Do not take our teasing to heart. We are all friends here."

After Andrik dealt four Minor Arcana to each player, face down, he dealt a separate Major Arcana, also face down, which the rules stated could not be looked at by the player. The players picked up their Minor Arcana.

Drogo, sitting next to the boy, let him look at his cards, eyeing the disapproving Smith. "He's got to learn sometime.

Would you keep him ignorant of the ways of the world?"

As dealer, Andrik had first offer option. "I have a Pentacle for trade." He scanned clockwise around the table.

"I shall trade," Kedda said. The recipient did not have to state what he was trading. That was the risk, and strategy, of Jun.

The other players had their turns. Each player then bet his hand. Since Kedda had brought few coins tonight and each of his gems was worth many gold, the players permitted him to call bets without actually placing a coin on the table. Drogo appointed himself to keep track of what Kedda owed.

To everyone's surprise, Kedda had the World card, an automatic win, rather than the Death card, which migrated into his hand with more regularity than chance predicted.

Kart brought them a pitcher of ale and filled Andrik's empty glass. "Perhaps Kedda's luck has changed."

"Why do you say that?"

"I sense a difference in here tonight."

Before the second game began, four longshoremen entered and approached the bar. Now dark outside and half a watch past their normal quitting time, they grumbled, "Why should we care about his schedule when he only pays regular wage for extra hours."

"Quastor pays twice what Rysten pays."

"I heard that some sorcerers showed up in Quastor and a few townsfolk are missing."

"Probably just the Thieves' Guild's keeping in practice."

They ordered and took a side table. Kart paid them no further attention and watched the stranger in the corner booth.

The Smith sent the boy home. The longshoremen left after two more drinks. Kedda's unluck had finally manifested itself.

While the card players paused for a snack, a bard entered. "A song for anyone?" he inquired.

"Sing one for our favorite loser." Tarsk indicated Kedda and tossed the Bard a gem from his own pile. The Bard's eyes brightened at his sudden wealth.

Drogo snarled at Tarsk. "Are you ill?"

"Perhaps honest wealth has reformed him," Andrik suggested.

The Bard strummed his lute. The players listened to his haunting tune and verse:

> *I sing of a youthful wanderer*
> *Born under troubled stars;*
> *Fated from birth for all his years,*
> *His soul imprisoned and forever drenched*
> *With endless stinging tears.*
> *His grief was woven from the thread of his soul,*
> *A shroud that enwraps him in strife.*
> *Will he find One to unravel his curse,*
> *And rekindle the fire of his life?*

Kart momentarily forgot his preoccupation with the stranger and asked, "A self-portrait, Bard?"

"A tale, embellished a bit, of one I met in my travels."

"Well, Tarsk, I hardly think that your ill-spent money bought good cheer," Drogo said.

Tarsk flipped a gold coin at the bard. "Sadness reminds us that the world is not always bright."

Drogo growled.

The game resumed. Kedda's remaining wealth quickly transferred itself to the others. Tarsk won the most, further adding to Drogo's displeasure, but Kart knew that would be forgotten after he and Tarsk completed their patrol tonight. While some nights were better than others for them, Kart had never seen the two thieves return empty-handed from a foray.

The Smith left. The thieves finished their ale and bade farewell. It was nearly midnight. Andrik had the next watch and would be leaving soon. Rysten paid its guards well to ensure that it was a decent place to live.

Kart cleaned up more slowly than usual, hoping that the stranger would soon leave. *Does he know that I can see him? If not, perhaps I could gain surprise.* Despite his elaborate precautions, he feared that the Brotherhood would one day regain their memory of him and seek him out. He worried for Alir.

Kart forced his attention back to Kedda and Andrik. "You're a strange one, Kedda. I think you lose to us on purpose."

"Mysteries make life interesting."

Andrik smiled. "What has life revealed to you?"

"That every man should have three goals: to stay out of trouble, to remain free to enjoy the time given to him, and to die with no outstanding obligations."

"A noble philosophy. I'll keep that in mind during my watch. Good night to you." Andrik left.

Alir came out. She had straightened her hair. "Good night, Father." She kissed him, then walked over to Kedda and lifted his arm from the table. "A million stars and two full moons await us." She escorted him outside.

Kart had never seen her this happy, but he was sure the relationship was temporary.

The man in the corner arose and approached. Kart's frustration flared as the man stepped from the shadows. "What do you want of me, Mage?"

"I did not expect to encounter an Adept capable of penetrating my Concealment."

"You're not here for me?"

"I require the services of the one you know as Kedda."

"He is not a Mage."

"No."

Kart had hoped for more. "Take me instead. He makes my daughter happy. Let him remain. My power is not insignificant."

"If it were sufficient, I would accept your offer, but forces greater than you understand are at work. It is best that you remain ignorant of them." The stranger drew back the hood that had covered his ears and most of his face. In the dim light the aura around him became obvious. "I am Arion."

"An Elf? Then it's *true* that your bodies glow?"

"We do not boast about it." Arion replaced his hood and left the inn.

Kart stared reverently after him. What affair was so grave that an Elfaeden sought another's aid?

Six days ago, another Mage had come here just after midnight, seeking lodging. Kedda had been the only one still in the common room. The Mage ordered ale and walked over to Kedda. "A game of cards, sir?" He placed a Tarot deck on the table as he seated himself.

Kedda had appeared uninterested. Nevertheless, the Mage shuffled and dealt. To Kart's surprise, the Mage lost game after game. Finally, he accused, "You have cheated!"

"It's your own deck, sir, and you dealt," Kedda said.

"You aren't the innocent you pretend to be!"

"That's true. I come from another world around a distant star."

The stranger's gaze fell upon Kedda's ring. "What stone is in that ring?"

"Not a Mage-stone, sir, else you would have divined that." Kedda pointed at Kart. "This innkeeper is an upstanding resident of this town, and I consider him a friend. He wishes no trouble, nor do I." Kedda got up from the table, left his winnings behind, and walked up the stairs to his room, smiling at Kart.

The Mage delayed before taking the money and going to his own room. Kart hadn't seen him leave the following morning.

Were the visits of two Mages here, days apart, coincidence? If this were Quastor, he would understand. Its illicit trade included objects that enticed Mages to visit, but Rysten held little attraction for Mages of power. Kart had reassured himself that he was safe because the other Mage had been a minor practitioner, unable to read Kart as Mage.

Kart picked up a mopping cloth and made his rounds to wipe down the tables and extinguish the lanterns. The lingering scents of his patrons hovered subtly in the air. The odors on a man's clothing sometimes revealed where he had recently been. Not so with Kedda.

By the time he finished cleaning up, the night breezes and the nighttime quiet of Rysten's streets had cleared out the residues of the day's activity. Only the two lanterns flanking the bar remained lit. The cool light of the twin Thalaran moons coming through the double front doors gave a blue-gray cast to the rest of the room. During the warm months he left the doors open. He never locked them. His guests needed free access, and what good was a lock against a determined thief? Or a Mage?

Kart removed his apron and draped it over a hook behind

the bar. For others it was time for sleep. Despite the Elf's professed purpose here, today's events had unsettled Kart. He would not allow his past to taint Alir. He walked into the kitchen, down into the cellar, and stopped before a blank wall. He spoke a Word. A hidden door slid aside.

* * *

Upon returning with Alir, Kedda sensed Arion—concealed by Magick—waiting outside the Silver Spectre. After escorting her inside and bidding her good night he returned to where Arion, now visible, stood.

"I am Arion—"

Kedda regarded him. "You are a Mage of the Elfaeden, and you dislike telepaths. You've located one of the items I seek. I detected it one time, some months ago. Since then it has been shielded from me." Kedda smiled knowingly. "I would like to meet these friends of yours whose powers were able to find it. Did they tell you that Kart also possesses an artifact?" He noted Arion's surprise.

"A S'pharn has found a Tri-Lith, and I will be the first target of his revenge," Arion said.

"You have a serious problem. You will need my help."

"Meet me on the North road out of town in the morning just after sunrise."

9

TRAX

Three Years Ago: Planet Thalar, Town of Jocathan

Trax leaned against the brick sidewall of the bakeshop and chewed a stick of dried meat while he scanned the morning streets of Jocathan for the promise of funds. The girl—her name was Nistenna—who had made him a man last night on his sixteenth birthday, deserved something very nice.

Before that, over supper, Mylane had once again pressed him to select a legitimate trade. He'd already decided that. Even though the Thieves' Guild wasn't officially recognized in Jocathan, it operated much as the others did, except that *its* apprentices didn't openly boast or announce themselves. Of course, Mylane wouldn't let him apprentice there, but then she wasn't his *legal* guardian. At sixteen he could apply for membership, which he planned to do after he finished this little job. He knew they'd put him through some sort of test. The best young thief in Jocathan didn't see that as a problem.

He thought that Mylane wasted her money paying certain individuals to protect him from unwise or careless actions. He was never careless. Beneath the angelic façade that he carefully maintained—and motivated by years of teasing from boys who had legitimate parents—guile and craftiness served him better than the education Mylane provided.

It wasn't that he didn't appreciate her concern. She loved him. He returned that love, within limits. He couldn't let his friends think that he depended on her. After all, she ran a house of courtesans. He suspected that he was the careless result of one of her girls. Despite her profession he respected her. She was good at what she did. Like he was.

Everyone in Jocathan knew Mylane, one way or another. While she no longer actively engaged in the profession herself, her business prospered. She provided for his needs. His skills provided for his wants.

He spied a white-haired old man hobbling along the street. The tall, ebony walking staff was a sure sign of wealth. *Such fine, rich robes. Such a burden he's carrying.* He decided to help the man cross the rough, cobblestone street and lighten his burden at the same time.

Trax took another bite of his meat stick and wrapped it in a piece of glazed paper before he stuffed it into a pocket of his black leather pants—a good thief is never messy. He straightened his gray tunic, and put on his most helpful smile.

Some minutes later he stood in an alley fondling the pouch of coins. Long, heavy garments rarely challenged his skills. The graybeards were so unimaginative. If he couldn't tell by a man's gait where the money was stored, then there wasn't enough to concern him. This would buy Nistenna a handsome gift.

He recalled last night and sighed. He had come home at his usual late hour to find his bed already occupied. Drawing his knife and holding it close to his face in readiness, he narrowed his eyes into the dim light cast by the lantern beside the bed. He'd seen Mylane talking to this girl a few days ago.

"You have kept me waiting," she said with a soft sweetness that dissolved his caution.

He dropped his knife when the girl folded down the blanket and got up from the bed, naked. She came up to him, pulled his body against hers, and pressed her lips tightly upon his. The tingle of that kiss crept down his neck and torso, then pulsed inside his leather pants. The shivers kept him from moving while she undressed him and took him to bed with her.

At first he was angry with Mylane. This was something a young man should plan on his own. But after Nistenna pleasured him three times, his anger had melted. Despite pretending to shield him from the ways of the world, Mylane was a canny woman. She would know that sixteen-year-old, virgin boys weren't respected by their peers. Of course, being the best, Trax had no peers.

Trax fingered the pouch of coins, counting them through the soft leather—more than enough. He listened to them contacting each other. Gold? Not silver? Gold would assure him many more nights like the last one.

He shot a glance around the corner, spied the old man limping away, then opened the drawstring to verify what his nimble fingers and keen ears had told him. A moving shadow made him snap his head left. There stood the old man looking neither decrepit nor unconcerned. Their eyes met, and the old man spoke words that Trax didn't understand. A terrible moment later, when his muscles refused to obey him, he knew that he had pickpocketed a Mage and that he would never again experience the pleasures of last night.

If only he had listened to Moka. His friend was three

years older and had spent a year as apprentice to a Mage, before the Mage died in an unfortunate accident. Moka was currently apprenticed to an apothecary and fond of telling Trax, "Mages can trap your soul. If you ever pickpocket a wizard, your life will be his."

Trax cast his eyes down at the ring on his finger, his prized possession. Moka had also warned him that it would be useless against a Mage. He wished he'd never won it in that card game last year. As the Mage led him out of the alley, he remembered, and regretted, every detail.

Hemla the gambler had taught him the gambling card games. Mylane didn't approve of Hemla's teachings. Trax had properly sooted his cheeks and put on worn, baggy clothes to hide his well-fed appearance. At that particular game sat Ilkaf, Hemla, and a traveler who had come to see Jocathan's new printing presses. Ilkaf was one of those whom Mylane paid to watch over Trax. Among the stranger's silver and gold coins Trax spied the ring. It might have been a simple wedding band for all its plainness. Trax's keen eyesight spotted the rune engraved on its inner surface. Moka had told him that runes and Magick slept in the same bed. Trax liked that description.

Trax convincingly lost each round of cards. Down to his last two coins, he pointed at the ring and said with a doleful voice and moisture-laden eyes, "I've never had a ring."

He saw the stranger look to the other men. "Very well, but you must win it." Trax cheated, of course, but the man either didn't notice or didn't care. Trax didn't worry about the few silver coins he'd lost to gain the ring. He could easily replace those. He had something far more valuable.

The next day, he went to see Moka. "This rune indicates detection Magick," Moka told him, proud of his knowledge.

"But it's probably weak Magick, otherwise its rightful owner would have come after it. Perhaps the card player stole it and killed its owner."

Trax doubted that.

"He may have been unaware of its powers, as you claim, or he may have tricked you into winning it," Moka said.

"Tricked?"

"It could be cursed. Sometimes the only way to rid yourself of a curse is to have another freely accept it."

Trax didn't see how a curse could work that way.

Moka narrowed his eyes. "As for the ring's ability, you may have to wear the ring to discover what it is. Of course, that would activate the curse. Ask yourself, why was your benefactor not wearing it?"

"What type of curse?"

"There are no *true* curses, but certain spells can summon evil things. Powerful Mages delight in the suffering of others."

Trax wanted to know if all powerful Mages were evil.

"When you have that much power, there's little distinction between good and evil. They cast potent and unpleasant Magicks upon their things. You already know about the Pocket of Woe."

Not personally. Some of his friends had related their experiences. If you didn't speak the correct Magick Word before you put your hand in, sharp teeth bit you. It was a sensory illusion, Moka had explained, but the pain felt real, and your scream delighted your would-be victim. Of course, the Pocket was always empty, adding to your embarrassment.

Moka resumed his explanation, "Curses are simply baneful Magick. I learned this from my Mage. If you pursued an honest craft like Magick, you would know this, too."

Trax had found Moka especially annoying that day. "If Magick is so powerful, why is your Mage dead?" Moka looked at the floor. While Trax didn't appreciate Moka's constant attempts to reform him, Moka was still a friend. "I'm sorry," he said. Trax closed one eye and held up the ring to peer through it.

"Don't tempt the Fates to shorten your life."

"If I don't tempt them, my life will be one of missed opportunities." He slipped the ring onto his left hand.

"A cursed item may have a spell of Permanent Possession to prevent you from removing it."

Trax gasped, then saw Moka laughing. He yanked the ring off his finger.

"The Fates must be asleep. Replace the ring and look around. Tell me what you see."

Trax scanned the apothecary shop. "That shelf." He pointed behind the counter at a shelf of colored glass bottles. "Those bottles are glowing."

"Ah, remove the ring and look again."

Confused, he did as Moka instructed. "They aren't glowing anymore. Is this some trick?"

"Put the ring back on." He took a bottle from under the counter. "Do you see this one glow?"

"No."

"Trax, my friend, you are most fortunate. For a thief," Moka scowled, "such a ring is a windfall. It's a ring of Magick detection. When its wearer spies anything with Magick upon it, he sees it glow. Someone must have bribed the Fates on your behalf today."

"I can expand my plunder to Magick."

"Of course, Mages have spells that can detect the ring's power and even block its use. They do not take kindly to being spied upon or to having their pockets picked."

"So, I should never use the ring on a Mage because the ring wouldn't tell me he was a Mage?"

"Not unless you were a more powerful Mage."

"Then I might as well not use it or pick *any* pockets!"

"Another well-spoken truth, my friend. Thievery may be profitable, but it's never wise. There ends your lesson."

Trax stomped out of the shop and ignored Moka's warnings. His friends would get caught stealing, but he never did. "I can *smell* Magick," he boasted.

As the Mage led Trax helplessly along, he knew that Moka had been right, but it was too late for regrets. This Mage was taking him to his doom.

They walked beyond the western edge of the town proper and stopped outside a modest dwelling. Trax knew the house had belonged to Moka's deceased Mage mentor and had lain empty for a year.

Mylane stood in the open doorway. "Come in, Trax."

Has this evil wizard captured her too? The Mage nudged him inside. Trax felt his body again under his own control, not that it mattered now. Inside the dim, sparsely furnished house he followed Mylane into the parlor where he saw two chairs and a small couch. Mylane sat on the couch and indicated a chair for him. The Mage sat next to her. When Trax opened his mouth, Mylane put a forefinger to her lips.

The Mage turned to Mylane. "Is he ready?"

Trax thought that he sounded more youthful than he looked.

She stared at Trax. "I'm the one who isn't."

"You have raised him well."

"The fire of youth inhabits his soul. What you ask of him will require more discipline than he shows," she said.

"A fiery spirit will serve him all the better."

"Then I give him to you."

Trax blurted out, "What! Mylane, how could you sell my soul to this sorcerous viper!"

"He is hardly that."

"I trusted you!"

✳ ✳ ✳

For three days, Trax sat alone in a second-floor room and refused to eat. He knew that even if he managed to escape, the Mage would find him. So there he sulked until his empty belly and the lack of a reaction from the Mage caused him to reconsider his method of protest.

He left the room and wandered downstairs, stumbling twice on the stairs from weakness. He couldn't recall the last time he was this hungry. He considered the front door and remembered Moka telling him that Mages can create locks no thief can pick.

A wave of lightheadedness passed over him. He staggered into the kitchen. On the table he found a loaf of bread, a jar of jellied fruit, and a pitcher of water. One scent of the fresh bread and instinct took over. He greedily stuffed a chunk of the bread into his mouth. He picked up a spoon next to the jar and smeared the fruit onto another chunk of bread. He tilted the water pitcher to his lips, not caring that more water spilled down his chin than into his mouth. At some point he must have sat. He had consumed most of the bread before he realized it. He rubbed his hand across his belly and heard himself sigh.

The Mage had still not appeared. Moka had told him, "They can make themselves invisible." Trax turned his head both ways to listen. Had they left him alone? He again considered the front door, but decided that exploring the house might be a safer course of action. Behind a door in the hall leading to the kitchen he discovered narrow stairs leading down. Luminous globes like ones in the shop where Moka worked lit the stairway.

Trax found himself in a room ten to twelve feet wide and four times that in length. Bookshelves lined one of the long walls. He had never seen so many books together. Near the far end he saw a small reading desk and chair. A small alcove on the same wall as the stairs interrupted the stretch of shelves. A stuffed leather chair occupied the alcove.

Trax scanned the books. Most of the titles were in a script he neither recognized nor understood. The few that he could read dealt with histories and various crafts. As he looked at the volumes, he became aware that some of them glowed. These were Magick books! He rubbed his ring. Why hadn't the Mage taken it? He took one large volume from the shelf and opened it. Strange symbols filled the crisp pages. Magick *spells*? His excitement grew as he searched book after book for one that would explain the language and symbols.

"This one might answer your questions," said a voice behind him.

A startled Trax dropped the book he was holding. Behind him stood the Mage.

From a small chest in a corner next to the reading desk the Mage withdrew an elegant, leather-bound volume, which he placed in the middle of the desk. "Or, you are free to leave. It was wrong of us to keep you here."

Us? *What does he mean*?

Mylane called down, "Supper is ready."

The Mage went upstairs. Trax replaced the book he had dropped and followed.

They ate in silence. After supper, he returned to the library.

Trax sat down at the reading desk. He dragged his fingers down the suede-textured cover of the book the Mage had shown him before, then carefully opened it. On the first page was inscribed, "The Elfaeden." Moka had told him about the Elfaeden, the keepers of Magick. Why was this book here?

$$* * *$$

Trax rubbed his eyes and wondered what time it was. He went upstairs and peered out a window at a clear, night sky. The position of Thalar's two moons, the larger one overhead and the smaller one just rising, told him it was an hour before midnight.

A dim light flickered in the study. He peered through the cracked door. The Mage sat on the floor turned away from him. He must be meditating, Trax decided. His hood was pushed back, and his skin had a radiance that didn't vanish when Trax removed his ring. This Mage wasn't from Thalar, not with pointed ears he wasn't. And he wasn't an old man. He was an Elfaeden.

Trax held his breath as he tiptoed back to the stairs and down into the library. Only when he had sat down did he dare to exhale. He tried to read but couldn't concentrate, so he curled himself into the stuffed chair.

"Your bed is surely more comfortable."

Trax slitted his eyes open at the Mage. "Why did you bring me here?"

"To help you learn."

"Learn what?" Trax stretched himself upright.

"That is up to you."

"Will you teach me Magick, sir?"

"Not many who begin that difficult study finish it. Are you willing to invest the time?"

Trax felt bold. "Will you teach my friend Moka also?"

"We have an agreement. My name is Dayon."

✳ ✳ ✳

Moka appreciated Trax's unexpected generosity. After a month of diligent study, Moka had mastered his first spell while Trax had barely learned to read the Magick scripts. "I'm smarter than Moka. Why is he learning faster than I am?" he complained to Dayon.

"Moka already spent a year in training, and spends his time wisely."

Trax held up a pouch of coins. "I must keep my other skills honed."

"Have you forgotten the lesson that you learned at our first encounter?"

"Teach me the spell you use to change your appearance."

"Unless you increase your study time, you will be Moka's age before you are ready for that."

"Three more years?"

"At least."

Moka had never told him it would be this much work, but he badly wanted that spell to use in his other profession. He forced himself to study and the following spring, two months after his seventeenth birthday, he learned how to change how others saw him.

"Now, I will show you how to see past the spell," Dayon told him. "Use both skills judiciously. Deception breeds mistrust, and one who can see through it gathers both friends and enemies."

Trax had expected the Truesight spell to be simple to master, but he kept failing. "What am I doing wrong?"

"It is easier to confuse another's mind than to clear one's own. Nothing is certain in Magick. Overconfidence is dangerous enough in ordinary life. The more potent the spell, the more concentration you must exert to effect it. Magick summons and shapes energy. A failed spell may cause damage, sometimes to yourself."

"Have you ever had such an accident?"

"Once."

Trax didn't ask for elaboration.

When Mylane visited, she brought the girl Nistenna with her. "The well-being of the body is vital," Dayon told him. "One cannot think clearly if one's mind is on other things."

"When will you take me out to test my Magick?" Trax asked him one day.

"Before me stands a fine young man with more education than most men in Jocathan, and many skills, perhaps some of questionable value, and who has here those who care about him. For now the gaining of knowledge is sufficient."

"No! I belong out in the world, not inside reading books."

"When you learn to ask the right questions and to seek what is worthwhile, you will be ready for the world."

He *was* ready. He'd been out on his own. He'd done very well out there. Dayon went back to his books, and Trax knew that his further objections would come to nothing.

* * *

That winter, on a cold snowy day when Moka was absent and Trax had just mastered the spell to determine the strength of Magick in an object, Dayon took him into the library. From a concealed compartment in what Trax had thought was an empty wall at the rear, Dayon produced the black walking stick that Trax had only seen once before, that day he picked Dayon's pocket on the street. "Try your new spell on this one," he said to Trax.

"This is not Magick." His ring told him it wasn't.

Dayon set the staff against a chair. "Cast the spell."

"My ring says it has no Magick!"

"When you first encountered me, you learned the ring's limitations."

Trax performed the spell and announced, "There is *no* Magick in it."

Dayon picked it up and held it out.

Trax grabbed it with both hands. A moment later, he felt his body vibrating.

Then he fainted.

* * *

When Trax awoke, he was lying on his bed, inexplicably famished. Through the window he saw darkness.

Dayon entered. "You're fortunate. You've been unconscious for a day and a half. For me it was longer. It must like you."

Trax sat up. A wave of dizziness pushed him back down.

Dayon helped him sit up again. "The Staff of Chaos is concentrated with Mage-stone, but it is not an item of

Magick. I will teach you what I know about it. Perhaps it will reveal more to you than it did to me."

"I don't understand," he said weakly.

"Nor do I. Once you master it, the staff can take you to other worlds. Come downstairs and eat."

As he followed Dayon, he smelled Mylane's cooking. He sat at one end of the table. Mylane and Dayon sat opposite each other. He didn't wait until everything was on his plate before he began gorging himself.

"You haven't been feeding him," Mylane said.

"He eats when he wants."

"He makes me cook," Trax complained through a mouthful of his favorite heavy yeast bread.

"A boy his age requires survival skills."

Mylane nodded. "He thinks he has those already. What will you teach my son next?"

Trax swallowed hard.

"To chew his food more thoroughly."

Trax snapped his head at Mylane. "Your son?"

"He can carve his own destiny," Dayon said to her. "Or he can let fate drag him where it will. Giving him the staff may not have been wise."

"Your father is probably right," she said to Trax.

10

SIRENS OF ADVENTURE
Day Two: Planet Thalar,
Outside Rysten, Morning

Kedda found Arion waiting on the wooded North road leading out of Rysten. Clouds partly covered the rising sun and hinted that it might rain later. Kedda whispered to Arion, "A thief named Drogo followed me here. He needs to be taught a lesson, but I also have a use for him. Form the Gate for us while I block his mind from perceiving it."

After Drogo had unknowingly passed through the Gate, Kedda confronted him. "You're outside Jocathan," Kedda said. "Rysten is that way, two days' journey from here, sufficient time to consider your error, Drogo."

"What have you done to me?"

"Taught you to be careful who you follow."

"Who *are* you?"

"I'm Kedda, the one who has provided you with plenty of coin and who could have my Mage friend send you to a place where the law enforcement officials would consider you and Tarsk nice little boys playing in the street compared to what they normally deal with." Kedda read the panic in Drogo's mind moments before it showed on his face.

Drogo pointed at Arion. "He's a Mage?"

"A powerful one with a particular distaste for your kind. Only because you and I are friends will he not harm you." The small lie would reinforce the lesson.

Drogo nervously looked over his shoulder. "Rysten is that way?"

"Yes." Kedda held out a pouch of coins to Drogo. "This will ease your suffering on the way back." As Drogo reached for the pouch, Kedda held it tightly. "I require a favor."

Drogo eyed him with suspicion.

"Watch over Kart and his daughter. See that no one harms them."

"Why would anyone harm Kart?"

"Do as I ask and two more full pouches will be yours when I return. Do not fail me." Kedda indicated Arion.

Drogo grabbed the pouch and hurried off. Kedda said to Arion, "You and I are not the only ones who keep dark secrets."

＊＊＊

Trax was in the basement library engaged in his morning studies when Moka came to get him. "Two gentlemen wish to see you. One is an Elf."

Trax looked up. "An Elf? . . . Show them into the parlor and have the servant prepare refreshments." Moka left. Trax marked the page and saw his hands trembling as he shut the oversized volume. He let his hands steady themselves on top of it before he set it aside and rose from the chair. From a rack near the stairs he took the blue velvet robe that Mylane had made for him and put it on. He pondered for awhile before he retrieved the staff from its hidden compartment at the rear of the library.

He approached the parlor shaking. The two sat on the couch against the opposite wall. With the staff gripped tightly in his left hand to suppress his nervousness, he held it out of sight behind the doorway. "I am Trax. How may I help you?"

The Elf stood up. "We seek Dayon, who possesses the Staff of Chaos." Being only the second Elf he had met, Trax couldn't be sure of his age.

"May I know your names?" He hoped that formality would help him maintain his composure.

"I am Arion. My companion is Kedda."

Neither one seemed threatening, but how did they know of the staff? It had shields against detection except when in use. He hadn't used it since his father and mother left a month ago. Should he trust these two? He casually brought the staff into their view and came into the room. He took the corner chair to the right of the doorway, across from them holding the staff upright next to him.

The servant arrived with a tray of refreshments. Trax watched him hand out napkins and sweet biscuits and pour the herb tea. After the servant left, Trax calmly picked up his cup of tea and took a sip. "How do you know Dayon?"

"I require his assistance," the Elf said.

"My father is on his honeymoon. I don't know where he is." Not that he hadn't tried to find out. "My father told me that someone might come seeking this staff. For your own safety, I recommend that you not touch it." Trax twisted his lips into a smile.

The other one—Trax had forgotten his name—said, "The Staff of Chaos is not a Mage's staff." He said to the Elf, "It's the object I seek."

Who is this other one? Trax wondered.

"You are Dayon's son?" the Elf asked.

Trax felt his tension dissipate. He leaned the staff against his chair. He picked up his biscuit, coolly took a bite then took another sip of tea. "My father has been gone over a month. He has covered himself with a Privacy spell." Trax saw an opportunity. "In his absence, I offer my services."

11

HE'S JUST A TEMP
Day Two: Planet Stracos, Early Afternoon

The lighthole continued to form a short distance away from the fountain. A few moments later Arion stepped through into Freetown. He motioned the four of us back through the lighthole. On the other side we found ourselves back at his place. He said, coldly, "Refresh yourselves, then we will meet." Pissed off and not hiding it well.

An hour and a half later I'd changed back into my jeans and denim shirt and was in Jake's room, with the door open. We'd been discussing events in Freetown when Jen-Varth entered. "Arion is ready for us."

Jake sighed. "Play time's over."

Jen-Varth led us through the corridors and around several turns to a plush sitting room. Arion, standing at the front, invited us to select seats among the dozen elegantly padded chairs arranged in a semicircle. The hood of his crimson robe—the same one Jake and I had first met him in—was shoved back and I could clearly see his copper-streaked hair. His penetrating, golden eyes captured mine. I quickly looked away. He was pissed about something, maybe more than one something.

The carved furniture was the color of semisweet chocolate. Six paintings of alien landscapes adorned a deep stucco wall behind him. The other three walls, including the one with the door, were lined with longitudinally cut half-columns six to eight inches wide and spaced about two feet apart, as if someone had embedded logs into plaster. But the walls weren't plaster, and the columns weren't wood. Both were smooth, light-gray stone. I said absentmindedly as the work captivated my attention, "Must've taken a lot of time to carve these walls."

"I'm glad that you appreciate them, Scott."

Two strangers entered the room. The young one in a dark-blue velvet robe carried a black walking stick and strode along as if we should be impressed by his entrance. He took a seat at the right end of the semicircle, putting four empty chairs between him and me. Obviously a social misfit.

Words popped into my head, *"He calls himself Trax. He is the Staff Bearer."*

Where did that come from? The second stranger's eye caught mine with a knowing gleam. He sat next to me, without a word, bringing the aroma of leather with him. Short and compact, he wore snug-fit, walnut-brown chamois slacks. His periwinkle shirt had tight cuffs, loose sleeves, and a fastened, banded collar. The shirt, not tucked in, touched the chair. Over the shirt his black leather vest was laced up the front. Close-cropped, sandy hair topped a beardless, rounded face with a flattened nose. Eyebrows darker than his hair arched over his violet eyes. Interesting.

Before I could introduce myself, Arion began, "It is unfortunate that one planned member of your team is missing.

We have a replacement until he can be located." He pointed at each of us, starting from his right. "Jake Kesten of Earth, Jen-Varth of Xenna, Scott Madison of Earth, Kedda of Erebor, Trax of Thalar." He gave us a moment to look at each other.

Which one was the temp?

"Please observe." He waved his hands and the room lights dimmed. The three-dimensional image of a planet burst into the midst of us. "Millennia ago, a race of beings called the Yorben roamed the stars gathering knowledge of other cultures." The picture before us zoomed through clouds to a pair of miniature Empire State Buildings joined by a bridge. "They constructed these outposts as bases for their explorations."

The scene changed to an interior, showing a semicircular arch in the middle of an otherwise empty chamber. In the darkness around us, for the first time I noticed the glow of Arion's skin.

He resumed, "Mages and Psis are able to create Gates of limited duration, such as I used to bring each of you here. Long ago the Yorben learned how to stabilize Gates indefinitely, barring physical damage or destruction. Many of their Gates still exist. You will utilize them on your journey.

"If the Yorben had limited their discovery to stabilizing Gates, your presence here would be unnecessary. An artifact known as a Tri-Lith has fallen into the hands of a S'pharn named Vraasz. He seeks revenge against my race, but will not stop there. With his natural Psi powers the S'pharn could easily kill all of you. With the Tri-Lith he could destroy an entire world. In Freetown you felt the results of his exercises."

A stifling silence filled the room. The holographic scene faded and the lights brightened.

Arion resumed his monotonic lecture. "For centuries the S'pharn have borne enmity toward the Elfaeden. My people are peaceful, but dispassionate. I warned our Elders of the impending danger. They will not act. Vraasz will not stop with decimating the Elfaeden. Further, he seeks to free another S'pharn, one whose evil is without limit. You must prevent that."

I raised my hand. "You said that one member is temporary?"

"Trax, until we can locate Dayon."

Trax the Temp arose and glared at me. "I'm here, make the most of it." He smacked the end of his staff on the hard floor. As he sat down, a chill passed through me.

Jake cleared his throat.

Arion ignored the interruption. "You have at most ten days to reach Vraasz and retrieve the artifact. He will remain where he is until he has mastered its power. Once he leaves the world that he is now on, he will be difficult to locate and you will lose the advantage of surprise. Jen-Varth's intuition and skills will guide you through uncertainty. Trax possesses the Staff of Chaos, fashioned by those who made the artifact. You must help him to use his skills wisely. I invite your questions."

I considered asking, "If you're the powerful one, why don't you just flatten the Evil Dude's ass?" But I was a guest here. I glanced around to see if anyone else was wondering the same thing.

"An excellent supper will be served shortly," Arion said. "Afterward, you may socialize. You should retire early to prepare yourselves for what lies ahead. While you may wander freely around the keep, please respect your companions' desires for privacy." He nodded to Kedda and left.

As we walked out, I said to Trax. "I apologize if I offended you."

Trax regarded me as if he were looking down at me rather than up. "Your *presence* offends me."

What was chewing on his ass?

He turned up his nose, gripping his staff firmly. I felt that chill again. If the little shit didn't watch his step, I'd turn Trax the Staff Bearer into Trax on a stick.

12

YOU DON'T LOOK LIKE
A MIND READER
Day Two: Planet Stracos, Late Afternoon

Supper. In my teen years it became the high point of my day because study time followed, bedtime came after that, and both meant a respite from the Colonel's ludicrous suggestions that together we would make a great military pair. Every day of my life he had pushed me in that direction. When I first started to walk, Mom said he tried to teach me to do it in cadence. Trying to about-face in a walker is an experience every child should have the opportunity to savor. Not that I remembered it, but Mom's amusing descriptions made me wonder how I'd grown up normal.

She lavished great quantities of sympathy on me when Dad wasn't around. If not for her, I would have been deeply neurotic by age five. Every morning after Dad left, she turned me loose. During my incursions, the enemy never prevailed. Destruction was thorough. Mom told me years later that she spent the two hours of my nap time every day undoing the devastation before Dad came home. He never knew about the battles that took place in his absence and Mom's struggles to reverse his indoctrination. She believed that a kid should choose his own path. My brother Adam, on the other hand, had shown promise early on. Dad wanted to send him to a military prep school. Mom vetoed that. "Brothers should grow up together," she told him. The Colonel did instill self-discipline in me. That enabled me to get decent grades while some of my buddies partied themselves right out of college.

Supper. Arion had not understated its excellence. Jake and I still took turns cooking even with separate apartments. Neither of us was a slouch in the kitchen, despite his earlier intimations about my propensity for fast food and microwave meals. Since being on Stracos, food that was orders of magnitude above the roadkill stew served in college dorms had romanced my palate. The dessert in front of me now, berry-laden and covered with the richest chocolate I had ever tasted, had no equal. This raised a question. Had aliens brought chocolate to Earth, or had they taken it from us during one of their visitations?

Supper. It was also a time to reflect upon the day's past events, a time to plan for tomorrow.

"Dragons coming tomorrow," Fehlen said eagerly after he downed the final bite of his dessert.

"Dragons?" Jake raised his eyebrows.

"Big dragons." Fehlen stretched his arms wide. "They shine like pretty stones."

Jake smiled politely at Fehlen then leaned over to me. "Don't worry, you're too skinny to make a decent meal even if he's right."

"You don't believe him?"

"I believe that Fehlen believes dragons are coming. No doubt Arion's guests are arriving in vehicles which Fehlen calls dragons."

"Do they breathe fire?" I asked Fehlen.

"Fehlen not see them do that. Maybe they let Fehlen ride them like last time."

"Didn't I tell you?" Jake whispered.

Fehlen got up from the table. "Sleep now."

"Fehlen speaks the truth."

I jerked my head toward Kedda. It had to be him, and not Trax, poking into my mind, given the relationship that Trax and I had already established.

"Problem with your neck?" Jake asked.

"Yeah, you're a pain in it."

"Would any of you care to join me for a game of cards? I find no better way to acquaint oneself with new friends," Kedda said.

Trax, who had been silent all during supper, uttered, "You may waste your time as you see fit. I have to practice my Magick." He headed for the door.

"He needs practice because his Magick is less than he lets on," Kedda said.

Trax snapped his head around at Kedda. "My staff says otherwise." He strode out.

"Did you find him under a rock?" I asked Kedda.

"The façade is how he deals with his fears."

"He doesn't look afraid to me."

"He fears failure." Kedda pulled out a deck of Tarot cards. I had some coins left over from the market and felt them magnetically being drawn to Kedda. For me, the game promised to be a short one.

Kedda taught us to play Jun. Given Jake's wisdom in the ways of probability and statistics, I figured he had a fighting chance, but he never needed to engage his gray cells. After two hours of playing—a half hour of that spent learning the game—we had effortlessly relieved Kedda of his coins.

And gemstones. Jen-Varth offered to return Kedda's money. Kedda insisted that he keep it.

As far as I could tell, no one else knew about Kedda's telepathic abilities, except maybe Arion, who seemed to know everything. Maybe Kedda was his answer to, "Do I look like a mind reader?"

The others retired. I stayed behind to talk with Kedda. "Are you the one who's been poking comments into my brain?"

He smiled. "In the short time that most of us exist, we must try to make our lives meaningful."

This might prove an interesting adventure.

Dev Antos entered the room hanging his head like a bad puppy. "I'm sorry I put you in danger back in Freetown."

"Was anyone hurt?" I asked.

"Nothing more than a few headaches. I should have trusted Arion's judgment."

"How pissed was Arion?" He gave me a puzzled look. Maybe the translators couldn't handle the slang. "Angry?"

"He wasn't angry. He simply told me that taking you to Freetown exposed you to danger."

"What's really going on here?"

"Arion will not tell me. He said that he will explain it to me after you leave Stracos."

Enough pussyfooting around. "Where can I find Arion?" If I was the bait and cannon fodder for this mission, I had a right to know.

"He won't answer your questions." Kedda said.

"I want to talk to him. Now!"

"He often meditates in his study," Dev said.

"Show me the way."

13

CAN SCOTT COME OUT TO PLAY?
Day Three: Planet Stracos, Morning

Morning brought Jake knocking at my door.

"Go away."

He entered.

"I thought Arion told you to respect my privacy."

"Know what day this is?"

I grumbled. "Does it matter?" My confrontation with Arion last night had resulted in, "Please trust us," before he dismissed me to bed.

"Suit up."

Tuesday. Martial arts practice. "I'm not awake."

"Wrong excuse. Your body's still running on Earth time, and back there it's noon."

"I have a headache. Besides, I didn't bring my *gi* and I don't have a cup."

"*Gi* not required, and I taught you how to avoid groin kicks."

"Not *yours*!"

The imminence of agony and the zero chance of pain avoidance motivated my lies.

"The memory of failure will encourage you to put forth

166

greater effort. Of course, we could begin right here."

I was out of the bed, on my feet, and dressing in quick time. Once, a year ago, when we were roommates, I'd refused to leave the comfort of my bed for practice. In minutes my bedroom became a shambles, not from Jake, but from my puny attempts to dodge his blows. The myriad of welts and red marks on my body afterward convinced me that I hadn't avoided any of them.

* * *

"Good job," Jake complimented as we exited Arion's rec room. I was proud of my performance. He took me down four times. It was usually double or triple that.

Lo, did I see the aspiring Trax-kabob approaching?

He glared at me. "I was hoping you'd stay in your room until after I'd eaten."

I forced congeniality. "What did I ever do to you?"

He studied me. "I don't deal with peasants."

Jake stepped forward, his barefoot, six-one, muscular body arched over Trax. "We're supposed to be a team."

Trax squared his shoulders. "I've handled things more significant than either of you."

I put my hand on Jake's shoulder. When he turned his head, I winked and took a step toward Trax.

Trax thrust the staff out as if I were a vampire and it was the dreaded silver cross. I felt a chilly tingle, like when I touched the statue in Freetown. Was this a good thing or a bad thing?

Thoughts formed in my mind. *"Our young companion doesn't know that the Staff of Chaos cannot harm you, because of what you are. But I advise you not to touch it."*

Over my shoulder I saw Kedda standing behind Jake. Was Kedda a Magick person too? Bolstered by the encouragement, I took another step forward. "Don't threaten us, you little worm."

He snapped back, "Touch me, and I'll make you uglier than you already are."

I took two more steps, stopping a foot from his face. "Hey, I'm not the ugly one here."

He mumbled something, derogatory, I was sure.

Kedda poked words into my brain. "*I will assist you with young Trax. Don't be alarmed.*"

Moments later, I was levitating off the ground. Trax's mouth flew open. With Kedda's tenuous reassurance, I kept my cool and centered my best penetrating stare into Trax's wide eyes. Moisture beads formed on his forehead as I included some head tics and a bout of writhing torment. When gravity tugged me back, I relaxed. After touchdown, I frowned then smiled. "We're here on a grave mission. Since you know nothing about me, I realize that you had to test my reactions in a threatening situation. It was a good test." I proffered my hand. "No hard feelings."

Trax's wide-open mouth closed.

"And to prove it, I'd like to show you one of *my* forms of recreation. Ever hear of a skateboard?" I put my hand behind me and motioned Jake and Kedda to move back.

Trax's eyes narrowed into a laser beam stare. Finally, a cautious "No" crossed his lips.

I'd make a great used car salesman. "It's a small board about this long," I illustrated by gesture, "with four wheels. On Earth, young people use it to master poise and balance— not that you require either one. Since I didn't bring mine, we'll have to pretend." I demonstrated by standing on one leg to simulate the balance.

Jake chuckled. "You skateboarded?"

Unknown to the Colonel. I'd find a drill squad, skate alongside, and mimic their maneuvers. To a kid who'd learned to about-face in a walker, that was a piece of cake. Sometimes the drill sergeant let me call the cadence. "And very well," I said over my shoulder.

"You try it," I said to Trax. "Use your staff for balance." I illustrated. "Terminology is very important if you want to be a boarder. Your skateboard is called a stick. The various moves have names. Pretend you're on your stick." I balanced on my left leg.

He hesitated.

"Try it."

He slowly copied me.

"Perfect." Having limbered up with Jake, I whirled around and swept Trax's legs. He hit the ground ass first.

"That, my dear Trax, is what we call a *beef*. Insult any of us again, and I'll show you what *face paint* means."

As we walked away, Jake said, "Not bad."

Kedda smiled. I think I impressed him as well.

Gotta love indoor plumbing. The warm bath also let me wash out my clothes, which I'd packed too few of for what was obviously not an overnighter. I strolled into the dining hall, ahead of the others, wearing loose-fit peasant garments that Arion had provided. Fehlen was already at the table quietly shoveling. Dev and Arion stood off to one side talking. They didn't acknowledge my presence.

"Why can't you transport the people out of Freetown until the danger is over?" Dev asked him.

"Vraasz would detect the use of that much power."

"Can't the dragons help us?"

Dragons?

"Not directly. They take a great risk in coming here. Marhesse told me to seek the Staff of Chaos on the world of Thalar where Dayon had brought it. I assumed that Dayon still wielded it."

"I sense that something more bothers you."

"They knew years ago that these events would occur. I found nothing among Karaydeon's scrolls to explain how they could have gained such knowledge. One day, perhaps in a century or two, they will tell me. I didn't want to alarm you about why the disturbances are so strong here. Vraasz found the artifact on the second planet in our system."

Dev's brow furrowed. "On Nyallos? One world away from us?"

"If Vraasz learns of the dragons and that they once guarded Orfo as a prisoner, he will find and kill them. The Magestone that permeates their hide makes them especially vulnerable to the artifact's power. Karaydeon promised that they would live to breed and repopulate their kind. I intend to honor his promise."

Arion turned to me. I felt my face flush. "This is why you must begin tomorrow. Only the shield around my keep prevents Vraasz from detecting me. He brought it down once by accident. I have already left here twice, necessary risks, but I dare not leave again until you have defeated him."

"Exactly what's *my* role in your grand scheme?"

"To defeat Vraasz. You alone can control the artifact and prevent him from using it."

"Lately, I can't even control myself."

"Kedda will help you. Once Vraasz masters the artifact's power, he will come after me to learn where I hid Orfo. I won't be able to prevent him."

"You expect *us* to defeat something *you* can't handle?"

"Yes." He walked past me and out the door.

"Forget that shit!" I said to Dev, "What's to stop me from leaving?"

"He would not let you, and you would not want the dragons as enemies."

"Are we talking real dragons?"

"We should eat before they arrive."

Dev headed toward the table. Dragons. Right. They had me convinced for a moment, just like when I was twelve, into my growth spurt, and embarrassed by spontaneous erections. The Colonel tried to convince me that military school would teach me to control them. I saw through him then; I saw through Dev and Arion now.

Pleased with that insight, I joined Dev. Jake, Kedda, and Jen-Varth entered a few minutes later. Trax followed with his eyes downcast. He took a seat at the far end of the table. Kedda had changed into a Robin Hood outfit with a rich green tunic, forest-green cape, black leggings, fine hard boots, and a pointed, tan leather cap. His garb made his amethyst eyes and sandy hair stand out even more. As Jake sat down next to me, I said, "Get a load of Kedda."

"What about him?"

"His outlandish clothes."

"He's wearing the same brown tunic and moccasins he had on a little while ago."

"Look again."

"Did I hit you in the head during practice?"

When I looked again, Jake was right. Curiouser and curiouser. No way could Kedda be my mentor.

While we helped ourselves to the chow, Fehlen filled his plate with seconds. Instead of his usual distressed leather vest and pants—which I took to be the local facsimile of T-shirt and jeans—he had on a crimson-and-cream striped tunic and new, black leather pants. Drape some chains over his shoulder, put him on a gnarly Harley-Davidson, and he'd be the leader of the pack.

I was munching a piece of toast when Arion entered. "Please assemble outside."

Fehlen jumped up. "Come meet friends." He was out the door while the echoes of his voice still lingered in the room.

With a remnant of toast in my hand, I scooted my chair back and said to Jake, "Let's go meet the big guys."

Except for Trax, who lagged behind, we did a group exit from the dining hall and wended our way through the maze of Arion's hallways. Arion met us by the outside doors. He stayed inside watching while we stepped into the warm sunlight. Jen-Varth and Kedda moved to one side and talked quietly. They turned away so I couldn't see their faces. Jake stood next to me.

Trax interrupted my thoughts. "Is this going to take long? I have spells to practice." He was looking back at Arion in the doorway.

Low-frequency, rhythmic vibrations rumbled in my gut. If a sound can be enormous, this one was. Two creatures, sparkling in the sunlight and dwarfing adult whales, descended. They halted just above the ground then gracefully touched down and folded their wings.

And Jake—Jake the stable, Jake the composed, Jake the imperturbable—exhaled, "Fuck."

"Isn't this a great Monday-morning surprise?" I whispered to him. Although it was Tuesday back on Earth, he got my meaning.

A deep, male voice reverberated in my mind. From their reactions, the others heard it as well. *"Arion has provided us with dinner as agreed."* His narrow, reptilian head scanned us. In two heavy steps he covered a hundred yards. He picked up Trax with his forelimb and wrapped his claws around Trax's torso. Trax turned white as the dragon turned to his companion and said, *"An appetizer."*

A voice I judged to be female entered my mind, *"You shouldn't play with your food, Marhesse."*

"True. Fear gives it an off-flavor." He put the faded Trax down and rejoined the other.

Smart-ass dragons. Perfect foils for straight-laced Arion.

Fehlen ran up to the female and began to pet her. The male regarded Arion in the doorway. I saw Arion's subtle facial expressions and assumed that they were conversing mentally. A lot of that going around. The male turned to the female. *"Our meal will have to wait. The Elf insists that we conduct business first."*

He mentally communicated to us, *"Honored guests, I am Marhesse. My mate Fezeccah and I greet and welcome you to Stracos, home of Arion, Master Mage of the Elfaeden."*

Arion cringed.

Marhesse narrowed his already narrow eyes and gave Kedda a dirty look.

"I don't think it's in your best interest to piss him off," I said to Kedda.

Marhesse gave me a dragon-ish snarl. *"Don't interfere or you'll have the pleasure of cleaning my teeth."*

I froze. No way did I want to be on intimate terms with

dragon mouth and dragon breath.

"*You show spirit, Scott Madison. We will excuse you from dinner.*" He roared then looked at Arion. "*Be patient, Mage.*"

Marhesse sighed aloud and continued, "*Alas, these are grave times. Each of you has at least one skill vital to the success of your venture.*"

"I'm all they require," Trax stated with cocky confidence.

The female pursed her lips as well as a dragon can and blew Trax over backward. "*Believe what you will, young one. Compared to your foe, whose very thoughts could shatter your body, we are puny. Dragons don't admit that more than once a millennium.*"

"I have the Staff of Chaos!"

"*If you could control its power.*" She raised her head, emitted a throaty rumble, leaned back, and brought the tips of her talons on both forefeet together. Trax shot upward with the speed of an arrow, abruptly halting thirty or forty feet above us, and began to twirl on his toes like an ice skater. A moment later, his twirling stopped and he shot downward. I gasped when his toes stopped barely two inches above the ground. A trembling Trax clutched his staff with both hands.

The female said, calmly, "*The opponent you go to face would not have stopped your descent. I didn't intend this demonstration to diminish the value of your skills or to embarrass you. Your Magick is useless if you are caught unprepared. If you were sufficient, the others would not be here. As for the rest of you, watch over him. He may save your lives.*"

The male raised his head nervously to the sky. At the same time I felt the chill again. "*We must leave.*" He told Arion, "*It lies in their hands.*" Before the dragons backed away, the female gave something to Fehlen. He grinned from ear to ear as he hurried toward us.

They unfolded their wings. Without flapping them, the pair rose effortlessly. They hovered far above us while a huge lighthole opened before them. Marhesse projected down to us, "*If you lose your way, Jake, follow the equations. And may your dreams enlighten you, Scott Madison.*"

They vanished into the lighthole.

I stepped into Jake's line of sight and said, helpfully, "Maybe it's a puzzle to keep us from getting bored?"

He looked past me and aspirated, "Shit."

Before I could probe him for an explanation, Arion said, "We must hurry inside."

Fehlen ran up to us and held out his hand. "Tooth from her baby." He touched the crown with his fingertips and the tooth transformed into a hologram of a baby dragon, alive and moving. "Me show Arion." Fehlen lumbered ahead of us.

Twenty feet from the door my stomach began to churn. A vise squeezed the sides of my head while electricity prickled along my nerves. I shut my eyes. A voice exploded in my brain, "*Who are you!*"

I felt as if fiery spears had shot through my eyelids, struck the back of my skull, and were bouncing around inside my head. My vision faded. Distant shouts and voices echoed my name. I was moving, my feet scooting across the ground. A body slammed against my back. I landed hard and everything got real quiet.

A pair of hands rolled me onto my back. I felt pressure on my temples. "Your sight will return in a moment." An unpleasant buzz drilled color and fuzzy images into my brain. "Focus your eyes, Scott." A moment later, I saw

Kedda's purple eyes staring down at me. The headache faded.

"What . . . happened?"

"A psychic shock. You felt our enemy's mind."

I didn't hear the others. "Where's everyone else?"

"Still on Arion's world."

"Then where are *we*?"

"Arion cast us through a Gate to prevent your mind from fully linking to Vraasz. The others will join us shortly."

"What *are* you?"

"For now, it's safer that you don't know. The shock has activated your power."

"What power?"

"You should sleep." He touched my forehead. My eyes closed themselves.

14

APPLIED CHAOS THEORY
Day Three: First World, Before Noon

I woke up to see Kedda and Jen-Varth with their backs to me, looking off into the distance. I didn't see Trax.

Jake sat next to me. "Have a nice nap?"

"How long was I asleep?"

He checked his watch and shrugged. "We've been here half an hour. Kedda said not to disturb you. You left us over three hours ago."

"I was evicted."

"Arion said it was necessary. He gave me a map and gave Trax several large marbles. He called them spell spheres, whatever those are, and told Trax not to squander them."

I spotted Trax a hundred feet away sitting on a large rock and chewing something. My evil self shouted, "Hey, Trax, I heard you got some balls." He didn't turn around.

Jake laughed. "Arion said he would continue to search for Dayon, but couldn't promise anything since he couldn't leave the keep because of the danger. Trax claimed he knew everything Dayon knew. Arion told him, 'In that you are wrong. Heed Kedda.'" Jake did a good imitation of Arion's long, solemn face.

"What did the bad boy say to that?"

" 'I trust my Magick.' Arion said back, 'Where you'll be traveling, your Magick will be of little use.' He gave us an extra translator for Dayon."

"Where do we go next?"

"We find the Gate that's supposed to be on this world."

"Did he tell you the name of this planet?"

"He said it was the first world on our journey."

In the absence of notable landmarks to name it after, I unimaginatively called it First World.

A midmorning sun smaller than Earth's lit a desolate landscape that was littered with large boulders and scrubby plants under a cloudless, blue-green-gray sky. The colors were pale, like a color TV picture with the color control turned way down. Clumps of gray-green, alien crabgrass made up most of the plant life. The few taller plants—none over two feet—had gray-brown leaves drooping on woody stems. If they photosynthesized, their pigment was something other than chlorophyll. I didn't see them inclining toward us, so I presumed they weren't carnivorous.

Unending monotony stretched to the horizon. No rivers or streams flowed over on this Midwestern, overgrazed prairie that showed more, loose, rocky soil than plants. We saw nothing Gate-like between us and the horizon. The map gave direction but no clear indication of distance.

For our gear, Arion had provided two canteens and a bedroll each. Plus whatever we'd brought with us. I still had on the mud-brown shirt and pants from Arion. Trax complained that too much encumbrance reduced his ability to cast spells. I wanted to suggest that he take off his heavy robe. Jake and I carried some of his stuff to stop his grousing.

Jake walked on my right. On my left Jen-Varth's blue eyes scanned the terrain. "The world on which Arion found me was much colder," he said. He'd strapped a holster across his right shoulder. I noted the knife sheathed on his right boot. No one else had weapons, not that I saw.

Trax and Kedda walked fifty feet ahead. Trax made it clear that he couldn't stand Jake or me. He didn't trust Jen-Varth for some reason neither of us could fathom. Something about Kedda, the only one who hadn't insulted or zapped him—not that Trax knew about—seemed to fascinate him.

I asked Jen-Varth how he met Arion. After he told the story I asked, "Does Arion always get what he wants?"

"I have seen no indications otherwise."

"Are you unhappy that you're here with us?"

He thought for a moment. "No."

I said, "Back home, if Jake doesn't have all the facts in advance, he won't accept a job. Arion's got too many secrets." Out of the corner of my eye, I saw Jake nod. An image flashed in my head. I blinked and said to him, "I just got this picture of you bending over a skeleton."

He stopped short. The color drained from his face. "How the hell do you know about *that*? Did Arion tell you?"

I overreacted. "No! Weird shit is happening to me. Stuff pops into my head! I don't *know* what it means!"

Kedda radiated to me over the mental airwaves, "*Trax is about to do something foolish.*"

I calmed down and pointed. "Kedda wants us."

"How do you know that?"

I ignored him and jogged ahead. Jake fast-walked close behind. Trax and Kedda had stopped in front of some tall rocks. Trax was bitching at Kedda, "Arion should have put us closer." He took out a marble.

"I wouldn't advise that," Kedda warned.

"What I do is none of your business!" He threw it as far as he could. Not far enough. It burst with concussive force. We reeled from the shock wave; intense heat smote my face. Recalling an early teenage experience that involved a hammer and rocket engine, I felt for my eyebrows—still there. Where the fireball had exploded stood a small crater.

I yelled, "What the hell was that, you little shit! You want another skateboard lesson?"

He said, smugly, "I needed to test the strength of the spheres Arion gave us."

"He warned you not to waste them!"

"It's a minor spell. Mine are far more potent."

I marched up to him. "That's what you keep telling us. What's your level of competence, anyway? From the way you brag, it had better be something special."

Silence.

"I haven't seen anything to back up your claims and threats. I think you don't want Dayon here because you're afraid a real Magick dude will show you up. Give me an answer—right now—or I'll mangle your body into something your mother will disown!"

Trax sputtered out a word I couldn't understand.

"I didn't hear that."

"Two," he coughed.

"Two *what*?"

"Twolevelsofcompetence," he muttered between his teeth.

"Unless that's on a scale of one to three, it doesn't sound to me like you're a Magick someone I should be afraid of."

Trax set his jaw, turned his back to us, spread his feet, and gripped his staff vertically, one hand above the other. Over his shoulder he glared at me with disquieting determination. He straightened his head and began to chant. Colors started to ripple along the staff. My body began to tingle in that foreshadowing, calm-before-a-disaster way.

Kedda shook his head at me. "He thinks he's invoking a test to prove his competence. He's about to learn how the Staff of Chaos earned its name."

"Should we duck?"

"Not this time."

An emerald green aura spread over the staff. Seconds later, two heavy-duty, armed and armored warriors popped into existence. Their swords were long enough to pole vault with.

Trax rotated the staff forty-five degrees. His wrists went limp, as if he wanted to drop it. The panic on his face said he couldn't. He squeaked out a call for help.

I saw Jake brace himself to attack.

15

DAYON

Day Three: Somewhere on
Planet Thalar, Earlier

Dayon and Mylane sat in the forest clearing surrounded by vibrant green trees. Beams of sunlight filtered through the trees on their thirtieth day away from Trax. Amid sylvan serenity, the torment of a past Dayon had never shared with her edged itself to the surface of his thoughts. He had violated Elfaeden cultural mores on two occasions. That he had sired a child by a human he did not regret. That he had taken a life years before, an event that indirectly resulted in Trax being born, now made him doubt his life path. Trax had grown up without the benefit of a father and was struggling to discover himself. Another part of his torment came from having abandoned his friend Jen-Varth, whom he had not attempted to contact since.

"I have wondered if our son might have behaved differently during his early years had he known he was less mortal than his friends," Mylane said.

"You raised him well. I should have stayed with you."

"You weren't ready for that and neither was I." She smiled. "That surprises you? When you met me, I'd already seen more than women twice my age."

"You made me see myself."

Mylane blushed. "Did you like what you saw?"

"I am not what I should be—should have been."

"The reclusive Elfaeden who care only for themselves? I love you because you are not that way."

He wanted to blame her for changing him, but he was changed long before he met her.

"After me you'll find another, and you will love her as you have me."

Her perceptiveness constantly amazed him. He was twice her age, but in her he saw more wisdom than in the eldest of his people. Her mortality haunted him at times. She would be gone before his life had begun. He vowed never to love another short-lived human.

Occasionally a forest creature would approach them. The Barrier that he had placed stopped any intrusion, and the Privacy kept their curious son from eavesdropping, as he had done initially. After Trax gave up scrying, Dayon moved them to another location. He maintained the Privacy.

"You never told me how you came to my world," she said.

He lowered his eyes. It was time to tell her the story of eighteen years ago that had led him to her. "I am not proud of that day. I fought for my life and lives of others."

"But you survived."

"Not without a price."

He told her the story.

"As I approached the lair, I saw no evidence of Shadow Master's presence. Did he consider me a minor annoyance beneath his attention? Or was he watching with the self-assurance he had shown in the past? Shadow Master had not gained his name or his reputation by being under-cautious.

He had placed his sanctuary in the dense woods nestled at the base of steep mountains to hinder approach from behind. The expanse of grassland in front and to the sides offered no concealment for presumptuous assailants.

"I looked at the sky. I had hoped to meet my foe in fuller light. Even with the spell-absorbing medallion that I wore beneath my tunic and the Magick weapons I carried, I felt unfit for the encounter. My abilities were far too meager. Nevertheless, I had to continue.

"Tavans and Elfaeden had shared this world in peace for a century. Although Tava was a Magick world, Tavans knew little of the Art and they were content. Until the necromancers arrived. They instilled distrust of us and wooed the Tavans with promises of teaching them Magick, building on our selfishness to share our knowledge. When the necromancers enslaved many Tavans, we Elfaeden, who prize personal freedom, let our isolationist dictates rule us. The Elders taught that we follow the natural order of events. We do not upset the course of history.

"For me matters were not that simple. The necromancers had also captured and killed my brother, Arel. 'Why then, if not to stretch our vision, did we leave our homeworld of Ador?' I argued.

" 'Some returned in recognition of our folly for leaving it, as did your father.'

"My father was among those who led us here, and I knew that he had gone back to persuade others to venture out, but they hardly considered me wise at eighty years of age.

"I was near the middle of the clearing when the rattling of bones overhead made me tilt my head upward. I unsheathed my brother's sword, which had passed through our family for generations and now to me, after his death.

With both hands I aimed it at the sky. The sword sparkled under the reddening Tavan sun. Points of light flickered along the edges of the carved runes that adorned the sword's length. Did my purpose justify stealing it from the reliquary?

"Shadow Master's creature prepared to strike. The enchanted blade in my hands seemed inadequate against something many times my own size. And how could I kill the animated skeleton of a dragon?

"The creature began a steep dive. I poised the sword, but the beast passed over me and I swung the sword at empty space, leaving a fading glow where the sword's Magick had rent the air. As quickly as the dragon had plunged, it ascended. Rising still, it circled for another dive. Live dragons did not inhabit Tava. Where had Shadow Master obtained the intact skeleton of one?

"The dragon came in lower this time, its bony fingers extended. The sword rang as tempered steel struck a leg bone and cleanly removed one forefoot. Severed from its source of animating Magick, the foot lay unmoving on the grass a few paces away. Unfazed, the creature rose to circle again.

"I heard youthful voices. 'We will help you, Elf.' From the woods came two Tavan boys. Each one brandished a long dagger and had no idea of the danger they faced.

" 'Go back!' I shouted in their language.

" 'We'll slay Shadow Master and bring back his head.'

"The bony rustle made them look upward with widening eyes. When I saw the beast adjust its course, I realized that Shadow Master had heard their boast. He was nearby controlling it. Its angle of attack was such that it could not aim at them. Again it rose.

"He needed clear sight and concentration to direct his mindless abomination. I scanned for his hiding place in the hope that his vanity would betray him. Among the rocks, the light of the low sun caught the gold embroidery on his black velvet robe. While the boys stood transfixed, I let my sword fall to the ground and prepared a spell. When the dragon reached the steepest part of its descent, I cast my Fireflash in Shadow Master's direction. A moment later I heard the crash and shatter of bones.

"My tactic had gained a little time, but Shadow Master would not permit himself to be taken by surprise again. Even if I defeated him, there were other necromancers on Tava, and they could no doubt summon more. I picked up the sword.

"The youths stumbled toward me blinking their eyes. 'Did you kill the monster?'

"Both went rigid. An annoyed voice came from the woods, 'They are mine, Elf, and you will be mine next.' I saw fourteen Tavan youths issue from behind the rocks where he was hiding. Each was armed with a small pointed weapon doubtless tipped with one of the few drugs to which Elfaeden are vulnerable. Shadow Master would not kill me. An Elf slave was too great a prize. His slaves came closer. I waited until they were within the range I needed to encompass them all.

"To my surprise Shadow Master left his hiding place. Ignoring him, I stuck the sword's tip into the ground at my right and began to utter a necromantic counterspell. He would not expect me to know such a spell and even less expect me to employ it. I extended my left arm and fingers at the Tavans and heard Shadow Master's curse of comprehension a heartbeat after my spell shot forth. He reacted too late. I sidestepped his energy bolt.

"The Tavans jolted when my Stun hit them and freed them from his control. Their weapons fell from their grasp.

"I pulled the sword from the ground and raised it.

" 'Your weapon is no more effective against me than it was against my dragon.' I heard the irritation in his voice. 'You surprised me. Now I will return the favor.' He stepped aside to let the figure in a tattered shirt behind him move forward. 'Your brother has served me well.'

"My brother Arel stood before me. Through a sardonic smile Shadow Master said, 'Replacing my dragon will be difficult, but the acquisition of a second Elf will ease the loss. *One* of your kind would sell for a handsome price. A pair will finance my ventures for a long time.' He gestured and spoke a Word.

"I felt the Magick energy strike me and dissipate into my medallion. Nevertheless, I dropped the sword and stiffened my body.

" 'Bring me his weapons,' he commanded Arel.

"Arel came toward me. When he was a dozen paces away, I moved quickly to retrieve the bow over my shoulder. I pulled the special arrow from my quiver and nocked it.

" 'You annoy me, Elf.'

"As the bowstring reached its full extent, my purpose fled from me. My body trembled against the thought of what I was about to do. The Elders would have known that Arel was alive. Why had they never told me?

"I sighted past Arel at Shadow Master and loosed the arrow. Shadow Master's eyes expanded when the bolt pierced his Shield and stuck squarely into his chest. He reeled, disbelief filled his face. In those last moments of life he withdrew a small sphere from his robe and dropped it.

White flames engulfed him. His body disintegrated into ash to prevent his resurrection or the corruption of his remains.

"The Tavan boys who had followed me here led the others back to their village. After they left, Arel approached. 'All of this puzzles you, Brother.'

"Two years ago, when I found the arrow tipped in precious Mage-stone lying on the cot in my dwelling, I had realized that someone among my people expected me to counter Elfaeden apathy with it, but I never discovered who had laid it there. Scrolls and books of necromantic spells shunned by my people found their way into my private cubicle at the library.

"Arel's words dislodged me from my reveries. 'It's time for you to find your true destiny.' He picked up the arrow from Shadow Master's ashes and handed it to me. 'This was my gift to you.'

"I was confused. Had Arel only pretended to be a slave while covertly executing this plan? How had he made the arrow without Shadow Master's knowledge? Shadow Master would have detected a piece of Mage-stone nearby.

"As if reading my thoughts, Arel said, 'You have much to learn about Magick. The Elfaeden are its caretakers, not its owners. We have shunned the practice of necromancy, but it is no more evil than any other aspect. The user of the tool determines how to employ it. I'll show you another secret.'

"Arel led me into the mountains behind Shadow Master's lair. Night had fallen when we arrived at the cave. 'Our special sensitivity to Magick led me to this place.' I felt it also, emanating from a tunnel in the rock.

"We entered. A few paces in, the tunnel made a sharp bend. Beyond where the outside air penetrated, the chalky smell of cold, damp rock permeated the tunnel. Only the echoes of dripping water and our own footsteps broke the silence. The air began to warm. The farther we walked, the more the warmth and moist, mineral smell increased.

"Around a curve the tunnel opened into a cavern ringed with small pools. A mist hung over them. I saw where Arel had worked in secret each night while Shadow Master slept beneath Arel's Unwake spell. I wondered why Shadow Master had not detected the spell upon him.

" 'His command of spells was more limited than he believed,' Arel said. He pointed to a black staff stuck upright in a hole in the rock floor. 'That is what drew me here. Although it beckons me to touch it, I have never done so. There is more than Magick in it. I believe that it was not meant for our kind and that whoever takes it will be charged with finding the rightful owners. The questing spirit of our father and our uncle resides more in you than in me.'

"I was unsure.

" 'We are becoming a new race, Brother,' Arel said. He reached into the torn pocket of his shirt and withdrew a sphere. 'Shadow Master kept this in case he ever needed to escape.' He let it fall from his hand. A Gate opened next to the staff. 'Take the staff and follow this Gate to your destiny. I will finish here with what we've begun.'

"How could I go? We are taught not to make hasty decisions. We meditate on the ramifications of our intentions. The balance of the universe must not be upset.

" 'Find your destiny and ours.' I heard urgency in his voice. 'Before the Gate closes . . .'

"I didn't hear the rest of his words. From somewhere inside an unexpected spontaneity made me reach for the staff. Its power surged into me. I don't know if that propelled me into the Gate or if Arel pushed me.

"I opened my eyes under a night sky filled with strange stars, vaguely aware of the staff loosely clutched in my hand. I thought at first that I was lying in a valley where cliff faces rose sharply above me. Was this Shadow Master's homeworld?"

Concluding his story, Dayon looked over at Mylane. "When my vision cleared, I knew I was lying on a narrow cobblestone street with old buildings rising above me. The hunger in my belly said that I'd been there several days. I sat up, then saw you come around the corner. I never knew what brought me to your world and to that alley near your house except that, as I later discovered on my own, the staff protects its owner. When I touched it, it adopted me, and perhaps directed me to where you found me. After I left you pregnant with our son, I discovered some of its abilities, but I did not learn its origin or how it came to be where it was. More than one stranger expressed interest in it during those years."

"Your story ended well, but you said that you paid a price for your actions."

Dayon regarded her. "The Council of Elders forbade me to act against Shadow Master. Because of my disobedience, I am forbidden to return to Tava, even to see my brother. I am equally unwelcome on the homeworld of Ador. My brother rid Tava of the necromancers."

"Yet your Elders did not banish him?"

"He didn't disobey them."

"Would Arel approve of me?"

"Perhaps."

She looked at the sword lying on the ground next to them. "Your people dislike violence, yet your family made a weapon and put spells on it."

"We are artists and artisans. To an Elfaeden the sword was a piece of art. Enspelling it enhanced the worth of the craftsmanship. We would not consider it anything else."

"You took it to use as a weapon."

"We should return to Trax. I worry about him having the staff," he said.

"He has survived this long without you. A few surprises will teach him humility."

"I placed a small Magick item inside the lining of his robe to enable me to trace him in case our wayward son decided to set out on his own."

Dayon was still concentrating on Mylane's impish smile when the disruption brushed him. He turned his head from side to side. "My protection spells have been nulled." He looked skyward. ". . . I am needed."

✳ ✳ ✳

They confronted a profusely perspiring Moka. "Trax is not on Thalar. I wish to know *why* he left," Dayon said.

Moka shivered. "He m-made me p-promise not t-to tell."

"I am here, Trax is not."

"You shouldn't threaten him for the loyalty you taught him to show," Mylane said.

"Nevertheless . . ." He heard Mylane sigh, and said to Moka, "The guilt will be on your conscience if Trax suffers harm."

Moka's stuttering evaporated. "Two gentlemen came here yesterday morning asking for the owner of the staff. The robed one was a powerful Mage and an Elf. The other wore the garb of a commoner, but I know he was a Mage in disguise. The Elf was surprised when he learned that Master

Trax owned the staff."

"Trax went with them freely?"

"He was *eager* to go."

"Did the Elf give his name?"

"Arion."

"You have been helpful, Moka."

"Is Trax in danger?" Mylane asked.

"Trax is in no danger from Arion," Dayon said.

"Who is Arion?" she asked.

"My uncle."

16

BONES OF CONTENTION
Day Three: First World, Noon

Jake went hurtling through the air, feet first, his boots aimed at the head of the warrior closest to us. An invisible barrier stopped him short, but he did a gymnastic flip and was standing upright again before I could blink. He showed more concern for Trax than I thought the little weasel was worth. A cracked rib or two, a little pain, and a few non-fatal wounds would be a good lesson in mortality.

Trax had taken an awkward, pseudo-defensive stance with his staff. The warriors approached him from both sides. One flick of a warrior's sword knocked the staff from Trax's grip. Jen-Varth pulled out his gun and fired. I heard a slight buzz and saw a spot of light flicker and dissipate on the spherical barrier around Trax and the warriors. Just as the second warrior was about to gore Trax, the staff flung itself back into his hand. The sword deflected off it, but caught and slit the left cuff of Trax's robe.

The first warrior moved behind Trax. Trax turned sideways, so they'd flank him, and nearly tripped on a rock. Even if the staff sprouted knives on both ends and the warriors hadn't been armored, their swords were so long that Trax couldn't get within two feet of hitting them. Unless a miracle or a your-wish-is-my-command genie showed up, these food processors were going to slice, dice, and mince Trax. None of this made sense. It was *his* staff. Yet, as far as I could tell, *it* had conjured up these attackers. Panting, Trax dodged two more sword swipes.

"Can't we do anything to help him?" I asked Kedda.

"He's in no real danger."

"He's about to die!"

"No."

Jen-Varth adjusted his weapon and fired again. This time a faint cone of light issued from his weapon. The light passed through the barrier and engulfed everyone in the bubble. Only Trax collapsed.

"What the hell are you doing!" I said.

The warriors and the bubble popped out of existence.

We looked incredulously at Jen-Varth. "I rendered Trax defeated. His opponents were no longer required and went back to wherever they had come from. The barrier was transparent. I reasoned that if light could pass through it, a diffuse, visible radiation from the DN-32 might also." This was the first time I'd heard him call his weapon anything, a military name. Was there a Military Rule Book somewhere in the Universe?

He bent over Trax, who had begun to move, and coaxed a leaf into his mouth. "Chew this." Jen-Varth stood. "He will have a headache for several hours. You may wish to rest. I'll go search for the Gate."

No one objected, but I pointed out the rapid passage of day on this world. There weren't more than two or three hours of daylight remaining.

Jake pulled out Arion's map and studied it. He pointed

to the horizon where the sun was heading, "If I'm reading this right, the Gate is maybe an hour away." He pointed at some distant rocky hills. "There."

Jen-Varth departed in that direction

"What exactly happened here?" I asked Kedda.

"The staff has several tests built into it and uses its power to create them. Trax has not learned how to select which one he calls forth."

I went over to Trax, not sure why I cared, and squatted next to him. The staff lay a couple of feet away. Out of curiosity I reached for it.

Warm, rumbling thunder filled my head. My hand tightened around it and not-exactly-voices echoed in stereo a question I didn't understand. Next thing I knew, it fell from my hand and the storm clouds parted. I looked into Trax's eyes and blinked hard. "What the hell was that?"

"You *felt* something?" His expression said he was more surprised than I was.

"Like I stuck my finger in a light socket."

"But, you're not a Mage."

"And you're not much of one!"

He looked at the ground.

"Sorry."

Jake was leaning against a large rock and still had Arion's parchment map next to him. He wasn't looking at it.

I went back to him and asked, "Did Arion say why he didn't put us closer to the Gate?"

"His need for hasty action after your unexpected encounter compromised his accuracy. Or so he claimed."

"So, Arion's fallible?" I said. Something was bothering Jake. I sat and pulled some fresh vegetables from my pack. I munched on an alien carrot. "I could go for a greaseburger, large fries, and chocolate-flavored, liquid plastic. Think we'll reach our destination?"

"Too many variables, and I don't have the equations."

"Any idea what the dragons meant?"

"I do now." He grew serious. "That skeleton was four years ago, when I was twenty-six, before I became the Jake Kesten feared by hackers everywhere."

"I'm listening."

"Bryce Duncan and I met in grad school our first year at SUNY Stony Brook. That's the State University of New York. Bryce was studying Indian archaeology. In my second year of grad school, he and I were roommates. I was searching for a topic for my doctoral thesis. That summer Bryce invited me to explore Mayan ruins in the Yucatán with him. I found the Mayan calendar and ideograms interesting and came up with my thesis topic: language-decoding algorithms. My advisor, a purist mathematician, thought I was a lunatic. He said, 'Others have spent entire careers on that subject with limited success.'

"But I was young and impetuous. 'It's a Diophantine problem,' I told him, ignoring his disdain, 'and I'll prove it.'

"Several long years later, I finished my work. My thesis committee, not being enlightened individuals either, grilled me beyond the humane, but they granted me my degree." Jake shrugged his shoulders. "What can I say? It was brilliant. Although three journals declined to publish the resulting paper. A fourth, new and short on submissions, accepted it as a curiosity piece. After that came the postdoctoral position in the computer science department at Illinois."

"How did you go from being a stuffy academic to working for the Army?"

"Well . . ." He told me the story of how Bryce found the cave, the skeleton in uniform, and the briquette-shaped object.

"This has something to do with our mission, doesn't it."

Jake gave me a hard look. "In more ways than one. I hadn't gotten very far along that morning when my boss came in to remind me that we were presenting a paper in a few weeks. I worked on that during the day and on the scroll at night. By Saturday, my brain was dissolving, and I knew only one thing that could help."

"Passionate sex?" I said.

He nodded. "On Friday our female lab assistant asked me what I was doing that weekend. I told her I'd be right here working. Just as I was ready to go home Saturday evening, she stopped by and wondered if I was interested in dinner.

"Sunday morning, a persistent knock on the door of my on-campus apartment brought me out of a deep, healing sleep. The knock came again, harder. In a stupor, I slid out of bed and shuffled to the front door.

"Two men in khaki, short-sleeved shirts stood outside my apartment. The stocky one with buzz-cut, sandy hair asked as soon as I cracked the door open, 'Dr. Kesten?'

" 'Who wants to know?'

"They identified themselves as representatives of the U.S. government. 'Uh, we need to talk,' the stocky man said.

"His stare made me realize that I'd answered the door in my white tank top and lemon-colored bikini briefs. I invited them in and offered them a seat on the couch while I retrieved a robe.

"I'd barely sat down in the ratty chair across from them

when the second man said, 'We're here about Bryce Duncan.' His muscular arms told me that he spent many hours at the gym. Except for his narrow, wire-rimmed glasses, he could have been the cover model for a romance novel. He had a thin briefcase tucked next to him. I pretended concern. 'Has something happened to him?'

" 'Don't be coy, Dr. Kesten,' the stocky man barked. 'We want to know why you visited him, what he told you, and what he gave you.' He reminded me of a drill sergeant.

"Rivers of sweat ran down my sides, luckily hidden by my robe. I tried to sound calm. 'Gentlemen, you are in my apartment at my invitation. Unless I am being accused of a crime, you have no right to make demands. I have a guest in the next room who will call Campus Security, or the police, if you don't change your tone.'

" 'There is no need to get upset, Dr. Kesten,' the cover model said. 'You're not accused of anything, but we'd like to confirm what Dr. Duncan told you about his find.'

" 'Confirm? Did you forcibly extract the information?'

" 'Not at all. We asked for input and collaboration, just as we would like yours.'

" 'Bryce and I were roommates in college. My doctoral work was language-decoding algorithms.'

" 'We know this.'

" 'He wanted my help in deciphering some primitive writings.' Partly the truth.

" 'And he gave you some photographs.'

"I was surprised, but then I said, 'Yes.'

" 'What specifically?'

" 'Photographs of the writings.' Bryce had provided them as a cover. He said the wall writing wouldn't fool an expert, but it would buy time if they asked why I was there.

Apparently Bryce had spilled his guts.

" 'Where are those photos now?'

"I set my jaw. 'In my office. Safely locked up.'

" 'We want to see them now,' the drill sergeant monotoned.

" 'I'd like to shower and eat breakfast first, Gentlemen.' I was in no mood for their shit.

" 'Perhaps a compromise?' the cover model offered. 'We'll wait while you get ready. We'll go with you to pick up the photos, then we'll buy you breakfast and we can talk.'

"I agreed. While I showered, I counted the ways I could inflict pain on Bryce. Before I left, I informed my overnight guest where I was going and whom to contact if I didn't return.

"My office consisted of a desk, a bookshelf, and a filing cabinet in the corner of a windowless computer lab. I convinced them I wasn't going to attempt an escape, so they waited by the door. The cover model was amiable; the drill sergeant was all business. I didn't want to show them the scroll photos, but these guys were smart enough to see a lie. I pulled the manila folder out of my top desk drawer and put it in the rarely used briefcase that I kept next to the desk.

"While we waited for our food at a small truck-stop diner on the edge of town, the cover model scanned the photos and asked what progress I'd made.

" 'I'm still encoding the data into the computer.'

"The drill sergeant glared. 'What did Dr. Duncan tell you about the cave, Dr. Kesten?'

" 'Perhaps, if you told me exactly why you're here, I could be of more help.'

" 'We presume that you saw the skeleton,' his partner, the cover model and apparently the one in charge, said.

" 'Well preserved for as old as it was,' I said.

" 'Did Dr. Duncan propose any theories to you about the nature of his find?'

"I sipped my coffee. 'Gentlemen, I'm not a naive, sheltered academician. Bryce Duncan is my friend. What we did—or did not—discuss is our affair. For all I know, you might be lying to me, holding him somewhere under forced interrogation, and may already have extracted from him his entire life story. You may be empowered to do the same to me. However, as long as I am able to act under my own volition, I'm not going to offer further information until I have spoken with Bryce. In private.' I took another sip of coffee.

" 'As we told you, Dr. Duncan is freely assisting us.'

"I pointed at the drill sergeant. 'Why the good Fed/bad Fed bit?'

"Cover model said, 'That wasn't our intention, and we did not intend any insult. Dr. Duncan speaks highly of you. We respect his and your integrity. I'm sure you can appreciate our concern. Have you spoken with anyone else about these photos?'

"I shook my head.

" 'That's what Dr. Duncan told us to expect.' He opened his briefcase and handed me a sealed envelope. 'The United States Government is interested in your services. Please consider this offer.'

" 'That's it?' I asked.

" 'For now.'

"I knew it wasn't that simple. 'May I have a couple of days?'

" 'Of course, but we'd appreciate a decision as quickly as possible.'

" 'If I refuse?'

" 'We don't think you will. That offer is very generous.' He handed me a business card—name and phone number, no company name or position.

"The size of their offer nearly made me forget that I wanted to strangle Bryce. I later called him from a pay phone in the Student Union. 'What have you done to me!'

"His calm voice was unnerving. 'You've seen the highway signs about your tax dollars at work? Think of this as a rich Uncle Sam putting you in his will.' "

Jake looked straight ahead as he finished his story. "That's most of it, Scott."

I remembered Bryce Duncan calling Jake that one night at my apartment. "Why didn't you tell me about Bryce before?"

"They bound me under a non-disclosure agreement."

"Did they do anything nasty to him?"

"After he got his ass chewed all around for not reporting his cave discovery immediately, he agreed to cooperate. They appreciated how he'd gone to extra lengths to keep everything secret and decided he'd be an asset to their team."

"What happened to the black stone?"

"The briquette. That's what we called it. Someone, somewhere is supposedly studying it. That's all we know."

"What was on the scroll?"

He glanced sideways at me. "Equations."

"That's what the dragons meant?"

"It didn't click with me then because I never figured out what the equations meant. I think they might be the spatial coordinates of the Gates."

"Did you figure out how the skeleton got there?"

"Yep. Bryce showed me a side cave off the main one

before he buried it with two quarter sticks of dynamite to hide what was in there."

He had more mystery in him than an Agatha Christie novel.

"Well, what was in it?"

He took a slow breath. "I think it's the same kind of Gate we're after here."

"A *Gate*? On Earth?"

"Why not? Do you remember the day we met in your father's office, two years ago?"

"Sort of."

"We'd just left the office to get breakfast. I was driving the jeep. You said something and I slammed on the brakes. Do you remember what you said?"

I thought for a moment. "Something about wanting to dissect your nuts?"

"Exactly. Bryce had used that same expression, not one I'd ever heard before. The déjà vu caught me off guard."

"I thought I made it up."

"Your pre-psychic abilities, I suspect. I never told you how I came to work at Fort Bragg."

"Now that you've told me what you really do—investigate extraterrestrials—it makes sense. Except that my father isn't involved in that."

"You're sure? Maybe his transfers sent him to where he could take charge of investigations."

"Yeah, I'm sure. He doesn't keep secrets well. What doesn't make sense is why anti-hacker activities came under his jurisdiction. He's barely computer literate."

"The government works in mysterious ways."

"You're a bit young for secret government work."

"No one else who could do it."

"A little cocky?"

"Confident. Three days after the cover model and the drill sergeant visited me, I called to find out in what capacity I'd be working for the government. They gave me two choices: be a consultant or learn to play soldier. I don't take orders well, so consultant it was. They told me that I'd need a legitimate cover story in case I was ever questioned about what I did. I suggested that I help rid the world of hackers. They liked it and asked where I wanted to be stationed."

"I still don't understand."

He stared straight ahead. "*You* were at Fort Bragg. I first met Arion four years ago, just after I'd gotten back from my meeting with Bryce."

"What!"

His eyes met mine. "You might want to close your mouth before an alien insect flies into it."

17

MAYBE THEY LEFT THE
KEY UNDER THE DOORMAT
Day Four: First World, Early Afternoon

I closed my mouth. Jake had known about this mission four years ago and was the accomplice in my alien abduction? I took a deep breath.

"Scott, if I'd told you before, you wouldn't have believed me. I never saw Arion after that until he showed up at your apartment a few days ago. I wasn't sure I hadn't dreamed him."

"You trained me anyway. For the past two years."

"It hasn't done you any harm."

"So, I was just another assignment."

"It sort of started out that way, and it kept your father from harassing you."

My father never gave me a fist in the gut like this. I looked out at the landscape and tilted my head up at the sun. "I thought we were friends. Friends trust each other."

"Scott," rasped in his throat, "Arion made it clear that refusal wasn't an option."

I shifted my eyes back to him. "Did he force you at magic-wand point?"

Jake smiled. "Humor in adversity."

"Fuck you."

* * *

Jen-Varth came back an hour after he left. Jake got up to meet him. I didn't move. I heard him tell Jake, "The Gate is enclosed in a transparent barrier."

We packed up our gear and headed out. I walked a long way behind because I needed thinking space. For two years I'd worked with Jake. Most of the time he sat at his PC tracking a hacker or unraveling the hacker's code. Boring stuff. But if I peeked over his shoulder and asked, he'd show me what he was doing. I even enjoyed getting beat up twice a week during martial arts practice because I was learning. To keep myself otherwise occupied, I took courses at the University of Colorado. One more and I'd have enough for a non-thesis Master's degree. Mom still expected the phone call once a week although it had now slipped to once every other week. Sometimes Dad was home when I called. I think he realized that one soldier son was the best he could hope for.

When Jake's work required him to travel—sometimes to Fort Bragg—I usually went with him. In good weather Jake flew the Piper. Occasionally he had to attend a Washington meeting without me, which I understood because I knew how the Government liked to keep secrets even when there were no secrets to be kept. Except that *those* meetings must have dealt with the extraterrestrial stuff he hadn't told me about. One thing had puzzled me, however. Technically, he was my employer because my paycheck came from him and not from the government. I never asked. I figured that maybe he expensed me. He always treated me as an equal and, I thought, had trusted me and kept me informed.

The hacker assignments were nothing more than a cover, and I'd been another assignment—from a different boss.

Back on Earth it was Wednesday, twelve-ten in the morning. We'd left on Saturday around four in the afternoon. Arion's world ran on a twenty-five-hour day. This world ran close to twenty. Maybe interplanetary jet lag explained why I felt the way I did. Or not.

The alien sun was disappearing behind the low, distant hills when we came to the Gate. The brown-black hills were dull like everything else, and the dusk was an uninspired yellow-orange.

The Gate stood amid an expanse of rubble. We decided that the rubble was the remains of whatever structure had originally housed it. In the waning daylight, the bubble around the Gate luminesced faint pink. The Gate's blue-gray frame stood eight feet tall, a perfect semicircle on top of a trapezoid, which was in turn mounted on an irregularly shaped stone platform. The frame encased a lighthole.

Trax boldly went up to the barrier and touched it. "It is not Magick," he announced. He knocked on it, it sounded like Plexiglas. He pointed at Jake. "We aren't lost, so you're useless. Perhaps the time-wasting card player has a suggestion?" Meaning Kedda.

"This is unexpected," Kedda said.

Kedda didn't know about this? I remembered Trax's exploding spheres and said to Trax, "Maybe it's time to use your balls instead of your brain."

He glared back. "The boy who has no powers dares to insult those who do?"

I marched up to him, forked my right hand under his chin. I pushed up and back hard enough to hurt and looked straight down into his light-brown, cat-like eyes. I saw fear

206

in those eyes. "How about we build a campfire? I'll shove that stick up your ass and toast you over the flames while we sing happy songs."

Jake grabbed my arm from behind. I reeled around. "Fuck off!" I let Trax go and strode toward some tall rocks—the landscape had a plentiful supply. I scrunched up behind them and tried to calm down while I watched them set up camp several hundred feet from the Gate. Jen-Varth pulled out two small lanterns with solar-rechargeable battery packs. They gathered wood for the campfire, but it burned with the combined stench of smoldering rubber and road-kill skunk. After half an hour of that delightful incense, they moved to the other side of the fire. Trax asked why they didn't dump water on it to put it out. Jake said they didn't have any water to waste. I considered suggesting that Jake piss on it.

To take my mind off the knots in my stomach, I munched the alien trail mix we'd gotten in Freetown, not bad but certainly a comedown from the fare of the past two days. Jen-Varth told them that we carried enough nourishment to sustain us for seven or eight days if we didn't care about losing a couple of pounds.

They set out their bedrolls in a circle. I eventually retrieved mine and unrolled it some distance away from them. Jen-Varth put a lantern at the center of their circle and came over to offer me a second one, which I declined. "What happened between you and Jake?" he asked.

"A serious failure to communicate and lack of truth in advertising."

Perceptive guy that Jen-Varth was, he left me alone. I removed my shirt. Dev's medallion bobbed against my chest. I still had no clue about its function. I removed it, opened my backpack, found my jeans, and slid the medallion into the left front pocket. Then I lay down and threw the blanket over me.

Jen-Varth and Kedda lay on top of their bedding fully clothed. Trax glanced around before he removed his robe. Underneath the robe that I thought was too heavy for this climate, he had the same ivory-colored underwear Arion had given me: snug, boxer briefs and a sleeveless shirt. But no pants. I wondered if he'd brought anything for warmer climes. He exchanged the undershirt for a long nightshirt, crawled onto his bed, and tucked his staff—like a faithful teddy bear—in next to him, and pulled his robe over him.

I lay on my back under the moonless sky with my hands behind my head and browsed the alien constellations. If our sun were somewhere up there, what sort of constellation would it be in? Probably an insignificant one.

A shiver went through me. I hoped it was a night chill and not another premonition. The last one had led to Jake's revelation. His Pied-Piper approach had caused me to miss the clues. Just after I partnered with him, he scheduled me for a more-than-complete physical and a thorough blood analysis, plus a psych profile and MRI brain scan. Jake told me the latter had nothing to do with the physical. He said that some researcher friends were studying idiots to see what made them tick. Very funny.

The doctor said that I could stand to gain a few pounds. Jake promised that I would. The blood analysis, however, yielded a surprise. I had an unusual and rare blood protein. The hematologist assured me that there was no cause for concern, meaning that no one had discovered any nasty consequences yet. When I pressed him for details—on account of my biology background—he said that the level in my blood was considerably above what he'd seen before. Jake dug into the scientific literature and found that my blood level of this stuff departed from the mean, of those who had it, by over three standard deviations, which I knew was statistical terminology for really weird. I never asked Jake why he'd sent my blood for analysis. At their first meeting Arion must have told Jake that I was special, and Jake wanted to find out why. Screw him!

***

I came awake, after a dreamless sleep for a change, but with a stronger shiver than last night's. The air temperature felt fifty or fifty-five on my face. Sometime during the night I must have wrapped myself tightly in the blanket. I was warm enough so that the outside temperature hadn't caused the chill.

Light on the horizon meant the sun was awake. Just it and me so far. Trax cuddled his staff. Probably dreaming about the wonderful things that he wished he could do with it. My watch said I'd slept for seven hours. I pushed myself onto my elbows and noticed that Jen-Varth's sleeping bag was devoid of Jen-Varth. I spotted him in the distance a few feet from the Gate and threw off the blanket. *Nice piquant fragrance, Scott.* I fished around in my travel bag for my falsely advertised twenty-four-hour protection. I slathered it under my arms, stuffed it back in the bag, and pulled out my black briefs and black tank top from home. You can't go wrong with basic black.

I pulled on my jeans and sneakers. Dev Antos had bought me leather boots in Freetown, but sneakers added a touch of home to this alien place. I didn't bother with a shirt. The cool air felt good on my arms. The tank top absorbed enough sun to keep my chest warm, and the sporty lime scent of my freshly deodorized self ensured that I wouldn't offend anyone.

I wandered over to Jen-Varth sitting cross-legged on a clump of pseudo-grass. He stared at the Gate with puzzle-solving determination, a new layer of his personality. His personality layers had all been interesting experiences. Unlike Jake's latest layer—*Don't go there, Scott.*

"Looks like someone locked the keys in the car. Think Arion knew about this?" Jen-Varth didn't reply. "Any idea why he's sending us the long way around? Why didn't he just lighthole us to wherever we need to be?"

"I don't have the answers. Please touch the barrier."

"Is it safe?"

"It did me no harm."

I tapped it with my left forefinger. Nothing. I dragged my fingertips down it. Solid, with the resistance of static-charged plastic.

"Try longer contact. Close your eyes."

And feel the Force? No doubt Arion and Kedda had pumped his head full of nonsense. *What the hell.* I put both palms against the bubble like a fortune-teller pretending to read the aura around her mark.

Something flashed in my head. I pointed at a pile of rocks fifteen feet behind us. Jen-Varth agilely uncrossed his legs, got up, walked to where I had pointed, squatted there, and began digging in the rubble. I watched then offered to help, but he'd already found a green-black object the size of a computer mouse. The top half had a grid pattern on it and the bottom center had a thumb-sized indentation. "What's that?"

"What we needed." He held it up to the sun, aimed it at the Gate, and pressed his thumb into the indentation. The bubble around the Gate rolled up and over and buried itself out of sight in the ground.

"How did I know where that was?"

"You're a Pneuma. We would call you a Spirit Watcher on my world."

"What's a Pneuma?"

"One who senses the tenuous energies between objects and living things."

I pointed at myself. "You think I'm a psychic?"

"A Spirit Watcher is more than that. Trax said that the barrier was not Magick. Had it been Psi-activated, Kedda would have removed it."

"Did Arion tell you about Kedda?" I asked.

He shook his head once and his black hair flicked across his forehead. He brushed it aside. "I believe that we need all three of the powers with us. Trax is the Mage, you are the Pneuma. I am not a Psi, and Jake can't be one. Therefore, it must be Kedda."

"Why not Jake? Not that he is." *Unless that's another secret he didn't mention.*

"The component matter of your world determines what you can be. Your world is Pneuma. Only Pneumas can come from Pneuma worlds."

"You're right. Kedda telepaths to me."

"I suspected it from the expressions on your face. Some Psis are telepathic."

"I don't think Kedda wants everyone to know what he is. He would have revealed himself if he tried to remove the barrier," I said.

"He could have done it unnoticed while we slept."

"I don't understand these powers."

"Each world has only one. If you are gifted, you can use your world's power, and only that one. My world is Pneuma. I was not gifted to use it."

"What kind of world is this one?" I asked.

"Pneuma. Your power is active here."

"So, Kedda couldn't have removed the barrier because this isn't his kind of world."

"As a traveler, he will carry a Psi-stone of sufficient power." Jen-Varth pressed the control to restore the bubble.

"Why'd you do that?"

"To see what will transpire."

Sneaky guy. We headed back to the others.

He thought I was some kind of psychic? Better that than Scott Madison, Jedi Knight. I was only three when *Star Wars* came out, so that made me a second-generation *Star Wars* kid. Dad had encouraged my interest because the Jedi were soldiers.

I asked Jen-Varth what powered the flip top barrier.

"Perhaps solar batteries." He pointed to the grid on the remote control and slipped it into his pack.

"Why didn't Kedda or Arion warn us about this?"

"They may not have known."

"I don't believe that, and neither do you. Any thoughts on why it was sealed?"

"We may learn after we pass through it."

"I don't find that thought comforting."

He regarded me. "You and Jake must resolve the discord between you."

Out of respect for him, I didn't reply.

Kedda and Jake were up and moving. Trax resisted the arrival of morning. I saw him squirm and knew that he'd be up soon. He abruptly got out of his bag, grabbed his staff, and headed for the rocks. After he came back, he changed back into his sleeveless tunic and put on loose-fitting, draw-string pants, which answered one of my questions from last night about what other attire he'd brought. He smugly came over. "I have other things to do with my life than to waste it here. I will remove the barrier."

How many lessons would it take before he learned?

Jen-Varth asked if he could observe.

Trax grunted. "As you wish."

I grabbed my backpack—this could take awhile, and I'd get cranky if I didn't eat breakfast—and followed them to the Gate. Jen-Varth sat on the ground with his backpack next to him. He discreetly palmed the remote control we'd found. I sat next to him and munched trail mix while Trax flamboyantly gestured at the Gate. Jake and Kedda wandered over. Just when Trax seemed ready to quit, Jen-Varth pressed the button.

I shot to my feet and ran up to Trax. "You did it!" I shook his hand vigorously. "Our hero!" His wide eyes said that he knew it wasn't his doing.

The jubilation ended when a bad feeling tapped me on the shoulder. A lighthole was forming behind Trax.

18

ENELLE
Day Four: Planet Yandall, morning

Elect Sovereign Lord Enwan Hane stood on the rampart overlooking the Free City of Dandray and wondered whether he had made the best decision for his daughter's birthday. A few traces of night mist, not yet dispelled by the morning breeze and the warmth of the rising sun, hung over the forest to his left. He observed the citizens and transports moving quietly along below him. For safety, and to reduce crowding, he and the city administrators had prohibited personal, motorized vehicles inside the city. Many citizens walked or used the human-powered cycles provided at no charge and kept at convenient stations around the city.

Lord Hane's main problem did not lie with running Dandray. He had a motherless daughter whom he loved very much, so much that he had indulged her every whim and ignored the bad behavior that resulted from his years of overprotection. More than once he had considered remarrying. He was handsome, a popular leader among the people—they continued to reelect him—and rich enough to attract suitable women. But his duties always precluded long-term, intimate relationships. He feared alienating his daughter, although he knew he had done that long ago. So many times she wanted to accompany him on his trips to other Yandallan cities. He never took her. The power she'd been born with was too unpredictable. Perhaps when she learned to control it.

He had convinced himself that keeping her at home was best and would avoid public embarrassment for both of them. Of course, everyone in Dandray knew about her. They had been told that she presented no danger. Still, Lord Hane heard the rumors. The citizens would rather not have her around them. He paid six attendants three times standard wage for half the normal working hours to keep her amused and out of public places. When that failed, he declared a public holiday to permit the citizens to be away from their businesses.

Enelle was a comely young woman, one to whom any young man should find himself attracted were it not for her temper and bitterness. Perhaps, he considered, she had a right to be bitter. Counselors had tried in vain to teach her how to control her gift. She didn't see it as a gift. She believed it had caused her mother's death in childbirth.

Last year one of his advisors suggested that a virile young man might be able to tame her. Hane promptly dismissed the advisor. Lately, her behavior had become more demanding, her trips into the city more frequent. Declaring so many holidays was bad for business. Even her attendants suggested that Enelle required something more. Three months ago, Lord Hane had reconsidered his former advisor's suggestion. After discreet inquiries, he summoned a certain young man who reputedly had never refused a woman before.

After hearing Hane's proposition, the man said, "Lord Hane, if I may speak frankly . . ."

Hane nodded at the young man.

"I would cut off my manhood before I let *her* have it."

Hane felt the blood rush to his head. Had his guards been in the chamber with him, he would have granted the man's wish without delay. He took several deep breaths to regain his composure and said to the man, "I know of your reputation. My daughter is more beautiful than those you customarily bed."

"She is indeed."

"I will double my offer to you."

"Lord Hane, I do not disrespect you, but your inquiries about me must have told you that I act for whim and pleasure, not for money."

Hane felt his anger rise again. Lord Hane appreciated honesty, but this man tested that appreciation. "Are you suggesting that you find my daughter so detestable that you could *not* pleasure her?"

For the first time, Hane saw the man smile. "Not at all, Lord Hane. I don't recall when I last slept alone or a woman did not wish to have me again."

"Then explain your refusal!"

"If the knowledge that I had bedded your daughter became known, it would . . . damage my reputation." Hane opened his mouth to speak, but the man continued, "Lord Hane, I know that you disapprove of what I do. I simply indulge my lust and employ the talent I was born with. This proposal you make to me is not what a father should do for his daughter. Your people respect you, and no matter how closely you and I would try to keep this arrangement secret, someone would find out. While the damage to my reputation would temporarily compromise my lifestyle, your reputation would suffer irreparably. Your leadership of Dandray has brought too much good for it not to continue."

Such wisdom from this young man. The man shamed him.

"If I am asked why I was here, I will say it was to warn me never to come near your daughter, given that she will soon be of an age that permits me to do so without legal repercussions."

After the man left, Hane felt relieved. What he had contemplated bordered on moral depravity. When had he gotten that desperate? Yet, he was no closer to resolving the problem. He wanted his daughter to be happy, to marry. After his meeting with this young man, Hane realized that his daughter would never find that happiness in Dandray and possibly not anywhere on Yandall.

Some days later, a cloaked stranger brought him another proposition. "Will my daughter be in danger?" Hane asked.

"I offer no assurances except that those with her will have an interest in keeping her safe and possess the abilities to do so," the stranger said.

Enelle had always wanted to travel outside Dandray. Hane decided to make this trip her eighteenth birthday present.

✳ ✳ ✳

Princess Enelle Hane checked herself in the mirror twice more after dismissing her two attendants to their breakfast. Every strand of her dark brown hair was in place. It perfectly grazed her shoulders—she insisted on it. She examined the objects on the dressing table. Had they replaced every item in the locations she had designated? Yes. Everything was in its place today. She'd had them reprimanded enough times for past failures.

She returned to her image in the mirror. Was her makeup correct? She always thought that her slender face made her look too much like a boy. She made them apply judicious amounts of blush under her cheekbones and a light application of subdued lip color—not the gloss red other women painted their lips to advertise passionate kisses and the greater pleasures they could provide. No. A man should not want her solely for the pleasure he could extract from her.

Had they gotten makeup on her necklace again? To be sure, she fingered the pointed, irregular pieces of jet-black stone. The six multifaceted, red gems evenly spaced along the bottom of the necklace were each worth the considerable yearly salary of a city employee. The necklace had been her mother's, and it somehow helped control her curse.

The morning sun caught her attention. She went to the window. Her lavish room on the top floor of their six-story residence overlooked the city and afforded her a view of the surrounding forest and of the two distant rivers and the lake beyond. Just enough high clouds reflected the red, mid-morning sun to tint the sky mauve. While most of the other city buildings were lower and newer, the Hane family had maintained the older style of their mansion. She appreciated how the pale, redstone walls glowed in the setting sun during her evening strolls through the gardens.

As she pressed her hand along the windowsill, her fingertips caught in one depression, an imperfection some might think—imperfections filled her world—but she knew that a childhood temper tantrum had created it, an expensive toy thrown because her father went on a trip without her after promising to take her.

She wasn't really a princess, and her father wasn't a king, although he had the power of one. He used to call her his princess. When had he stopped? She liked to think of herself as a princess. A princess had status. She had none.

Three months ago she had been on the rampart when that young man arrived. She knew who he was. She wasn't the naive little girl her father believed her to be. She had snuck into the audience hall, secretly listened, and barely managed to contain her anger and tears until her father left. That evening at supper he'd acted as if nothing unusual had transpired that day. "I had the cook prepare your favorite meal. Why aren't you eating? Aren't you feeling well tonight?" How could he even look at her after he'd tried to turn her into a prostitute!

She'd hardly spoken to him since, and he'd been too busy to notice. She had considered spying on him again, then decided it was better not to know what worse, unforgivable things he might be planning.

Today was her eighteenth birthday, and she had determined to take control of it. She'd planned a trip into the central marketplace and had considered, for once, wearing commoner clothing, to wander about unnoticed. But if she wanted that, she could simply stay home. At least in formal attire they would notice her, even if most would not speak to her. So, she put on her finest white, high-collared gown. She expected that her father had already attempted to thwart her plans. Whenever she summoned her attendants to dress her and make her up, he knew her intentions and would alert the people and the merchants. Many times she'd gone into the city to find that he had declared a holiday.

She wasn't a danger to anyone. Why did everyone treat her like a child? She couldn't help that they made her mad with their pretenses and fawning just to please her father. She'd get angry, yell at them, and her curse would manifest itself, in an old way, or in a new way. It didn't matter. Some would turn their faces from her; others would faint or scream. Children would start to cry. Yelling, screaming, shouting. She couldn't concentrate. In her frustration and awkward attempt to flee, things would get damaged—never people—but that didn't matter. They labeled her a menace. They couldn't tell her never to come back, not with who her father was. She didn't mean for it to happen.

Another idea struck her. Maybe she wouldn't return home tonight. Maybe she'd leave the city on a trip of her own making. Of course, she wouldn't get very far. When she didn't return, her father would send his men out. They'd find her, bring her back, and nothing would change.

She glimpsed something behind her. A circle of light. It hung in the air, unmoving. *Why is this here*? The Psi Adepts among her people used Gates for travel to distant places— places her father never took her, so she'd never been allowed to enter a Gate. Was this the answer to her wish? Her father would expect her to go into the city. He was so predictable. If she stepped into the Gate, maybe she'd be somewhere her father couldn't find her. He'd begin to worry. Then, when she came back, he'd listen to her.

She stepped closer. Maybe on the other side she'd find someone who liked her.

※ ※ ※

The lighthole formed behind Trax, but nothing came through.

I yelled, "Trax! What stupid thing did you do this time?" I pointed.

He turned his head around. His face got red. He came back at me. "I-I don't think I did this."

A figure came through, and the lighthole snapped out of existence. For a frozen moment in time the new arrival stood there. She was Trax's height, about five-eight. The formal, white dress with the high collar and cape said that she'd made a wrong turn somewhere.

She finally blinked. "Where am I?" Being closest to Trax, she asked, "Who are you?"

About his age, too.

"I demand that you answer me!"

Brat boy and brat girl? Is she another lesson for him, or the second half of buy-one-get-one-free day for us? "Hi. My name is Scott," I said.

She cocked her head in a way that told me we had a language barrier. At the very least. She glanced around and declared with a haughty manner that matched her attire, "I don't like this place. I wish to go back to my room."

No one reacted.

"Send me *back*!"

Maybe we'd gotten her for pest control. Her shrill voice would certainly keep everything away. Something about her sent shivers through me.

"With pleasure," Trax said. He raised his staff and began to chant as if he knew what he was doing. His cool, confident expression gave me the opposite feeling.

I yelled, "Don't even try it!" and an instant later launched myself through the air in what I envisioned was a perfect, flying football tackle.

I struck him squarely. The staff flew out of his hands. I felt the rippling prickle of lightholing. Before I had time to contemplate the significance, we landed hard. I heard the *oomph* of his lungs emptying a second before I heard—and felt—the crunch in my left forearm.

19

LET'S HAVE A PARTY AND INVITE THE RELATIVES
Day Four: Somewhere Else

Shit, shit, shit! Pain lanced up my arm. Like stubbing your bare toe and smacking your shin at the same instant—multiplied a thousand times. Every heartbeat pulsed pain. I broke that arm playing baseball when I was twelve. This hurt a hell of a lot more than I remembered.

Trax pushed himself up, rolling me off him and onto my back. "Aw—shhhit!" I clenched my jaw and squeezed my eyes shut while my brain processed the deluge of neural impulses from my arm and cordially translated them in minute detail. "You little fuckwit!"

"Let me help."

Red and orange lights strobed behind my eyelids. "Go away!" Then I realized the voice wasn't Trax's and opened my eyes. Jen-Varth stood over me holding his backpack. I sucked air through my teeth. "Sorry, I thought you were Magick boy."

"I jumped through the Gate behind you. I thought it best to do so. I was not wrong." He set down his pack, rummaged in it, pulled out something, and shoved that something into my mouth. "Chew."

223

It had the texture of a raw mushroom and the piquant flavor of oregano. I barely noticed it over the screaming pain in my arm that had resolved not to be ignored. He opened his canteen and put one hand beneath my head to lift it.

Trapezius muscle in the neck, connected to clavicle . . . From anatomy class the name of every bone and muscle between my neck and forearm cascaded through my thoughts in that blitz of agony. I closed my throat to prevent accidental swallowing and a choking fit. Between the waves of pain I heard Jen-Varth say, "Chew more." I wanted to smack him. He tilted the canteen to my lips. "Now swallow."

I took a few more sips to rinse down the particles and squeaked out, "Was that a pain killer?"

He laid my head back down. "It will limit tissue damage around the injury site."

I moaned heavily. "I need a pain killer."

"You have broken your arm. Please try not to move it."

From my mental list of immediate things to do—throttling Trax had leaped to number one—I crossed off waving down a cab and made number two shoving bamboo shoots under Jen-Varth's alien fingernails. I wondered how he was sure it was broken.

He pointed to the ugly bulge of flesh—I still had on the black tank top—which didn't come close to displaying the amount of pain I was in.

"Do you know where we are?"

"Not yet."

"Who else is with us?"

"Only Trax. Apparently you redirected whatever Magick he was attempting."

"I'd like to redirect it up his ass." *Ow!* I had exhaled

too fast. I pointed at his weapon. "If you're not going to give me a pain killer, shoot me and put me out of my misery."

I thought he said, "In a moment."

"What!"

"I'll attend you in a moment," he repeated.

He was even following proper emergency room protocol: make sure the patient has adequate time to suffer before attending him. I knew there wasn't much he could do except set the bone—I knew that would be a joyous experience—and splint my arm.

While he helped Trax to his feet and checked him out, I turned my head sideways on the ground and scanned the landscape. Except for a distant copse of scraggly trees, this barrenness wasn't much different from the previous one. Jen-Varth returned. "Trax is uninjured."

Figures. "For now," I mumbled. "This ends *my* fun and frolic for today and my usefulness on this stellar adventure," I said louder. *Nice pun, Scott*.

He pulled some implements from his pack. "I will repair your arm."

I swallowed hard. "I hope you've got a real good anesthetic." He took his gun from his holster. "Hey! I was kidding before—" He pressed it against my forearm and fired. A jolt of numbing warmth spread through my arm. *Ooo*. He set it aside and positioned his hands along my arm.

Trax came over.

"If you even *look* like you're enjoying this, I'll make sure you know what it feels like," I said.

Trax turned his head when the bone popped.

The pain edged its way back. I gritted my teeth at Jen-Varth. "It's wearing off. Zap me again with that anesthetic stun gun of yours."

"Another shot would amplify the injury." From his kit he pulled out a dried leaf and held it to my mouth. "This t'anga leaf will help. Chew it and swallow the juices." Kind of hard lying on my back, but I managed.

I opened my mouth wide and closed it almost before his fingers were clear. I needed drugs, preferably the sensory-altering, mind-and-body-numbing variety. *Parsley flavor.*

Jen-Varth messed around in his backpack. Trax squatted beside me. "I—I'm sorry I hurt you."

I swallowed and pushed the leaf into my cheek. "Hurt? Did you ever break your arm?"

He shook his head.

"Ever get kicked in the nuts?"

He nodded.

"Well, imagine that, then imagine someone grabbing and squeezing hard." He winced. "This is worse." I swallowed. "I didn't know you could make a Gate."

"I can't."

"Sure looks like you can."

He shook his head. "The staff made it."

"Any idea where it dragged us to?"

Before he could answer, Jen-Varth tilted my head so I could spit out the leaf. I felt dizzy. He placed his pack beneath my head and said to Trax, "You will assist me."

I saw both reluctance and sympathy in Trax's eyes.

"You will feel this," Jen-Varth told me.

I locked my jaw. He straightened my arm and had Trax hold my palm flat against the ground. Real pleasant. Jen-Varth passed a rectangular object about seven inches long back and forth between my elbow and my wrist. It buzzed faintly while my arm got uncomfortably hot. When he finished, he said to Trax, "You must return us."

"I don't know how."

"You brought us here."

"The staff did it!"

While they argued, my brain and body disconnected. The sky turned gold, and rainbow curlicues circled the bright purple clouds.

* * *

I squinted my eyes open. The sun had progressed to late afternoon, and they'd moved me next to some large boulders. A red-eyed Trax sat with me. I was about to question him when Jen-Varth came over to examine my arm. He'd put on a flexible bandage. Minimal pain. "Are you comfortable?" he asked.

"Am I healed?"

"The bone will require a few days to mend completely. I can remove the restriction tomorrow."

Cool. It sure beat weeks in a sweaty cast. He scooted me up against a boulder. "What was that gadget?"

"It triggers cellular repair." He shoved two pills at me. "These contain mineral concentrates, growth factors, and herbs to mediate the healing. I will give them to you three times a day for the next two days. You will experience tingling at the injury site. Some find it unpleasant." He opened his canteen.

After I washed down the pills, I asked, "Are you a doctor on your world?"

"My father is. He taught me basic healing practices."

"Does he want you to be a doctor?"

"On Xenna each person chooses his own path."

"Must be nice. My father wanted me in the military."

227

"We spend the years of our education exploring and understanding possible life paths. Once we select one, we are expected to succeed and to excel at it. I won't return to my world because I failed at what I sought to be."

"But you doctored me up just fine here, Trax earlier, me in Freetown. How's that a failure?"

"It was not the profession I chose."

I looked over at Trax.

"I've been unable to persuade him not to blame himself for what happened," he said.

"You're too nice to him."

Trax turned his head away and rubbed his eyes. Several yards away, I saw a circular opening form in the air and pointed. "Is that Arion's taxi service?"

Through the lighthole stepped a man wearing leather armor, a scabbard slung across his back. Tapered ears—one of Arion's kind.

The newcomer regarded us. "Jen-Varth?"

I saw Jen-Varth begin to tremble. "Dayon?"

The newcomer nodded slowly.

"Hello, Father," Trax said.

Jen-Varth's legs collapsed under him.

$$* * *$$

I sat cradling my arm, which tingled as Jen-Varth said it would. Jen-Varth and our new arrival, Dayon, stood off to my left, unemotionally talking over old times. They hadn't included Trax or me in their conversation and had been at it for the past hour. Arion had been right about Dayon being alive.

Behind some rocks a few yards ahead sat Trax playing

with the ring on his right hand. He rotated it, moved it up past his knuckle, craned his neck over the rocks to look at Dayon and Jen-Varth, then angrily shoved the ring back down. He balled the hand into a fist and ground the ring into the palm of his other hand. Tears welled up in his eyes. He dropped his hands into his lap and lowered his head.

What's going on with him?

Jen-Varth caught my attention and motioned me over. Getting to my feet proved a chore with one handicapped arm and snug jeans. When I arrived, he said, "Dayon will tell you why he's still alive when I thought he was dead." That sounded interesting. They sat. I maneuvered into lotus position.

Dayon told me that he joined the Protectors after he had killed a man. Noting my open mouth he said simply, "You would have seen him as evil and deserving death. Elfaeden do not pass such judgments. Men should be free to choose and follow their own paths."

Jen-Varth tensed.

"Maybe you should remind Arion of that," I said to Dayon. *And Jake and my father.*

"It would not be my place to advise Arion."

"Why not? Somebody should."

He didn't respond to that, but told me how three years later he met Jen-Varth. Because the Elfaeden were nearly unknown on the worlds that the Protectors served, suspicion led to rumors about their relationship.

Jen-Varth interrupted, "They thought Dayon and I were sexually involved."

Dayon continued, "Our commander sent us to handle an incursion of slavers and told us there were four of them. We found twelve. Before we could act, one of them saw us and aimed his weapon, not a benign Protector DN-32, at me. The Staff of Chaos detected danger and transported me. The slaver's weapon discharged at the same time. Jen-Varth believed that it had caused my destruction."

This mission was getting more convoluted by the hour. "How can a staff know you're in danger?" I asked.

"I know only that it does."

I recalled Jake's tale of the skeleton and the briquette-shaped artifact, with the outline of something inside when they x-rayed it. Was it an artificial intelligence chip and did the staff have one as well? I noticed Dayon's translator. "Did Arion give you that?"

"Yes."

Good. "Then he knows where we are and that we got separated from the others. Can you get us back?"

"Yes."

"Let's get on with it."

"Trax must accept the responsibility for his actions and learn to solve the problems he causes," he said.

I unfolded my legs. "Look! If you've got a problem with him or with Arion, save it for later. We're on a life-and-death mission. Let's get the fuck on with it!" I absentmindedly leaned on my left arm. It didn't exactly hurt but I lost balance. My head slammed into the ground.

Jen-Varth helped me up. "You need to be careful with your arm, Scott."

No shit! I yanked my right hand out of his, shot a glance at Dayon, and strode off toward the trees.

A few minutes later, Jen-Varth came over carrying his backpack.

"I'm not in my best mood," I growled.

"When we find ourselves in circumstances not of our

choosing, we must support one another and cooperate to seek a resolution."

"Dayon doesn't share your enlightened viewpoint."

"He wants Trax to correct his own mistakes."

"We don't have that much time to waste." Father-and-son conflict was running a marathon through this adventure.

He brushed his long hair from his eyes. "When I knew Dayon before, he did not yet know he was a father. We were both searching for the purpose to our lives, but he carries an extra burden."

"What's that?"

His blue eyes narrowed. "Arion is Dayon's uncle."

Uncle Arion? I'd sure find it a burden trying to live up to Arion's sleaziness. If I still believed that I was dreaming all this, I'd swear that I'd been transported into a Charles Dickens novel flooded with secrets and revelations and where you find out that everybody's related to everybody else.

I asked Jen-Varth, "What about our recent female surprise? Whose kid is she? Yours or Kedda's?"

"Not mine, and I think not Kedda's."

"Why not his?"

"Kedda keeps many secrets, but I don't think that she is one of them. I also believe that Kedda is a female."

"No way!" *Kedda, a woman*? Kedda had probed my brain. I'd undressed in front of Kedda. I'd *peed* in front of Kedda! Well, sort of. "Are you sure?"

"A suspicion, a guess. I have seen the longing in his eyes as he looks at some of us, especially you."

"Maybe he's gay?"

"That look is different. For now, I cannot think of another answer for his secrecy. But it's unimportant. You need to help Trax. Perhaps *you* can convince him of his worthiness and skills. He feels a kinship with you."

"Not after what I've done and said to him."

"While you slept, he thanked me for healing you."

"So?"

"Although he came freely into this adventure, he came unprepared. He knew he was not the one sought. Now that Dayon is here, he realizes his inadequacies."

"He told you that?"

"Not directly. He's not stupid, Scott. He saw how Arion treated you."

"What do you mean?"

"Do you know why Arion selected you?" he asked me.

"Jake knows."

"I don't think he does. I believe that Arion expects you to develop on your own, the same way Dayon wants Trax to. You and Trax have more in common than you think. We were all brought here without sufficient explanation. The girl also."

"For sure. Do you know why *you're* here?"

"No. Only that I have no special powers."

"You're a pretty good doctor. Back in college some of the students played fantasy role-playing games on the week-ends or whenever they got tired of studying. Most would be fighters or wizards, but they always brought along a healer to patch up the injured and raise the dead."

He indicated my arm. "Perhaps that's my role."

"You can raise the dead?"

"Not that I'm aware of."

"Well, I'm sure you're here for more than just fixing us up," I said. "How old you are?"

"I'm not old enough to have gained the wisdom I need to

be here. I am twenty-eight."

Jen-Varth was a handsome guy, only an inch shorter than me, with a perfectly straight nose and slender face that rarely smiled. Nothing alien about him except the blue bodysuit. His bronze skin wasn't all that bronze. The contrast against his blue suit made it stand out.

"Jake's only twenty-nine," I said. "I'm twenty-four. If you're not old enough to be here, I'm sure not. Do you know where we are yet?"

"Yes, and so should you."

"I should?"

The sun was setting. He pulled a bag of trail mix from his pack and handed it to me. My own backpack was else-where in the universe. He inclined his head toward Trax. "Trax hasn't eaten and needs a friend."

Feed the hand that bit me? I don't think so.

Jen-Varth left. I held the bag and leaned against a tree scarcely taller than I was. Why should I know where we were? *What's that smell?* I sniffed the tree. *Skunk wood!* *Son of a bitch.*

Enlightened self-interest made me join Trax and squat next to him. "Hungry?"

He rubbed the sleeve of his tunic across his eyes.

I opened the trail mix bag and held it out to him.

He reached in for a handful, put a few pieces into his mouth, and chewed slowly. "I'm sorry for the suffering I've caused you and everyone else." He sniffled then took a deep, halting breath, almost a sob. "I don't belong here."

"Hey, I said some stuff I probably shouldn't have, and if I hadn't tackled you, we wouldn't be here, but I don't think leaving is an option for any of us."

"Dayon would send me away if he could."

"Why would he send his son away?"

"To protect me."

"But he can't send you away?"

"He can't make Gates either. I'm only his son by accident! My mother was a courtesan. He left after I was born, so she took care of me."

"Looks like she did a good job."

"My father came back to clear his conscience by turning me into a Mage. You told me before that you didn't think I was much of a Mage. Well, you were right. What I do best is gamble, pick pockets, and steal."

"Your mother let you do those things?"

"She had me watched, but I bribed her spies not to tell her or to tell her whatever I wanted her to hear. I got them drunk when I wanted privacy."

"You are wrong, Trax." Dayon had come up behind him. "Mylane knew everything, and she would have stopped you before you got into real danger."

"She didn't know about the night Moka and I thought about going to Quastor." Dayon didn't see Trax's sly smile.

"Why didn't you go?"

The smile vanished. "Moka drank too much ale and got sick."

"Your mother made certain that he did." Dayon walked away.

"I can't do what you want!" Trax said after him. Dayon ignored him.

Although I'd just met Dayon, he was full of contradictions. He was an Elf like his uncle, Arion, yet I hadn't seen Arion carry any weapons. The sword hilt protruding from Dayon's carved leather scabbard told me it was a fine, heavy weapon. He'd said that he'd killed a man. The way he'd said it told me that his concern over it went deeper than his apparent surface indifference. But having left Trax fatherless for most of his life didn't bother him? I couldn't believe that, unless Elfaeden considered it a mortal sin to mate with a human. According to Trax, Dayon couldn't make Gates and apparently he couldn't control the staff any better than Trax could. So why was he here?

Arion bore his own set of contradictions. If he was so powerful, why were we on this mission? What was that invisible statue in Freetown all about? Our legends of dragons and Pegasi fit what really existed out here, but we'd missed the mark in depicting Elves as happy, carefree beings. Swords-and-sorcery, telepathic powers, and Magick were commonplace out here. Why had Earth been left outside this reality?

Trax pulled me away from my ruminations. "I can't be what he wants." His eyes were red again.

I saw a scared young man who'd let the siren song of adventure and his youthful impetuosity yank him into a larger, less friendly, and unforgiving universe. Out here he had no safe places to run to, no friends, and a father pushing him into something he didn't think he was ready for. I'd had it easy. The Colonel never wanted me to be something I couldn't be, only what I didn't want to be. Trax and I had some things in common, and Jake's betrayal had brought me up one friend short for now. "I think I can help you get us back," I said.

He slanted his head at me. "You know how?"

"Were you a good thief?" I asked him.

"Yes." Confidence returned in his voice.

"Did you ever get caught?"

"Only once."

I'd have to ask him about that later. "How did you get so good?"

"I observed those who failed and made certain I didn't repeat their mistakes."

"You're a good observer?"

He didn't answer immediately. "Yes."

"How is this world different from the other one?"

He frowned. I handed him a twig I'd broken off a tree. "Smell this."

He sniffed it. "We're on the same world?"

Unless skunk wood was common in the vast realms beyond Earth, we were. The terrain, day length, and position and size and color of the sun should have clued me earlier.

"We don't know how far the staff brought us," he said.

"From the way Dayon and Jen-Varth are acting, it can't be all that far. Jen-Varth must have figured it out from the stars. Of course, we can't ask him for help without your father finding out. If this were your homeworld and you were lost, how would you find your way back?"

"I would use my Magick to locate a familiar object. It's one of the first spells I learned."

"You said this isn't a Magick world."

"The staff has enough Magick."

"So?"

He considered that. "The translators Arion gave us! We all have them." He was pleased with his insight.

"Won't the ones we have here confuse you?"

His enthusiasm faded. "They might."

"Any way around the problem?" I asked.

"If you stand close to my father and Jen-Varth, I can seek beyond you."

"Go for it. Impress your father." *I wish mine were that easy to impress.* "I'll keep them busy."

"Thank you, Scott."

"For what? You figured out most of it."

"For being my friend after what I did to you."

"Like I said, most of it was my own fault."

I stood up and strolled over to Jen-Varth and Dayon and pointed back at Trax, pretending to mock him to hide my coaching. "Magick Dude at work. Do not disturb." Trax had clutched his staff horizontally with both hands.

We small-talked. Jen-Varth asked about my arm. I told him it hurt a little. I asked Dayon what Arion had told him about our mission.

"That my son, as wielder of the Staff of Chaos, had come with you to battle a S'pharn, and that you would explain further," he said.

"Figures. Arion's not big on disclosures."

Trax's confident voice shouted at us. "We must go in that direction to find the others!" He pointed a few degrees left of where the sun had set.

I shrugged my shoulders. "He's full of surprises."

* * *

We arrived to find everyone awake and sitting near the Gate and a smelly campfire. Back on Earth it was Wednesday, seven p.m. Here, it was a couple of hours past sunset.

Jake stood up. "What the hell took you so long? Kedda said you weren't far away and that Jen-Varth would get you back."

A few miles, as the alien crow flies.

237

He saw my wrapped arm. "What happened to you?" he said.

"When did concern for my well-being become part of your personality profile?"

Jen-Varth answered him while I turned to Kedda and asked, "Did Her Majesty keep you occupied with diapering and feeding?"

I bowed to her. "Welcome to our humble planet. I didn't catch your name."

She pursed her lips.

"Enelle," Kedda said.

Standing near her gave me the creepy shivers. "I see you gave her the spare translator," I said to Kedda. "That must have been about as pleasant as bathing a cat." *Which meant she could understand me.* "Any idea how she got here?"

"She was in her bedroom getting ready to celebrate her birthday, when a Gate appeared and pulled her into it."

She yanked her head at Kedda. "How did you know that?"

"He reads minds," I said. "Oh, happy birthday. I can empathize with surprises." I told Kedda, "I'll bet the dragons' perverted sense of humor sent her here."

She shot me a puzzled look. "Dragons?"

Time to test her translator. "Yeah, fucking, bad-ass dragons." Her blushing face confirmed its efficiency.

"You should watch your language," Jake said behind me.

I fake-smiled at her. "If she wants to hang out with the guys, she'll have to learn to get over it." I turned to him with both middle fingers aimed up. "One for now. And one for later, in case I forget."

I indicated the Gate and said to no one, "Who's going to lead us onward and upward?"

We didn't have a designated leader. Jen-Varth had the potential—prepared, levelheaded, decisive—but preferred staying in the background. I still believed that Kedda had the greatest knowledge of our mission, although he also had left the initiative to someone else while providing occasional guidance only to me. Before Dayon's arrival, Trax had had the arrogance. Dayon displayed no desire for leadership. If Colonel Madison passed any command genes to me, they hadn't manifested themselves. But I knew how to be a gentleman. I thrust my good hand toward the Gate and smiled at Enelle. "Ladies and royalty first."

"I am not going anywhere!"

"You've already gone somewhere. If you care to stay behind here, I'll appreciate the peace and quiet of your absence," I said.

"I understand why you're being a prick to me, but why to her?" Jake said.

I had no idea. "In keeping with your example of honesty, I decided that I should no longer hide the evil monster beneath my innocent and trusting exterior."

While I hadn't appointed myself as leader, I needed fresher surroundings. I stepped through the Gate.

20

UH, TAKE US TO YOUR LEADER?
Day Four: Second World

I came out into a shallow cave. The air was fresh, damp, and thin. I found myself taking deep breaths to compensate. The gravity felt normal, so there must have been less oxygen in this atmosphere rather than less air. Forty feet ahead a ten-by-ten-foot-square opening framed a bright gray too diffuse to be night unless this world had a super bright moon. I walked toward the opening.

Behind me I heard, "Let . . . me . . . go!" Over my shoulder I saw Jake towing Enelle through the Gate. She yanked her hand from his. The others filed through behind them, Jen-Varth last. I saw him palming the remote control he'd kept that operated the barrier around this Gate. When he passed me, I whispered, "You sealed the Gate?" He nodded.

Enelle stomped forward and halted next to me. Her cape flew out behind her while she straightened the billowy sleeves of her dress. It hung well on her, gauzy and fairy-like. The high collar enhanced her slender face. She scowled. "What are *you* staring at?" Warmth rose in my neck.

I ambled forward and stood next to Dayon who was

looking out beyond the cave. A steady rain dripped from the sky—the kind of rainy-weekend rain that makes you want to stay inside and curl up with a good woman. Not with her, though.

Off to the left, hewn rock steps carved out of the hillside led down at a hefty slope. No railing. Ahead, over a mile away, stood a hill covered with dense, green vegetation. An otherworldly, conical tower with no visible openings poked above the vegetation and blended into the natural rock, as if the building had been stuck down into it. The overgrowth of mature vegetation completely covered the slope so that the boundary between the rock and tower was invisible from here. A modest town sprawled out in the valley below us.

Jake stepped up next to Dayon and me. He unfolded his map and tilted it toward the light. "The next Gate lies across the valley, probably in that structure. We'll wait until the rain stops."

It didn't seem as if that would happen anytime soon. I stuck my hand into it. Normal wetness, no stinging sensation. I stepped out onto a wide ledge and let the cool rain wash my face. When I came back in and saw Trax smiling, I figured this must be a Magick world.

Behind us, Jen-Varth said that we might want to rest for a couple of hours. Jake put his map away and he and Jen-Varth spread out their bedrolls. They fell asleep on them immediately.

Enelle hadn't done anything to get tired from. She sat on a rock and stared at the Gate. Kedda offered to undo his bedroll for her to sit on so she wouldn't get dirty. I didn't see what difference it would make. That dress was going to get dirty no matter what she did. She ignored him. He pulled out his cards and invited the non-sleepers to play.

RICK TAUBOLD

"I'll win," Trax assured Kedda.

Kedda's wry smile said otherwise.

My arm started aching. Using my bedroll as a pillow, I stretched out on the cave floor, rested the arm across my stomach, and reflected.

Our party consisted of two factions: those who knew some or all of what was going on—Kedda and Jake—and those who didn't—Jen-Varth, Trax, Enelle, myself. I wasn't sure about Dayon. Was Arion slimy enough to keep his nephew in the dark? Or was Dayon just as slimy at withholding information? Unlike the Vulcans in *Star Trek*, pointy ears in this realm didn't guarantee honesty and forthrightness.

Dayon sat next to me. "We should set a guard. This world is unknown to us."

He hadn't been very talkative, but why was he talking to me now?

"I don't think anything will come out in this rain," I said.

"Foul weather is the best time to attack, when it is least expected."

"Are you a soldier?" I asked him. "I noticed your sword."

"I am a soldier of a sort. I joined the Protectors to test and hone my skills. My people are pacifists, yet some of my family understand that vigilance is necessary. This is why Arion gathered you."

"Did he send you to help us hack and slash the bad dude?"

"I doubt that my sword or me would be effective against the enemy you face. Arion did not say why he wanted me."

"You're his nephew."

"That would not matter to him."

I certainly couldn't accuse Arion of nepotism. Another thing, Arion had given us a spare translator. But Dayon arrived with one already, which meant Arion knew that someone else—Enelle probably—had joined or would be joining us. Too many secrets for my taste. Further, every obstacle or problem we had faced, we'd solved fairly quickly, including my broken arm, too easy for what Arion had indicated that we'd face. Everything so far had been suspiciously low key. If I were reading this story as an adventure novel, I might have closed the book. Had Arion selected us to cover all eventualities? Or had we just been lucky? If the latter, when would our luck run out?

I remembered the medallion in the pocket of my jeans and pulled it out. Dev said it would protect me. For a piece of jewelry it was crude, not quite circular, and hastily polished, more like something banged out in high school metal shop for a C-minus grade. I maneuvered it over my head and positioned it on my chest.

* * *

Jake woke me. "We're ready to leave. How's the arm?"

"It's still there."

"Want to talk?"

"Not now, not here, and if parallel universes exist, not in any of them either. Leave me alone."

I dragged myself up. No one else was inside the cave. A lantern stood nearby. I squinted at my watch. *Five hours*? Jen-Varth's drugs must be messing up my sleep cycle. Back home it was midnight, Thursday. Day five of our adventure.

I walked outside. The clear sky had a hint of light left in it. From here the town looked quiet, but we were several hundred feet up and a half mile or more away. Looking down at the town unsettled me. It was too idyllic. I also felt someone watching us. I scanned the area, but saw nothing in the low light.

The others stood twenty feet away at the end of the ledge. When I joined them, they were discussing appropriate attire. I heard Jake suggest that since we didn't have time to scout ahead and the chance was slim that any clothing we carried was the native dress, we should go as we were and hope that "we're from another land across the mountains" would suffice. Jake had added a black T-shirt to his black jeans. I didn't think he was in mourning. Not for me anyway. Smear a little soot on his face and he'd be ready for a black ops mission. Not that I cared. I still had on my black tank top and considered changing it so I wouldn't look like him.

Kedda wore a gray tunic and darker gray cloak. "I have some experience in these matters. Now that Scott is awake, we should go," he said.

"Shouldn't we wait until morning?" I asked.

"It *is* morning," Jen-Varth replied.

I saw that the sky was lightening into a vibrant, deep blue canvas with high, wispy clouds dry-brushed onto it, the antithesis of the former, rain-induced pallor. "Must be short days on this world," I said.

We gathered our gear and headed down. Dayon noticed my medallion. "Who gave you that?"

"A friend of Arion's bought it for me."

"It is Magick."

"That's what he told me."

"Do you know its function?" he asked.

"Something about reflecting or absorbing spells."

"He fitted you for battle."

"Battle?"

"You should conceal it. It works best when your enemies don't know you have it."

"Battle?" I repeated.

"It would not make sense to wear one if you did not expect to encounter hostile Magick," he said.

When Dev gave it to me, I didn't think he had intended it for anything specific. "But what does the medallion *do*," I asked Dayon.

"You already told me."

His answer affirmed his lineage. Evasive answers ran in his family.

Negotiating the steps was no problem except for Enelle. She refused to remove her formal shoes, lest her feet get dirty, and complained that her dress was getting wrinkled.

"Take it off and carry it!" I said. "There's probably nothing worth covering anyway." She bared perfect, white teeth at me, the kind that took lots of money to have straightened. "Nice teeth, Princess." Genetically engineered? I decided not. She wasn't bad to look at, but she wasn't as perfect as a genetic engineer would have made her. About five-eight; a hundred and twenty pounds; a bust that added interest to her dress; dark eyes; petite nose; slender cheeks. I'd have made her lips fuller.

"Stop staring at me!"

She probably liked to be on top.

The steps turned into a gently sloping trail. The feeling of being watched didn't go away. Neither did it get stronger nor weaker, as if the watcher was moving with us.

I remembered that the Gate had been sealed from the *other* side. After I pushed away the unpleasant implications of that thought, another observation replaced it. Everyone we had met on this journey was human. Not humanoid. Human. Like Jake and me. Jen-Varth's bronze skin, blue eyes, and black hair might elicit a few stares on Earth—Arion's and Dayon's tapered ears definitely would—but all of them were human. Dev had said as much back in Freetown. And who met us at the bottom of the hill where the trail widened? Four humans. Waiting for us.

Two of them were dressed in stiff, oatmeal-cookie-colored caftans and bell-bottom pants, with dark chocolate (I was hungry) Roman-style sandals laced up the leg. I decided they were bodyguards or law-enforcement. The other two wore turquoise caftans with white sashes over the same arrangement of pants and sandals. They would be the honchos. White headbands kept their shoulder-length, dark hair in place. No visible weapons.

Kedda stepped forward in first-contact, ambassadorial fashion and bowed. "We of the distant lands of Arion greet you. I am Kedda."

The honchos looked at each other as if not expecting us to speak their language.

"Purpose journey-stream home-place cross?" one asked.

Colorful language. Or maybe my translator battery was running low.

Kedda indicated our destination. "Journey-end. Night stay, nourish rest, provision buy." He bowed again.

"Pleasure home-place guest dwell." With an excessively accommodating smile the honcho motioned for us to follow.

"Kedda has many talents," Jen-Varth said to me.

My translator couldn't be defective because I understood Jen-Varth perfectly. Was Kedda speaking their language? Had he been here before? Were these his people? I dismissed the latter because neither had acknowledged kinship.

The honchos led. Their lackeys followed us. "We don't have any local coinage," I whispered to Kedda. He rattled the pouch hanging from his waist. Precious metals and gems glittered the same on any planet. "Is there anything you're *not* prepared for?" I asked him.

He replied, straight-faced, "Enelle." After a pause he said, "And these people."

What did he mean by that?

As we approached the town, a premonition slithered underneath my being-watched feeling. Our hosts were neither obsequious nor aloof. No amenities, no tour of the town, not a sightseeing syllable spoken. I saw Freetown-like shops attached to a few of the houses. No business district. Most of the buildings resembled adobes with stone igloos atop them. Some were conventional cube shapes. None resembled the architecture up on the distant hillside.

We halted. Number One honcho gestured, "Nourish-place. Sunfall return." He left. His entourage stayed while Number Two honcho led us inside.

Lanterns dimly lit this cafe. Three short rows of stout wooden booths, snugly arranged like tables in the company cafeteria, led to a small bar. The place was neat and clean. Our host said to a man behind the bar, "Sunfall mountain-place-guest prepare."

Maybe a luau with lavish entertainment?

The bartender, or whatever they called him here, was a pleasant enough fellow, although he spoke very little. He alternately smiled and frowned. In his simple-complex language he told us where we could freshen up and said that he'd have food ready shortly.

When we returned, a bowl of rose-colored, apple-like fruit and a plate of yellow vegetables on the bar greeted my hunger. I grabbed a fruit and bit into it. It tasted like . . . an extra sweet apple. The vegetables crunched and tasted like water chestnuts. I picked up a goblet of purple liquid and sipped. Nonalcoholic, mildly tart, berry-flavored. Decent.

The booths accommodated only four people each. We selected two near the bar, across an aisle, and started to sit when Kedda suggested that Jake, Trax, Dayon, and Jen-Varth sit on one side of the room while he, Enelle, and I sit together on the other. He said that a smaller group might make Enelle feel more comfortable, but I was sure that he knew how I currently felt toward Jake—you don't keep secrets from a mind reader.

The bartender's furtive look sent the cold pricklies to search-and-destroy the surviving warm fuzzies inside me. I held up my glass to Kedda, "Is this drugged?"

"No. Our hosts have an interesting event planned for us."

"Are we in danger?"

"I can protect us as long as we remain together."

"Can you read everyone's mind?"

"Not all. The individual must be projecting his thoughts for me to read them clearly. Yours and Enelle's are easier to discern because of your powers."

Enelle, who had been ignoring us, flashed him an ugly look. "You can read my thoughts?" She wasn't bad looking when she wasn't scrunching up her face.

Kedda nodded. "Sometimes."

"Why have you brought me here?" she asked curtly.

"We didn't. Someone else did, so you must be important to us," I responded.

From her reaction I surmised that she liked to feel important. "You spoke of dragons. The legends of my world mention them. I want to know more."

I didn't appreciate her imperious tone, but at least she was talking.

After I described our meeting with the dragons, I found myself staring at her necklace. I shivered. Shivers, tingles, jolts, spasms, nausea, seizures, pain. Why hadn't college been this much fun?

A stronger shiver started in my neck and snaked its way down my spine. I saw her neck muscles tense, her eyes locked into mine. Half a heartbeat later, my own body's muscles violently snapped to attention. My injured arm had a fleeting moment to utter its distress before the red alerts and damage reports from every station of my anatomy overwhelmed me. Strobe lights.

Kedda shouted, "No!"

21

THEY DON'T MAKE DEMONS
LIKE THEY USED TO
Day Five: Second World, Morning

"Where the hell did they go!" Jake shot out of his chair, knocking it over. He felt his body stiffen in the next moment. In front of him, still seated, were Jen-Varth, Trax, and Dayon similarly paralyzed. A moment ago, across the room, Scott, Kedda, and the girl had been talking. He'd heard Kedda raise his voice a moment before all three vanished. From the corner of his eye Jake saw their host's hands poised at them as if he were about to conduct an orchestra.

An official and six deputies rushed in. They quickly tied everyone's hands behind them and took Jen-Varth's gun and his boot knife. After they gagged Dayon and Trax, the man behind the bar lowered his hands. Jake's paralysis faded. "What did you do with the others?" he asked the men.

The official slapped Jake across the face. Jake instinctively twisted his body sideways and shot one foot firmly into the official's chest, knocking him backward into a deputy. Both men staggered.

Jake felt a sharp point against the right side of his neck. A second deputy had also poised a foot-long, conical dagger over Jake's heart.

Having recovered, the official waved his hand at the table where Scott and the others had been. "Where go?"

Jake glared at him. "That's what I asked *you*."

The man's puzzled look frightened Jake. If these people weren't responsible for Scott's disappearance, who was? The official pressed against the dagger over Jake's heart and repeated his query.

"I don't know!" Jake rasped.

The man pointed at Trax. "Demon-symbol carry. Execute-ceremony first." He glowered at Jake. "Second."

Execute? "We mean you no harm!" Jake protested.

From behind, a deputy yanked Jake's tied arms back so hard that at first Jake thought one shoulder had dislocated. His anguished grunt seemed to please the official. "You are demons from the Place of Evil. The ceremony occurs at third moonrise."

Jake immediately noted the change in the man's speech pattern. Had they switched to a different language that the translators rendered better? If so, what had prompted the change? And why did they center their attention on him?

One deputy shoved Jen-Varth out the door. Another pushed Jake along behind him. While the dagger was no longer over Jake's heart, periodic scratches from the one at his neck kept him reminded of their sincerity. The ache in his pulled shoulder muscles and the recollection of swift and total paralysis advised against an escape attempt. Some minutes later, the other deputies came out carrying the tightly bound Trax and Dayon.

The procession ended at an open area where a dozen upright poles nine inches in diameter were arranged in a vague semicircle. They bound Jake to one pole and put Dayon and Jen-Varth on either side of him. Jake noted the extra care they put into Dayon's restraints. He was surprised that they didn't take away the translators.

They stripped Trax completely, without the decency of a loin wrap, and trussed him to a horizontal pole suspended between two uprights. His bare back hung inches above a fire pit, like a pig for roasting. Apparently, since Trax had wielded the staff, that put him first on their to-do list. The staff lay in the fire pit beneath Trax. Although they had left it in the tavern, after they finished securing him to the pole, the staff had suddenly appeared beneath him. Jake hadn't told Scott that the staff was the same color and texture as Bryce Duncan's briquette artifact.

Jake watched the townspeople industriously preparing for what he knew was a fourth of July celebration with them as the fireworks. This wasn't what making sacrifices in life meant to Jake.

The first moon, large and faint in the midday sun, had risen thirty degrees above the horizon. The second one had not appeared, but the speed of the preparations told him that ceremony time was near.

Four years ago, when Arion transported Jake to his world, Arion had told him, "Our knowledge of what will transpire is limited. We do not think that you are an essential element. We expect that Scott Madison will accomplish the mission without you, but your presence might aid his chance of survival. I will take him even if you decide not to train him." Back in his apartment, Jake remembered saying—no, shouting—at the collapsing circle of light he'd just traveled through, "Then why did you pick *me*?" Only Arion's sudden appearance just after Bryce Duncan's discovery had convinced him that Arion wasn't a lunatic. On a whim, he had asked Bryce if he knew anyone named Jefferson Scott Madison.

"There's a Colonel *Jack* Madison at Fort Bragg, one of the base commanders, not involved with my stuff though."

Jake also hadn't told Scott that he'd secretly followed him around campus at UCSD and had sat in on his classes before they ever met.

The dragons' remark about the equations had come as a surprise, though. Jake had believed that his only purpose was to protect Scott. He hadn't been very successful at that.

Jake saw a man approaching clad in a heavy, forest-green caftan and carrying an oversized book an inch thick. The man opened the book and walked past each prisoner in turn, looking between the book and the person.

He came to Jake and touched Jake's translator. "We know this lets you understand us. Tell me your name, Demon."

"Why should I? You're going to execute us anyway."

"I ask the questions!" He slapped the book. "This instructs us on how to make your banishment painful!"

"More painful than execution?"

The man came closer and said quietly, as if not wishing to be overheard, "They don't understand that you cannot die."

"That's news to me."

Jake wondered why the man hadn't spoken to the others. Why only to him?

"You are curiously stupid for a demon," the man said. He flipped several pages and read from the book, " 'The demon's soul resides in the heart of its human body. Remove it while the body lives and the demon's soul is forced back to the demon's place of origin where his soul must reside for a hundred-year before he can reincarnate. Burning the body prevents the demon from returning to it.' "

The man smiled as if he was proud that he knew these things.

"I can see why we're outdoors. That must create quite a stench," Jake said. "So, when did demons last visit you?"

"You do not know?"

Jake gave the man his best sheepish smile. "I'm just an apprentice. They don't tell me everything."

"This is *my* first encounter with your kind." He seemed proud of that as well. "Your last visitation was before my birth, half a hundred-year ago."

"If the banishment lasts a century, how can the demons have returned so soon? Maybe we're not demons," Jake said.

"I have determined that you are a new demon."

"How do know that?" Jake asked.

"I detect no Magick in you yet."

He thought that a curious mythology, something Bryce would appreciate. Jake cast his eyes at Jen-Varth. "He's not Magick either."

"He does not have the correct semblance for a demon. We know that demons have human slaves."

"How do you know *I'm* not a slave?"

"You attacked an overseer. A slave would not attack one with the power to set him free." He indicated the book again. "You would do well to tell me your name. We can delay your soul from returning to its realm while we inflict torment upon it if you do not cooperate." The man left.

Jake remembered Bryce telling him that many beliefs and superstitions had a basis in fact. Having seen mythology come alive in the past few days, Jake was certain that he didn't want to meet the motivation for this one. He looked over at Jen-Varth. "What do you think?" Jen-Varth inclined his head at Trax as if to indicate who had to make the next move. Jake turned to Dayon on the other side of him. "Do you have any suggestions?" Not even a nod or a head shake came from Dayon. Trax gave a snakelike wiggle. *Poor kid.*

Jake saw a couple of townspeople point at the sky and noted the rising of the second moon. He muttered, "Arion, if you're out there, we could use some help."

The man with the book, the demonologist, returned with a turquoise-robed official. The two were arguing. "They are *all* demons!" the official said.

"The last ones came from the *other* side," the demonologist retorted.

"How many of us does your book say they killed before we drove them away? Why do we proclaim at ceremony, 'Beware the objects of velvet black that steal your soul'?"

"If these are not demons—"

"We will banish them!" The official tramped away.

The demonologist regarded Jake, seeming less certain of his pronouncement than before. "The staff, it's just a walking stick," Jake offered.

"It follows him," the demonologist countered.

"It was a gift from his father." Despite their actions, these people seemed peaceful, moral, and scared. "We are not demons. Release us, and we will go in peace."

For a moment Jake thought that the man might do it, but he suddenly opened the book, flipped several pages, and read with renewed conviction, " 'They conceal their power until it is too late.' " He looked at Jake again. "We cannot chance even one demon going free. Why did the others vanish if they were not demons fleeing capture?"

Jake couldn't argue with their logic. Even if he knew where Scott, Kedda, and the girl were, how could he respond? He decided to try something that they might better understand. He began chanting and used mathematical terms for the words.

The demonologist frowned at him. "You are not a Mage."

Jake stopped chanting. "No, I'm not." He resumed.

Two robed individuals arrived, possibly priests, Jake thought. They listened. One of the men nervously asked, "What manner of demon spell was that?"

Jake paused again. "Just a musical tune I composed to pass the time. I'll be glad to repeat it for you."

The two priests looked quizzically at the demonologist and then at all four prisoners. One priest asked the demonologist, "Does the book mention this?"

Where had they gotten this book? Only the demonologist seemed able to read it. "You won't find the answers in there," Jake said.

They ignored him. Their consultations confirmed Jake's guess that the so-called demon visitations had not occurred during the lives of those here, but the efficiency of their preparations suggested that they followed this ritual on a regular basis even without demons to banish.

Noting their frequent glances at the horizon, Jake loudly announced, "I have cursed you all. Unless you release us your town will be laid waste before the sun rises again." That sounded good.

Some of the townsfolk paused their work to look at Jake, then resumed. Even if these people freed them, where would they go, and how would they accomplish their mission without Scott?

22

KART
Day Five: Planet Thalar, Kart's Inn,
Late Evening

Every night since Kedda's departure from Rysten, after his patrons had left and his guests had gone to bed, Kart went into his kitchen and down into the cellar. Usually he didn't get there until midnight, but tonight had been slow. Everyone had left three hours early. Holding his candle, he moved to the cellar's farthest corner where he uttered a Word. A blank wall slid open. A second command caused Magick illumination to fill the room. He sealed the door and sat at his small desk to reflect on the recent, troubling events while his past loomed before him.

One joined the Brotherhood for life. One swore oaths to them beyond one's natural lifetime. But Kart had left the Brotherhood and stolen their artifact. He had erased his name from their memories, although he couldn't be certain of the permanence of that.

The artifact had been among them for decades, discovered in a chance raid on a primitive world. It contained Mage-stone of unusual potency. After Kart had completed his apprenticeship, he was allowed to study the black cone with the hemispherical tip. As far as he knew, he was the first to discover the second power within it, Psi-stone, which he believed accounted for its exceptional strength. He presented those findings to his mentor, who declared, "Magick is the only power of value to us. Do not waste your time on others."

His mentor had found him as an abandoned young boy. Among the Brotherhood, most members kept young boys to satisfy their desires because, they claimed, women interfered with devotion to the Art. Had Kart not been gifted with Magick, his mentor would have used him that way.

Kart did not share their tastes. When he was old enough, he took a woman from a nearby village whose people served the Brotherhood in exchange for the privilege of being allowed to live. Weyda became pregnant. His mentor ordered him to get rid of her.

At that point, Kart realized that Magick was not the most important thing in life. If he didn't put her away, he knew that they would. He conceived a plan. The Brotherhood had recently been foraging on a nearby Psi world for victims for their mind-control experiments. Psi Adepts could erase memories. If Kart could persuade one to help him, then he could erase their memory of him. He could escape with his woman and unborn child and they would never know to search for him. He had just learned how to make Gates, so he could visit that Psi world himself. Secretly, he took his woman there, leaving her safe, and returned with an ally, a Psi Adept who agreed to erase Kart from the Brotherhood's memory if he could also erase their memory of his world. Kart readily agreed.

Kart's thoughts returned to the present. He found himself staring up at his shelf of books and scrolls. No one in Rysten knew him to be a Mage. Here, he and Weyda had raised their daughter, Alir, in peace. He restricted his use of the Power and kept constant watch. He knew all of import in Rysten and the neighboring towns, who of significance came and went, what Magick was present. With the artifact's power, very little was beyond his skill. He had restored Weyda when her heart failed four years ago even though he had feared that using its power might reveal his presence.

One night, not long after Kedda's appearance in Rysten, when Kart's late-night scrying had unexpectedly shown him Kedda's image, he suspected that the artifact held more secrets and that Kedda knew those secrets. He scried on Kedda and Arion after they left Rysten and saw them meet the boy Trax in Jocathan. They attached importance to the boy's staff, yet Kart detected no Magick from it, unlike his own artifact that had to be shielded against detection.

On Arion's world the Shield spell around Arion's keep blocked him from scrying inside it. Why did an Elf of Arion's skill require the assistance of others? Kart feared that something larger and more sinister was happening. He worried for Alir and Weyda. Kedda had the answers he desperately needed

* * *

A sudden damp coldness against my bare shoulders made me gasp. White lights scintillated inside my eyeballs, and triple-strength prickliness coursed through my body like cut-off circulation returning with a vengeance. I caught the faint smell of musty books just before I heard a stifled shriek. Enelle? Then Kedda's voice, sharp and angry. "Kart! Why have you brought us here?"

Who's Kart?

"I—I have . . . made a mistake," a new voice said.

A hand touched me and my vision cleared. Kedda knelt beside me. "Wh-where are we?" I asked.

Kedda said in the coldest tone I'd ever heard from him, "We are in the town of Rysten, in the cellar of Kart's inn. Not far away lies Jocathan, Trax's home. Kart brought us here. I have placed Enelle in Stasis to avoid complications for the present." He helped me sit up and pointed to a man sitting silently at a desk a few feet away. The man had brown hair graying at the temples and a squarish face with a small beard and mustache. "That is Kart. He has been watching us." Kedda got up from the floor.

"Then I wasn't imagining it?" I said.

"You felt him? Close your eyes. Do you sense it?"

"Sense what?"

"His artifact."

This was getting weird.

"Your powers located the Gate barrier control that Jen-Varth keeps with him," he said.

Was there anything he didn't know?

"Please try."

I closed my eyes. *Fetch, Scott, fetch.*

Nothing but the sound of Kedda's boots slowly clicking on the stone floor . . .

A white flash discharged in my head. I popped my eyes open. "What the hell was that?"

"This." Kedda stood next to the desk. On it lay an open, five-inch-thick book. "Come here."

I got up slowly and walked the couple of steps toward him. The old, hollowed-out book trick. Kedda pulled out a cone four inches high and nearly that wide at the base. The last top inch of the cone was a hemisphere. It had the same color and matte texture as Trax's staff. "Kart wants answers that he believes I can provide. He also believes that his daughter desires me."

Kedda? A ladies' man? The Cracker Jack surprises on this adventure still hadn't run out. But Jen-Varth thought that Kedda was a female.

"Jen-Varth is incorrect. I am male."

"*Damn mind reader*!"

"Please control your thought projection."

"I *wasn't* projecting!"

"The one who holds the Tri-Lith linked with your mind once. You must not let it happen when we encounter him."

"Fat chance when I can't even stop *you*. Back on Arion's world he peeled my brain like a cooked potato when he wasn't even there. And don't change the subject!"

From his pocket he withdrew a black . . . briquette. Unless I was seriously mistaken, it was a copy of what Jake said his friend Bryce had found on Earth.

"It is not a copy." Kedda held it out. "Take it to enhance your power and help shield your thoughts."

"Oh, no. Every black thing I touch zaps me, causes me pain, or knocks me unconscious."

"This is less powerful than the Staff of Chaos. It will give you brief and minor discomfort."

"Yeah, that's what the doctor says just before he does something that hurts like hell."

"You will need this to resist the S'pharn until you can access the Tri-Lith he holds."

"I can't wait," I sneered.

"The Tri-Lith will make you more powerful than Arion."

"Riii . . . ght. When do I get my superhero suit?"

At that point he got more serious than I'd ever seen him get. "You don't understand, do you?"

"How the *fuck* can I? Nobody will explain anything!" I stuck out my finger an inch from his flat nose. "If my ass is about to get fried, I've got a right to know!"

He stayed calm. "You aren't the one who's in danger."

I snorted. "*I'm* not in danger? Let's go over this again. In the past few days I've plummeted to the ground from a flying horse and narrowly escaped becoming road pizza on an alien planet; I've broken my arm; I've been knocked senseless more than once; I've had my stomach want to empty itself several times—I'm sure that's not over—and someone I've never met has long-distance dialing privileges to access and suck out my brain. Which redefines 'reach out and touch someone.' No danger? We haven't even gotten to the *hard* part yet!"

"The danger is to the rest of us. Our purpose is to bring you to the S'pharn. Whatever the cost."

He went over to Enelle and touched her. She unfroze and got hysterical. Well, not exactly hysterical . . .

"Don't touch me!" She started to cry. "You hate me."

Kart, who had sat silently during all this, raised his head. I looked at him, then at her. "We don't hate you." I knew I sounded condescending.

Her sobs lessened. "You should."

"These aren't the best circumstances for any of us. I wish you weren't here . . ." *Oops, that came out wrong*.

"You *do* hate me!"

"I meant, we don't have any control over what's happening to us. When this is all over—"

She bared her teeth, and I thought she was going to

slap me. "You'll *what*! Take me to bed because you think *that's* what I need?"

Whoa! Her emotions were flying around faster than a hard-smacked racquetball. "I meant, when this is over, our lives can go back to normal."

"I don't *have* a normal life!"

"Look, I'm just trying to be your friend."

"I don't have any friends."

"Then I can be your first . . . friend." I could do cordial friendship, but I had no idea what made me want to be cordial with her. Should I tell her that we were the pieces in a universe-sized chess game and that I was supposed to be a white knight?

She calmed down and said she was hungry.

Kart had said that we could find something to eat upstairs. I realized that we were in a secret room when he gestured and a section of wall moved aside. I was surprised that Enelle wasn't surprised when he did that. Kedda ushered us upstairs. Kart stayed behind. I figured he had more moping to do.

In the kitchen we found the snacks for guests who got hungry in the middle of the night. Along with the standard bread and cheese were some meat jerky and a bottle of wine. I didn't trust alien wine and said I'd prefer water. We loaded food onto a wooden tray and went out into the barroom.

We picked a table facing the outside doors. Two lanterns gave the room a warm glow with flickering shadows. This inn had an older look than the one in Freetown. The tang of beer and wine drifted around the table. Kedda went behind the bar and drew us mugs of water from a small pump. The water had a heavy mineral smell, but the taste wasn't bad.

We had just finished our snack when a surprised female

voice said, "Kedda? You have returned?"

I turned. A young woman stood by the front doors. She stepped into the light. Kedda stood up. He introduced us to Alir, giving our names but not our places of origin. Did she know about our mission? "Can you provide Enelle with traveling clothes? I must speak with your father," Kedda said.

After Alir took Enelle upstairs and Kedda had gone back downstairs to Kart, I munched on the remnants of bread and cheese and pondered the sparkle I'd seen in Alir's eyes when she saw Kedda here. In my mind it negated Jen-Varth's suspicion that Kedda was female.

Through the open front doors came the cool, leafy scent of early autumn. A different chill, the foreboding kind, followed it. I remembered what Kedda had said before we were zapped off the previous world. "I can protect us as long as we remain together." I told myself, *Don't worry about them. Jen-Varth knows how to handle things. That world is Magick. Dayon will be at full power, and Trax isn't completely helpless.* I knew they wouldn't let anything serious happen to Jake, but I hoped for a little suffering to make him appreciate what he'd put me through. A floorboard creaked behind me. I jumped.

"I didn't mean to scare you." Alir had returned alone. "She is changing her clothes. Is she yours?"

"What?"

"Is she your woman?"

"Hell, no. We're just traveling companions barely tolerating one another," I said quickly.

"Oh. Did my father summon you?"

"Accidentally, I think. By the way, how can you understand me?"

264

She showed me an amulet. "Father made these. Most of our patrons speak a common tongue, but they speak another when they wish to restrict who understands them." She smiled. "We alert our guests or the Town Guards before damage is done."

She didn't act or talk like a barmaid. "Did you go to school here?" When she frowned, I said, "Where did you get your education?"

"Father taught me to read. Mother taught me how to be a good woman for the man I choose."

Don't go there, Scott. I pointed at the doors. "You don't lock up at night?"

"Our guests come and go at all hours. The Town Guards keep watch. Come outside, I will show you."

I pressed my left hand on the table to get up. The arm was still weak, and I nearly lost my balance.

"Is something wrong?" she asked.

"A minor injury from the other day. It's still healing."

We wandered outside. The sky was very dark and I couldn't see any stars. Two lanterns hung on poles out front. I glanced at my watch. Four-ten a.m. back on Earth. We'd been here an hour. I asked her the time.

She looked at the sky. "Fifth hour, first watch."

I didn't see any timepieces around, but I suppose when you live on a clockless world you learn how to tell time in other ways. "How long is a watch?"

"Six hours."

From what little I could see, this was just another fantasy town, aged more and not as clean as Freetown. "Where are the guards?"

"They will pass here soon."

Two men in dark tunics and pants stepped out of the

shadows. One said in a low voice, "Which room is the gem merchant in? We have business with him."

Thieves?

"He's not interested in your kind of business," she said.

The man grabbed her and pulled her close. He said in a throaty growl, "I expect an answer, girl."

"*We've got trouble!*" I mentally projected. I hoped that I projected as strongly as Kedda said I did.

"*We're coming, Scott.*"

Sweet. Just like walkie-talkies. I assumed a martial-arts stance. "Leave her alone!"

The second thug pointed a finger and a ball of light flew toward me. I ducked aside, but the spot on the ground behind me where the lightball hit crackled and fizzled. Too pleased with my lightning reflexes, I failed to notice him fire again. His second lightball hit me squarely in the chest. *Aw, shit*!

But I wasn't flung backward, and I didn't collapse onto the ground. All I felt was a slight warmth from the medallion against my chest. I saw surprise on the thug's face.

Kart rushed outside. "Release my daughter!"

The first thug held Alir tightly. The second one's right hand glowed yellow-white two inches from her neck. "Swear our freedom or she dies. Guild oath."

Kedda came up behind Kart. Kart signaled him to hold and said to the thugs, "Harm her and I swear by the Shades that the demons of the Abyss will revile you."

The second thug—the one with the glowing hand— hissed at Kart, "Necromancer?"

The first thug pulled a knife and put it to Alir's throat.

"No! He'll do *worse* than kill us if we harm her," the second one yelled.

His confused partner lowered the knife and released Alir. The thugs watched Kart closely as they backed away and disappeared into the shadows.

My heart had slowed some but was still a candidate for a speeding ticket. "You're just going to let them leave?"

"They will not return," Kart said.

"Who were they?" I asked.

"Thieves from Quastor."

"Where is that?

"A town two days' journey from here. Business there must be slow."

I silently thanked Dev for the medallion. Those thieves had nearly taken me out. I didn't need this shit. Hell, I was only twenty-four. I wanted to get married and have kids. I wanted to live long and prosper, not live fast, play hard, and die young. And what exactly had Kart said that made them give up so easily?

Another man dressed snugly in black emerged from the darkness. As my heart came alert again, Kedda said to him, "Drogo, you disappointed me."

An associate of Kedda's?

"Scott, this is Drogo. I paid him to watch over Kart while I was away, but he prefers to relieve other people of their money dishonestly," Kedda said.

Even in the dim light, I could see the fear on the man's face as he mumbled over and over, "Kart is a necromancer? I'm a friend to a necromancer?"

"If he meant you harm, Drogo, you would be long dead. Kart is a good man," Kedda said.

I wasn't sure, but I thought the thief mumbled, "The only good necromancer is a dead one."

"Few are privileged to count a man such as Kart as their

friend." Kedda tossed a pouch of coins at the thief. He caught it and left.

I thought a necromancer was somebody who contacted spirits to predict the future. They must do something a lot more serious here.

"Now that my secret is known, Alir and Weyda are in danger," Kart said to Kedda.

"There is a place on Arion's world where one's past is not questioned. You and your family will be welcome."

I knew he meant Freetown.

"I offered Arion my services in your place because I knew of my daughter's fondness for you," Kart said.

"Father!"

"Please, stay here with her. I will go in your place, to repay the trouble I have caused you," Kart told Kedda.

Kedda shook his head. "My destiny is to go with them."

We went back inside. I saw Enelle, in comfortable clothes, and didn't realize that I was staring until our eyes met. And locked. *Aw, shit, not again.*

For me it wasn't as bad as before, just a couple of shivers, but she was gasping. Her body shimmered and changed. Into a cat-like creature.

"Her necklace contains the power matrix similar to Kart's artifact and Trax's staff. It stabilizes her. You disrupted it," Kedda said.

"I didn't touch her!"

"Please take her downstairs," he told Alir.

After they left, I said, "What was that?"

"Enelle is a shapechanger. And a Bahrat like you."

"A what?"

Kedda glanced past me, at the doors. "Your Bahrat ability is the reason you're here. They brought her to you."

"Who did?" I said.

Kedda shifted his eyes back to me. "Arion and the dragons. She is here to complete you."

"I hope you don't mean that in the Biblical sense," I said caustically.

"All Bahrats possess at least one special gift."

"Yeah. I find hidden objects."

"That's your Pneuma ability. Your gift has not yet revealed itself." He seemed preoccupied.

"But you knew about her."

"Because she knew. It was in her thoughts."

"I'll bet Arion knows."

"He didn't share it with me." Now he seemed cranky.

"He's not a sharing kind of guy. Well, if *she* turns into a cat, the next full moon should be an interesting event for me."

Kedda wasn't paying attention. I knew that things weren't going according to plan, but this was something else. He kept looking outside as if he wanted to go there. He didn't even seem to be reading my thoughts.

"Please go downstairs to Kart and Enelle. I will join you shortly."

Definitely cranky. He hurried out the doors. I headed to the basement.

Enelle had returned to normal and was crying. Again.

I felt responsible somehow and knelt in front of her. "I'm sorry I did that to you."

"You think I'm repulsive," she said through her tears.

"I think you're very pretty." She was, but I had no idea why I said it.

"I'm sorry that I brought you here," Kart said.

Everybody was sorry but it wasn't helping solve our

problem. I stood up. "You can't send us back, can you?"

"No. I found Kedda through his ring. The girl's necklace interfered with my attempt to bring him here."

"And we got caught in the backlash. You can't find that world again?"

"If I had Arion's skill, I could. I require a link. With Kedda here now, that link is gone."

"One of our other members has a black staff artifact. Couldn't you lock onto that?" I asked.

"It is shielded from me."

"And there's no other way?"

"There is one, if you and the girl are willing. It would be dangerous."

At that point, Kedda returned, looking more relaxed. "Kart says he can get us back," I told him.

"You, Enelle, and I will continue alone," Kedda said.

"The *fuck* we will!"

"The Staff of Chaos will protect Trax and enable his return home. The rest will be dead. Kart's intervention prevented me from saving them."

23

HI HO, HI HO,
SPELUNKING WE WILL GO

Day Five: Kart's Inn, Late Evening

Jake? Dead?

Kedda's eyes bored into mine. I felt him reading my thoughts, calmly picking out each objection before I could speak it. "Your anger will change nothing. The people on that world were organized against us. They caught Trax and Dayon unawares and disabled them."

A slow seethe rose in me. "How in *hell* could you know that?"

"Arion cannot help. He is not free to act." Kedda said it matter-of-factly, as if he'd accepted their deaths and didn't care!

"Unless you and Arion knew and didn't warn us!"

I told Enelle, "You might want to plug your ears for the next few minutes because I'm going to use some *really* bad language." I measured my words to Kedda, "We *are* going back there. Kart says there's a way, and you are going to go above and beyond your very fucking best to assist him."

"Arion chose this route as the safest one while your powers developed. He left all decisions regarding your safety to me."

"I don't give a flying fucking rat's ass what you and that glow-in-the-dark Pointy-Ears and his scale-skinned side-kicks agreed on, or who you *think* is dead or alive. I'm *not* giving you an option!" Something pricked my brain and I couldn't move.

"Do as we agreed," he told Kart.

I projected at Kedda, *"Damn you to fucking hell!"*

His body jolted. I was able to move again. His confidence dissolved when my eyes met his. "You shouldn't be able to do that yet, not on a Magick world and without an artifact in your possession."

I smiled back. "Guess what—you're wrong."

Kart gestured. I felt my medallion warm. I pointed at him. "I've got you covered, too."

Kedda's eyes narrowed. "Arion's decision may have been incorrect."

"Which of his many bad ones would that be?"

"Your powers are developing more rapidly than we expected. He chose this longer route to allow them to mature before you confronted the S'pharn."

"Then I think it's in your best interest to get us back to the others before I figure out what else I can do that you don't think I can," I said.

"I can't return you."

"Cut the shit! I *know* you can!"

"My power is limited."

"Yeah, right. On Arion's world you levitated me with no problem. I'll bet you can lighthole yourself anywhere and anytime you fucking well please!"

"It's not that simple, Scott. We require a link to them. I was that link when Kart was watching us."

"He says there's a way, you say there isn't. Who do you

think I'm going to believe?"

"His way presents an unacceptable risk to you."

* * *

I let go of Enelle's hands, dropped to my knees, and gave up fighting the waves of nausea. My midnight snack from Kart's inn, reveling in its newfound freedom on the grass, paid no attention to my heaving above it. Next to me, I heard Enelle whimpering and gasping, just short of retching.

I took a few deep breaths and leaned back on my heels to let my stomach unknot. Through the blur of watering eyes, I saw a crowd gathered around us. In the background I heard Jake's voice. "Untie us or there'll be more."

More what?

A few feet away on my left, Trax hung by his hands and feet from a pole. Two men rushed to untie him.

A hand touched my back. "You okay?"

"I appreciate the misery of morning sickness."

Jake helped Enelle up, then offered a hand to me.

I declined. "If I move, I'll get sick again. Send Jen-Varth and his Pepto-Bismol over."

Five minutes and a potion later, my stomach had settled. Jake, standing over me, said, "We'd better leave before these people figure out that I'm a charlatan. I told them I put a curse on them."

"How did you do that?"

"I sang."

"That'd do it," I said. He sang worse than a cat in heat.

"These people don't care if their sacrifices are virgins," he said.

I laughed a little and held my tender sides. I hadn't

forgiven him yet. At least he cared how I felt, which was more than Kedda did. "So, what happened?"

"I remembered something Bryce once told me. Many cultures believe there is magic in music, in the rhythms and rhymes. I chanted using mathematical terms."

"And?"

"They pretty much ignored me. Then you suddenly appeared through a Gate and all hell broke loose. While you were recycling your food, they set us free. Except, from the rumbling among some of them, I think they're having second thoughts." He pointed toward Kedda. "Who's the new guy?"

I looked up. *Kart*? He had a sack with him. A now familiar tingle told me that it contained more than clothing.

We decided to depart before these people regrouped. When one of their leaders balked about us heading in the opposite direction from which we'd come, I pointed to Trax's staff and gave them a warning shake of my head.

The midnight air had the feel of a summer night. Two glaring moons made sure I didn't think that I was back home. I noted our hosts' speech change and asked Jake about it.

Kedda, walking ahead of us, turned his head back, and said, "They're using a different language than before."

"Who the fuck asked you," I said.

"Why the attitude," Jake asked.

"He told us you were dead."

"We almost were."

I stared into his eyes. "He said that only Trax—because of the staff—would survive. He refused to bring us back. He wanted to go on without you. I couldn't let you die thinking I was an asshole."

"I never thought that. I know I betrayed your trust."

"That's why you're still on my shit list, but right now he's *way* ahead of you."

The street out of town was packed dirt, devoid of vegetation. Jake kept watch behind us. Trax walked ahead of me with Enelle. Farther ahead were Kart, Dayon, and Kedda. Jen-Varth, next to me, filled me in on what I'd missed. Remembering Trax's predicament, I considered saying, "We had Trax on a stick after all." He was just as much a victim as the rest of us, and he'd been humiliated in front of his father. Instead, I caught up to him. "You didn't deserve what they did to you."

"My father thinks it was my fault," he said, quietly.

"If he couldn't stop them, how could you?"

"I have the staff."

"That's bullshit. What were you supposed to do all tied up? From what I've seen and heard, he isn't exactly a model Elf." Maybe I shouldn't have said that. Dayon *was* Trax's father. I wondered, how would the staff have saved Trax?

Twenty minutes after leaving town we reached the bottom of the hill. We labored up the slope, and my stomach threatened me again. Unlike the other hill, heavy undergrowth clogged the rock steps on this one. The climb and rarefied atmosphere left everyone panting. Kedda looked ready to collapse. *Good.*

The town's lights flickered through the trees below. The third moon, pale blue and gibbous, had just cleared the horizon. "Three isn't my lucky number," Jake mumbled.

The entrance to the tower was overgrown. Jake examined his map. "We're in the right place, but some annotation would have been helpful."

Behind the vines overgrowing the entrance we found a

long tunnel. "They periodically check the other cave," Kedda said. "They know about the barrier surrounding the Gate on the other world and believed they were safe until we arrived." He meant the barrier around that Gate, the one that Jen-Varth and I had found the remote control that opened it, but I was ignoring him. "At one point they considered sealing that cave, but feared a rockslide might endanger the town." Interesting tidbit. I still ignored him.

"How does he know that?" Jake asked me.

My turn for surprises. "Did I tell you that he's a telepath and reads minds?" Jake's eyebrows arched. I glared at Kedda. "And the next time he goes into mine, he'll find it hazardous to his health!"

I volunteered Trax and me to enter first.

Jake asked if Dayon would be a better candidate.

"Trax has the staff for protection," I said. I pulled out my medallion. "And I've got mine."

"I thought you carried your protection in your wallet," Jake smartassed.

I told him how it had saved me on Kart's world.

More eyebrow arching. "Be careful of your arm."

Jen-Varth gave us two lanterns, and Trax and I stepped into the murk of another adventure.

The tunnel didn't seem deep at first. Twenty feet inside, it turned sharply left. I examined the ceiling for bats and big hairy spiders—nothing anywhere except a few loose stones on the floor and some petrified animal droppings. Archaeologists call them coprolites to make them sound important, but they're still shit.

We turned the corner. The passage narrowed by a couple of feet. This part was still natural rock. I didn't think we'd entered the main structure yet. I bent to clear the low ceiling.

Ten feet farther along, the passage narrowed again and made a forty-five-degree turn to the right. A wall of boulders blocked our further progress.

Back outside I said, "Big rockslide blocking the way. If the Gate's there, it must be behind it."

"The Gates contain the same material as the artifacts. Your powers can verify its presence," Kedda said.

"Lucky for you I'm giving my powers a rest. Back on my world we had a comic book superhero called the Hulk. He was a had-it-together guy before the accident that changed him. After that, when he got upset, he turned into a big, ugly, pissed-off creature, not unlike the way you make me feel. You'd better hope that my powers don't turn me into the Hulk because you'll be first on my to-maul list."

Number one moon had just set, number two was ready for its nap, and number three had crept a little past overhead. All three were larger than Earth's. The eastern horizon showed signs of daylight. Dayon provided protective spells including the ability to breathe if any of us got buried alive. I wanted to help but Jen-Varth insisted that my arm was still healing. I asked him if his laser gun could drill through. He said it did not have destructive power. When I asked Dayon if he could Magick the rocks away, he said that with the helpers we had, manual labor would be faster and safer. So much for the power of Magick.

Kedda and Trax went inside first to dig away at the rocks. They handed them out to Jen-Varth, Dayon, and Jake. Enelle helped some and said nothing. Kart wanted to help, but Kedda said that heavy labor in the thin atmosphere might tax him. Except that Kedda's tone hadn't been one of sincere concern, and I detected irritation in him again.

After half an hour of working in the cave, Kedda came

out to rest and Jake took his place. Kedda was beat. He said he wanted to check out something down the hill.

"Go knock yourself out—literally," I said.

Kart and I chatted after Kedda left. He found my translator interesting because, unlike his, mine worked on non-Magick worlds. "Were Kedda and your daughter dating?" I asked him. Remembering my talk with Jen-Varth a few days ago, I hastily clarified my definition of dating.

"I had hoped that Kedda was the man for her, but he has made it clear that he is not."

"Who knows what'll happen after our mission is over?"

"What do you know about him?" Kart asked.

"Not much. He lets you know things when he's ready," I said. Kart had known him way longer than I had and apparently knew less than I did.

Kedda returned half an hour later. Despite his previous tiredness, and having just climbed the hill, he was refreshed—and mellow—like he'd gotten laid or found some local weed to smoke. "Two men from the town were watching us," he said. "I discouraged their activity."

"*I wish I could block your mind reading.*"

"You have the ability to stop me."

What? Shit. I must have projected that. I had to be more careful.

He pulled a translator from his pack and gave it to Kart. "You will require this on non-Magick worlds." He walked away.

Two hours later it was midmorning with no end of the digging in sight. By checking the sun against my watch, I concluded that a day on this world was fourteen to sixteen hours long.

After two more hours they broke through. Trax volunteered to go in. I needed some excitement and insisted on accompanying him. When I crawled through the hole, I made sure not to lean on my injured arm. The passage on the other side was tight at first. A rough-hewn corridor ended a few feet ahead. Trax, in the sleeveless tunic he'd stripped down to while working, walked ahead of me and disappeared!

I rushed up to where he'd vanished. There was no lighthole. In the tunnel floor I saw an opening into a vertical shaft. As I shined the lantern down it, I saw Trax receding. He stopped fifty feet down, stepped out of the shaft, and vanished again. *Shit*. I yelled down, "Trax!"

No response.

"Get your ass back here, you little shit!"

He poked his lantern into the shaft and followed it with his head. "Come down."

"I'm not jumping down!" I didn't need a broken leg, too.

The shaft went dark. Moments later a stone circle filled the hole in the floor. An elevator. Trax had made it down safely, but he had Magick and a staff that cared about his existence. I bravely stepped onto the platform and trusted Jen-Varth to fix anything I broke.

A smooth ride down brought me facing Trax, who was ten feet down a tunnel. He pointed at the wall on my left. Inlaid into it was a small panel with two colored circles. "Those control it from here," Trax said.

He took charge and motioned me to follow. Fifty or sixty feet later, the corridor came to a T-intersection. "Which direction?" he asked. "I know you can sense the Gate."

Maturity along with his one-eighty change in attitude? I closed my eyes. "Left." I wasn't sure that I should be his role model.

A little way down the corridor we found a door. "In here?" he asked.

"No."

We continued on. I got no twinges from the next two doors either. The corridor ended at a door. Trax reached out to press the panel next to it. I grabbed his arm. "Not a good idea. Let's go back for the others."

He gave a sheepish nod, then jerked from my grasp and pressed the panel anyway. After a hesitant creak, the door rose upward. "My Magick will protect us," he said. So much for the improvement to his maturity level.

He held up his lantern. In the middle of the ten by ten room stood a semicircle on top of a trapezoid. The semicircle enclosed a lighthole. When he marched toward it, I lunged for his robe and yanked him back. "You're pushing our luck," I said. This Gate was wide enough for us to enter side by side. "We check it out together."

We came out into a room forty feet square with light gray walls of carved stone blocks. A musty chill hung in the air. Among the shadows across the room we saw another door. This one had a conventional lock. I knocked on the door. Thick. "I guess we'll have to break it down."

Behind an evil smile he said, "This lock is not a problem for me."

The little slime. He'd told me about his cutpursery, but omitted the breaking and entering part.

He gestured. I heard noises from the lock. This next world must be Magick. He reached to open the door. I stepped in front of him and said, "*Now* we go back for the others."

"One more?"

"No. We've been lucky so far, and we've been down

here awhile. They'll be worried. Our group's been separated twice. I don't think 'third time's a charm' is apropos."

He reluctantly agreed.

Just before Trax and I headed back through the lighthole, I noticed something metallic on the floor. I held the lantern close to examine the flat, circular piece about three inches in diameter.

"Is this Magick?" I asked Trax.

He leaned over it. "Yes."

I picked it up. It was a quarter of an inch thick and metallic gray with a satin finish. The other side had symbols carved into it. "Anything you recognize?"

"No."

I stuffed it into my pocket.

We traced our way back to the rest where Jake had decided our next move. "According to the map, the Gate leads into a building. The next Gate is in the same building. Let's go." He picked up his backpack and shrugged it on. I showed him what I'd found. His eyes widened. "These markings look similar to those on Bryce's scroll."

"Can you read them?"

"Maybe. I'd have to study it. The language is different."

Kedda approached us. "Where did you find that?"

"Trax and I found it in the cave," I replied, curtly.

"We must seek a different path."

I heard angry shouts in the distance. Jen-Varth summoned us to the edge of the overlook. The townsfolk in procession were advancing up the hill.

"How fast can we get through to the Gate?" Jake asked me.

"The elevator takes half a minute each way. With eight of us—"

"We must find *another* path!" Kedda interrupted.

"No time, and you're outvoted," Jake told him.

But it was clear that Kedda wasn't listening to Jake. I heard a rumbling. The rocks we'd dumped over the cliff—most of them had fallen onto a wide ledge below—began to move. I saw Dayon gesturing while Trax watched.

I started tingling and turned around. *Oh, shit.* I saw Kart holding his artifact. Kedda stood beside him, concentrating. My stomach churned. I had to stop Kedda.

I lunged for the artifact. An invisible bolt leaped at me. Colors detonated around and inside me. Enelle screamed. Alternating waves of cold and hot, freezing and burning, cycled through me.

A flash and a thunderclap ripped away the world.

Before I passed out, I caught the scent of a forest in a drenching rain.

24

WE SHOULD HAVE CALLED AAA
Day Five: Third World, Early Afternoon

I woke up with a brain-hammering hangover that made the warm, steady raindrops feel like burning needles being shot into me. The two people carrying me set me down gently, but even that sent more jolts through me. They propped my back against what felt like a tree. I felt every trickle of water from my rain-soaked hair running down my face.

Very gently I brushed the water off my forehead and out of my eyes. Jen-Varth stood with his back to me, carrying Enelle. His bodysuit repelled the water, but with the hood down the rain had plastered his long hair against his ears and neck. Jake set out a bedroll next to me. Jen-Varth placed Enelle on it then said to Dayon, "We require shelter and a way to dry ourselves."

The rain suddenly stopped dripping on me. "This isn't a Magick world," Trax said simply, as if apologizing for Dayon's inaction, "but with the Staff I can hold this spell for a while."

Dayon, standing behind Trax, was still a mystery. He'd taken little action in all this—about the most he'd done was to help us in the cave—which made me wonder why he'd stayed. Was it to observe Trax?

Under Trax's invisible umbrella the air became sultry. We were near the edge of a forest. Daylight filtered through dense, gray and purple clouds. Jen-Varth removed his backpack and took out a lantern.

"I'll look for shelter," Jake said. Jen-Varth went with him. They melted into the forest.

I put one hand on the ground. Despite the steady rain, the half-soil, half-moss forest floor was barely damp. Kedda squatted next to me and touched the side of my head. The throbbing quit. "You should not have interfered, Scott."

"*You* were interfering. *I* was stopping you!" I looked at Dayon standing behind him and wondered what he thought. His face was as impassive as ever.

Kedda pointed to Enelle. "You must help her."

She lay trembling beside me. Her eyes were shut and her eyeballs darted beneath the lids as in REM sleep. Before I could stop him, Kedda put her hand in mine. Her twitching stopped. A blast of flashing images and overwhelming emotions burst into me: pride, anger, sorrow, and helplessness. Love and desolation intertwined with deep melancholy. Warm, comfortable despondency beckoned me.

I retched and yanked my hand back. *What the fuck*?

The distant echo of his voice said, "Help her."

My slow, deep breaths had partially calmed my stomach. "That's . . . *your* job. If I touch her again, I'll be sick."

He put his hand on mine. The nausea dissipated. "She has shut me out," he said.

"I'll have to find out her secret," I said.

"You don't understand," Kedda said.

"Sure I do. You can't get inside her brain and you want

me to restore your access. Our military guys would say, 'Foxtrot Oscar.' I'd just say, '*Fuck* Off.' "

"You must do it because you are the same as she is."

"Like hell I am!"

"Fight the battle with her, Scott."

His words invoked unpleasant memories from my grade school years. After a bully beating in third grade, I cried for Dad to do something. "Men need to fight their own battles," he told me, hoping that the instincts of a true military man would take over. The Army transferred Dad every year or two. I suffered for it. New kids, Army brats in particular, always got picked on. I learned to request extra projects from my teachers so I could stay after school and have Mom pick me up. I was okay until ninth grade.

"Madison!" Ball Breaker screamed from halfway down the hall. I froze. He'd earned his nickname. Before I could consider running, he was in my face. "That your name?" Instead of staring down at my helpless, little freshman face like he did with the others, he was looking straight into my eyes. I was five-eleven.

He covered his error. "Know who I am, kid?"

Don't let people bully you, Son. The Colonel's words sat comfortlessly in my thoughts. Ball Breaker expected one of two responses: a silent, obeisant nod of affirmation, or the lachrymose cowering of a freshman begging instruction regarding his station in life.

In ninth grade I was going through a reckless stage, and I was an inch taller than he was. I'd acquired a repertoire of smartass responses. Had I been wearing a cup, I might have said, "I could've been your old man, but the dog beat me over the fence." Or my personal favorite: "I heard you blow dead rats, but that's not true because I saw one of them move."

He looked around. "I'm lettin' you off this time, freshman. Just keep outta my way!" I was sure he let me go only because none of his crowd were around to witness the massacre. I won the battle because I *hadn't* fought. So much for the Colonel's advice.

"Scott." Kedda pulled me out of my reveries.

I closed my eyes and reached out for her hand.

Soft blackness engulfed me. In the distance, specks of light flickered. I felt myself tumbling. I expected to get sick. When I focused on lights, my body oriented itself. The lights drew me toward them. Barriers randomly popped up and dissipated an instant later. I slammed into a few before I learned to control my forward motion.

A single path shimmered into existence. Abruptly, it split into three. When I let my concentration falter, the three paths blurred and an uncaring stupor overcame me. The light specks vanished. The engulfing black velvet returned.

Something from behind grabbed at me and disrupted my complacency. I pressed ahead until a sturdier barrier blocked the way. I pushed against it. *Harder*! It burst inward.

Behind the barrier lay a sanctuary. Rebellion guarded it and warned me away. Off to one side I glimpsed an older man standing alone. As I looked at him, an image of Enelle's necklace girded my chest and started to contract. It slid up to my throat and contracted further until I could feel the points of its black stones pricking me.

The older man reached toward me. Was he her father? I projected at the sanctuary, "*Mother*."

A wave of anger slammed into me. The necklace squeezed tighter. A second crushing wave followed.

The necklace vanished. Angry daggers flew at me from the

sealed sanctuary, missing me but coming dangerously close. A wall of slashing swords appeared and curved around me.

"*Stop!*"

Had I shouted that order?

The swords vanished. A door in the sanctuary cracked open. From it came soft, eager whimpers and slow breathing. A cloud of warm sensuality descended around me.

The door opened fully. Intimate feelings enveloped me, aroused me. For the first time I became aware of the separation between my mind and my physical body and of the tenuous link joining them. Something like electricity shot along that link.

Vivid colors washed over me. Like a flood of cold water, they made me gasp. Gradually, the colors faded into warm pastels and to a lingering white haze. A fuzzy image formed behind the haze and brushed it aside. The image sharpened. I saw my own body braced against a tree. On the ground next to it I saw the empty bedroll where Enelle had lain. The angle changed. I was ascending, turning away to the left. A blur of forest green, then—

The eyes that weren't mine blinked. Before me lay a crisp panorama of dark green hills and blue-purple mountains. A white sun above shone through breaks in light gray clouds. For a moment I had sight with no other senses.

A switch flipped. My other senses came alive: the feel and roar of the wind rushing by, the scents and heaviness of the air after a rainfall. She made a long turn, a gentle bank. Below us, two rivers came together at one end of a narrow lake. We descended and flew along it until it plummeted over a dual waterfall. We dipped down through the cool mist, then circled through it again. Up and down we darted on this roller coaster ride through nature.

Ahead, a forest. We skimmed the treetops, brushing them as we passed. Droplets of water fell from the wet leaves. We slowed and descended into the forest. The rest of our group, standing together, came into view. We glided in and landed next to my body. I felt a mental nudge a moment before my vision went dark. I opened my own eyes. In front of me sat a graceful, eagle-like bird with dark brown feathers tipped in purple and magenta. The bird morphed into Enelle.

Above the trees a lost, warm sun shoved aside the remaining clouds and reasserted itself. The forest floor released its stored-up moisture as a smoky mist rising into the sunbeams. Forest creatures skittered from shelters to resume their rain-halted activities. With all that had happened, the trauma, the bouts of retching that had wracked my body, the lack of proper sleep and weakness from an empty stomach, I should have been ready to pass out. But I felt better than I had in the past couple of days, since before we went to Freetown.

Jake and Kedda stood a few feet away. Behind them Trax was speaking with Dayon. The rest were scattered around, looking at us with assorted expressions. Jake knelt next to me. "Scott? What happened? Kedda told us she was in a coma."

I looked at her as she sat with both legs to one side, weak and pale but okay. "We flew together."

"You never left here," Jake said.

I blinked and took a long breath. "My mind did."

Jake's mouth started to open and stopped. His jaw hung there for a long time. "Like out of your body and into hers?"

I shrugged my shoulders uncomfortably. "I guess so."

"It's my fault that you're here," he said to her.

She stared at him. "*You* brought me here?" she said.

"Not directly," I said. "You're here because of me, and I'm here because of him." I glared up at Kedda. "Go find somebody else's brain to suck on!"

"I never introduced you," I said. "This is Jake Kesten, my mentor . . . and friend. Jake, meet Enelle Hane."

Kedda, who hadn't left, interrupted our meet-and-greet. "It is urgent that Jake solve the equations."

"We're lost, and he knows it's his fault," I said to Jake and stared at Kedda. "It's *your* problem to solve, not Jake's. Leave us alone before I'm forced to use more bad language in front of Enelle."

I saw the tense readiness in Jake's body as he stood up and confronted Kedda. I pointed to an isolated spot away from everyone, "Why don't we talk over there?"

Jake helped me up. As soon as we got there, Jake said to Kedda, "*You* fucked us over and you expect *me* to fix it?"

I silently applauded Jake's proper use of the f-word.

"With our combined skills we can reach our destination," Kedda said. His coolness was unnerving.

"I'd bet on a snowball's survival chance in hell versus us leaving here anytime soon," Jake mumbled.

"You underestimate yourself."

"Not likely. I know my capabilities."

"There is a mathematical pattern in the Yorben Gates. The equations contain the coordinates of our destination." Kedda was insistent, if anything.

"I don't *have* the equations."

"Your map shows the location of several Gates. Arion chose you for your ability to find the equations from that information. When night comes, Jen-Varth will analyze the star patterns to determine our current location. With that information and the end point from the equations, Kart can form a Gate to our destination."

Jake's facial muscles locked. "Sorry to disappoint you, but I need a computer to do what you want—if it's possible even then. No offense to Kart, but I don't think that mathematical coordinates are going to be much help to him." I'd never seen Jake this tense. "What about you, the mysterious Mr. Kedda? You have more knowledge about this mission than all of us combined. I'll bet *you* told the dragons about the equations and omitted the part that you didn't have them. Right? Give me the time and the tools and I'm confident that I could do what you ask, but time is short and the toolbox is empty. Scott and I don't hop around the galaxy like you do. We've never been off Earth before. Until a few days ago, we didn't know any of this was out here."

Kedda took out the briquette. "Didn't you?"

The blood drained from Jake's red face. I grabbed his arm. "We need to talk. Alone."

I dragged him to the forest edge, about fifty feet away. He pressed his back against a tree and bored his eyes into me. "Did you know Kedda had that?"

I nodded.

"Un-fucking-believable," he said.

"That's not in your normal working vocabulary."

"My normal vocabulary expanded five days ago."

"Did you know that Kedda had a second spare translator? He gave it to Kart while you were digging inside the cave," I said.

"I know Kedda is somehow connected with that skeleton Bryce found in the cave. His having a briquette just like the one Bryce showed me is too much of a coincidence otherwise." He flexed his jaw muscles and shook his head very slowly. "What else is he hiding? By the way, what happened between you and Enelle?"

Good question. I looked out at the hills that she and I had seen from the air. Something from the Bible-as-Literature class I'd taken popped into my head. Jesus said that thinking about having sex with a woman was the same as having done it. As we were leaving class that day, I overheard one guy say to the girl next to him, "I dreamed you and I did it last night. How about we do it for real this weekend?" She slapped him. It made an impression on me around the time I was being peer-pressured into losing my virginity. I think I was fifteen when the Colonel told me, "Scott, there's nothing wrong with sex when the time and person are right. Without it your brother and you wouldn't be here." I took it to mean that Adam and I were not accidents, but I wondered if he also said it to soften the message from the graphic Army training films he'd shown me a few years before. Of course, he had shown me the old ones. The updated ones take a sensible approach.

"The closest approximation would be having sex," I told Jake. But it wasn't sex.

He laughed. "It gives new meaning to screwing your brains out."

My neck and face got hot.

"Scott, I'm sorry for what I did to you."

"You mean, kidnapping me after my college graduation and wresting me from my father's clutches?"

He laughed again. "For not trusting you with the truth from the beginning."

"As you suggested before, if you had told me, I probably— no, definitely—would have thought you seriously deranged. Our friendship and wonderful working relationship would never have begun, and I'd never have gotten your martial arts training or experienced the sadomasochistic pleasure of your kicking and bruising my body into shape. Shit, I might still be a virgin."

"You still are."

"Did you forget my slipup in Freetown? What really sucks is that I don't even remember if I enjoyed it."

"That's because it didn't happen."

"What?"

"You fell asleep before anything happened. Your virginity is intact."

"How do you know that?"

"Dev told me. She came to Dev because she was afraid she'd be blamed for insulting a Blue Robe if word got around that he didn't or couldn't perform in bed."

"Should I be relieved? Or insulted?"

"Your choice."

"And you didn't tell me about this earlier because . . ."

"Judgment call. I figured if you thought it was out of the way you'd concentrate more on the mission."

He was right, but not for the reason he said. Guilt—and the other problems we'd faced—had temporarily repressed my sex drive. Until that mind bond, or whatever it was called, with Enelle brought it back in full force.

"Maybe Kedda pissed you off to bring us back together."

That wasn't Kedda's style. "Before I accept your apology," I said, "is there anything else you neglected to tell me that relates to my future?"

"Only what convinced me to take Arion seriously from the start. It wasn't at magic-wand point as you so colorfully suggested. He said that he'd take you whether I trained you or not."

"But you didn't know who I was then, did you?"

"No. I said to him, 'You'll take this Scott Madison, knowing that he might fail?' " Jake took a long breath. "Arion replied, 'I did not say that he would fail, only that without your help he will not survive.' "

"You came to the rescue of a total stranger."

He said, soberly, "You're not a stranger now, but given what you've been through already, I see no evidence that anything I've done or taught you has made any difference. Right now, I'm praying that I don't have to watch you die."

"Kedda and Arion claim that I have a super power poised for the proper moment, but if I detect my imminent demise, I'll warn you in time to turn your back."

"Don't joke about that, Scott."

"Look, we can't change the past and we can't change that we're here. We've a bug to squash and a universe to save. What's our next move?"

"I could use your advice."

"You're asking *me* for advice?"

"Yeah."

"If you had your cell phone, we could call AAA."

He threw back his head and laughed heartily.

A moment later, Enelle screamed.

25

RAISING THE DEAD
Day Five: Third World, Late Afternoon

Jake swept his backpack off his shoulders, unzipped it, thrust a gun into my hand, dropped the backpack at my feet, said, "Stay here," and ran toward the others.

My eyes followed him. I saw four, dark-furred creatures, fast and slinky like mongooses, attacking. Kart pulled Enelle behind him. Two of the beasts came at Jen-Varth. He drew his gun. They leaped. He fired once. Both dropped three feet in front of him.

A third creature darted at Kedda and Dayon. Dayon drew his sword—the first time he'd used it among us. That creature also leaped. He swung the sword two-handed and sliced off the beast's head.

The fourth bounded at Trax, who stood a few feet closer to where they had come from. Catlike, it hurled itself at him. He awkwardly knocked it aside with his staff. The fallen creature gave a guttural hiss, scuttled to its feet, and sprang again too fast for Trax to react. With its long snout wide open, it bit into Trax's bare right arm. Trax gave a cry and fell to the ground. The staff flared blue. Seconds later, the creature went limp with its teeth locked onto Trax's arm.

A fifth beast came out of the woods. Kedda narrowed his eyes. The creature stopped as if it had run into a brick wall. Dayon neatly skewered it with his sword.

Then it was over.

I dropped the gun and ran to Trax. Milky saliva drooled along his shaking arm. I grabbed a stick to pry open the creature's jaws and pulled it away by its bushy tail. Trax gave several short gasps and quit moving. I yelled, "Help over here!"

Jen-Varth arrived first. He knelt and put his head to Trax's chest. He said without looking up, "Venom. His heart has stopped."

Dayon was there next. He said nothing.

Behind me Kart said, "I can restore him."

Dayon turned sharply at Kart and spat, "You will *not* do that to my son!" He told Jen-Varth, "I put him in your care," and walked away.

What the hell?

A hand touched my shoulder and a tingle shot through me. I stood up to see tears filling Enelle's eyes. She put her head on my shoulder. I put my good arm around her.

She whispered in my ear, "Can they save him?"

From a venom that had stopped his heart that fast? I didn't see how they could. "I don't know." She trembled against me. She had a right to be scared. It could have been her lying there. Why did I think that our being on this world was my fault after all?

Over her shoulder I saw Jen-Varth open his medical pack. He took a sample of the creature's saliva and mixed it with something in a small tube. A minute later he went over to Kart, said something to him, and walked toward Dayon. Kedda sat a few yards from Kart and brooded at the ground.

What was going on with him?

Jake caught my attention. "Let's go see Jake," I said to Enelle. I pulled a tissue from my pocket and wiped the running makeup off her cheeks. It was hard to judge her age, but I didn't think she was over twenty. What was I to her now? A friend? A lover?

When we got to Jake, I pointed at his gun lying on the ground. "I didn't know you'd brought that."

He bent to pick it up. I saw his hand shaking. He straightened up and tucked the gun into his backpack. "How much more suffering before we're done? If we can't find a way back, will Arion come to pick us up, or will he leave us to rot? Is she okay?"

"Very scared," I said.

"I promise I'll get you home. Both of you."

I saw Jen-Varth bring Kart over to Trax. What was he doing? He unfolded a small, plastic-like sheet on the ground and arranged various implements from his pack on it. He reminded me of my late-eighties TV hero, MacGyver. I watched the show regularly during my mid-teens. MacGyver used whatever was on hand and stretched the limits of science to get out of a predicament. Despite the purported bad influence of television, MacGyver fostered my own interest in science. Jen-Varth moved deliberately, with definite MacGyver-ness. I heard him tell Kart that this might work. Just what MacGyver used to say, except that it *always* worked for MacGyver.

Jen-Varth lifted Trax's shoulders, poured a liquid into Trax's mouth, and massaged his throat to coax it down. He picked up a hypodermic device—a needle, not the transdermal spray I expected from advanced, alien technology. He clicked a vial into the hypo, injected part of the contents into

Trax's arm, and repeated the operation with a different vial. Next, he pulled out his gun, adjusted it, and shot Trax in the chest! Trax's body jolted. Jen-Varth shot him again! Trax's eyes flew open then shut. Enelle gasped. Jen-Varth put an ear against Trax's chest and nodded. I'd never seen MacGyver raise the dead.

Jake let out a breath. "More unbelievable by the minute."

While Jen-Varth repacked his stuff, Dayon approached him. He didn't say anything. He didn't thank Jen-Varth.

I walked closer and squatted beside Jen-Varth. "Pretty amazing the way you jump-started Trax's heart."

"A dangerous procedure. I could have killed him."

I felt my jaw drop. "But he was already dead."

"No, he wasn't. Anaerobic metabolism in the Elfaeden brain will preserve function for a considerable time."

"Like in muscle when it's fatigued?" I suggested.

"Yes."

"So, what was the problem?"

"Because Trax is half human, I could not be certain of the energy setting I needed on the DN-32. Too little and I would have failed, too much would have killed him," he said.

"I'm confused. He would have been dead anyway without your help."

"Kart had the skill to save him without risk, but Dayon forbade Kart to act in that way."

"What did Kart want to do?" I wondered.

"Necromantic Magick. Dayon killed a necromancer."

I tried to follow the logic. Dayon clearly didn't like necromancers. Kart was a necromancer, yet Dayon put Trax in Jen-Varth's hands? Jen-Varth had a one-in-three chance of saving Trax. According to Jen-Varth, Kart could have saved him for sure. Had Dayon known those odds?

We set up a camp outside the forest edge and moved Trax there. The few small animals and birds we saw ignored us. Jen-Varth removed the flexible cast from my arm, weak as if I'd overexercised it but otherwise fully functional. Two of us now owed our well-being to Jen-Varth.

The day length on this world seemed close to Earth's. As sunset approached, the gathering clouds promised more rain. We needed them to hold off so Jen-Varth could check out the stars. According to Kedda our problem wasn't getting off this world but getting to where we needed to be in time to act. We were about to begin mission day six. "Arion said we had ten days," I reminded him sarcastically.

"Arion is an optimist," he said. "He did not anticipate the time we have lost. Once Jake decodes the equations, we must select a new path to our goal."

We sat around and ate supper. Kedda left after eating, probably to pee in the bushes or whatever he needed to do. I quietly asked Kart, "Why can't you use Enelle and me, like before, to put us back there?" I wasn't anxious for a repeat of the regurgitation experience.

"Kedda has forbidden me."

"We'll see about that."

It wasn't dark yet, but the food and the stress of the day had made me sleepy. My last nap was the five hours inside the cave on the second world while waiting for the rain to stop. Fatigue had taken its toll on everyone except Dayon. I lay down on my bedroll, staring up at the sky and trying to keep my thoughts away from Kedda. On the other hand, the weird dreams weren't helping.

* * *

I awoke to the smell of wood smoke, not skunk wood this time, and saw a campfire a couple of yards away. It was nighttime. Clouds had covered half of the sky. Two tiny moons—or asteroids on a collision course—populated the visible half, along with considerably fewer stars than in Earth's sky. Since Earth is already on the edge of the Milky Way, this place had to be out in the boonies. I saw Jen-Varth standing a couple hundred feet from the campfire, methodically surveying the sky. My arm ached, so I wasn't going to get back to sleep right away. We'd been on this world for six hours. I'd slept for two of them.

I pushed myself up and walked over to him. He said to me, "We are in quadrant six, Castill system. That," he pointed to a strain-to-see, blue flicker of light thirty degrees above the northern horizon and on the verge of being consumed by the advancing clouds, "is Ranor."

26

MARTIAL ARTS, WET DOGS, AND ALIEN SURPRISES

Day Five: Planet Ranor, After Midnight

We arrived on Ranor after midnight local time. Light gravity, thin air, and nose-hair-freezing cold. Jen-Varth knew exactly where we were. He said we were lucky that the air was calm. Even with a brisk pace, the hour-long hike was beyond miserable. Every time I shivered, I prayed that I wouldn't split down the middle.

Before we left the poisonous mongoose world, Jen-Varth had insisted that we add many extra layers of clothing. "When the sun sets on Ranor, the air becomes icy." I rummaged through my backpack and was surprised to find an old pair of knit gloves in the bottom. Lucky for me. When we originally packed for this adventure, Jake had asked Arion about clothing. Arion said that we required nothing heavy. Jake, never one to listen to the advice of others, had brought a fleece jacket. With only a denim jacket I was in deep shit.

Enelle had gotten extra garments from Alir. I gave her my gloves and put my extra pair of sweat socks over my own hands. Really deep shit.

Our luck was teetering on empty because we also found out that Dayon couldn't make Gates. This explained why he had stayed, having no way to leave. Trax was here because he had control of the Staff of Chaos and Dayon didn't. Arion had told us early on that Trax was temporary, but when Dayon popped in, Trax wasn't popped out. Right now, though, it was too cold out here to think about it.

Having Kart with us had kept the shit from sucking us in over our heads. We didn't know how to get to where we should be, but we knew—Jen-Varth at least did—where we were.

Jen-Varth brought us to the Protector outpost. Its four Quonset-hut buildings unpleasantly reminded me of an army base. Three of them were dark, barely visible silhouettes against a moonless sky sparse with stars. The fourth building, a two-storied structure set apart from the others, was over a hundred feet wide and three times as long. Lights rimmed the double-wide entry. Jen-Varth led us to it and keyed some buttons next to the doors. The doors parted in the middle to reveal a tunnel some twenty feet long. "Please enter ahead of me," he said. The slo-mo speed I was moving at would have given a ninety-year-old man time for a game of checkers before I reached the doors. I was the last one inside. The doors slid shut.

Warmth crept beneath my clothing, as if I'd been put into a microwave oven and was heating from the inside out. The entry tunnel had flat, metal sides and a semi-cylindrical ceiling ten feet above. The walls held a stack of three, foot-square, light panels every six feet or so. The topmost panel was pink, the middle light green, the bottom light blue.

I gingerly withdrew my hands from my jacket pockets and maneuvered the socks off my hands. I expected my brittle fingertips to detach at any moment.

After we completed our defrost, I noticed that Jen-Varth

had drawn his stun gun. "Expecting trouble?" I asked.

"No, but do not speak until we are alone."

I had thought we *were* alone.

He wanted us to walk ahead of him again. I shuffled forward. Beyond the transparent doors at the tunnel's far end, a young man in a metallic green-gold bodysuit sat at a semicircular desk that sloped upward toward us. His eyes darted back and forth at something on the desk. We approached. He raised his eyes, acknowledged Jen-Varth, slid his left arm sideways, then returned to whatever was on the desk. The doors opened.

With a wave of his gun Jen-Varth motioned us onward. I kept my eyes on the guard while I walked. Thick, spiky, brown hair, patterned like mink, covered his ears and the back of his neck. Lean, black sideburns traced down his face, along his jaw, behind sunken cheeks, and across a short, triangular chin. The sideburns looked fake. He looked alien.

I stopped next to the desk. A widescreen monitor held the young guard's attention. Two dark blue rectangles flanked the screen. His fingers curled over those rectangles and moved in time to the images darting across the screen. If aliens were the bad guys in *our* video games, who were the bad guys in theirs?

An earthy-woody fragrance with a hint of wet dog emanated from his direction. I couldn't decide if it was the furniture, his body chemistry, or alien cologne. The screen flashed white, and he spewed out a string of creatively foul words. He struck his right fist hard on the desk. Then he jerked his head at me and cursed me, my ancestors, and my manhood. Jen-Varth had asked us not to speak so I politely shrugged my shoulders. He grunted something and drew his gun. Behind me I heard someone gasp a moment before I heard a buzz.

My back arched violently; my hands flew open. "Son of a *bitch*!" It felt like he'd hosed me with a flamethrower.

The pain dissipated quickly, but muscle tics continued while his laughter echoed at me. I raised a shaking hand with the middle finger aimed up. His mirth dissolved. Up came the stun gun. Jake's martial arts training told me to *mawashi-geri* thrust-kick his nuts. My disabled body refused to cooperate.

I'd barely completed the thought when the kid's green eyes went wide. His gun fell to the floor with a dull thunk. Anguish rippled across his face. With a stifled grunt he dropped his hands to his groin and folded forward.

Jen-Varth leaped in front of me, gun in hand. "These are under my protection!" The moaning kid leaned sideways against the desk, his eyes half-closed. "I'm sorry he did that to you, Scott," Jen-Varth said.

"W-why sh-should y-you be? Th-this is an historical, f-first c-contact, ce-celebratory . . . occasion." I took a deep breath and pushed out the words, "I'm the first Earthman to experience an alien obedience instrument."

My muscle tics subsided. The kid was still caressing himself when Jen-Varth led us away through the central gallery. The girdered ceiling arched to a gothic point. Closed rooms lined the two long walls. Above us more rooms and a walkway ran the length of the building on each side. Three deserted crosswalks joined the two side ones. We came to a side room at the far end.

White ceiling panels lit the white walls as we entered. Bolted along the right wall were a dozen semicircular chairs with the dull gray finish of a plastic composite. The unpadded seats had a faint mesh pattern. Jen-Varth keyed several buttons on the wall next to the door. After the door slid shut sideways, he said, "You may speak freely in here."

"What the hell happened out there," Jake asked.

"This facility also serves as a prison. I drew my DN-32 to make him assume that you were in my custody so he would not question you."

"What gave that little prick the right to shoot me? All I did was shrug my shoulders!"

"He is impulsive."

"That hurt like hell!" I'd probably have nightmares about it for years to come.

"The DN-32 briefly incapacitates. You are recovered?"

Except for the buzz in my brain and the tingle in my arms. "Next time I see him, he's roadkill. Anyway, thanks for shooting him before he fired a second time."

Jen-Varth frowned. "I did nothing."

"But he doubled over—"

"This is a Pneuma world. It fueled your power," Kedda said.

Jake arched his eyebrows at me. "What did you do?"

"Nothing! I *thought* about kicking him in the nuts."

Jake smirked. "The power of positive thinking."

"That's not funny. Jen-Varth had his DN-32 weapon out."

"DN-32?"

"That's what he calls it."

"I didn't see him use it."

I'd heard the buzz from the guard's gun. I hadn't heard anything from Jen-Varth's. But the buzz wasn't very loud anyway, and by then intense pain had captured my attention.

Jen-Varth opened a corner closet next to the door. Hanging inside were dozens of monochrome overalls in white, black, and two shades of gray. He pulled out a black one and gave it to Kedda. The rest of us got white ones. Mine was five inches too short. Enelle changed inside the closet while we changed outside it.

I checked out the walls and ceiling and asked Jen-Varth, "Is there any surveillance equipment?"

"I deactivated it."

Next question: "How many prisoners are here now?"

"Very likely none."

"But you said this was a prison."

"This is a multi-purpose facility. It houses Protectors assigned here and provides guest quarters. Anyone under our jurisdiction can also request asylum. Crimes are judged and punished under local law. Ranor is mostly peaceful, but at the request of the inhabitants, we will imprison trouble-causers for a short term and provide rehabilitation counseling. Long-term imprisonment occurs offworld."

The place wasn't exactly high security. "How do you ensure that your occasional prisoners don't escape?" I asked. *Stupid question.* They had their DN-32 stun guns that could drop the most intransigent of felons, so they'd also have implant chips and obedience collars.

But he simply said, "Where could they go?"

"The closest settlement?" I suggested.

"Is over six hours of brisk walking." Remembering our frigid trek here, I got his point.

The white overalls labeled us as visitors so that no one would think we were criminals. *A little late.* "Why is Kedda wearing black?" I asked. Although I thought it fit the newly revealed blackness of his personality.

"He is our technician."

"I don't see anyone else around," Jake said.

"This is our sleep period," Jen-Varth said.

He brought us to another small room where we dined on pungent veggie patties. He told us they were high in protein and made from the local crops. I found them barely edible. The milk-like beverage was slightly sweet and mint-flavored, also a plant product.

While I forced down the swill, an anomaly struck me. Did the various peoples we'd encountered have similar nutritional requirements? That made sense because, as far as we knew, the chemical elements were the same throughout the universe, contrary to how the low-grade, sci-fi movies spoke of metals unknown on Earth. Health conscious Jen-Varth would surely warn us of digestive or nutritional problems with the local food. I hadn't seen him or Kedda or Trax popping pills, and no one had complained of intestinal distress from eating the food or drinking the water. This didn't square with my biology training that said it was next to impossible to avoid such problems. That I was dreaming once again made sense. If that were the case, then I didn't have the reality and responsibility of super powers.

Jen-Varth mentioned transportation.

"You mean as in off this planet?" I said.

"To where we may find what we need." He said that he could obtain a vehicle for four: Jake, Kedda, himself, and me. He put the others in a budget-motel guest room.

White-clad nobodies had no security clearance and weren't permitted to ride in official vehicles, so he procured bodysuits for Jake and me. The green-gold one was too close to olive drab for my liking.

"Does color indicate rank?" I asked.

"Yes."

"What rank is mine?"

"Rank one."

The asshole guard had the same color.

"Couldn't you give me something higher?"

"These will attract less attention. Your height limited my selection." He pointed to the red insignia on Jake's shoulder. "Technical specialist, rank three." Because Kedda was too short for a Protector, none of the uniforms fit him. Jen-Varth said that black technician's overalls would suffice. We clipped our translators onto the side pockets.

I found the tight suit incredibly comfortable. The air in the building was slightly cool and the suit automatically compensated. It also outlined my gender. I felt self-conscious in front of Enelle, but it didn't bother her. She must be used to suits like it on her world. The outline of my medallion showed under it. I slipped my medallion into my pack. Dev said it would protect me from Magick, but this wasn't a Magick world and it sure didn't work against high-tech stun guns, which also proved that alien stun guns were not Magick.

Before going to the garage, Jake and I needed to use the restroom. Jen-Varth pointed us to the unlabeled, color-coded room. Jake went in first and returned with a smirk. "Interesting."

I went in. Their toilets were a close copy of ours, but wider at the back. The bodysuit had a Velcro-like fly front that was invisible except from up close. For other business, however, it had to come off. A few minutes later I stomped out. "You might have warned me! High-tech toilets that *scrub* you clean?"

Jake roared. "Be glad they don't have urinals. *Those* could be a shock."

Just before sunrise the four of us headed to the motor pool, which was attached to the main building by a barely heated, underground tunnel. Jen-Varth again cautioned us not to speak. With our official attire the men on duty would expect us to speak Trade Common, which Jake and I didn't.

The guy in charge was an ordinary-looking human. Jen-Varth introduced us. "These are Jake and Scott, archaeologists from Earth, and Kedda, their technician." Almost the truth. "We require a transport."

"You didn't return your skimmer," the man said.

"A power cell malfunction. We will retrieve it." Jen-Varth's tone was cold.

"I hear you're not reenlisting. I don't think we'll miss you." The man laughed as he led us to our vehicle.

Noting the man's blue uniform, the same color as Jen-Varth's, I quietly said to Jen-Varth, "He doesn't like you."

"I don't care."

"Has he been here as long as you have?"

"I have fulfilled my ten-year term and may leave whenever I wish. His contract has eight years remaining."

The same rank as Jen-Varth who had eight years on him?

"Do you use Gates to get off this planet?" I asked.

"Ships visit once a year."

We passed by several hovercraft. "Why don't we take one of those?"

"They seat only three," he said. We stopped next to a satin-finish, steel-blue ATV made of a plastic-like substance with a clear dome—a futuristic Volkswagen Beetle with space inside for four undernourished people. The three-foot balloon tires put its top at my eye level.

We loaded our packs into the rear trunk. Jake sat in front next to Jen-Varth. Kedda and I sat in back. We harnessed ourselves in while Jen-Varth guided our ATV out of the garage at old-farmer-on-a-tractor speed. After he cleared the entrance he put on the brake, set the controls, and punched a button. The whisper-quiet, electric engine smoothly accelerated the ATV into haul-ass gear. Good shock absorbers kept the ride smooth. Bouncing high in the light gravity made it a bit scary.

At one point Jake commented, "I didn't see any women around the outpost."

"Women rarely join Protector service. Enlistment is for ten years. The length of assignment to a particular world is uncertain, and female Protectors are expected to sexually satisfy the males. Some find that unacceptable," Jen-Varth said.

Remembering our conversation aboard the pegasid a few days ago, I knew he wasn't talking marriages and monogamous relationships. I kept that to myself, but I did say, "The guys must get real horny otherwise."

"The local men and women provide for our needs, an unstated agreement in exchange for our services."

I hadn't seen any evidence of women's lib out here. "What's the role of women on your homeworld?" I asked him.

"I don't understand your question, Scott."

"What's their rank in your society?"

"They are equal to the men."

A forty-minute ride brought us to Hastain settlement just as light was appearing on the horizon. We parked at the edge of the settlement. Jen-Varth told us to wait by the vehicle while he contacted someone who could help us.

"How many settlements are on Ranor?" I asked him.

"Six."

Being early in the day, there wasn't much activity. The few locals we saw mostly ignored us. A couple of them stared. I browsed the sci-fi frontier town. Prefab buildings lined the main street. No sidewalks. Green sealer overlaid the crushed stone pavement on the streets and made it resemble turf. Although there were many different smells, I couldn't pick out any specific one. They merged to give the settlement a unique scent identity.

Fifteen minutes later Jen-Varth returned with a boy dressed in a ratty, sleeveless top and badly worn hide pants. Only his high-top moccasins with a half-inch sole were almost new. He carried an animal fur folded under one arm and looked underfed. I guessed him around fourteen. "Esak will take us to the library," Jen-Varth said.

Before I could ask what library, the boy said, "I am pleas-ss-ed to meet friends-ss of Jen-Varth." Amazing how the translators added his speech inflections. He acted younger than he looked.

On our left the local general store had just opened up. Jen-Varth took us in to buy food. "Can you get us anything non-vegetarian?" I pleaded. "I need meat."

"The animal life on Ranor is inedible."

"Couldn't be any worse than the plant life."

"Yes, it is," he said with conviction.

The store had refrigerators for the perishables. "They should leave it outside," I said. "After sitting out at night, it would stay frozen all day and then some." In the store I whispered to Jen-Varth, "Why do we need the kid? Is he the only one with a library card?"

"He has explored the buildings where we're going. We do not have the time to waste searching them."

"How long have you known him?"

"Less than one day."

Jen-Varth paid for the supplies with some sort of credit card, and we got back in our ATV. Kedda and I sat in back with Esak squeezed between us. It wasn't enough separation for me.

* * *

Two hours later I pointed out a pair of tall, conical buildings on the horizon. "Like the ones in Arion's video."

"Yorben structures a millennium old," Kedda remarked.

Jen-Varth drove the ATV through the opening in the left tower. Outside, I noted a hovercraft-like vehicle. "Is someone else here?"

"That is the surface skimmer I left behind when Arion took me." Jen-Varth popped the bubble dome up and back, and got out. We unsquished ourselves. "The second tower holds what we seek. Esak knows the route."

The air inside was warm. "Where's the heat source?" I asked.

"I don't know. Be alert. Some of Ranor's predators aren't shy about venturing into human habitations, and these structures would provide an ideal base for slave traders." He didn't seem convinced of any real danger to us.

Jen-Varth and Esak wasted little time except to detour us through a forest that Jen-Varth said he wanted us to see. I think *he* wanted to see it. "Who tends it?"

"Robotic units." He pointed out one among the trees.

"For centuries?"

"The structures have endured, why not what lies within?"

I didn't argue with his flawed logic. Buildings weren't the same as mechanical devices, like pyramids versus automobiles. Egyptians knew how to make things last; Detroit engineers didn't. But we weren't dealing with either here.

Esak led us across the bridge between the towers. The library wasn't far from there and wasn't what I expected. After seeing the forest, I had envisioned a huge room with elaborate consoles and circular, holographic platforms. Sci-fi land should be big and showy. The room was less than forty feet square and contained real books. The pages and bindings were plastic-like and in pristine condition.

We found some CDs in the library, slightly smaller than ours. Nice to find an advanced civilization after all the frontier ones we'd visited. Since Kedda was the presumed expert on the Yorben, I expected him to take charge. His knowledge, however, was deficient in the techie stuff. While he knew a little about the layout and how to find what we needed, he couldn't read the language. He rummaged through a long drawer and pulled out some charts. The Yorben had two languages. He knew their everyday one, but not the technical one.

"Looks like cuneiform without the wedges," I said.

Jake's eyes widened. "This is the language from the scroll that Bryce found, just written differently." He traced his finger along one line of writing. "Same material, too."

Was their skeleton a Yorben?

Jake continued, "These are the equations." He pointed to a symbol. "This is the same shape as the first Gate we came through and the shape of the entrance to this building."

The trapezoid with a semicircle on top, I noted.

"The symbols above it are vector designations followed by the number twenty, maybe the number of solutions. I'll bet the entire Gate matrix is in these equations." His excitement rose. He pulled out his own folded map and examined it. "The map is incomplete—wait a minute."

While his eyes darted back and forth between his map and the equations, I realized something he hadn't. Our translators had so far rendered writing into English for us, but here they didn't. For some reason, they didn't—or couldn't—render Yorben. The only reason I could think of was that they *were* Yorben. If that was true, how had Arion gotten hold of them?

Jake pointed to a column of symbols down the side of the chart. "These are the translation keys, and it's not just coordinates. If I'm right, we may have solved a few mysteries. Damn! I wish I had the scroll here to confirm it." He turned to me. "I might be able to find out who Bryce's cave skeleton was, but I'll need to look at my copy of the scroll. For now, we've got other things to worry about."

Then, he said to no one in particular, "Lead me to the computers and I'll have us back on track by morning."

"You're a mathematician, not an astronomer or a navigator," I said.

"At the root of astronomy is physics, and physics is applied mathematics—never say that to an astronomer or a physicist; they get nasty if you do. Astronomy plus physics plus mathematics equals navigation."

Kedda found the computer room, but had no idea how to work the complex controls.

Jake shook his head. "All this technology and no instruction manual."

Jen-Varth interjected, "There's a computer complex in the Protector outpost. I don't have access to it."

"Who does?" I asked.

"The cadet at the security desk."

"The sadistic asshole prick who shot me?"

He smiled. "That would be Pirro."

27

WOULD YOU LIKE A PIECE
OF MY MIND?

Day Six: Planet Ranor, Late Morning

Jen-Varth's hovercraft-slash-surface-skimmer got us back to the outpost a little over an hour later. Only Jake and Jen-Varth were needed, but I insisted on going along to settle a score with the cadet. Kedda stayed behind with Esak.

I asked Jen-Varth about the space ships they used out here. "When we can, we employ Mages to open Gates to travel between worlds, but Mages are rare in this region of space. Until a century ago our space vehicles limited our travels."

"You didn't develop faster-than-light drives?" I wondered.

"No." He set the hovercraft on autopilot and told us the story.

The Protectors began a century ago in a solar system of three inhabited Pneuma planets. One world had a Yorben Gate. A warrior race looking for new worlds to conquer discovered the other terminus of that Gate and found this particular world to their liking. Without faster-than-light vehicles and with no Magick or Psi, help arrived only after many inhabitants had been slaughtered. A wealthy individual who lost his wife in the raid founded the Protectors and set up a trust fund for their continuance, but with no faster-than-light travel, the technical problem became how to transport Protectors to the worlds needing them.

At the time no one in that region of space understood how the permanent Gates remained stable. A brilliant engineer placed a huge frame of dense Psi matter in space. A trained Psi Adept aboard a craft could generate a Gate inside the frame and the Gate would remain stable long enough to pilot the vehicle through it. They linked eleven solar systems.

"Is there a Yorben Gate on this world?" I asked.

"Perhaps in the building we just left, but no one has explored for it. Ranor is an isolated world in the Castill system. Men unhappy with their homeworld come here to escape past lives. The inhospitable environment ensures that few outsiders bother them. On occasion, slave traders or pirates invade from one of the larger worlds. The Protector outpost is here for that reason."

Just before noon, the outpost loomed ahead. Jen-Varth parked behind the smallest building.

"How do we get this asshole to help us?" I asked.

"Perhaps you or Jake can offer a suggestion. He runs the computers alone from a room in this building. I don't possess the entry code for the outside door."

"There must be another way in," I said.

"Through the main complex. I cannot take you that way because there would be questions we cannot have asked."

Cagey MacGyver has no plan?

Jake challenged me, "Let's see what you've learned during our association. What would you do?"

"Where's the door?" I asked Jen-Varth.

"In front."

"How does someone without the code gain access?"

"There is a signal panel next to the door and a security monitor, but he will have no cause to admit us."

Inspiration struck. "What's his name?"

"We call him Pirro. His full name has six additional parts, one for each living individual in his lineage at the time of his birth."

Seven names? That had to suck. I had him teach me a couple of words in Pirro's language. I removed my translator so I wouldn't hear them in English. "You and Jake stay out of sight. I know we need him conscious, but if I get into trouble, shoot him and make sure he knows what pain is." If Jen-Varth's or my reflexes weren't fast enough, my ass would get fried again.

Fully equipped, I marched up to the door and pressed the metal contact plate. A monitor screen above it came on. Jen-Varth had said that the women here used the middle finger for three different meanings. Pointed up it meant, "How about you and me get it on." That explained why Pirro wanted to shoot me a second time when I gave him the finger. Pointed sideways, "If you want it, go play with yourself." Pointed down, "I heard you can't get it up." *Sweet.* When I saw Pirro's face I showed him the inverted finger.

His image vanished. Moments later, the door opened and his pissed-off self marched through, gun drawn but angled at the ground. I raised my hands to my shoulders to show I wasn't armed. When he halted a few feet from me, I said, in Trade Common, "Eat me."

The gun came up more quickly than I expected. I knew what to do, but before I could react, his mouth formed an oh, his gun fell to the ground, and he grabbed his groin and doubled over.

Jake and Jen-Varth hauled him inside.

Halfway down a narrow corridor we entered the computer room. Pirro's earthy-woody fragrance pervaded it. Jake supported him. Jen-Varth sealed the door. The two side walls were blank and glowed blue-white. A workbench ran the length of the wall opposite the door. Underneath the left side of the bench was a rack of circuit boards arrayed end-on. On the wall above the bench were mounted three, three-foot-square flatscreens. Below each screen sat a four-section keyboard with no visible wires. Each position had a tall swivel chair. They helped Pirro into the center one. "Thanks for shooting him," I said to Jen-Varth.

"I didn't need to," he said.

"What do you mean?"

"Your abilities go beyond those of a Pneuma."

Jake put his hand on my shoulder. "That's what I call giving someone a piece of your mind, karate style."

I turned around. "What the hell's going on with me?"

Jake flexed his jaw muscles to hide his incipient smile. "I think you kicked his ass. Well . . . not his ass."

"I don't find that funny."

"Imagine what you'll be able to do after we get back to Earth and I train you some more."

"*If* we get back."

"Seeing you in action has raised my confidence level."

"I think Jen-Varth did it and he's covering it up. Alien humor," I said.

Jake tilted his head. "He never touched his weapon."

"Do *you* believe I did it?"

"You got inside Enelle's mind."

Thinking about that gave me the shivers, but projecting my thoughts as a physical force *at* someone? That scared

317

the hell out of me. "There must be another explanation."

"Feel free to offer one."

"Kedda's been messing with my head. I think he gave me a temporary power transfusion."

Jen-Varth touched a panel above the circuit board rack. The room walls brightened and became less blue. He handed Pirro his translator and motioned Jake over. "Pirro is ready to assist us."

Pirro gave me a rat-killer stare. "I didn't know they let Psi-freaks join the Protectors."

His disparaging reference to what he perceived as my Psi ability summarized, I was certain, not only his current world view but also a chapter from his book of life experiences. At least our ruse was working. He believed I was a Protector.

Pirro said to Jen-Varth, "Let me train him. I'll tie a leash around his sex to make him behave." He sneered at me. "If you've got any. You must not be worth much if they sent you here."

I glared back. *"You're* here."

"There's good fucks and bad fucks."

Jake unfolded his map from Arion and set it on the bench. He unrolled a chart we'd brought from the library. "We need your help with these."

When Jake mentioned the Yorben computers, he got Pirro's attention. "After we finish here, you will take me to them," Pirro said.

Arrogant little prick.

Jen-Varth and I sat on the floor against the wall behind them. Without his translator, I knew that Jen-Varth couldn't understand me. When I started to hand him mine, he just put his hand on it. I suggested quietly, "Why don't we visit the others while we're waiting. The misfit prefers my absence."

"We are in a security section. The detectors would initiate an alarm if we passed into the main building. I have no authority to be here, and you have no identifier."

"What's to stop *him* from turning us in?"

"Because he admitted us improperly, they would add to his punishment term."

"What do you mean?"

"Ranor is the least desirable world to be assigned to. He constantly provokes other cadets into fights hoping the Commander will transfer him."

"Why don't they?" I asked.

"Ranor does not attract technical experts. He's the only one they have to maintain the computers. He was given two years' assignment here. For each infraction, they add to that. He has already increased his assignment term to three years."

"How long has he been here?"

"Six months."

"Why'd he join in the first place? From what I've seen, this isn't his kind of company."

"Pirro did not join by choice. His father is a Protector high official. The enlistment kept Pirro out of a correctional facility."

"What makes him tolerate *you*," I wondered.

"Pirro likes to visit the settlements. For good reason, our Commander will not let him go unescorted. I volunteer to accompany him."

"Why would you hang out with a social misfit?"

"The men of his race emit potent pheromones. When we walk the settlement streets, he attracts more women than he can use for one night." His dark blue eyes met mine. "Pirro and I are not all that different. We both earned assignments here." He removed his hand from my translator and said no more.

Jen-Varth hung out with Pirro because the little fuck-up was an alien stud-muffin who procured for him? No, that sounded too tawdry. For Jen-Varth sex was simply a physical need that he dealt with. During our birds-and-bees talk aboard the pegasids he'd told me about his male-pill herbs that rendered unwanted conception not a problem for him.

His second remark intrigued me more. He had earned this assignment? I could see that Pirro belonged here, but Jen-Varth? He was quiet, kind, and caring. He reminded me of my brother Adam, after he changed.

During Adam's junior year in high school, not long after the M. Adam Madison name degenerated to Madam Madison and spread throughout the school, he developed an attitude that he wasn't going to take shit from anyone. Dad got calls from upset parents about their beaten-up kids and promised them that he'd talk to Adam, but he was proud of Adam for defending himself. The kids finally left Adam alone, but the attitude remained.

Christmas vacation of my senior year in high school, Adam's second year at college, he came home in his ROTC uniform to reassure Dad that college hadn't turned him from the One True Path. I instantly detected something different— no attitude. Adam was good-looking in or out of uniform and had no problems with dating. As of the previous summer he was still a virgin. I knew he'd been struggling with that and figured that he'd given in. That night I asked him. He told me that he'd joined Campus Crusade for Christ.

Adam? A Jesus freak?

My parents were quiet Presbyterians and believed that religion was your own personal peace with God. When

Adam and I were young, they encouraged our attendance at Sunday school, but rarely attended church themselves. Adam told me that he hadn't said anything to them because he figured Dad might take it in a negative way. "The Army has chaplains," I said.

Adam said that Dad didn't consider them military men and reassured me that born-again Christians weren't required to become ministers or missionaries. All the Bible stuff from Sunday school now made sense to him.

"You got religion," I said.

"Christianity isn't a religion, it's a relationship," he said. No one had pushed him, so he wasn't going to push me. "We're to be an example to others. When they see the difference in us, we share our faith with them." It wasn't that I didn't want to believe. I saw the amazing change in him. He found the appropriate moments to tell Mom and Dad—Mom first, Dad later.

After I started college, I rarely saw Adam, even during vacations. His school was on quarters, mine on semesters, and we both had full-time summer jobs to help pay college expenses. After he graduated, he joined the Army. Of course.

I saw him briefly after boot camp and before his overseas assignment with the Army Corps of Engineers. He isn't much of a letter writer. When he writes, once or twice a year, he always ends with a Bible verse. I keep his letters.

I think I took that Bible as Literature class because of him. Religion and my biology studies always seemed to exclude one another. At UCSD I saw my share of the God squad around campus. When I passed by, they'd stuff a tract into my hand or between my textbooks. Depending on my mood I'd ignore them or thank them and wonder if Adam had done this same thing on his campus.

It wasn't only Jen-Varth that had triggered my thoughts of Adam. Over the past few days I'd seen similarities of lifeforms that pointed to a common origin and evidence of the power that could have created it all. I wondered, where were heaven and hell actually located?

I looked sideways at Jen-Varth as he pensively observed Jake and Pirro. Adam's inner peace had been tangible and whole. Jen-Varth's lay in broken shards, as if whatever he once believed in had deserted and forsaken him.

From the hard floor I stared up at the empty third chair and craved its padded comfort. Pirro was civil with Jake and actually listening to him. For Pirro this was probably the closest he had ever come to appreciating a talent other than his own. Despite the allure of the chair, I decided to put my discomfort aside and stay where I was.

Whenever Jake sat at a computer hacking against the forces of evil, how he said "shit" told me what was going on. Staccato meant his adversary was better than he expected, drawled meant a revelation, and three in a row usually led to an onsite visit. "Shit on you" meant that the target hard drive was now placidly reformatting itself. Here, I heard all except the latter. The three in a row puzzled me because we were already onsite.

Nearly an hour after they'd begun, Jake swiveled his chair toward us. "We should find three Gates on this planet. One of them links to the first world on our journey."

"But the only Gate we found took us to the joyous world of those demonophobic party animals, not here," I said.

"If you recall, what housed that Gate was destroyed and took the second one with it. One destroyed, one sealed. I wonder if Kedda knows why."

"I expect he does."

Pirro asked who Kedda was.

"A gambler we met along the way," Jake said.

I thought, *And maybe secretly gambling with our lives.*

"As far as I can tell," Jake said, "there's no fundamental difference between a Gate like Arion makes and a permanent one. Both bridge two points in space. The Yorben figured out how to make your basic lighthole permanent. Apparently, nobody has done it since them. Too bad we won't be able to spend more time in their library."

"Maybe in our next life." I pushed myself up and stretched, noting Pirro's evil eye.

Jake continued, "Their equations are amazing. Do you know what fractals and the Mandelbrot set are?"

I knew what the Mandelbrot set looked like and couldn't resist an opportunity to rib him. "You mean those multicolored, op-art, spiky spirals?"

He cringed. "Their simple appearance masks their deeper beauty. We don't create fractal equations, we just discover them. The Yorben equations have a similar beauty, but they've been created. I believe that after the Yorben made their Gates, they constructed these equations to describe the coordinates for their Gates, among other things."

"That doesn't sound so hard."

"There's a PhD thesis in these equations. It's a whole other language with more nuances than I've ever seen in any Earth language. We know how to generate best-fit equations for data points, but they're usually an approximation. One Yorben equation generates *many* sets of exact, three-dimensional coordinates, and it has *only* those solutions."

Pirro interjected, "I could make them."

Jake squinted at him. "Really."

I started toward the empty chair. Pirro's right hand immediately went to his gun. Although I still wasn't convinced of my alleged powers, I narrowed my eyes at his crotch. "I can think faster than you can move."

"I heard that's how you Psi freaks do yourselves." he sneered. He made a jerk-off gesture at me.

"Enough." Jake meant it.

Jen-Varth came up beside me and took back his translator from Pirro. "Your duties require you elsewhere."

"You will take me with you," Pirro declared.

"We are not on Protector business."

"You owe me! I want off this shit-sucking planet!"

"You signed a contract."

"I was ass-fucked!"

"You could have gone to prison," Jen-Varth said.

The long hair down Pirro's neck bristled and his wet-dog odor intensified. "Better that than having my woman pleaser stuck in the dirt here!" He swiveled his chair toward the console, shot his right hand out, and poised it above a control. With a snarl he said, "I touch this and you stay here with me."

Jen-Varth said, calmly, "If you come with us, you will never be able to return here or visit any world under Protector jurisdiction. You will be a fugitive."

"I don't see a problem with that."

Jake's facial reactions to Pirro had been interesting. "We're already overcrowded," he reminded Jen-Varth.

Jen-Varth told Pirro, "Forge the Commander's authorization for a transport, pack what you wish to bring, and meet us at the garage entrance."

"Is that an *order*, sir?"

Jen-Varth smiled. "You have chosen to break your

enlistment contract. I have suggested the most expedient means to accomplish it."

We stepped outside. Jake asked Jen-Varth, "Why are you bringing that filthy-mouthed—"

"He wishes to leave Ranor."

"We're not here to rescue . . . riff raff." I saw Jake struggling with his choice of vocabulary. "He could jeopardize our mission."

Jen-Varth gave Jake a hard stare. "I have no desire to stay on Ranor. I have helped you here beyond my authority. Pirro knows this. He must come or he will ensure that you suffer here with him. In that case, your mission fails."

Jen-Varth had never given us a reason to mistrust his judgment. Jake nodded. "Bringing him is a mistake."

"Leaving him here to breed might be a bigger one," I said. I thought it odd that Jen-Varth had spoken as if he weren't a member of our team.

We headed toward the main building. The midday weather was pleasant, temperature in the low sixties. I looked up at the clear sky and down at the dusty ground. "Does it ever rain here?" I asked.

"A few times a year. Violently."

The guard desk was vacant. Except for two blue-uniformed men talking in front of one door, we saw no one else on the main floor. From a crosswalk above, a man in yellow pointed down at us. Jen-Varth crossed his hands over his shoulders and bowed his head. After we passed beneath the man, Jen-Varth said, "My Commander's deputy. We have an appointment to establish my official date of departure. I will not keep that appointment."

We entered the guest quarters where Dayon, Trax, Kart, and Enelle were waiting. Enelle's tired eyes brightened when she saw me. She looked lost and scared. And like she wanted to hug me. "How are you doing?" I asked her.

A shadow crossed her face. "Trax's father cares about him and Kart misses his daughter. My father won't notice that I'm not there."

"That's not true, and you don't believe it either."

I sensed that she wanted to tell me something else, but Jen-Varth interrupted. He told them about our newest addition. Trax gave Jen-Varth his translator. "My father told me that the staff has one built into it."

Then why had Arion given Trax one? Every suggestion that any part of this mission was outside Arion's knowledge or control scared the shit out of me.

Jen-Varth said that we had to leave before someone noticed our presence and questioned us. On our way to the garage he said, "If Pirro has done his work, the men on duty will not question us."

Pirro met us at the entrance with three bags of gear. Jen-Varth gave him the translator.

Pirro indicated Enelle and asked Jen-Varth, "Is she an apology to me?" One of his scents, not the wet-dog one, intensified. I heard Enelle inhale sharply. "I'm Pirro," he said to her. "I can make you very happy."

Jen-Varth told him simply, "No."

I wondered if Pirro required a translator because "no" was the only word that he really had to comprehend.

The day was half over. The two men on duty inside had already succumbed to boredom. We kept our heads down and Enelle stayed close beside me so they wouldn't notice her. When they spotted Pirro, one said, "Hey, Pirro, I haven't seen you in the settlement for several days. Must be lonely in the computer room playing with yourself."

Pirro went for his stun gun. Jen-Varth warned him, "That wouldn't be in your best interest."

The low minibus had twenty black bucket seats lining the sides of its primer-gray interior. The cylindrical top was tinted darker gray and one-way mirrored. Jen-Varth got into the driver's chair at the front center and strapped himself in. I took a seat behind him. Enelle sat with me. Pirro sat across the aisle from us. "It'll be quieter in back so you can sleep if you want to," I suggested. *Away from his pheromones.* She moved and sat next to Kart. She seemed comfortable around him. Maybe he'd become a stand-in father to her. Pirro stayed where he was. Which surprised me.

Jen-Varth drove us out of the garage. I looked back at Enelle. My gut told me that Arion—or someone—had sent her to us. As much as I hated Arion's emotionless and commanding air, he seemed to have our best interest and protection at heart. I also suspected that he didn't know everything that was going on, and that the dragons' involvement was far from passive. I saw too much coincidence for any of this to be coincidence. This smacked of intricate, behind-the-scenes work. But whose work was it? Perhaps neither Kart nor Pirro was here by chance.

By the time the outpost had vanished from sight, the others were asleep. Nearly everyone here had secrets. From my observations, Kedda had the most and perhaps harbored ones more sinister than Kart's. Dayon, as Arion's nephew, had a dark past that fit with the dark secret Arion kept in Freetown. Trax was just a kid. Granted, he was Dayon's kid, but *his* clandestine past seemed limited to being a street thief. If that were true, he and I were the only ones here without a serious past. Jake had expertly shielded his secrets from me. I didn't think that he'd told me all of them yet.

Jen-Varth was a quietly fascinating character. While he didn't see himself as having a purpose among us, he had saved Trax twice and helped me several times. Despite the hurt buried inside him, he hadn't let it stop him from helping us. When our mission ended, I decided that I'd miss him the most.

Only on the surface was Enelle the typical spoiled child. It amazed me how fast her attitude had changed by being among us. That's what happens when a lonely person is thrust into a group of people who don't ignore her. Where had she gotten her power? Did I want to ask the same question about mine?

Then there was Kedda. He was no longer the fun-loving guy from several days ago. I had thought that he and Arion were working closely together, but I'd seen him brooding. Did he have an agenda different from Arion's? Had he imbued me with my power? I didn't know which scared me more, that he might be trying to alter Arion's plan, or that he might be using me to help him alter it.

Pirro abruptly swiveled his chair to face me and asked, "Does she service you well?"

Trying to pretend that I wasn't appalled, I said, "That's none of your business."

"She is dreaming about *me* now."

"What makes you think she's interested in a crude little shit like you?"

"She sniffed me. One sniff makes them interested, two and they crave me." He licked his lips. "Ranoran women are sensitive. Only takes one sniff to have me naked and fired twice while other men are still negotiating. Do you Psi-freak a female before you stuff her?"

"What!"

"Slow and gentle, to make her *beg* for you. If you teach me how to Psi-freak, I'll get you women like I do for Jen-Varth." Not waiting for my reply, he said, "If you don't want a woman, I'll let you have me."

On the one-to-ten scale of crude, Pirro was a twenty. I was glad that Jake was asleep or he would have thrown Pirro off the bus. Jen-Varth's lack of reaction amazed me. Maybe his race secreted a chill hormone.

I was about to tell Pirro to leave me alone when he changed the subject. "Tell me about your business." A demand, not a request.

"Why are you talking to me? I thought you didn't like me."

"I don't, but I'm bored and she's asleep."

Thrasonical malapert came to mind. My senior year in high school I'd taken an English elective in creative writing. For one assignment the teacher gave us a list of character traits. She said to select one and write a short story about a character with that trait. I chose "braggart" because Dad had recently acquired a first lieutenant fresh out of OCS with that personality profile. I modeled my character after him. To impress my teacher with my vocabulary, I scoured a thesaurus and found the adjectives *thrasonical* and *malapert*. I couldn't decide which one I liked better, so I combined them. My English teacher (I think she had to look them up) red X-ed them and said they were too pretentious. Not for Pirro they weren't.

His earthy-woody fragrance was filling the minibus. I saw Enelle moving uneasily in her sleep and leaned forward at Jen-Varth, "Does this thing have a ventilation system? Pirro is scenting the air." He pressed something on the console.

"You're spoiling her dreams," Pirro said.

I glared at him. "Let's make something clear. *She* is a lady, not someone you can whore around with. While you're with us, keep your alien sex organs and pheromones away from her. I'm just learning this Psi stuff, and frankly I'm finding it a bit hard to control. If I hear any of your filthy language or suggestive remarks in her presence again, I'll purposely *lose* control in your direction."

"You can't give me orders," he sneered. "You're a first-rank like me."

"That's not an order. It's a promise. Would you like a painful reminder of what I can do?"

He grumbled, "I didn't say I wouldn't share her." He repeated his request to know about our adventure.

I decided that it couldn't do any harm and it might keep his horny thoughts and pheromones in check. He kept interrupting with how he would have done things differently. He also didn't believe that the dragons were real. "They convinced me," I said. "Does your world have Magick?"

"I don't believe in Magick."

"Well, three members of our group practice it, and Kedda, the one we mentioned before, he reads minds if you're not careful. I'll have to ask him what's in yours besides a testosterone-frosted pile of shit." When I told him about the Yorben computers, he claimed that he could operate any computer.

"The improper exercise of that particular skill sent him to Ranor," Jen-Varth said.

28

GROUP DYNAMICS
Day Six: Planet Ranor, Afternoon

Nearly two hours had passed since we left the outpost. Kart and Dayon were awake and talking to each other. They must have patched up their differences during their time together at the outpost. I said to Pirro, "Stay here and keep Jen-Varth out of trouble," and joined them.

"What's up, guys?"

"We are concerned about why Kedda wanted to change our course," Kart said.

"Arion told me that he gave you specific instructions and that Kedda knew the path to follow," Dayon said.

"I wasn't there at the time, but I'm sure he included a contingency plan," I said.

"There would be no need."

"Despite popular opinion, including his own, Arion is not infallible," I said.

"With the resources available to him for this task, he is," Dayon said.

I hadn't expected that one. I looked at Kart. "So, why did you agree to help him change our path?"

"He told me that my interference had delayed you too much."

"He lied to you. Where did he want you to take us?"

"He didn't tell me."

"Is there a way to block him from reading my mind?" I asked.

"If you were to carry my artifact, unshielded, it would interfere," Kart said.

"Yeah, interfere with my breathing," I said.

"Your sensitivity is a rare gift," Kart said.

I understood how Enelle felt. The line between gifts and curses had almost popped us out of existence. Still, shapechanging didn't knock her senseless.

Jen-Varth parked the minibus outside the second tower. We disembarked and made our way to the computer room where we found Kedda waiting and Esak peacefully asleep on the floor. Kedda regarded Pirro. Mind reading? Assuming Pirro had a mind to read, if Kedda wanted porn, he'd found it.

As if anticipating someone's question, Jen-Varth said, "I'll send Esak back in the transport that we left inside the other tower. It has automatic guidance."

Esak came over rubbing his eyes. "Pleas-ss-e take me with you."

"It's too dangerous. When I return—"

Pirro smirked. "You're not coming back."

Tears filled Esak's eyes. I grabbed the front of Pirro's uniform with my right hand. Looking down at his shorter self, I yanked the stun gun from his shoulder holster and jabbed it underneath his nuts.

He grinned at me. "You won't."

"What makes you think I won't?"

"Jen-Varth needs me to get his women. If you shoot me, he'll spend the rest of his nights alone, and you'll have to get on your knees and suck my woman-pleaser before I'll forgive you." When I heard Enelle gasp, any doubts I had about the efficiency of our translators evaporated.

Forcing myself to stay cool, I said, "I'm sure Jen-Varth did fine before you came along, and I warned you about the language." I pulled the trigger.

His eyes went wide. He didn't scream, just retched. Better self-control than I expected. His wet-dogness intensified as tears streamed down his cheeks. I held him firmly. "Gives you a rush, doesn't it? Are those tears of joy?" I pressed the gun up into him. "If it were my choice, I'd kick your sorry ass outside and let you walk back in the ball-freezing cold." I took a deep breath and measured my words, "As long as you're with us, you *will* remember three rules: you are an unwelcome guest, you have no rights, and you will treat *all* of us with respect at all times. Are these clear?"

He swallowed and exhaled a string of maledictions. In the way that Earth Eskimos have many words to capture the subtleties of different forms of snow, Pirro's language was rife with sexual obscenities. I wasn't sure the translators conveyed all the nuances.

"That wasn't the reply I wanted." I pulled the trigger again. This time his heart-rending scream reverberated splendidly throughout the room

I felt a hand on my shoulder. "Scott, that's enough."

"For now," I said to Jake. I slid Pirro's gun back into its holster and let him collapse. "If you'd heard his remarks while you were asleep in the minibus, you'd cheer me on." I lowered my voice so Enelle wouldn't hear. "He's the crudest little fuck I've ever met. And wish I hadn't."

"He helped me with the equations," Jake reminded me.

"Only because he wanted something. Do you know what he did to put him here?"

"Insubordination?" he said.

I smiled. "He's an alien computer hacker."

"I kind of figured."

"Jake Kesten, the foe of hackers, worked knowingly and willingly alongside one?"

"Chalk it up to an engaging personality. Maybe you and I could channel his talent. I'd be his mentor, and you'd keep him in line. He respects you."

At my feet Pirro dramatically grunted. "Not a chance," I said. "He's got a short attention span, a shorter retention time, and we've already got an assignment."

"Consider the challenge of rehabilitating him."

"No challenge. A quick trip to a vet will fix him."

We heard Esak sobbing loudly and Jen-Varth saying, "I promised your caretaker that I would bring you back."

"He . . . is-ss dead."

Astonishment crossed Jen-Varth's face.

"He . . . was-ss . . . very ss-sick. I told him . . . you c-came back . . . f-for me. H-he . . . w-was g-going to t-take . . . a . . . medicine . . . to end . . . his-ss ss-ss-suffering."

Another coincidental addition? How could Esak belong with us? We weren't scheduled to stop here. On the other hand, Kart's world hadn't been a scheduled stop either. As for Pirro—the chance fertilization of an innocent ovum by a reprobate sperm cell—if he was a planned addition, then the planner had a sick sense of humor.

On the other end of the emotional scale, Dayon said, "Kart and I can take the boy with us back to our world. Trax has the Staff of Chaos and will assume my role among you.

I believe that Kart's artifact poses a danger to you."

"No offense to Trax," I said, "but you and Kart are the only powerful Mages we have. Arion sent you, and Kart's the only one who can make a Gate."

Trax nodded in assent.

We ate and discussed the situation. Kart and Dayon agreed to stay with us until we found a way off Ranor. They restated their intent to take Esak with them.

Esak objected. "I won't go!"

"You're a young boy. You don't realize the danger. You could be injured or killed," Jake told him.

"Among my people each has the right to select the course of his life," Jen-Varth said. "I won't decide another person's fate for him. The validation of good decisions and the regret of poor ones make us what we are. Arion took Esak from me once in violation of our personal rights and his own racial ethic. Esak can choose. I will honor his choice. I ask that you do likewise." Jake nodded. Jen-Varth turned to Esak. "Any of us, you or I as well, could die on this journey. Dayon and Kart are good men and can see that you are safe and cared for. If I survive, I will come for you."

"I want to stay with you."

Jen-Varth suggested that Jake become our leader for the rest of the mission.

"A Protector should lead," Pirro mouthed off.

"If this were Protector business, you would be right," Jen-Varth said.

"Our training makes us the best qualified!"

My evil self muttered, "For you, that must've been pet obedience training."

Faster than I thought possible for him, Pirro sprang at me and knocked me onto my back, cursing his little heart out.

A moment before his fist connected with my jaw, he collapsed on top of me. Jake pulled the unconscious Pirro off me. I smelled like wet dog.

Dragging and carrying Pirro for the next two hours along the winding corridors and into and out of the elevators wasn't fun, but better than having him awake. Four-inch-square, blue night-lights came on and off automatically at our passing. Jen-Varth persuaded me to exercise my new powers to point us in the right direction while Esak guided us past unimportant corridors and dead-ends to a door five levels below ground.

"What's next?" Jake asked.

Pirro, now unfortunately awake and still irrepressible, said, "Use the Psi-freak's head to smash it down."

Given his boasts of sexual prowess, I almost suggested the part of *his* anatomy we should use as a pry bar. But Enelle was present, and he'd probably take it as a compliment.

Kedda walked up to the door, set his fingertips into a pattern, and pressed against a small panel next to it. The door hissed open sideways.

Thirty feet of corridor later the ten of us stood in front of another sealed door. Next to it was a small slot about two inches wide and the thickness of several credit cards. Kedda produced an object and pushed it into the slot. The door slid open. *He had an access card?*

Three Gates mounted on circular platforms occupied the otherwise empty, circular room. Dominating the center of the room, two Gates fully twelve feet high stood next to each other. Off to the left and close to the wall stood a smaller Gate five feet wide and just over human height. At the far end was a door large enough to drive our minibus through. All of the Gates had lightholes. I said to Jake, "I thought one was supposed to be nonfunctional."

"Interesting," Jake said. "Well, we can figure out which one went to our first world." He walked to the small Gate and halted.

I yelled, "Hold it! If you jump through and nothing's on the other end, you'll be lost in space."

"Not true." He removed his backpack, fished around in a side pouch and held up a penny. "May be worth something out here." He tossed it through the Gate. It vanished. "Must be one of the other two."

"What do you mean?" I asked.

"If there's no Gate on the other end, the penny won't vanish." He walked back to the large Gates, took out another penny, and flipped it through the left one. That penny also vanished. "Let's be sure," he said. He handed me a third penny. "Your turn. I got my two cents worth."

I pitched it through the right Gate. And it vanished! "Did you forget a minus sign somewhere?" I asked.

"I don't think so. The calculations were right, so I guess I'll have to take a look."

"What if a hungry hostile or a bottomless pit is waiting to swallow you as soon as you step across?"

He pursed his lips.

"I sense danger," I lied.

"Really." He said it in the same disbelieving way as when Pirro claimed he could reproduce the Yorben Gate equations.

Jen-Varth volunteered. "I am the best candidate."

"Trax is," Dayon said. "The staff protects him."

Jake pondered a moment. "Trax goes through alone, takes a quick look, comes right back." He nodded at Trax. "Okay?"

We were already in front of the large Gates. Trax chose the one on the right. Minutes later he returned.

"What did you see?" Jake asked.

Trax stared at him. "It's safe enough to look."

Jen-Varth went in. Jake followed. I yanked Pirro along with me. "Join the Protectors and see the universe."

The Gate on the other side was also mounted on a platform. A transparent dome surrounded it, like the one on the first world, and Jen-Varth still had the controller that opened that one. Would it work here also?

No description fit what lay before us. Melted, twisted lumps, some partially fused into one another, made up the landscape. What must have been buildings had run together and frozen into amorphous grotesqueries. In various places the ground itself was glazed. Directly overhead a reddish sun in a gray-blue sky illuminated the scene. A few loose bits of debris tumbled past us to indicate a moderate wind. Jen-Varth pulled an instrument from his pack and scanned the area. "The radiation exceeds safe levels, the atmosphere is acceptable." He took out the remote control and pressed the button. The barrier rolled up and over, exposing us to the harsh environment. A sinus-clearing, acrid smell of ozone and burning electrical insulation hit us, the lingering scents of civilization. "My radiation measurements indicate that this occurred over three centuries ago," he said.

"Where did he get the garage door opener?" Jake asked me.

"We found it on the first planet. It's how we opened that barrier."

"Why didn't you tell me?"

"I wasn't talking to you then."

Jen-Varth pressed the button again to close the shield. We went back through the Gate. Jake pointed at the smaller Gate and told Trax to take a lantern and check it out next.

He mumbled to me, "It makes sense now."

"What does?"

"Wait until he returns and confirms it."

Trax came back less than a minute later. "I was inside a sealed cave. I didn't see any way out."

"You were in Upstate New York," Jake said.

I snapped my head at him. "What!"

"The side cave off the one Bryce found. The man who belonged to the cave skeleton came from, or had visited, that melted planet where the radiation altered the carbon-14 content of his body. He probably died from radiation poisoning, not from the crack in his skull, which might have come from a falling rock after he was dead." He stroked his chin. "But was he a victim of the destruction, or the cause of it? Well, one more Gate to check out."

Trax stepped through the last Gate and was gone a long time. When he reappeared, he said, "Our problem is solved."

29

DÉJÀ SCREWED
Day Six: First World, Before Dawn

Jake had been right about a Gate leading back to our first world. We'd assumed it had been destroyed only because we didn't know it was in a room below the other Gate. Trax spotted an elevator shaft like the one we found on the demon banishers' world. The small elevator brought us, one at a time, outside the Gate platform up top and into pre-dawn light. We hadn't seen the elevator before because debris had covered it.

Jen-Varth used the remote control to open the bubble barrier. His lantern revealed shoe tread marks that weren't ours on the platform. "The demon banishers?" I suggested.

"That's my guess," Jake replied. He asked Kedda, "Why do some of the Gates have barriers around them?"

We hadn't spoken much to Kedda since our return from the outpost and he had been silent. He probably knew some of us were pissed at him. "I don't know."

I believed him. If he'd known about the bubble barrier and didn't have a control, he would have told Arion and they would have done something different. But I no longer trusted Kedda anyway.

"They could be waiting on the other side," Jake said.

"Why would they expect us to come back through this one when we left through the other one?" I offered.

"Maybe not us, but if we got through, they might expect someone else could. If they've destroyed or blocked the Gate on their end, we're screwed."

"We can toss a rock through to test it," I suggested.

"And attract their attention if they're guarding it."

"Their Mages may have set traps," Kart said.

In true MacGyver fashion, Jen-Varth offered, "I can prepare an anesthetic gas."

He and Esak sat on the nearby rocks while he worked. Jake and I sat on the edge of the platform and snacked. The rest hung out. Out of my hearing Kedda talked with Kart and Dayon. Trax offered Enelle some of his meat jerky, which she accepted. They seemed a good match. Pirro had strategically positioned his lustful self near them. I imagined that I saw his pheromone molecules circling above him and looking for an opening to swoop down and attack her.

Jake said to me, "I see a million questions floating around in your head."

"Only a thousand, too many to make sense of and most I don't expect ever to get answers to."

Kedda signaled Jake to join him. I stayed behind and zeroed in on Jen-Varth's activity. In Freetown he'd purchased a small carry pack. From that pack he'd unwrapped a hand-grenade-sized glass container into which he put various powders. He added water and quickly sealed it.

Jake came back over to me. "What was that all about?" I asked.

"Kedda feels that this is the appropriate time for Dayon and Kart to leave. The demon banisher Mages will detect

Kart's artifact and be able to use its power against us," he said.

"Kart was there last time and they didn't detect it."

"Kedda says one of them did."

"If Dayon and Kart leave, the demon banishers will have Magick, and we won't," I said.

"We have Trax," he said.

"That didn't help us before. How do we get across to the other cave without being stopped?"

"Dayon says the safest way is for Trax to use his staff's short-distance Gate spell. He can engage it out on the ledge, and we will step through to the other side, bypassing the village."

"Yeah, and last time he tried Staff teleportation, it wasn't short-distance and some of us ended up with a broken arm. Has Trax been checked out and certified on this spell?" And if he didn't aim it far enough, we could end up in the hands of an irate citizenry, who I was sure didn't appreciate having their previous demon-banishing festival canceled.

"Kart will keep an eye on us," Jake added. "He and Dayon will also contact Arion to let him know our progress."

I snickered. "I'm sure Arion knows exactly where we are, what's going on, and is betting that our next move will be more stupid than the last."

Jake raised an eyebrow.

I monotoned, "I know, if he tries to help us it'll alert the Evil Dude. Arion's nonintervention is just a convenient excuse to keep his nose clean."

"What's made you so cynical?" Jake asked.

"Going around in circles and putting up with a lot of shit. And not even getting paid."

"Is that all this is to you—a job?"

"Since we left Arion's world, we haven't heard a peep from the Evil Dude. Makes you wonder if all that stuff back at Arion's was nothing more than special effects."

"What would be his purpose in that?"

"To get us out and about," I said, "to give the universe an infusion of new genetic material—I almost did that in Freetown. Instead of sleeping our way to the top, he wants us to sleep our way around the universe and have interplanetary relations. He added Pirro the Pimp to help us get laid."

"Then we should get started."

Jake called everyone together. We'd been here less than an hour, but it felt longer. Kart and Dayon said brief good-byes, wished us well, then relinquished their translators. Kart lightholed them back to his world.

Pirro, who had said that he didn't believe in Magick, watched them with a semblance of awe. His reverence was short-lived, however. After they'd gone, he said, "I could learn to do that."

We ignored him.

Jake reviewed our situation, then asked, "Who should deliver the gas?"

I instantly pointed at Pirro. "The cannon fodder."

Imagine that you own a dog whose favorite outdoor pastime is patrolling the neighborhood for fresh dog shit to roll in. He does this knowing that he'll need a bath afterward. He likes baths because he has learned the pleasure of spraying you with water.

You also own a cat. The dog's second favorite pastime is antagonizing the cat. Although the cat is clawless, a bath is not something that the cat will tolerate without tranquilizer pills. One sunny summer day, dog and cat are both outside.

Your shit-covered dog has returned from a successful mission and has located the sleeping cat. Shortly, the cat will also require a bath. Imagine the chaos of bathing them together, without tranquilizing the cat first.

Whether Pirro's retention time really was too short to remember what Jen-Varth and I had done to him previously, or his tenacity made him not care, with killer-crazed eyes and fluent cursing, he ran at me. Jen-Varth's first blast hardly fazed him. The second one slowed him down. A third made him collapse to his knees inches in front of me, choking down his pain. Jen-Varth fired again. Pirro flopped over into fetal position at my feet amid spasms and gasping sobs.

Jen-Varth hadn't used the knockout setting of his stun gun. He'd used the nerves-on-fire one. He said, in response to my unasked question, "The first shot of the DN-32 causes brief, intense pain that quickly dissipates." I already knew that. "A second sensitizes the nerves and doubles that pain." Now I understood why Pirro had screamed when I shot him the second time after I delivered my rules to him.

"What happens after four?" I asked.

"The intensity and duration will ensure that he retains the memory of it this time. Do not touch him unless you wish to increase his suffering."

I looked down at Pirro. He was either badly overacting or seriously hurting.

"I don't approve of torture," Jake told Jen-Varth.

"The Protector code forbids it, and I find it distasteful. Pirro required this lesson." His expression affirmed his words as he holstered his gun and walked away.

Jake shook his head and told everyone, "Whoever wants to use the bathroom or change clothes, do it now."

We sent Enelle below while the guys changed up here. I

was still wearing the comfortable Protector uniform. But it *was* a uniform. I changed into my trusty jeans and wrinkled denim shirt. The uniform folded and compacted well. I stuffed it into my backpack for a souvenir of the trip.

I squatted in front of Pirro. He had uncurled himself and sat with his arms wrapped around his knees, still quivering half an hour after the incident. The defiance had faded from his bloodshot eyes. "Jen-Varth hates me."

"If he hated you, you wouldn't be here with us."

"You enjoyed watching me suffer."

"No. You and I were even before." I hesitated before adding, "If I'd known how painful two shots together were, I'd have stopped at one."

He shivered. "I didn't deserve this."

"You attacked me."

"You insulted me! You insulted me the first time we met."

Inadvertently. I'd only found out later that the finger was a homosexual invitation.

"Jen-Varth never liked me," he said softly. "He used me to indulge his pleasures and punished me to impress you."

Wait. I gave him the finger *after* he shot me. Before that, I'd merely shrugged my shoulders. The little prick shot me out of frustration because he'd lost his video game.

"Jen-Varth doesn't need me anymore. You're a Psi-freak. He has you to do women for him now."

I stuck my finger in his face. "You perverted . . . little . . . shit! You made me feel sorry for you and got *me* to apologize for what *you* started." I grabbed his stun gun from its holster and aimed it at him. "Give me a good reason why I shouldn't pull this trigger."

He pointed at Enelle. "It would make me want your

woman more than I do now." He removed his hands from around his knees and folded his legs in front of him so I could see the reason for his assertion. "I can make her want you after I'm done." His earthy-woodiness had gotten very strong.

Jake came up beside me. He took the gun out of my hand and examined it. "This reminds me of those drug commercials that warn about possible sexual side effects."

I unsquatted myself and said to Pirro, "I hope it stays hard until it hurts." Jake handed the gun back to me. I dropped it in front of Pirro. "Here, play with your sex toy."

"Want to stick around to see if he's into S & M?" I asked Jake, who raised an eyebrow. "He must have been genetically engineered. Evolution and natural selection wouldn't screw up that badly. I'll bet his engineer is paying for the crime in some unpleasant place."

Some days everything goes right—very few for us lately—and this wasn't one. We'd planned everything right, tried to consider every possibility, yet here stood Trax and I on the other side of the Gate helplessly watching Jen-Varth's anesthetic gas swirl up around us.

Our brief, decision-making session had decided who would cross the Gate threshold: Trax, because the staff protected him like it hadn't done before, and me, because we were entering a Magick world where my medallion should protect me (according to Dayon). Trax had had the gas grenade, and I'd had Pirro's stun gun ready. We stepped through the Gate. Four bright lanterns, Magick ones judging from the glimpse I had, illuminated the cave. Outside it was dark. Two guards seated at the cave entrance looked up from their card game. I fired at them, and I missed.

Well, I didn't exactly miss. The beam would have hit them had it not struck an invisible barrier across the cave mouth first and reflected back at us. The reflected beam coming back, slightly dispersed, wasn't strong enough to knock us out, but the numbing sting made me drop the gun and Trax drop the gas grenade.

For some bizarre reason, I remembered one particular day during my junior year in college, shortly after the start of the semester. I was sitting outside on the grass enjoying a little sun before my next class. A coed planted herself next to me and proceeded to tell me about the music of the spheres, the harmonic resonance of the universe, and how she wanted to have sex with me to find out if I was her soulmate. I clung to my virginity, thanked her for sharing that, and politely set off for class. Over the past few days I'd learned that her placid music of the spheres was more like Heavy Metal, and the four-part harmony of the universe was chaotic caterwauling. These were my last random thoughts before Jen-Varth's sleepy-time vapors cradled me to sleep.

✳ ✳ ✳

I awoke—sans headache or drug hangover—to a charming déjà vu setting. To the smell of fresh air. To a night sky with two bright moons and lanterns hanging everywhere. To Trax a few feet away. To people around me.

Angry people.

Lynch mob people, protesting that Trax and I were hanging in pig-roasting position not because they thought we were being treated unfairly—gagged, naked, arms and legs

aching from being cruelly lashed to our respective poles—
but because the fire pits beneath us were still unlit. Trax and
I had conveniently delivered ourselves into their hands.
Once again.

I hoped that, when Trax and I didn't come back through
the Gate, everyone else would come through to investigate.
I thought-projected my panic. "*Kedda!*"

No response.

"*Kedda?*"

Silent airwaves were not good. Either the others never
came through the Gate, or they were—Kedda at least—
unconscious somewhere.

The mob quieted to agitated murmurs as three men
approached us. One carried a lantern, which he set down to
remove my gag. The second, an official-looking official
carried my translator and placed it on my bare stomach.
Before I could ask if he had a light, he pointed to the neck
of the third man, one of the peasants, and asked, "Which of
you did this?"

The first man raised the lantern so I could see the marks
on his neck. What I imagined vampire bite marks would
look like in real life. The tumblers of my mental lock
turned; the combination fell into place. *Oh, shit!*

On Ranor, after our unfortunate acquisition of Pirro and
subsequent return to the library where we'd left Esak and
Kedda alone, Esak had come over yawning and stretching
and sleepy-eyed. I'd casually observed a mark on his neck,
but I'd figured it was a birthmark or a latent love bite. I'd
been unconscious and alone with Kedda at the beginning of
our adventure when Arion thrust me into that lighthole to get
rid of me. I hadn't noticed any irritation or tenderness on
my neck, but with no mirror to check it out, I couldn't be

sure I didn't have fang marks myself.

Pushing that thought aside, I regarded my inquisitor. I could have him check out my neck. If he found bite marks, maybe he'd consider me an unfortunate victim as well and release us. Or consider us doomed and light the flame of purification. Whatever, this nicely confirmed Kedda's secret. For sure, him being a her would have been easier to deal with.

"Here's the deal," I told the inquisitor. "Set us free and I'll tell you who put the bite on your guy." Before Kedda put more bites on one of us.

My inquisitor pulled out a nasty dagger and pointed it at the clamoring mob.

"Okay," I said, "I'm willing to compromise. How about you leave us rare instead of well done?"

"We will have an answer from you before the third moonrise." Two moons were already high in the sky, and I heard the ugly crowd demanding a conflagration. He walked away. Maybe I could contact Enelle instead. I projected my thoughts to her.

At first, nothing came back. Then, "*Scott? Are you all right?*"

"*Not exactly. Trax and I are the main course of their outdoor barbecue. Is everyone there with you?*" The walkie-talkies worked with her as well. I just hoped that Kedda couldn't listen in.

"*Yes,*" she projected back. "*We are trapped in the cave. We came through the Gate and saw them taking you and Trax down to their village. They have guards outside the cave.*"

"*Ask Jake what I should do.*"

Long minutes later I heard Jake in my mind. "*Kedda*

says that you can use the power in Trax's staff."

"Jake?"

"Yeah. If I touch her, I can talk to you."

"This is really weird. Well, you tell Kedda that I know what he is, what he did to Esak, why these people are super pissed at us, and if he did the same thing to me, he's in deeper shit than he can possibly imagine."

"What do you mean?"

The din of the crowd was growing. I heard raised voices and a commanding one above the others.

Jake came back on the line. *"Scott?"*

"I'll explain later. Gotta go."

A man in a high-collared, leaf-green gown approached us.

"Where I come from the executioner wears black," I said. "I don't mind waiting while you change."

The translator had fallen off my stomach. He picked it up and put it back. "You have created an awkward situation for both of us," he said. "It's fortunate that I was able to convince them to let me question you. Your previous escape and subsequent return have both angered and concerned them. I told them that only one of you is a demon, that the rest are his unwilling slaves, and that I have the ability to discover which of you is the demon vampire."

Vampire? That's how the translator rendered what he said. "I'm not in a talkative mood," I said through my teeth.

He picked up Trax's staff and displayed it to the crowd. *It didn't zap him?* "They fear this," he said. "I would like to know how it came into your possession, but you do not know its origin and would not tell me in any case. If you project your thoughts to me. When I speak to you, I use my own language, not theirs, so they will not understand me."

350

"Who the hell are you?"

He leaned close and whispered, "You must trust me. I can take you and your friends safely away from here."

"I'm supposed to believe you?"

He set the staff on the ground and withdrew my medallion—the one Dev had given me and which had already saved my ass—from his pocket and put it around my neck. "They know that this affords you protection from lesser Magick. It would not protect you from my power in any case, but having you wear it will convince them of my power. Please forgive what I must do to convince these people to release you into my care. I do regret having to do this."

He placed one hand on my forehead and the other on my chest. A jolt of unbelievable pain—searing heat and electricity—surged between his contact points. The crowd acknowledged my loud, choking gasps. He repositioned his hands behind my left ankle and at the base of my spine. I felt the rip of my leg muscles contracting in unison against the bonds holding me to the pole. The crowd cheered at my scream. Why was he torturing only me, not that I wished Trax harm?

After my pain had abated, he leaned over me and said quietly, "The situation is complex. Because he carries the staff, they are convinced that he is a demon. I have told them that I am a powerful Mage who specializes in demons and have come to their aid. I also told them that you are his servant, and that you are not a demon yourself."

"Then why am I strung up like he is?"

"To prevent him from acting through you. I have examined their book on demons. Their mythology is very curious and not always consistent. According to it, Magick can restrain a demon, but it inflicts pain upon him. I tortured you to convince them that you are no demon. Your performance has validated my claim."

"Performance?" I choked out.

"Whatever. If they suspect my true identity, I won't be able to prevent them from killing you. I will have your friends brought here. Please encourage them to cooperate."

30

WHERE YOU FIND DRAGONS, EXPECT DUNGEONS

Day Six: Demon Banisher World, Nighttime

This guy in green had gained the crowd's attention and respect by torturing me. He told them to untie the two of us. When they balked, he demonstrated that he had us under his full control by gesturing at me. The jolt arched my back. I knew he wasn't using Magick because his power felt exactly like Kedda's mental probes. The crowd ah-ed in awe of his power. They trusted him. Did I? Hell, no!

The crowd parted when my compatriots arrived under heavy guard, chain-gang style but unbound. The guards arranged them in a lineup in front of us, Jake at one end, Enelle at the other, the rest in between. Trax and I, still naked, stood next to the torturer. (He hadn't given his name so I called him Green Robe.) He had the peasant brought forward, the one with the bite marks on his neck. Green Robe asked the man, "Which one of these defiled you?"

I squeezed the translator in my left hand.

The peasant scrutinized Trax, then me, then the others. He shrugged his shoulders. Green Robe put a finger on the peasant's temple. Comprehension fell across his face. He pointed at Kedda.

Murmurs cascaded through the crowd. The peasant stepped back into their midst. Green Robe stretched out his hand. Kedda stiffened and zombie-walked toward him. I felt sure that Kedda was faking, but what the hell was going on?

After Kedda arrived on the other side of him, next to the fire pits, Green Robe turned to me, "Your debt is paid."

What did that mean?

He bid Trax and me to join our friends. I noticed that Enelle had been staring at us with curiosity instead of averting her eyes in embarrassment. Was it because Trax and I were circumcised? We hustled to Jake's end of the line. Green Robe held up his hands and addressed the crowd, "Your means of banishment will not work on a demon of this type." He waved a hand at the fire pits. "He will feign banishment, then he and his minions will return to plague your town with such evil as you have never before experienced. I will rid you of him permanently." Like a showman, he swept his left hand at us. "I have broken his spell upon these innocents. Permit them to depart in peace. They wish to return to the lives they had before this demon enslaved them."

A leader that I recognized from our previous visit said, "How can we be sure that other demons won't come?"

Green Robe reached into the pocket of Kedda's tunic and displayed a computer-mouse-sized object to the leader. "This enabled him to open the barrier beyond the cave." He dropped it on the ground and smashed it with his boot. I knew it wasn't *our* remote control. Ours was greenish-black. The smashed one was light gray. Green Robe hadn't taken it from Kedda's pocket. He'd palmed it from his own.

He lapsed into concentration. A waist-high, horizontal ring of flame sprang into existence around Kedda and him. The ring expanded outward to force back the crowd. Behind him a lighthole appeared. He stepped into it and pulled Kedda with him. The flame ring vanished. Trax's staff rose from the ground next to the fire pits and flew into the lighthole. Trax gasped. The lighthole vanished.

"Mind telling me what happened here?" Jake whispered.

"We got screwed up the ass."

He looked askance. "I hope you don't mean that literally."

Despite Green Robe's promise to the crowd, he was gone, and we were still here. Someone pointed at the sky. The third moon. "We need to leave, right now," I said to Jake.

"You and Trax should put your clothes on before you embarrass yourselves further."

"I would if I knew where they were."

Pirro stepped forward from the other side of Jake and said, wistfully, "If they unclothed me before this many females, my scent would overcome them. In their frenzy they would empty me."

"I understand now," Jake said quietly to me.

Around us things were happening. Jen-Varth had Esak next to him and was talking with two officials. Another official brought our clothes. Some crowd members were inciting others. Every minute we delayed here gave these people time to digest and assimilate current events. Since our anonymous benefactor had departed, we had no way to stop them. With a flick of the wrist, they could Magick us into submission.

Trax was dressing. When I didn't move to do likewise, Jake said, "This isn't a nudist colony."

I knew I was blushing and pointed up at the clouds crossing one moon. "I'm hoping for rain. I need a shower."

"You have a good woman pleaser," Pirro said. "You should show her that you want her." He pointed behind me.

My heart stepped up its pace and sent a surge of blood to the last place I wanted it to go. *Shit.* I picked up my denim shirt from the ground and tied it around my waist.

She tapped my shoulder and I turned around. She held out the black briquette. "In the cave, before they brought us here, Kedda told me to give you this."

"Keep it for me." I didn't want any black things in my possession right now.

Jen-Varth, followed by an official, came over. "The people are demanding action against us. The leaders are divided over the issue and their Mages will do nothing to protect us." The official signaled. Guards promptly surrounded us. "They will hold back the citizens if we leave at once." Jen-Varth looked worried.

One guard handed Jen-Varth the weapons.

Pirro reached to grab his, but Jen-Varth held on tightly. "Give me mine," Pirro demanded.

"After we have left the village."

"We can leave as soon as I get dressed," I said.

The crowd noise increased. Someone rammed into a guard, causing him to wobble. Jen-Varth said, "Now."

I grabbed the rest of my clothes and backpack from the ground, clenched them tightly, and started running with the rest. Over my shoulder I saw the mob push through the guards. Trax was behind me. He reached into his belt pouch and threw a sphere over his shoulder. *Boom*! He picked up speed and caught up to me. Panting, I gave him a thumbs up and nodded. Quite a transformation in him.

When we reached the bottom of the hill, this planet's thin atmosphere had taken its toll. Trax, Enelle, and I were ready to collapse. Jake was sucking air like a vacuum cleaner. Jen-Varth, Pirro, and Esak, used to a thinner atmosphere, were simply exhausted. I braced my hands on my knees to catch my breath—which wouldn't catch—and looked at the situation in the distance. Trax's explosion had delayed but not deterred the mob. The thrill of the chase had renewed their resolve. The shouts were coming closer. Torches bobbed through the trees and bushes. Had the crowd recruited the guards, or had they trampled them?

Jake panted. "Up the hill!"

I panted back. "No way."

Jen-Varth gave Pirro back his stun gun. "Set it wide, at full power." He motioned us up the hill. "We will make them reconsider their pursuit." Pirro didn't object. He enjoyed dispensing pain. When Esak also wanted to stay with them, Jen-Varth sternly told him, "No."

We weren't very far up the slope when I heard muted screams. I knew what that felt like. I stayed behind Enelle so she wouldn't be staring at my bare butt and to make sure she didn't fall backward. The night breeze was pleasantly cool on my sweaty body.

We reached the top faster than I expected given the difficulty of the climb and our level of exhaustion. Looking down the hill I saw Jen-Varth and Pirro not too far away. The crowd wasn't pursuing. Was their fear of something up here greater than their desire to render the evil out of us over an open flame?

"Do you know what happened to Kedda and to Trax's staff?" Jake asked me.

"Not for sure."

"Feelings or premonitions?"

"We're in deep shit and in need of serious sleep."

"Shit we can handle."

"Not this shit."

"Depress me with the details later. Into the cave."

We found a clear path to the Gate, no new blockages. Jake asked Trax, "Can you seal the tunnel behind us?" Trax pulled a sphere from his pouch. "Do it," Jake ordered. "If we're unlucky enough to end up on this world a third time, they won't let us make it this far anyway."

One by one we went down the elevator. After Enelle had gone down, I got dressed while I waited for my turn. Trax came down last. The elevator had begun its descent with him on it moments before I heard the explosion.

"No going back now," Jake said.

"Already deleted that vacation spot from my list of favorites," I said.

"You never told us exactly what's on the other side of this Gate."

"What goes with dragons?" I said.

Jake and I went through the Gate first, leaving the Demon Banisher World behind and stepping into our next world. Our lanterns revealed new footprints inside the dungeon. "Trax unlocked the door the last time we were here," I whispered.

After everyone was through the Gate, I noticed that Pirro had stopped his lewd remarks. He must have been tired.

"Sleep now?" I suggested to Jake.

He asked if Trax could secure the door with a spell, then apologized for forgetting that his staff was gone.

"I don't need it. This world is Magick. I can place an alarm in case someone touches it from the other side."

His expression told me how he felt. "We'll get your staff back," I said.

Something about this world had increased my sensitivity to alien artifacts. I separately detected—and knew what they were—Enelle's necklace, the black briquette she currently carried, the Gate we'd come through, what I suspected was the next Gate not far away, and farther still, Trax's staff and Kedda's ring. I didn't like this power of mine.

31

WHEN FOUR-LETTER WORDS FAIL
Day Six: Fourth World,
Somebody's Supper Time

Three hours later Jake woke me. I saw Pirro standing behind him. Pirro's fragrances drifted down over me. "I need a woman," he said.

I considered replying with, "Go back to sleep and try for a wet dream," but I saw Enelle waking up next to me. I couldn't believe how much the past six days had complicated my life, or that the semi-romantic attachment back home had nearly faded from my memory. I told myself that Enelle was an unwilling traveling companion who needed a temporary anchor. She was closer to Trax in age and temperament, but he'd shown no interest in helping her through this. Pirro, on the other hand, was busily secreting aphrodisiacs.

Somewhat refreshed, we entered a corridor made of dark gray stone blocks, six feet wide with twelve-foot ceilings. Dungeonesque architecture, fairly new or recently refurbished. If it wasn't, the caretakers had put a lot of time into keeping the place clean. Unlit torches stood in wall sconces every eight to ten feet. The corridor went left and right. Farther down, in both directions and on both sides of it, were wooden doors with barred windows. Instead of the expected mustiness, a gamey smell permeated the air.

"I'll look for the Gate," I said. I took a lantern from Jen-Varth and walked left where I sensed it. Although it felt farther away, I peered into the first cell that I came to. No Gate there.

I wandered toward the next one. From around a corner twenty feet down the hall came the source of that gamey smell. Four fuzzy-faced bipeds—taller than me—with flattened, flared noses and prominent teeth, carried shields and wielded four-foot swords. Their hair was shoulder-length, trimmed in front at mid-forehead, and silver-streaked. They looked intelligent, competent, bellicose—and hungry.

An energy bolt—from Trax?—flew past me, struck them, and promptly dissipated. Around the necks of all four dangled three-inch medallions that glowed briefly. *Spell absorbing like mine?* From where I stood, the medallions were identical to the one I'd found in the cave on the previous world our first time there.

My mental lock tumblers whirred and clicked. A new combination fell into place. Kedda had recognized the medallion and had known these guys were here. Because of that, he'd vehemently insisted that we go a different route. Then he and Trax's staff had disappeared with Green Robe. My Jedi-Knight and Spiderman senses told me that Kedda (his ring at least) and the staff were nearby.

I heard two stun-gun buzzes behind me. The shots hit the two furballs in front. They shuddered and shook it off. *Immune to those as well?* One creature stepped forward and slashed his sword through the air less than a foot away from my chest. The guns fired again, both beams striking him. He snarled at the annoyance. *We're fucked.*

RICK TAUBOLD

A thousand-watt flash bulb went off. I couldn't tell how it affected the creatures because I went blind. I heard growls, snarls, and scuffling ahead of me. The confused voices behind me fell silent.

My vision slowly cleared. Two more werewolves had joined their buddies. The new pair had brought their pets, two large lizards the size of small ponies. With sparkling eyes. Suddenly, I was transfixed and couldn't avert my gaze from the lizards. My body stiffened. *Basilisks*?

During my college freshman year, before my courses had gotten really hard, I'd succumbed to the evils of fantasy role-playing games. On one adventure our party encountered a basilisk. It turned my character to stone.

The werewolf guards laughed their ugly heads off while we helplessly petrified. *Please, let this be a big, bad dream.*

"Enough!" an angry female voice commanded. "I will not have our guests welcomed in this manner!" At first I saw no one, not surprising because I couldn't turn my head. "Return the Lisorans to their cells. In the future they are to be released only upon my command!" I heard toenails clicking on the stone floor, moving away.

A tall, striking woman stepped into my field of vision, fully human, gorgeous, and captivating. She wore a long, black cape with a high collar. Underneath that were slate-gray knit slacks and a turtleneck top that outlined a fit, trim body.

She looked at me. "I apologize for this inhospitable greeting. My guards are usually less stupid." Her voice was warm and soothing.

Suddenly, I was able to move. I heard moans and movement around me. Our host took a step back and bowed slightly. "I am Adana. Welcome to our humble castle."

Jake asked slowly, "What happened to us?"

"The Lisorans can induce paralysis when they perceive a threat to themselves. They are vegetarians despite their fierce appearance. We have four of them. Unfortunately, we have not been able to breed them here. The guards endangered them and will be punished for their stupidity. Now, you will dine with us and rest for the night. My servers will cater to your needs."

I had dirty laundry in my pack. "We have fresh clothing for you," she said.

"We appreciate the offer," Jake said, "but we're on a somewhat urgent mission. Our information says that there's another Gate in your building. If you'll show us where it is, we'll leave and not bother you further."

The guards growled in unison. She said, through what I considered a sadistic smile, "They want you for supper—as an apology for their poor treatment of you. They are of a single mind on this matter. It would be difficult for me to persuade them otherwise."

Her penetrating eyes shone black in this light. Beneath her smile I saw prominent incisors. With werewolves and basilisks, I'd be really disappointed if she wasn't a vampire. I considered revising my assessment of Kedda. Was the mark on Esak's neck really a birthmark? And had whoever put the bite marks on the peasant from the demon banisher world come from here? After all, we had opened the way for them.

"Please, come with me," she said.

We did. Jake walked in front. Enelle and I followed, with Trax, Jen-Varth, and Esak behind us. The werewolf guards brought up the rear. Pirro came up panting on my left. "I almost exploded when she looked at me," he said.

"She's not your type." I pointed at the physical evidence of his raging lust. "And quit showing off." His wet-canine fragrance, which I took for his equivalent of human nervous sweat, had gotten stronger and more pungent. I pointed my forefinger at his streaked hair, then pointed my thumb at the guards behind us. "Relatives of yours?" When he didn't reply I said, "Why don't you go ask them?" He still didn't take the hint. I didn't like him. He was smart enough to know that I didn't like him. Why was he hanging around me? I pinched my nose at him. "You smell, move away." He lowered his head and moved back. Did he have hurtable feelings?

The vampiress led us down the corridor, around a corner, up stairs to a landing crossed by another corridor, and up more stairs. We climbed and arrived at sealed, double doors with a slot beside them. She pressed an access card—like Kedda's—into the slot. The doors parted.

She paced ahead of us into the room and stopped halfway through to let us catch up. Ornate swords and artifacts of violence wallpapered the long room. She saw Jake browsing them. "You appreciate these?"

"They're unusual."

"Morthen will give you a tour later. Many years and many worlds have built our collection."

I remembered what Kedda had told me about the briquette blocking my thoughts. I let the others pass Enelle and me so I could talk to her. "Do you have that black object handy?" She pulled it out of her pocket. I palmed it before I had time to consider the consequences.

The jolt and lightheadedness weren't as bad as I had expected—*about time I got used to this shit*. Our hostess hesitated and turned her head sideways. Apparently she sensed something different, so it must be working. I shoved the black briquette into the front pocket of my jeans.

Past the armory we entered a modest dining room, no cathedral ceiling or chandeliers, bare except for a dark red, wooden table with ten chairs around it. A male and female werewolf dressed in an approximation of early American frontier clothing hustled into the room from somewhere. Vampire Lady smiled at us. "They will show you where you may refresh yourselves. We will serve the meal when you return."

We followed the servants. I whispered to Jake, "That suave bitch is a Psi. She reads my thoughts, and my brain is flashing red alerts. We're in more trouble than we know."

Jake nodded once.

A male wolf-servant showed us to individual rooms, mine last. Outside each door was a small table with an unlit lantern. The servant lit the lantern and carried it into the room. The room wasn't much larger than the dungeon rooms and sparse: a bed with its headboard against one wall, a freestanding rack with pegs for hanging clothes to its right, a nightstand with a small lantern on its left. Two more lanterns hung from chains near each side wall. The servant lit all three.

My room was the last door along the corridor. I saw one more door at the end. The room wasn't luxurious, but utilitarian and comfortable. The warmth in the air surprised me. I had expected damp chill. The place must be heated.

The wolf-servant pointed out fresh clothing and two towels on the bed. They had expected us. When the servant told me about the bathing facility, the room at the end, I forgot my concern and was shedding my trail-worn overgear and undergear onto the floor before he'd closed the door behind him. I wrapped a towel around me, put on the sandals I found at the foot of the bed, and padded my way next door. If somebody was going to have me for supper, I figured it was good alien etiquette to wash the food first.

The dingy, stone walls in this section were not new like the ones in the dungeon. Minimal lighting came from oil lamps on pedestals spaced every ten or fifteen feet on alternating sides of the hallway. I entered the bathroom. It was about twenty feet square and contained three tubs lined up across the room. Each tub had a pump next to it. One tub was already filled. A male wolf-servant in the room was filling the second. I approached the full tub and tentatively stuck my hand into the water. Perfectly toasty. I didn't ask him how they heated the water. The guy wouldn't understand me anyway. I noticed a door in one corner, what I assumed was the indoor outhouse. I needed to use that first. The toilet had a water pump that swung into place over it for flushing and rinsing, bidet style. The water was chilly. However the plumbing was handled, it worked well because the toilet odor was faint.

Trax showed up about the time my prune-skin fingertips signaled the end of my bath. He'd brought his translator. I said hi, he said something, and I pointed at his translator and made rapid, nonsense gestures. He laughed at my humor.

I'd just wrapped myself in the towel when Enelle walked in fully clothed and carrying her towel. As soon as she saw us, she inhaled sharply, turned away, and left. I didn't understand because she'd already seen our anatomic details.

Jen-Varth entered a few moments later wearing his bodysuit. He stepped into the bath without undressing. *A wash-while-you-wear fabric*? I thought back on an earlier observation. He hadn't changed his suit, not that I'd noticed, and he wasn't exuding the human aromas that arose after days of no bathing. Maybe the suit had a natural deodorant property, or his race was blessed with a miraculous physiology. He'd brought his translator—and had worn it into the bath—I borrowed Trax's and asked my question. His answer was an herbal rub. With a sample of that and his male-pill herbs I could start my own drug company to revolutionize sex and the personal hygiene industry on Earth. I could become rich. If I were so inclined and I ever made it back to Earth.

When I got back to my room, I saw the fresh clothing, the second towel, my watch, and the translator all still on the bed where I'd left them. My sneakers were on the floor. My backpack was gone, along with the clothes I'd removed and left on the floor. I'd left the briquette in the pocket of my jeans. Which I'd laid on the bed. They were gone. I wondered if Pirro's language had an appropriate adjective because the only English one that came close—fucked—seriously understated our situation.

She entered without knocking. Vampire Lady. Dressed in a black velvet robe. "I've wanted you since I first caught your scent."

"I thought the bath would take care of that."

"I wanted your friend Jake for an appetizer," she said, "but I couldn't resist your blood scent." Her voice was velvet.

I looked at the translator on the bed.

"I am speaking your language," she said.

And reading my mind? She didn't reply. Had I finally figured out how not to project my thoughts?

"You and Jake are from the same world, aren't you?"

"Yes."

"Your scent is so different from his." Her gaze locked

me in place; the towel unwrapped itself and fell to the floor. I couldn't move. She came forward, lifted my right arm, and pressed her fingertips along my forearm. "Young, firm skin." I felt a burn, like a paper cut. She pulled my arm to her lips and gently sucked.

When she raised her head, I saw the tiny cut with a trace of blood around it. She licked away the residue. "Your blood has a flavor I have never tasted before."

Those blood tests Jake had run on me?

Her eyes and Psi power dug into me, turned my will to mush, and made me horny in a way I'd never been before. My mind flashed back to Freetown, to The Vampire's Den Inn and the fantasy I'd had of the lusty vampiress on the motorcycle. *Oh, shit.* The face had been hers. That was about the time my premonitions started.

"A man who struggles excites me," she said.

"You won't let me struggle," I rasped.

She lessened her mental restraints. I thought about bolting for the door—it slammed shut. She removed her robe to reveal the white, silky nightgown underneath. "I haven't decided which of the young ones will be dessert, but I look forward to a full main course in you." My abdominal muscles tensed and pressure built in my groin. "You are a virile young man who won't disappoint me."

"Yes, I will," I squeaked.

She sighed. A blast from her mind slammed me backward, onto the bed. She pushed the straps of her nightgown down over her shoulders and let it fall to the floor.

She never bit me, just lightly sliced through the skin on my neck with her sharp fingernail and alternately lapped and sucked, not taking much, but relishing every drop. She painfully tensed my groin muscles whenever I tried to break free. After sating herself on my blood, she straddled me. "Ask me," was all she said.

As corny as it sounded, every sex fantasy I'd ever had was in position and ready to deliver. And most of me wanted her. Badly.

"I can convince you," she said. She leaned back and focused her gaze on the part that wanted her most. Muscle contractions rippled through my groin. Deeper inside me something else pulsed. I knew exactly what she'd targeted. I drew a loud breath.

"Ask me," she repeated.

Was this like the vampire legends that said vampires couldn't come into a house uninvited? Did I have to consent before she could take me?

"No," I whispered.

"You are more durable than I expected. Virgins seldom resist."

Was my virginity that obvious?

"Tonight you will beg me for pleasure."

She got off me and off the bed and began to put her clothes on. I started to sit up. Once again she slammed me back onto the bed. "With you I will show patience, but here is a taste of what I can do."

She concentrated at me and repeated the mental muscle massage in my groin. The pressure built, and I couldn't stop the inevitable. Once the contractions started, she kept them going and reinforced them until they became painful. Tears streamed from the corners of my eyes. "Please . . . please . . . stop."

At some point she did stop. By the time my panting slowed, she had finished dressing. "For now, your friend Jake will supply what I seek. Later, you will beg me to pleasure you—" With a glance she sent one final blast of power at me. I choked down my scream. "Or you will suffer."

She smiled and turned toward the door. "My servants will shortly announce supper. I suggest that you attend. You'll need all of your strength if you expect to resist me the next time. I recommend that you not try."

She opened the door and strode out without closing it.

32

BUILDING INTERPLANETARY RELATIONSHIPS
Day Six: Fourth World, Evening

"Scott?"

I opened my eyes. Jake had come into my room. In his underwear. While his eyes surveyed the scene, I pulled a towel over me and sat up on the bed. A couple of moans escaped my lips.

"What the hell did she do to you?"

I sighed. "When I didn't cooperate, she triggered me with her mind. For about two seconds it was incredible, but then she didn't let it stop. It felt like dry heaving only farther down."

"I know what you mean."

"Oh, no, you don't."

"Yes, I do. She took out her frustrations on me. Three times. The first was fantastic. The second and third just plain hurt. The blood sucking before the sex took me by surprise, but it seemed more like kinky foreplay. I've given more at the doctor's office."

"She was here right after I took a bath," I said. "Did you get one?"

"I was resting when she came in. Before she left, she

told me I should check up on you."

"Like she really cares." I tried to laugh, but I ended up coughing instead.

While he went back to his room to grab his towel, I put my clothes on. I walked with him to the bath. After he was soaking in the tub, he said, "Maybe they don't *need* blood. Maybe it's an aphrodisiac or an aperitif before sex."

"Interesting theory, but I disagree," I said, feeling a bit relaxed. "Do you remember our first visit to the demon banisher world, when we were clearing the rocks out of the cave? At one point Kedda came out of the cave to take a break because he was beat. While Kart and I were talking, he went down the hillside. When he came back, he was all happy and energetic. I thought he'd gotten laid. Now, I think he refreshed himself on peasant blood. Kedda and the staff are here in this castle or whatever it is—I feel them." I also told him that Kedda had given the black briquette to Enelle, that I'd taken it from her, and that it was missing.

One of the servants came into the bathroom to announce supper. "As long as they're offering to feed us, we'll partake," Jake said. "Then we'll figure out our next move."

"And how to stop Vampire Lady from making her rounds with the rest of us?" I asked.

"That, too."

* * *

Jake and I entered the dining room. The rest of our group were already seated along the table. Her Vampireness, in a forest green gown textured like gauze, stood at the far end and said as we entered, "I am pleased that you joined us for this fine meal." I noted the caution in Jake's eyes and didn't say what I was thinking. I carefully avoided thought projection.

Jake and I sat across from each other. For a castle, this room, the entire place for that matter, was unadorned. Hewn stone blocks, steel gray, composed the walls. I saw no mortar or cement holding them together. Neither did I see evidence of wear. Everything looked fairly new. Even the odors of the place suggested recent construction, that fresh stone, chalky, earth smell instead of mustiness.

Adana extended her arm at the door where we'd entered. "Ah, here is Morthen."

Jake and I together turned our heads and stared at the man who walked through the door with Kedda—Green Robe. He was carrying Trax's staff. "It's our pleasure to have you with us under these more pleasant circumstances," he said.

By whose standards? "You stole some things that belong to us," I blurted out.

Smiling, he took the seat at the end of the table, opposite Adana. "Brother Kedda does not belong to you. Please, enjoy the fine meal first and do not let unpleasantness spoil our appetites." Kedda sat on Green Robe's right, next to Jake.

Green Robe signaled the servants. They brought trays of tiny glasses filled with liquids of various colors, one tray for each of us. "You are new to our world and will be unfamiliar with our drink."

"I know what blood is," I mumbled.

"Please sample these to find one that suits your taste, and the servants will fill your glass with it."

I didn't press the issue. After Adana's forced exercise, I didn't feel like arguing.

None of the beverages were familiar. I chose the lime green one with a pear flavor and a light kick—alien wine cooler. Jake chose water. Jen-Varth and Trax selected the yellow vegetable juice. Pirro took the one that had smelled to me potent enough to induce a coma. I was content to stop at amnesia.

For the first course they served a thick, meat and vegetable soup, borderline stew. By the time I'd finished half of the bowl, Pirro had consumed two glasses of the drink and his eyes were barely open. Before the servants could refill his glass, he passed out.

"Do you wish him taken to his room?" Morthen asked.

At first Jake said yes. "No. I want him in my room tonight."

"Adana thought you would prefer a woman."

Jake doesn't blush. He did this time.

Salad, plus warm, doughy, yeast bread—unmistakably yeast—came with inch-thick steaks. The steak had a beef texture but was far more tender than any beef I'd ever had. The flavor reminded me of lamb. I hoped it wasn't were-wolf. Mildly tart berry pie completed the meal. I had to admit that the food was excellent. But I refused to compliment them.

Conversation had been nonexistent during the meal. Morthen broke the uneasy silence. "While I'm glad to show you our hospitality, I regret that my brother has dragged you into his fantasy." Jake gave Morthen a puzzled look. Morthen addressed Kedda, "You did not tell your companions that you—and we—are Yorben and that you and I are brothers?"

Jake's eyebrows rose. My mouth flopped open.

"Your astonishment tells me that he did not," Morthen

said. "I am baffled at this." He regarded Kedda. "Why would you hide this fact from those whom you have asked to follow your fantasy?"

Kedda said nothing.

"My brother has always been introspective. He chooses to follow the philosophy of our ancestors, who preferred to remain outside mainstream civilizations and to pursue their exploration in a secretive manner. I cannot fault him for this. When our civilization was at its height, the Yorben were misunderstood and even maligned. Our advanced technology frightened lesser civilizations. For that reason, we avoided them."

Morthen was a smooth talker, but he was hiding far more than Kedda had hidden from us.

Jake spoke up. "Not wishing to seem ungrateful, but you haven't exactly made the best first impression on us."

Jake? Being a tactful diplomat? Had something crawled into his brain and taken over?

"We ask your forgiveness." Morthen oozed politeness. "Adana and I have kept ourselves isolated here for many years. Only two Gates lead to this world. The one, which brought you here, we sealed long ago. My brother told me that he resealed it. We have found the inhabitants of that other world antagonistic to us and our purpose here."

What a load of bullshit.

"My brother and I share a different view of how to retrieve the lost Yorben artifacts. Adana and I sensibly enlist the aid of others who share our vision. Kedda sees no need to involve outsiders. Finding him in your company, or vice versa, was unexpected. He has not been forthcoming regarding the reasons for his alliance with you. Perhaps you will enlighten me?"

I didn't like the smell of this. Kedda wasn't talking, and I had no idea what he'd told Morthen. I hoped Jake had better sense than to say anything.

"Kedda is a traveling companion, one we met on our journey," Jake said more diplomatically than I expected. *Good for Jake. And it wasn't a complete lie.*

"Then, may I ask the purpose of your journey," Morthen asked.

"My people chanced upon one of your Gates on our planet and decided to explore where it led. Our galactic neighborhood is boring. We needed some excitement."

"Yet Trax carries one of *our* artifacts." Morthen indicated the staff.

"That staff belongs to me," Trax said, coldly.

"No, it does not."

"It obeys me!"

"It may seem to, but our artifacts have safeguards against misuse," Morthen continued. "They are attuned to us. We can override their attachment to others—as I have already done for your safety.

"A hundred generations ago our family began a quest to find the lost Yorben artifacts, fearing they would present a danger by falling into the wrong hands. I believed that a joint effort among our people would serve better. Now, these many years later, Kedda has realized this and has returned to collaborate with us."

Flickers and prickles inside my brain told me he was lying, which I'd never felt from Kedda. Was my suspicion that Kedda was trying to sabotage our mission wrong?

Morthen looked at me. "You and the girl are a puzzle." He asked Enelle, "What is the name of your homeworld?"

"Don't tell him!" I blurted out.

"What harm is there, my friend?"

"Don't you *dare* refer to us as your friends! Sucking blood from people and forcing them to have sex are *not* acts of friendship!"

"You have misjudged us. In our culture the sharing of blood is the highest form of personal acceptance." He studied me. I felt him picking his way into my thoughts. "Your people use a blood oath."

"We don't *suck* it out!"

"We should not let this minor difference in our cultures taint what we intended as hospitality."

"Well, in *my* culture nonconsensual sex is illegal. It's called *rape*."

Morthen rose. "We have been presumptuous and indiscreet. How may we remedy this?"

"Return what you took from my room for one."

He said soothingly, "So much misunderstanding of our good intentions. Our servers took your clothes to be washed. They thought you would appreciate that. They are accustomed to seeing to our needs without being asked. I will see that next time they ask you first."

"And no more blood letting!"

"Only with your permission. Is there something else?"

"The staff. It belongs to Trax."

"I must decline that request. It is a dangerous item . . . but we are willing to compensate you for bringing it to us and for having to sacrifice. Now, you must be tired. Let sleep restore your bodies and purge unpleasant memories. We will talk again in the morning."

"I'd like to look over your weapon collection tonight," Jake said.

"Of course. It contains many fine pieces. Although I

treasure all of them, perhaps your compensation might come from it. I have other matters to attend to or I would accompany you. On a lectern in the armory, you will find a small history that I compiled on the weapons. Many of them have been in my family for centuries. Of course, it is written in my language, but I will be happy to translate and discuss it with you in the morning, after breakfast."

"We plan to leave here in the morning. We are engaged in important business of our own."

"Surely you will stay with us and enjoy our hospitality for a few days. We so rarely have visitors." It didn't sound like a request. "Until the morning, my friends." Morthen bowed his head and left.

Adana remained in the dining hall, watching us in the uneasy silence that pervaded the room. She said nothing, studying each of us, but her gaze kept returning to me.

"Mind if I join you?" I asked Jake.

He and I simultaneously pushed back our chairs and arose from them. We strolled toward the far end of the dining room, the direction in which we'd come from the dungeons, where two werewolves stood guard at the double-wide exit. Over my shoulder, I watched my teammates disperse out the other door, presumably and hopefully to the semi-safety of their rooms, leaving only Adana staring at me. As Jake and I passed into the armory, Adana also left the dining room.

"What do you think she'll do tonight?" I whispered to Jake.

"No doubt she'll have one or more of us."

In the armory I spotted the lectern Morthen had mentioned and pointed it out. "Think you can read it?"

"Pretty sure. And Morthen's not expecting it. I noticed

this and caught a glance when we passed here earlier. I'm hoping it'll give us some answers."

While he studied it, I wandered around this museum perusing the nasty things arrayed on the walls and laid out on tables. Among them were the usual swords, some plain, some with finely detailed etchings on the hilt and blade. I was drawn to one that looked similar to Dayon's. The etchings were in English—which meant they weren't Yorben. Was it Elfaeden? Where had Morthen gotten it?

I was just turning my attention to the non-sword pieces when Jake called me over. "You're not going to believe this," he said. "I just found the key to Bryce's scroll writing." Jake pointed to a set of symbols. "Some of these were on the scroll, but here the context is different. The Yorben language is dual-layered! The scroll had *two* interpretations, not one." He pointed to one group of symbols. "These I couldn't decipher on the scroll because they're names. Right here is a sort of family tree. This is 'Morthen.' This is 'Kedda.'" He stared into my eyes. "The name 'Kedda' was on that scroll as the name of the person carrying it—the skeleton person."

"That makes no sense at all," I said.

"It does if it's a family name."

"Which it is," whispered a voice behind us.

I turned around. "Brother Kedda! If you're here for blood, I already donated."

"You're in danger."

"What was your first clue?"

"Let him talk," Jake said.

"Sure. His friends haven't fucked us over enough, so let's give him a chance to finish the job."

"Is there someplace more private we can talk?" Jake asked.

"Your room."

Jake shut the book, we walked in silence to his room. Halfway there, we encountered Adana. "I hope you sleep pleasantly tonight." I gave her a fake smile.

She came up to me and whispered, "I will come to your room later," and sent a pang through my groin that made me gasp.

"What was that about?" Jake asked after we'd turned a corner and were out of her sight.

"She invited me to another seminar on interplanetary relations."

"Be careful."

* * *

Pirro was out cold on the bed in Jake's room—and still clothed—when we got there. At least they'd kept their word about moving him here. "Close the door, Scott," he said.

"Why bother? You can't lock it from inside." I closed it anyway.

Kedda held out the briquette to me. "Take this back so they can't read your thoughts."

"I didn't know this place was fancy enough to have a lost and found."

"The servers took your clothes to launder them. When they came for mine, I sensed and retrieved it before Morthen discovered it."

"It won't do us much good. They can still read everyone else's thoughts," Jake said.

"They can read only Scott and Enelle clearly," Kedda said, "and while Enelle wears her necklace, it shields her thoughts from them."

I snatched the briquette from Kedda. "I'll take it. Just to keep *you* out." I struggled to maintain my funky mood. Otherwise, I'd require strong antidepressants. "You vanished with Trax's staff, which Morthen now has and doesn't intend on giving back. I don't trust him, but at least I know where we stand with him. *He* didn't betray us."

"I didn't betray you."

"Could've fooled me."

"Arion chose Kedda," Jake said.

"I'm not sure we can trust Arion either," I grumbled.

Jake sat on the edge of the bed. I shoved the briquette into a pocket of my pants and sat with him to listen to Kedda.

"I left Erebor, the homeworld of the Yorben people, twenty years ago. I had joined a group of our people who sought to restore the knowledge and eminence of our race."

"How old are you?" Jake asked.

"The equivalent of sixty of your years. The average life span of the ancient Yorben was over three hundred years. Today our life spans are somewhat less. Much has changed in us."

I sneered. "But you're still vampires."

"The blood of most human species contains a substance that Yorben bodies require but can't produce."

"All your wonderful science couldn't fix that?"

"Our ancestors reportedly developed a synthetic supplement, but the blood of each race and species has a different chemistry. The Yorben sense of taste is able to discern—and appreciate—the differences. Some find particular pleasure in tasting new bloods. A legend says that this originally motivated Yorben explorations. One speculation of Yorben decline says that they lost the knowledge of making the supplement."

"Is that true?" Jake asked.

"We don't have the supplement today and haven't found the records of how it was made. The Yorben today are a mockery of what we once were."

"Vampires with werewolf servants," I mused to Jake. "I guess we've found the basis of our legends." I told Kedda, "I *know* you sampled Esak."

"I caused him no harm."

"How many others have you done? What about me? You had me alone and unconscious on our first world. Or weren't you desperate then?"

"Only the boy."

"Continue your story," Jake said.

"The Yorben structure on Ranor is the largest I have seen. We didn't know of its existence. Its library may contain the lost knowledge we seek."

"Arion showed us one like it," I reminded him.

"I have visited it. That one had a single underground level, and its power source was expired."

"Where does the power come from?" Jake asked.

"I'm not a scholar of the old technology. The most educated among my group possess an incomplete understanding of the old knowledge. Yorben records were scattered. What we find is often incomplete."

"Not even on your homeworld?"

"Our ancestors took their knowledge with them. Their greatness existed on other worlds. Erebor retained scarcely more than the legends. Our world is dark because it is distant from our sun. Yorben civilization developed underground. The forest in the Ranoran structure attests to the science of our ancestors. The few outsiders to have seen Erebor crafted legends that black demon fires carved the landscape and that the Yorben were tall, black-haired, black-eyed, dark-skinned, sinister beings with bony faces and deep-set eyes. Because they bore no resemblance to their fictional image, they could travel freely and not be recognized. They were not a prolific species. They paid more attention to scientific exploration than to siring offspring. With long life spans they saw no urgency to breed. Aging colonists assumed that others from Erebor would replace them."

"Where do the artifacts enter into this?" Jake asked.

"As our ancestors roamed the universe, they discovered the true nature of matter. Magick, Psi, and Pneuma matter are always separate and never combined except by chance or intelligent intervention. All worlds are naturally made of only one matter type. We do not know why this is so. Together these three make up what we call the Bahrat power, the power of creation and destruction. Because the Bahrat power is impotent without intelligent direction, our ancestors hypothesized the existence of a Creator. We have legends that religious Yorben went forth in search of this Creator, but no records to substantiate it. Our ancestors experimented with combining the three matter forms. One such combination led to making Gates permanent. This was a turning point for other races as well. Permanent Gates enabled travel over great distances that was impossible before.

"They did not stop with Gates. Any Adept—Mage, Psi, or Pneuma—loses his power on worlds that do not contain his matter type. There exist naturally dense and concentrated forms of each matter that an Adept can carry to give him limited powers on foreign worlds. My ring contains a Psi-stone to give me limited Psi powers on non-Psi worlds. The old Yorben were not content with these limitations. Their experiments yielded power batteries that gave them the complete range of their abilities.

"There is a biological component of the powers. Not all can be Adepts, and not all Adepts achieve the same level of power. Elfaeden are one exception. All of their males have Magick. None of their females do.

"My understanding falters here, but our ancestors employed a means to focus and direct the power in the batteries and keyed the artifacts to Yorben mental patterns to discourage misuse. The Staff of Chaos is one of these. Morthen wants it because it will provide him full power wherever he goes."

"Embedded circuit chips," Jake muttered.

Kedda resumed. "Only the Creator, they surmised, had the ability to access the Bahrat power, but that speculation didn't stop their experiments. Incomplete records suggest that Yorben biologists attempted to engineer the genetic pattern for a Bahrat. One of our philosophers has stated that the universe continues to exist only because they failed in that endeavor. Vraasz has found a Tri-Lith artifact, which combines all three powers in perfect proportion. He is not Bahrat, but neither is he a normal Psi Adept. He can tap enough of the Tri-Lith's power to destroy worlds."

"What's a Bahrat?" Jake asked.

"He says that Enelle and I are Bahrats," I chimed in.

I saw Jake's lips forming the f-word at the same time the realization hit me.

"Scott was right to stop Enelle from telling Morthen the name of her world," Kedda said. "Her home is Yandall, a sister world of Erebor. Rumors say that some Yorben migrated there in the past. She may have Yorben blood in her. I don't know how Morthen or Adana will react if she does."

"Who *is* Morthen?" Jake asked.

"My younger brother by twenty years. He and Adana came here after I left Erebor. What you saw in the armory they stole from Yorben. They secretly brought material, some of it Psi-stone and likewise stolen from Erebor, to build this castle. While inside it, his powers are strong, yet if he ventures out of the structure, he loses most of them because this is a Magick world. The lower part, what you called the dungeon, is original Yorben architecture. They built on top of it, using the local people as slaves."

"The werewolves," I said.

"I have spoken with them. These people were a peaceful race until Adana came to terrorize them. They serve Morthen and her to avoid the consequences of refusal."

"If this is a Magick world and Morthen's and Adana's powers are limited to the castle, how can they terrorize the population?" Jake asked.

"She has a Psi-stone pendant that gives her sufficient power outside the castle. This world has no Mages powerful enough to challenge her Psi powers."

"I'm sure Morthen and Adana are the demons that were feared on the Demon Hunter world," Jake said. "Somehow their access was blocked. Since the people didn't seem to know why no demons had visited for a while, I'll bet it was a natural cave-in."

"Yes, that was before they knew this world had a less rebellious populace. While my brother is not an innocent, Adana is the real threat to us. She is a dangerous woman."

Jake narrowed his eyes. "How dangerous?"

"Life-threatening if she is not given what she wants."

"And what does she want that she hasn't had, or won't have before this night is over?" I wondered.

"For all of us to stay here."

"For how long?"

"They don't expect us to leave."

We'd obligingly brought Adana and Morthen the Staff of Chaos, which would provide them the power to expand their reign of terror. The briquette would be a bonus. They didn't have it only because they weren't aware of it yet. Jake and I seemed to interest Adana. She'd keep us around to extract her pleasure from us. As for her using the others, Jen-Varth had too much pride to let her use him. He liked his sex, but he didn't let it dominate him. While he'd lost control of his life, I'd seen his quiet determination to regain it. I was sure he'd fight her.

Trax was a Mage, and this world that Morthen and Adana were on was a Magick world. She'd tread carefully until she found out that he was no threat. His cooperation, or lack of it, would determine his fate.

Esak had nothing to offer her except mundane blood. Adana would break what little spirit he had, and she'd find him too pliable to interest her further.

Pirro's hubris would be his undoing. His sexual exploits were aimed at pleasing himself, not his partners. Adana might find him amusing. Once he figured out that he was her plaything, he'd become recalcitrant and she'd no longer find him serviceable. I wanted to see his reaction when he found out he was disposable.

Morthen and Adana would fight over Enelle, I was sure.

As for our next move, Jake intended for us to be gone before Kedda's predictions came true. Jake wanted to pair us up tonight for protection; he'd be with Pirro, Jen-Varth with Esak, Kedda with Trax, Enelle with me. "She trusts you enough," Jake said.

I said that if Adana decides to visit me again, which I hope she won't, Enelle would be in worse danger. Kedda agreed. He wasn't going to sleep, so he'd keep watch over Enelle's and Trax's rooms, which were next to each other. We had sort of reinstated Kedda to our circle of trust.

Kedda laid another weight on me. He said that Enelle and I held the only key to our leaving here. Jake asked him to elaborate and he replied, "Scott and Enelle must learn that on their own."

$$* * *$$

In my room only the bedside lantern was lit. Finding my clothes hanging on the rack and my pack on the bed did not alleviate my depression. I moved my backpack to the floor. I needed sleep, but I doubted that I'd have much success. First, I required a trip to the bathroom.

Back in my room and standing at the foot of the bed, I slipped off the sandals. I'd worn them instead of my sneakers, not because I was fashion conscious, but because I hadn't wanted to be ungrateful or rebellious to my hostess, who did pay attention to such details. She'd proven her ability to manipulate my body with her mind, for pleasure and pain, though the pain part had been more discomfort than serious hurt. I didn't want to find out what she could do if I pissed her off.

I'd just started removing my tunic when I heard the door swing open behind me and felt her mental prod. Panic surged through me. The briquette in my pants pocket would block her from reading my thoughts. She'd wonder why I'd suddenly gone from an open-minded guy to a closed-minded guy, then she'd play a game of truth or consequences with me.

Filling my mind with horny thoughts, I quickly shoved down my pants, to seem eager so I wouldn't alert her. I stepped out of them, kicked them aside, and turned around. On a normal tall person, my tunic would have covered my hips and tented over my erection. On me the tunic stopped an inch above it.

Her long nightgown was parted in front, just short of her breasts. Translucent. Traffic-light green. Nothing beneath.

I was in hell.

"Supper has replenished you and weakened your resolve."

Don't count on it. I can't fight hormones, but I'll do my best against you. I held out my arm. "This is as much as I'm offering."

"Is it?"

She sent a muscle twitch at my groin.

"*Yes!*"

Her upper body pitched backward as if she'd been struck or punched, not enough to throw her off balance, but she visibly staggered. Adana registered surprise a second before she viciously reciprocated. Her mind blast knocked me back, onto the bed, and every muscle in my body clenched, like what I imagined touching a live electric wire would do, brief but memorable.

"You impudent, ungrateful human!"

She did it again, this time it was stronger. My body jerked into fetal position, knotting with pain. My scream was automatic and unavoidable. No way could I fight her. I figured she could snap my bones if she wanted to. Already the arm that Jen-Varth had mended was aching. Unless . . .

"All right," I said as I exhaled. "Please stop." But she didn't. Her next show of force rolled me off the bed onto the floor. My stomach muscles were in spasms. I struggled to breathe.

Through my half-open eyes I spotted my jeans next to me. With the briquette in the pocket.

Would it help? Did I dare go for it?

"Your power, what is it?" Her demand didn't suggest an option for my refusal.

"I . . . don't know." I took a breath, held it, let it slowly out. "It just . . . happens. I can't control it."

"I can be forgiving when my lovers cooperate. The bed," she said, as she pointed, "will be more comfortable for you."

I slipped my hand into the pocket of my jeans, grasping the briquette and feeling the tingle as it touched me. Had she noticed? I sat up and pulled the jeans onto my lap. My erection had nearly subsided—pain has that effect. "You know you arouse me," I said, "I'm more than a little tempted, but my culture teaches that sex is the wrong thing to do when you're not married." It was a stretch, but for me it was true.

With my hand still in the pocket of my jeans and around the briquette, I stood and held my jeans to one side to show her proof of my current lack of enthusiasm. With my other hand I rubbed my stomach. "I need a little while to recover. Come back later and I'll do what you want."

"But you force me to satisfy myself elsewhere. Three young ones await my attention."

Let her have at them. Jake didn't have my misgivings. Pirro, if he was sober, might provide short-term entertainment and give her a good bang for her buck. Since this was a Magick world, Trax could probably protect himself from her if he was so inclined.

But she'd said, "young ones." Did that include Esak?

He was an innocent kid. Blood sampling was one thing, but I couldn't let her do the other to him.

"Okay," I said, "I'll give you what you want, right now."

But she'd already left.

* * *

Morthen was seated at his bare dining table, with no one else in the room. I saw a lighthole forming off to one side. Through it came a S'pharn that I recognized.

Morthen pushed back his chair, rose from it, and bowed. "Lord Vraasz."

Behind Vraasz came a second S'pharn grasping the handle of a large crate. After the crate had passed through the lighthole, a third S'pharn exited carrying the other end of the crate. The two set down the crate and returned through the lighthole, which promptly disappeared.

"As agreed, Morthen, the blood of thirty humans. I hope it will give you the same satisfaction that it gave me watching it being taken from them. You have the artifact?"

Morthen held out a scroll. "These coordinates will lead you to the planet where it is hidden."

Vraasz furrowed his thick brow and pointed a clawed finger at Morthen, who forcefully sat down in his chair. "That was *not* our agreement!"

Morthen slowly stood again "And it was not my intent to change it, Lord Vraasz," Morthen said coolly. "Unknown to me, years ago, my brother removed it from our family archives. He took it elsewhere and shielded it against detection. I invested much time extracting the memories of those closest to my brother to piece together his movements those many years ago. Even then, I did not learn why he moved it. I was able to determine only its general location. That world is designated on this scroll." He held it out to Vraasz again. "The world holds one of our ancient outposts. The artifact is shielded. Once you arrive on that world, your power will enable you to locate it."

Vraasz's face contorted.

"This information is reliable, Lord Vraasz. I will honorably forfeit my life to you if it is not." Morthen bowed deeply. "I praise the return of Lord Orfo!"

Vraasz turned. A lighthole appeared moments later, and he vanished into it.

Wake up, Scott. Before the dream scene faded out, I saw two ghostly dragon heads floating in the background.

33

THE MORNING AFTER
THE NIGHT BEFORE
Day Seven: Fourth World, Early

"Wake up, Scott." Someone jostled my body. I opened my eyes to Jake, not Adana, standing over me. "What happened last night?" he asked.

"I just had the strangest dream," I said, still groggy.

"Never mind your dream. Was Adana here?"

But the dream was important. I blinked a couple of times. "Yeah, the S & M vampire nympho Queen herself paid me another visit." I saw the smile lines tighten around Jake's eyes. "She started her muscle torture, then I fought back."

"You what?"

"I used my powers to put her off having sex with me. Still, she retaliated viciously before she gave up."

Fully awake now, I tried to sit up, but my sore abs refused to let me. I gritted my teeth and fell back onto the bed. "Intact virginity, but real sore body. I still haven't recovered from computer monitors exploding all over me and a broken arm."

"It was only one monitor. You'll have to postpone recuperation. Jen-Varth's rounding up the others."

"Did Adana visit you?"

"No."

"She said she was going to get her satisfaction elsewhere. What time is it?"

"Near dawn. I found a window to look out. There was no one in the hallways and no sign of Kedda."

I rolled onto my side, eased my body upright, and cradled my head in my hands. I had a headache as well. "That was a mighty potent wine cooler. Pirro must have one hell of a hangover."

"He was gone when I woke up."

"Did you check the bathroom? Might be puking his head off."

"That was my first thought. I checked there. No Pirro."

"Well, after Adana left me she said she was going for the 'young ones.' I'll bet she dragged his oversexed self into bed with her."

"Do you think you can find the Gate?"

"The way my head's throbbing, I'm lucky I can see."

"Get dressed. I'll be in the hall waiting for Jen-Varth."

"Tell him I need drugs."

A few minutes later, Jake knocked and came in with Jen-Varth, Esak, Trax, and Enelle. No Pirro or Kedda. Enelle looked exhausted. Jake began, "Kedda said that Enelle and Scott are the keys to getting us out of here, but he didn't say how. Scott, any ideas?"

"Not a fucking clue." I turned my head at Enelle. "Sorry, but that's how I feel." She looked exhausted.

"We need to find Kedda, Pirro, and the staff," Jake said.

"Can we settle for two out of three?" I said.

"Pirro is part of the team."

I slipped my backpack on. "The end part."

"Will your weapon work on them?" Jake asked Jen-Varth.

"It had no effect against their guards. They would have taken it from me if it were a threat."

"Let's go find the Gate."

I loudly sniffed the air. "Woof, woof. Canine Corps ready to fetch, sir."

Jake arched an eyebrow.

"All work, no play, and not even a dog biscuit," I said.

Kedda entered and quickly surveyed us. "Where is Pirro?"

"We can't find him," Jake said.

"We have another problem," I told Kedda. "I need to tell you in private."

I took him out into the hall and told him about my three dreams with Vraasz. "What do they mean?" I asked.

"I've heard of dream projection among Mages, but have never observed or experienced it. I believe that the dragons have imparted information to you that even I did not know. It seems that my brother Morthen is allied with Vraasz. I knew of a cult of Orfo worshipers among the S'pharn. I already assumed that Vraasz was among them, but I didn't know that Morthen was. I must ensure that you don't reveal your thoughts to him." He placed his hand on my forehead. A flash rippled through my brain and my thoughts became scrambled, like I was drunk. "I have blocked your memory of the dreams, but it is not permanent. We must move quickly."

✳ ✳ ✳

Enelle walked beside me on our way to the dining room. We marched through its rear door and into the armory where a squad of armed werewolf well-wishers awaited our arrival.

Behind us, more guards blocked our retreat. Halfway down on the right stood Kedda, Adana, and Morthen. Morthen held the staff. He was not smiling. "You spurn our gracious hospitality." He stretched out his right arm toward the far end of the room. The guards blocking the far doorway parted to reveal a t-shaped support from which hung Pirro stretched in crucifixion position. He'd been beaten.

Jen-Varth drew his gun. It immediately flew from his hand. Esak rushed at Morthen, who mentally slammed him onto the floor. From his boot sheath Jen-Varth whipped out his knife and flung it at Morthen. The knife made it less than halfway to him before it clanged to the floor.

"You have no right to keep us here!" Jake shouted.

"I do whatever I please."

"I thought we were guests!"

"You changed that when you chose to keep secrets from us." Morthen pointed at me. "Give me the other artifact."

I glared at him and reached my hand into my tunic pocket to feel the briquette. "I don't think so."

He raised the staff. "I appreciate how this amplifies my power." Pirro was a good twenty feet away from Morthen and wearing only a waist wrap. Morthen pointed his finger at Pirro. A cut appeared on Pirro's thigh. It lengthened and spread downward to his knee. A trickle of blood followed the cut. Pirro's leg muscles tightened, his face contorted, and tears ran from his eyes.

Enelle squeezed my hand. "That's enough!" I said.

Morthen twisted his lips. "Then give me what I want."

I squeezed the briquette. "And if I do?"

"I will not punish him further."

"What happens to the rest of us?" I asked.

"You will stay here and enjoy our hospitality for as long as we desire it."

"No way is that happening!"

He raised his hand again at Pirro, but Kedda intervened. "I offer a compromise."

While Kedda and Morthen talked, Adana came over to me. "Do not fight him." She narrowed her eyes at Enelle. "It has been a long time since a man exhausted me in bed."

Jake snickered derisively.

"Tonight I will let you try to best him," she said to me. "Competition excites me."

"Won't Morthen be jealous?" I asked her.

"He and I do not share that pleasure," she said dryly. "Give him what he wants. He won't release you alive. Stay and become my consort."

She went back to Morthen. Though alien and evil, Adana was a beautiful woman who gave the kind of gratification that made men sell their souls, which was exactly what she still expected me to do. With her powers, sex on demand became a reality. What she'd done to me so far, distasteful though it was, had sent waves of pleasure through me like I'd never experienced before. I could only imagine what else she could do. On the other hand, seeing what they'd done to Pirro, I didn't want to piss her off. She'd lock me in a dungeon cell and let me out only when she wanted to pleasure herself with me. That was not an item on my to-do-before-you-die list. "She can try all she wants, but I'll fight her," I said to Enelle.

Kedda came over to me. "This is the only way I can protect you. You must trust me."

"Morthen said that. I believed him, and look where it got us."

He laid my left hand on Enelle's right and put his own on top. A buzz shot through me like being in a vibrating chair turned up full. Lights flashed in my brain. I felt his other hand go into my tunic pocket and saw him holding the briquette afterward. Then he let go of us. By the time my brain haze cleared, he was handing the briquette to Morthen.

Morthen took a deep breath. "Cooperation is less painful than disobedience. I have let Kedda persuade me to a fair compromise. Know this: His mission to save the universe from some imagined evil is a fantasy constructed to enlist your aid in retrieving our artifacts."

"Kedda didn't enlist us," Jake said.

"The Elf joined him in the deceit and hopes to expand his own power with our Tri-Lith."

Jake didn't reply right away, but finally said, "You owe us more for what you did to Pirro. We want the staff back."

"Do not overestimate my generosity."

Jake shrugged his shoulders at Trax. "Let's go."

Morthen pointed at me. "You will stay as Adana's pleasure-giver, and the girl will stay as mine."

"No! We're *all* leaving together!" Jake's voice resonated in the large room.

Morthen raised a hand and the guards came to attention. "For the rest I have offered the choice to leave. Those who stay will become slaves. Or die."

Happy thoughts buzzed in my brain. I put my hand on Jake's shoulder. "You guys go on. We'll be fine."

He angled his head and gaping mouth at me and my serenity. "I refuse to leave you behind."

I looked at Enelle then back at him. "We're cool."

He said in a throaty whisper, "You have a plan?"

I pointed at Pirro. "He needs you. Take care of him." I

shook Jake's hand. "Maybe we'll see you around sometime."

I felt like I'd been given pacifying drugs. My ears registered my words; my eyes registered his shocked expression. Placidly, I said, "Please get your ass out of here and through the Gate before he changes his mind and you have casualties on your conscience."

Without further protest he motioned everyone toward the exit. Jen-Varth picked up his stun gun and holstered it. Several guards watched him while others untied Pirro.

Two guards led the way with Kedda immediately behind them. Jen-Varth wrapped Pirro's arm over his shoulder to support him. Esak and Trax followed. Jake went last. Enelle and I held hands and waved good-bye to him. Adana lingered a moment then followed them.

Enelle whispered to me, "How do you know she won't lock them up or kill them?"

"They'll be fine," I said. *Why did I say that?*

* * *

Jake fought his emotions. One part of him didn't want to leave Scott behind. Another part knew he had no choice. Scott was right. *Not* leaving would endanger everyone. He reassured himself that after he and the others were safe, Scott would carry out a plan and return. He looked back at Adana and the guards following them. Was this all pretense, and before they could enter the Gate would she kill them, or take them prisoner and lock them in cells? Would Scott sense if that happened? He turned his head forward. What game was Kedda playing?

The guards up front led them back to the dungeon cells. Adana came forward with a key and opened one cell. "The

Gate is in here." Two guards took lanterns inside. Jake felt relieved when he peered in and saw the Gate's glowing center. He motioned the others ahead of him. From behind him Adana's soothing voice said, "I will miss you."

"Why'd you leave my room in a hurry last night?"

"Your companion's blood scent excites me unlike any I have encountered before."

That she'd keep Scott alive as a blood donor slightly reassured Jake as he stepped through the Gate.

This new world was stranger by far than any of the previous ones. Arcing left and right from the Gate he'd just exited were more Gates, two dozen by his estimate. They formed a circle that reminded him of Stonehenge. The Gates lay along the perimeter of a foundation of black stone, the same he'd seen in the Yorben buildings on Ranor. One spot in the ring of Gates was vacant. A path led out from it, through a shallow valley, and toward a distant group of hazy buildings. Jagged hills and dark green and brown vegetation composed the rest of the surrounding landscape. On Jake's left a dim yellow sun, a third the size of Earth's, angled forty-five degrees above the horizon. Barely clearing the hilltops, it cast its light upon the scene. Jake slid his backpack off and set it on the ground. He took several steps toward the center of the circular array and found himself taking progressively shallower breaths of the pure, cool, moisture-laden air. It both exhilarated and calmed him. An oxygen-rich atmosphere plus no light-scattering pollution would explain the sky's deep blueness.

"Where are we?" he asked Kedda.

"My homeworld of Erebor."

A few yards away Pirro sat on the ground with his legs straight and still wearing only the loin wrap. Jen-Varth wasted no time in tending to him. Jake walked over and squatted beside them. Pirro flinched as Jen-Varth sprayed something on the lash wounds on Pirro's back and blotted them with a small sponge. Jen-Varth offered him a painkiller, but he refused it. The long cut on his leg had stopped bleeding. He had a couple of bruises on his face. Jake saw two particularly cruel cuts across Pirro's shoulders and wondered why Morthen hadn't simply used his mental powers on Pirro. He concluded that Morthen's intent wasn't interrogation, but to inflict evident, lasting pain that neither an onlooker nor Pirro could deny.

"I'm sorry this happened to you," Jake said. "Why don't you let Jen-Varth give you something for the pain?"

"You would have to carry me if he did."

"What about a local anesthetic?" Jake asked Jen-Varth.

"The duration would be too short to benefit him. The spray will promote rapid healing."

"Thank you for rescuing me," Pirro said to Jake.

The rebel kid with raging hormones had more inner strength than Jake had suspected. Jake had no idea where it came from, but it impressed him.

Jake stood up and surveyed the Gates. Not all of them had glowing centers. If his understanding was correct, it meant that the link between here and their destinations had been severed. He focused on the one they had exited and saw Kedda next to it, holding a long rod that he was inserting into the left side of the frame. Not sure if this was a good thing, Jake hurried toward him. "What are you doing?"

"Preventing them from following us."

Kedda pushed the rod through the frame. Jake saw it protrude into the glowing center, which abruptly ceased glowing. Jake's tenuous emotional restraints dissolved.

"You . . . asshole." He spun around and propelled himself feet first at Kedda's chest.

* * *

I picked up my backpack and said to Morthen, "We're hungry. After breakfast, we'll do whatever you want."

"Of course you will. We'll make your stay with us comfortable," Morthen said pleasantly.

"That means you'll put soft padding in our dungeon cells," I mumbled.

"You have the freedom to go wherever you wish on this world. We will deny you nothing." He saw us holding hands. "Not even each other." He dismissed all but four of the guards and led us into the dining room.

My brain buzzed again. I slid my hand into my pocket and slipped Kedda's ring onto my finger. How did I know it was there? Anxious thoughts, fenced in by tranquility, skulked on the edge of my consciousness.

Enelle and I sat at the dining table. Morthen rested the staff against a chair on his right and took his seat at the head of the table. The servants came in with enough food for six people. I was famished, but I ate slowly. No point in rushing what would come next.

"Is the food not to your liking?" Morthen asked.

"I'm not used to breakfast," I lied, sensing the need to cover my uncharacteristic behavior.

Adana and her werewolf security pack returned. Morthen rose. I could tell they were speaking by mental cell phone. Morthen said to us, "When we decide to leave this world, you will accompany us. Adana and I will not forsake you as your friends have."

Enelle grabbed my left hand with her right and squeezed it tightly. Brain buzz again. My body began to tingle, then tremble. Someone hit the power switch. The staff rose from its resting place against the chair and flew over the table at me. Morthen grabbed and missed. My right arm shot up to catch it. *Oh, shit!*

Several lightning flashes sent away the brain buzz along with my sight. Morthen bellowed commands; furniture clattered. Then everything got quiet.

Neither pain nor death followed. When my sight returned, werewolves had enclosed us from behind. On the other side of the table stood Morthen and Adana. Both looked like they were shouting, but I couldn't hear anything except Enelle gasping. A bubble, like the one that had enveloped Trax during his earlier slice-and-dice encounter, had surrounded us. Both of us trembled as the werewolves' ineffectual weapon blows bounced off the bubble. "Are w-we g-going to die?" Enelle asked me.

"I hope not." She put her shaking hands on the sides of my face, pulled me toward her, and kissed me.

Morthen raised his arms. The wolf pack backed off. For a long time no one moved and nothing changed. When our shield vanished and external sounds returned, I quickly said, "This isn't our fault! It just happened!"

He sort of smiled. "I underestimated my errant brother. He implanted instructions in you. Adana and I shun using that power. There is no sport in forcing our will on others." I heard the strain in his voice.

"She didn't ask my permission when she forced me to have sex with her!" I interjected.

"Had Adana chosen to do so, she could have made you a docile participant, but she sensed your desire and need. She enhanced your performance to intensify your pleasure. Now, give me the staff and no punishment will follow."

The lingering seethe on his face told me not to trust him. I imagined what Dorothy in *The Wizard of Oz* felt when the wicked witch tried to take the ruby slippers and couldn't while Dorothy was still alive. I didn't see an ultimatum hourglass around for Morthen to flip over. *Why the hell not*? *What kind of worthless fucking fantasy was this*? I said to him, "Why do you need our cooperation? Your Psi power can force us."

"We want you to trust us."

"That's not going to happen," I mumbled. Louder I asked, "Then how come your guards attacked us?"

Adana waved them away. "They are stupid. Your friends no longer require you or they would not have destroyed the Gate after they left."

What?

"My brother prefers to work alone," Morthen said. "He freely conscripts others, but only for as long as he requires them to achieve his ends."

I tilted my head up at the ceiling. "Hey, Arion! You enjoying the show?"

"Who is Arion?" Enelle asked.

I squared my gaze at Morthen. "The dude who sent us. He's probably sitting in front of his crystal ball, kicking back with his dragon buds, sipping a potion, and laughing his Elf nuts off."

I lifted the staff, turned it parallel to the tabletop, and shoved it at Morthen. "You want this? It's yours."

34

STRESS RELIEF
Day Seven: Various Locations

Dev Antos sat at one end of the long table in Arion's dining room. He was worried and imagined the same emotion from the impassive Arion at the other end of the table. Between them sat Fehlen. It was just after midnight and Dev had arrived here at Arion's keep three hours ago. The servants had told him that Arion was in his study. He had found the study door sealed and had waited in the library for most of those three hours.

Fehlen finished eating, wiped his chin with his napkin, and said to Arion, "Fehlen see people get sick in Freetown today." Fehlen had witnessed them collapsing onto the streets. "Why you not go help them?"

Dev wondered the same thing. That was why he'd come here with Fehlen so late. He'd told himself that it was to protect Fehlen, but he couldn't deny that selfish emotions had brought him here. He was more than worried. He also resented Arion's complacency. He was sure that Arion could stop what was happening. Freetown was Arion's responsibility more than his.

"It is time for your sleep," Arion told Fehlen.

"Fehlen wish Arion good dreams." He obediently got up from his chair and left the room.

Dev stared down at his own half-empty plate. "Your late return here was unwise," Arion said to him.

What did Arion mean by that? That Dev should have come here sooner, or that he shouldn't have traveled at so late an hour? He also wanted to confirm what lurked above the fountain in Freetown. Despite his anger, he didn't ask because he still hoped that he was wrong. "Nikki asked why you haven't come to Freetown to deal with these problems."

"How did you respond?"

He had wanted to say that Arion's life was more important than theirs, that Arion had dismissed his responsibility and relegated it to someone else, that their Elf protector wasn't as powerful as they thought he was. "I told him that you were ministering to others."

"Why did you lie to him?"

* * *

Morthen and Adana had graciously let us take a walk together after breakfast. They had suggested a stroll around the castle for us to get acquainted with our new home and said that we'd feel more comfortable doing it together. We carried our packs with us, figuring to put them in our rooms when we got there.

The werewolves didn't follow us, but they were watching. We passed them at several guard posts. I'd smile, and knowing that they couldn't understand me, I'd say stupid things: "Have you ever met Little Red Riding Hood?" "Oink, oink, oink, do the three little piggies live anywhere around here?" "Know where a guy can buy a good wolfsbane beer?" "Mind if I join your howl-along at the next full moon?" Enelle laughed at the last one. She told me about dog-like creatures on her world that looked like these guys and did the same thing. I pondered that. Was it a point for or against our current Theory of Evolution?

We found a stairwell leading up into a tower and decided to explore it. Four flights of stairs ended at a lookout with a wall that came chest high on Enelle. This castle—although we hadn't seen it from the outside until now to verify what it was—was situated on a shore. A huge body of water stretched endlessly in front and to the right of us. It curved away from the shore on the left where we could see a town in the distance. Behind the castle were Colorado-like mountains, but the valley between them was greener than real. Above the valley hung a light mist. The sun hadn't cleared the mountaintops. The pinkish sky was streaked with gray and white clouds. A cool-warm breeze blew from the direction of the town and carried scents of the water, wood smoke, and roasting meat.

Enelle pointed at the sky. "If we come back here tonight, perhaps we might see your home."

"It'll be the second star to the right and straight on 'til morning," I said.

"You know that?"

"I know that I'm never, never going to get back to Earth." I told her about Peter Pan and the Lost Boys and Never-Never Land.

"They will rescue us."

"First, they gotta find us. We're lost in a big universe. And I don't think Morthen's about to let us go easily."

"Do you think I'm a brat?"

"You're a Bah-rat, not a brat." She smiled. I was

surprised that the translators rendered my play on words.

Her dark eyes joined with mine. "I want you to make love with me."

"What?"

"We've made love in our thoughts."

I felt the blood rush to my face. I'd been hoping she'd forgotten that. But I hadn't forgotten. Why should I expect that she had?

"If my father were here, he would ask you to do it. After his attempts to calm my temper failed, he sought a lover for me. I know that every eligible young man in the city of Dandray—and the male prostitutes—refused him. Do you have a wife on your homeworld?"

"No!" I responded more sharply than I'd intended because of what she'd said before that.

"I hope I won't disappoint you. I know you've experienced many before me. You're an appealing young man."

The conversation with Jen-Varth while he and I were riding the Pegasid had been disconcerting. This one was embarrassing. My face had to be redder than the sky. "I know you're scared. So am I," I said, "but this won't make our problems go away. Wait until you find the right person to share yourself with."

She laid her head against my chest. I brought my arm around her neck and stroked her hair. I hadn't thought that a person could change as much as she had in just a few days. Or maybe it wasn't a change at all, just the release of what had lain repressed beneath her anger and hurt.

"I knew you were the right man when we first linked our minds." She began to undress herself.

"Here?"

"I want you to be my first, before he has me. No matter

what he does, I'll have your gentleness to remember."

Being gentle wasn't what concerned me. I was nervous and nervous led to . . . "What if someone comes along?"

"Our lovesharing will make them jealous of us." She removed the last of her garments.

While I was a dorm advisor, on Friday nights I'd watch the parade of guys with their dates saunter past my open door. Sometimes I'd stand in the doorway to amuse myself with their reactions and expressions: guilt, uncertainty, coyness, winks, thumbs-up, the shoulder shrug that meant, "It's better than what you've got," when the kindest description for the girl was fugly, the fuck-you finger behind the back if I gave a disapproving look, or, "We're just going to watch TV." Once, a guy who came in with the same coed every Friday night handed me an envelope as he passed by. Inside it I found three sealed condoms and a poem:

> *These will grant you three wishes,*
> *But if they don't come true,*
> *Rub your magic lamp real hard.*
> *The magic genie likes that too.*

Jake had a standard list of items to pack for a mission, with consideration for the number of days he expected to be gone. I never packed the condoms. I wasn't sure why he did since we always shared a motel room.

Enelle pulled my tunic up over my head and undid the drawstring on my pants. And I knew this was the right thing for both of us.

* * *

Thump, ba-boom, thump, ba-boom. Body-shaking bass, the young kid's car next to yours, the killer stereo in the apartment below. Thump, ba-boom, thump, ba-boom. The worst headache Jake had ever experienced. He was sitting, bent slightly forward, and winced when a hand touched the back of his head. He opened his eyes. Jen-Varth was squatted in front of him. Pirro sat next to Jen-Varth. A short distance away he saw the pulsing images of Trax on top of his bedroll and Esak wrapped in a fur. "Your head struck the ground," Jen-Varth said. "I found no serious injury."

Jake slowly remembered . . . cursing . . . launching himself at Kedda. And why he had.

Jen-Varth held out a fluorescent yellow, cylindrical tablet to Jake. "This will relieve your discomfort."

"It's not discomfort, it's pain!" It hurt to speak. "I thought you used herbs," Jake said, more quietly.

Jen-Varth shrugged his shoulders. "The one I would choose is not available. The synthetic will serve." He handed Jake a water pack.

Jake popped the pill and washed it down. "Where's Kedda?"

"Seeking counsel."

Jake massaged his temples. "He's going to need more than that."

* * *

Dev Antos believed that he was closer to Arion than any non-Elf had ever been. He had known Arion for years, yet he now realized that the friendship he thought he had shared with Arion was illusion. The Elf's motives were more elusive to him than ever. Dev had lied to the people of Freetown to protect Arion. And Arion was ungrateful! He said angrily to Arion, "I protected your stature among the people. Freetown is the only hope many of us have. You're the one who protects our hope!"

"I have been forbidden to act."

By his own people? By the Elfaeden who never interfered in the affairs of others? Karaydeon, then Arion after him, had acted against Orfo to save the Elfaeden from slaughter. Arion was their savior! "You'll do nothing while everything we've built is destroyed?"

"I have not done nothing. I sent those who can stop it."

Dev nearly snorted. "A weakling Mage, a healer, two incompetent fighters, and a gambler."

Arion either didn't catch the sarcasm or chose to ignore it. "Others have joined them," he said. "Kedda, the gambler, is their leader. He will forfeit his life for them if required. Only if they fail will I intervene."

"You sit there and follow the orders of blind fools while Freetown panics!"

"Blind fools?"

"Your people."

"My people will not involve themselves in this."

"Aren't they the ones who forbade you to act?"

"No."

* * *

You hear about sweet love when you're in high school. If you listen to the oldies on the radio, you hear it echoed in the teen pop songs from the sixties. You know it's wishful thinking. Love is only that sweet in your adolescent dreams. Or, if it does hit you in real life, it doesn't last long enough to matter. Sweet love is Santa Claus and the Easter Bunny and the Tooth Fairy. In high school you believe; in college you learn the truth. I was finding out that a considerable part of what I'd learned in college was false. No one bothered us. The morning breeze chose the perfect moment to blow over us and enhance our shivers. The sun warmed my back as I lay on top of Enelle. Pure, sweet love.

I'd layered our garments beneath us as a shield against the cold stone. I didn't have space to roll off her without touching it. I pushed myself up. She pulled me back and kissed me hard. When she finally released me and I sat back, the brain buzz hit me. Her semi-vacant expression told me that it had hit her too. It made me get up and look over the wall. I saw Morthen walking quickly along the beach toward the village. The brain buzz escalated to major mental turbulence. Another *Wizard of Oz* flash came, the ruby slippers—there's no place like home.

* * *

Jake felt calmer, relaxed, less confrontational about Kedda. Jen-Varth's yellow pill had eased the headache, and Jake suspected that it contained something in addition to the analgesic. The five of them sat quietly eating their alien trail mix. Kedda hadn't returned. That was fine with Jake.

He'd always considered himself in charge of his life. In some ways he wasn't all that different from Scott. His own father, an electrical engineer, had made his feelings clear about Jake's choice of professions. He'd once said to Jake, "Scientists and engineers make the world a better place. As for mathematicians, we already know how numbers work. Who the hell needs to know why?"

But unlike Scott and Colonel Madison, Jake and his father were no longer on speaking terms. Jake's only sibling, his brother, Alex, three years younger, had been killed in an accident eight years ago during Alex's freshman year at Penn State. Jake was a senior then, having skipped a grade in high school. Alex told Jake that he'd been invited to "The Annual Art Film Fest" hosted by one of the fraternities on Saturday night. Alex grinned. "I heard they're porn films and the guys all get laid."

The film fest was legendary, but not in the way that Alex believed. Jake enlightened him. "They're stoke films, and it's an all-guy party. After a few beers loosen you up and the films get you horny, the contests begin—who can shoot first, the straightest, the farthest, the most times."

"Did you ever go?" Alex asked.

"I heard."

The night of the party Jake remembered a few stories that his father had told him about Alex's high school exploits, the number of different girls he brought home to study with, finding *two* half-full boxes of condoms in Alex's bedroom, and Alex's quirky sense of adventure.

It had been raining all day and was still raining a little after six o'clock when Jake decided to take Alex out for pizza and a movie. He called Alex's dorm room. Alex wasn't there. His roommate said he'd just left. Jake knew the party started at seven. He put on his raincoat and headed for the party. From a block away, he spotted the ambulance and police cars. Alex had been crossing the street when a driver saw him too late and skidded on the wet streets.

Jake's father blamed Jake. Despite some healing, they rarely spoke. At college Jake had wanted to take the rest of the year off. A counselor persuaded him that jeopardizing his academic standing would solve nothing. Jake knew that Alex wouldn't want him to drop out either. Grad school and meeting Bryce Duncan had helped. The commission to train Scott had given him a new focus.

Jake had not forgotten one short conversation with Scott shortly after they'd moved to Colorado. Scott had asked why he'd hired him. "To train you," Jake replied.

"For what?"

"For your future, whatever it turns out to be."

Jake remembered his next words, "You're the brother I never got to appreciate," and Scott's tentative nod and apologetic expression. Jake had never spent much time with Alex when they were younger because Jake always had his nose in a book. That year at college had been the chance for them to spend time together. Jake had kept that part of his life from Scott. Right now, Jake wished that Scott were here so he could change that.

Jake let himself be distracted by those around him. Jen-Varth lay on the ground, pack beneath his head, staring at the sky. Esak asked Trax, "Show me ss-some Magick." Trax had lost the staff that would have enabled his power on this non-Magick world and sullenly shook his head.

Pirro got up to put on a pair of pants. As far as Jake could tell, Pirro's uniform had been left behind as well. He found the pants unusual, a leather-like, blue-gray material with a satin-finish. Probably synthetic. Spaced two inches apart around the legs, inch-wide vertical stripes of dark, metallic blue fur ran from waist to cuff. Not unexpectedly, the snug, low-cut pants contoured around Pirro's hips and outlined his sexual equipment. He didn't put on a shirt. Pirro was lanky and well muscled for a kid who sat at a computer all day. The weak light of this world made the horizontal stripe wounds on his back appear dark red, in stark contrast to the pants. For a moment, Jake imagined himself back on Earth, mindlessly channel surfing on his TV. He paused on a heavy metal music video where Pirro was the lead singer. Jake found himself enjoying the music.

He saw Kedda in the distance. Although Jake's emotions predisposed him otherwise, his rationality told him that a less aggressive confrontation than before might be more productive.

∗ ∗ ∗

Dev thought that Arion seemed approachable right now. Just short of pleading, he said, "I need to understand what is happening to us."

"Magick, Psi, and Pneuma are being disrupted."

"I know that!" Dev shouted before he could stop himself. Anger wouldn't help. He tried to look apologetic, not that he expected Arion to notice. He asked, more calmly, "What reassurance can I give our people?"

"Tell them it will not endure much longer."

"What's causing it?"

"The one who wishes to free Orfo."

He was mayor of Freetown, a haven for refugees, fugitives, runaways, and expatriates, and he was responsible for their safety. Arion owed him answers! "Who has the power to forbid your interference?"

"Marhesse and Fezeccah."

The dragons? Dev had thought that Arion's power far exceeded theirs. "What gives them that right?"

"My pact with them and the survival of their children."

414

* * *

I was holding my pants, ready to put them on. Enelle stood at the wall with her head turned to watch me. I picked up a translator and pressed it into her hand. "We have to get the staff back."

Her naked body shimmered. The next moment she was a large bird. Before I could protest or stop her, she was circling wide around the castle. She flew behind it and dropped lower. I lost sight of her until she reappeared and headed toward Morthen. The town was less than a quarter-mile away. He was two-thirds of the way there. He'd toast her before she even got close! He was carrying the staff vertically. She'd have to roll sideways to get her talons on it, and I'd never seen a bird do that.

She glided smoothly down and strafed his right shoulder. He stumbled and dropped the staff. Good for her! She made an impressively tight circle and came around lower, just a few inches above ground. He recovered fast. Moments before she could pluck the staff off the ground, Morthen turned. She wobbled as if something had hit her.

"Fuck you!" I yelled at him.

He turned his head up at me just long enough for her to recover. She screeched and took off. He snapped his head back. Her wings froze in place. She made a sloppy, glide-in landing several yards from him.

Enough of this shit! I stretched my right arm out over the wall and concentrated. *Come . . . to . . . Scott*. Enelle screeched again as the staff rose into the air.

I went blind.

When my sight returned, my visual perspective had changed. I was seeing Morthen through her eagle eyes. He had noticed the staff rising. His head flipped back and forth between it and her/us. We took to the air and headed straight for it. His mental power grazed us, but only made us briefly dizzy. Just before we latched onto the staff, it hurtled away and toward the castle, drawn to my body, I assumed. Unless Morthen's vampire skills included bat transformation, it and we were clear of him.

We approached the rampart and saw my body collapsed behind the wall, eyes open and the staff clutched in my right hand. We landed. My mind flipped back into my body. Hazy-eyed, I watched her turn human. I sighed. *"That . . .* was interesting."

"We have to leave before they find us," she said.

"I've already found you." Adana's voice was acerbic—"biting" had a disagreeable connotation. She stepped from the shadows onto the rampart. I pulled Enelle next to me.

"I thought that I sufficiently pleasured you last night. I'm disappointed."

"Life's packed full of disappointments."

I felt pressure in my groin.

Adana cooed, "You respond so well to my ministrations. She cannot do that for you."

"She doesn't suck my blood!"

She did her muscle contraction thing that made me gasp. My grip on the staff tightened. "You know the pleasure that I can give you. Of course, your defiance requires punishment. Morthen will insist on that."

Embarrassed and angry I said, "Bite me!"

"A tempting invitation. I may be able to assuage his anger if you give me the staff before he arrives."

"Not while I'm alive."

"We can take whatever we want." Her self-assurance

faded. She must have fired a Psi-blast and was surprised that nothing happened. Was the staff protecting us?

I felt bold. "It's not gonna be that easy."

"Don't defy me."

I gambled that she couldn't read my thoughts as long as I held Kedda's ring and the staff. I projected to Enelle, "*Grab our stuff and climb up onto the wall.*"

Adana's eyes met mine. "Morthen has returned to the castle. I don't wish to see him harm you. He was not angry when he had the other one beaten. That was for show. But he is angry now. Hand me the staff."

I joined Enelle up on the wall and said to Adana, "Tell Morthen to try anger management therapy. And that we won't be staying for dinner."

For my last birthday Jake took me on a helicopter ride. He made me wear a parachute while we dangled our legs out the side of the chopper above the passing scenery. Then he suddenly jumped off and yanked me with him. I'm not fond of roller coasters, either.

Enelle and I held on tight to our stuff and to each other, and jumped.

✳ ✳ ✳

Jake watched Kedda approach. Despite his determination to remain calm, Jake found his state of mind toward Kedda less than amiable. "You left two people behind."

"To enable the rest of us to escape."

From the corner of his eye, Jake saw Pirro draw his weapon and rush at Kedda. "You let them beat me!"

"My attempt to prevent Morthen from doing so would have caused worse problems."

Jen-Varth had come up next to Pirro. "I doubt that your DN-32 will affect him."

Pirro fired anyway. Jen-Varth made no move to stop him as he fired three more ineffectual blasts at Kedda. Jake finally said, "That's enough." Pirro quit, but kept his gun raised. Jake motioned Trax and Esak to join them. He scanned the faces of everyone, then stared at Kedda. "We all agree that we won't leave until and unless Scott and Enelle are with us."

"I have the same intention," Kedda said.

Jake didn't believe him, and he certainly didn't trust him. "When do you expect that's going to happen?" Kedda pointed over Jake's shoulder. Jake turned his head to see Scott and Enelle stumble through a lighthole. Naked?

Jake wasn't the hugging type, but he rushed up to Scott and hugged him. "I was worried about you."

"I know you were."

"What the hell happened?"

Scott smiled. "I don't kiss and tell. Excuse us while we slip into something less comfortable." He discreetly turned Enelle away and told her to put her clothes on while he did the same. After buttoning his jeans, Scott walked over and handed Trax the staff. "Brought you a present."

Jake heard Kedda say, "We must leave at once."

Jake felt the rush of blood to his head. His heart raced and his breathing became rapid and shallow. He wheeled around at Kedda. "*I'll* let you know when we're ready to leave!

35

MY MIND WOULD BE
A TERRIBLE THING TO WASTE
Day Seven: Erebor and Beyond

Over my shoulder I saw Jake's scarlet face as he marched up to Kedda and halted inches from him. "Before we go anywhere else, we're going to clear up a few things. First, *you're* not the designated decision maker here. Second, you've put us in danger too many times already, and I'm not going to allow you to do it again! Maybe you can force us to do whatever you want, but as long as we have free will, we're not going anywhere until we *all* agree on our next course of action."

I slung my pack over my shoulders. Enelle and I walked over to Jake. "Kedda pissed you off, too?"

"Damn straight. You two okay?"

"On a scale of one to five, with three being 'okay,' we're about a two-point-five, but don't let us interrupt your ire at Kedda. He deserves it even if he did get us back to you."

"*He* brought you here?"

"Actually, the staff did, but he let me know that it was our ride home. The hard part was wresting it from Morthen—Enelle deserves the credit for that. Still . . ." I stared at Kedda for several moments, ". . . he's pond scum."

I took a deep breath. "The *only* thing keeping his sorry ass attached to his body is the fact that I think he's the only one who knows how to get us to wherever we need to go next."

Jake relaxed and asked Kedda, "How many more worlds do we have to cross?"

Kedda pointed at one of the active Gates in the circle. "That will take us to Nyallos, the world Vraasz is on."

"Why have we seen or heard or felt nothing from him since we left Arion's world?"

"We're too far away to feel the effects. This path avoided contact. When he linked with Scott, had Arion not severed that link, he would have learned our intentions and used Scott to kill all of us. Scott did not have the power to resist him."

"And he does now?"

"Yes."

I shrugged my shoulders at Jake. He said to Kedda, "You knew Morthen was on the world we just came from and you let us go there."

"I didn't know he was there until Scott found the pendant in the cave. I warned you that we needed to find another route. You ignored me."

"You should have explained."

"We were being pursued. I acted to save us." I found it amusing that fate had undone Kedda's intentions. "Many Gates lead to Erebor. Your skill found another path here."

"How could you not know where your brother was?" I asked.

"When I left Erebor, Morthen was still here."

"That fancy castle didn't get built overnight."

"I left Erebor twenty years ago."

"Will we encounter Vraasz as soon as we cross the Gate?" Jake asked.

Kedda said no and explained that all of these Gates led into Yorben structures. Vraasz would not enter a Yorben building because the tales said that Yorben places were well protected against intrusion. Centuries of legend had increased the reputed power of the Yorben so that even the arrogant S'pharn were wary. A dead S'pharn had no hope of conquering the universe.

"Does the Tri-Lith protect him like the staff protects its owner?" I asked.

"We don't know, but it affords him the power to vanquish any who oppose him."

"Where do I come into this doom-and-gloom scenario?" I asked.

"You will project your mind into his."

"Why would I do something that stupid?"

"In the moments of confusion while your mind battles his, we will take the Tri-Lith from him and give it to you. Once your mind returns to its body, you will command the power."

"He's not gonna stand still while you take his toy."

"Vraasz is Psi, the world is Magick. He will carry a Psi-stone, but its power will limit him."

"I don't think this guy travels without plenty of protection and defense."

Jake brought himself back into the conversation. "Sounds too risky. We'll come up with something better after Jen-Varth and I do reconnaissance."

"That won't be possible," Kedda said. "As soon as you cross the Gate, he will detect your presence."

I held up Kedda's ring. "What about using this?"

"It would block only the reading of thoughts."

"What's *your* plan?" Jake asked Kedda.

"I will pass through the Gate first and prevent him from detecting any of us."

Jake glared at Kedda. "Your previous behavior says we can't trust you."

I said, "I agree, but he's all we've got."

Jake pointed. "Okay, you, me, Jen-Varth. The rest stay here."

"We need Enelle also," he said.

"No," I said. But I knew that she was my backup.

"All right," Jake agreed.

"I'm going with you," Pirro declared. Apparently he decided that he didn't like being left out and said so.

"You're injured," Jake reminded him.

"You saved me and I owe you."

"You can repay me by staying here and watching Esak," Jake said.

"And this," I said, setting my backpack next to him.

Pirro shot Esak a look of disdain. "I'm a *Protector*, not a baby watcher."

Esak's eyes flared. He bared his teeth and flew at Pirro, knocking Pirro onto his back. He ground Pirro's bare shoulders against the stone pavement. Pirro yelped. Jen-Varth plucked Esak off. Pirro quickly arched his back and pushed himself onto his elbows. "Keep that birth accident away from me!"

"His parents were killed by slavers," Jen-Varth said.

Pirro snorted. "Nothing that ugly was planned." Esak strained against Jen-Varth's grasp. "If he attacks me again, I'll make sure he can never fuck a woman," Pirro said, evilly.

Interesting translation. The f-word must be a universal linguistic element.

Jen-Varth asked Esak, "Will you accept an apology?" Esak nodded. Jen-Varth told Pirro, "Apologize to Esak."

Pirro had sat up fully. I saw his back bleeding. He snorted again. Jen-Varth released Esak who was instantly on top of Pirro, straddling his chest. Pirro gasped and vainly tried to arch his back. "Get him off me!"

No one moved.

Esak placed his hand on Pirro's chest, pressed down, and wiggled himself forward and back to rub Pirro's back against the ground. Pirro emitted a string of quick grunts. "I'm . . . s-sorry." Esak pressed down harder. Pirro gasped out, "I'm s-s-sorry I insulted y-your p-parents."

Esak didn't move.

"What else do you want?" I asked him.

While Esak thought about it, Pirro offered, "I'll teach you how to do women."

"Nice offer," I said, "but he's too young yet."

Esak smiled at me. "I like his-ss pants-ss."

"*Good* choice," I drawled. "And I think he's your size." Pirro's eyes widened. "No!"

I squatted and told Esak, "You can get off him." I slid my hand behind Pirro's head and sat him up. Pirro drew up his legs. "Your back's bleeding again," I said. "Must hurt pretty bad." He gave a short nod. I slapped his back. He inhaled a long, vibrant gasp and quickly straightened his legs. "Good boy."

Esak removed the pants.

Jen-Varth tended to Pirro's back. Whatever he put on the wounds must have stung fiercely. Pirro's arms shook, and he drew halting breaths through quivering lips. Jen-Varth finished up and told Pirro, "You will become Esak's brother and mentor." I saw the opposition in Pirro's eyes. Jen-Varth yanked off the loin wrap that Morthen's people had given him and which Pirro hadn't had time to change. "Or I will geld you here." Pirro looked down at himself and nodded quickly three times. Jen-Varth inclined his head up at me. "Scott will help ensure that you keep your promise."

I again squatted next to Pirro and whispered, "Don't worry. I won't let him perform surgery, because if he did I'd no longer be able to Psi-freak you there." I placed my hand on the back of his neck and squeezed. "Jake thinks you have the potential to become a productive member of some society somewhere. I bet him that you don't. If you go with us and you don't survive, then I win the bet. I know you don't like me, so the best way to get back at me is to keep your miserable self out of trouble and alive. That way, you win and I lose. You're in no shape to battle the guy we're after. My Psi-freak powers are *nothing* compared to his. He could sever your nuts with a glance." I released my hand from his neck. "Thought you'd like to know that useful bit of information."

Jake had walked outside the circle of Gates. I joined him. "What's on your mind?"

"How helpless I feel. How I have no control over what happens next." He turned his head at me. "How much I wish you weren't here."

"While you're in a soul-baring mood, I've wanted to ask you a question for a while. What if I'd refused your offer that day you visited my dorm room? Would you have walked out of my life?"

"Hell, no."

"What was plan B?"

"I didn't have one. My investigations had told me that you'd accept."

"What investigations?" I asked suspiciously.

"I visited UCSD several times—buzzed my hair, sat in your classes, talked to your friends. I screwed up when I asked Troy Marshfield about you. I'd met his father, Major Marshfield, at Fort Bragg and knew that Troy was attending UCSD with you. I *didn't* know that Troy was more anti-military than you were. When I flashed my government I.D. at him on campus, he thought your father had sent me to spy on you."

"What did you do?"

"I noticed that Troy was holding hands with a black girl. I remembered how the Major boasted about his deep Southern roots, so I pulled out my camera and snapped Troy's picture. 'I'll give your father this snapshot of you on campus.' Troy paled. I said to him, 'Scott Madison submitted an application for a summer job with the government. I'm doing the required background check. Not a big deal.' I waved the camera at him. 'I'd appreciate you not saying anything that might take his mind off his studies.' By that time I'd learned enough about you. I saw the spirit of adventure beneath your studious exterior."

Jake was unsure what our next move should be. He gathered us and asked for everyone's input. While Jake didn't exclude anyone, Pirro remained silent, wearing Esak's old hide pants, no shirt, and an expression of defeat. For the first time, I noticed his half-inch-wide stripe of chest hair, unevenly colored like the mink-patterned hair on his head. The stripe began just below his collarbone and ran all the way down. It wasn't dense, just dark enough to stand out. I imagined his women stroking its length. Did I have fur envy?

The mysteries around Kedda didn't go away. He didn't divulge how he knew what he knew, only what we could expect. "Orfo is a S'pharn whose imprisonment Arion extended ten years ago. Orfo's desire for revenge upon the Elfaeden has no limits. The Tri-Lith will enable Vraasz to defeat Arion and to free Orfo to rule or to destroy as he chooses."

"I don't think Arion will go down that easily," I said.

Kedda shook his head. "Orfo will destroy Arion's world. That's the reason Arion sent us."

"Where is this guy Orfo?"

"Imprisoned above the fountain in Freetown."

My jaw dropped. So did Jake's. Kedda had not yet joined us when we'd visited Freetown, and Dev had suspected this.

"Where is Vraasz?" I asked.

"When we step through this Gate, we will be on the world next closest to the sun from Arion's. You needed to be away from the reach of his power until your own became active. While it will take years for your full powers to develop, we are hoping that what you have will be sufficient."

"And if they aren't?"

"You have Enelle's power to augment yours."

"She is *not* coming with us! I won't endanger her."

"Bahrats are a threat to Orfo. He will find and kill them all unless you stop him now."

This superhero thing had grown way out of proportion. I'd felt Vraasz screw my mind long distance. I didn't want to think about what he could do to me up close.

We passed through the Gate a few minutes behind Kedda, one at a time. Enelle and I went through last. Pirro and Esak stayed behind on Erebor.

We came out into a large room with blue-glow walls. Something yanked my attention elsewhere, not something I saw but sensed. "How far away are we from the artifact?" I asked Kedda.

"Several levels below the surface. You sense it?"

"Ohhh yeah." All the others—the briquette, Enelle's necklace, Kart's artifact—I'd had to concentrate on to be aware of them. This one pulsed red in my brain all by itself.

Once my eyes adjusted to the dim light, the pulse faded but didn't go away. The room resembled the Gate room back on Ranor, circular and bare except for the lone Gate in the center. According to our plan, we'd travel to the surface in two groups. If something went wrong, Kedda could contact me, and Enelle and I could escape.

Group one consisted of Kedda, Jake, Trax, and Jen-Varth. After Enelle and I joined them, Trax would render everyone invisible. Kedda made it clear that except for minor Magick from Trax, no one was to use any powers or telepathy until the last moment. Otherwise, Vraasz would detect us.

"Why is there only one Gate here?" I asked Kedda.

"Nyallos was a terminal world established in the latter days of Yorben expansion. We must be careful. Vraasz possesses your ability to detect the combination of two or more of the powers in conjunction," Kedda said.

"Won't he detect Trax's staff?" I asked.

"The Tri-Lith is much stronger and will mask the staff. You will steal the Tri-Lith."

"Why me? Thievery is Trax's specialty."

"I trained you in covert operations," Jake reminded me.

"Wouldn't it be more polite to walk right up and ask if we can borrow it?"

"Trax will make you invisible," Kedda said.

"Invisible or not, when the bad guy sees his toy floating away—"

"We will distract him, and you will create a replica to replace the one you are taking," Kedda said.

"Who's going to teach me how to do that?"

"You are Bahrat. When you touch the Tri-Lith, you will be able to create whatever you imagine."

"I imagine body-splatting pain when the evil dude makes the molecules of my body fly apart."

"What happened to your resolve to save the universe?" Jake asked me.

"It vanished when Kedda demoted me from superhero to thief and copy machine."

"You will need to prepare yourself for contacting the artifact," Kedda warned me.

"You mean, for my mind to explode out the top of my head and my personality to split into several parts. I'd rather be electroshocked."

Jake arched his eyebrows at me, then told Kedda, "It's too dangerous. I want alternatives."

"Glad you agree that my impressionable young mind would be a terrible thing to waste," I mumbled.

Trax offered, "With Magick I can create the duplicate, as an illusion, and make the original invisible. Scott can remain at a safe distance, and I will bring it to him."

"There will be no time," Kedda said. "Vraasz will sense his source of power being withdrawn. Scott must retrieve the artifact and use his power at once to kill Vraasz."

"No killing," Jake said.

"To let him live will endanger the future."

I wondered, "If the Tri-Lith gives me so much power, why can't I imprison him and let Arion deal with him later?"

"Vraasz is more dangerous than you believe."

"But," I said, "he won't have the artifact. If I can do all

you say I can, we'll take his Psi-stone, strand him, hustle ourselves back through the Gate—"

"And destroy it from the other side," Jake added.

"Yeah. Then we phone Arion to come get us."

"I am willing to try your plan. We have Enelle if Scott is disabled," Kedda said.

I put up my hand. "Oh, no. She stays down here where it's safe. If I'm disabled, as you euphemistically put it, we'll be so well fucked and far from home that it won't matter."

Jake made Trax test the invisibility spell on me. It would have been cool if it had worked. I noted Trax's surprise as he tried again. No luck. Then I remembered my medallion and pulled it out. "I think this absorbed your spell." Probably the only thing that was working right. I kept my serious misgivings to myself.

Despite Kedda's objections, we agreed that I would follow them in fifteen minutes—just me. When I asked how I'd find my way, Kedda took out a bag of stones that he'd gathered on Erebor and had Trax enspell them to glow. He'd use them to mark the way. I tried to smile as they left.

"Don't worry about me," I reassured Enelle. If I get into trouble, I'll send a mind-gram and you can come running. Okay?"

"Do you regret our joining? I know that you have a woman back on your world. You think you've betrayed her."

"How do you know that?"

"When you are in my mind, I am also in yours."

What other secrets did she see? I felt myself blushing and hoped that the blue light masked it, or that my being eight inches taller put my face far enough away from hers.

My Mom read romance novels. Once, during a moment

of boredom, I read one and afterward proclaimed it an unrealistic fantasy. But here I was, trapped in the throes of its predictable plot: Hunk and woman hate each other at first sight. They weave through a sappy plot, which, despite the mistaken ideas that love covers a multitude of sins and time heals all wounds, proves that it's the sex drive that surmounts the insurmountable. The contentious couple overcome their differences long enough to surmount each other in a steamy bedroom scene where the hunk, who has abstained from sex longer than is humanly possible, becomes a superhuman gentleman holding back until the woman gets her pleasure before he lets loose. (Premature ejaculation doesn't exist in romance novels.) Finally, several bedroom climaxes later, the stubborn pair realize that fate has brought them together, and the fairy tale ends.

"Time for me to head out," I suggested.

She pulled me toward her and was about to kiss me when Esak bounded through the Gate and ran past us. Next, Pirro charged through fully clothed, with his weapon holster across his chest and stun gun in hand, shouting, "Come back here, you little fuck fault!"

I clotheslined Pirro across the chest. He fell backward onto the floor and exhaled sharply. I glared down. "We told you to stay. Pets mind better. Esak, tell me what happened."

Panting he said, "He tried to take back his-ss pants-ss."

From the floor Pirro said, "They're not his!"

"They are now."

"He told me Jen-Varth was-ss never coming back for us-ss. He hated us-ss. That's-ss why he left us-ss there."

Pirro sat up and snorted. "He baby-cried."

Esak pointed at Pirro's gun. "He ss-stung me."

Pirro got to his feet. "I was protecting him. His howling

would've summoned attack animals."

"He kept ss-stinging me and wouldn't ss-stop."

I backhanded Pirro across the cheek and stared into his eyes. He jerked away and covered his groin.

A deep rumbling began inside me. Seconds later a sonic boom blasted through my head. Enelle choked on her scream. Another blast ripped through me and shook the building. My legs collapsed. Pirro fell to his knees. A familiar nausea made everything go in and out of focus. I leaned over, pressed my hands against the floor, and locked my elbows, taking deep breaths to keep from throwing up.

After a third explosion knocked me over, a thought-voice more powerful than the dragons' filled my head, *"WHAT FOOLISH CREATURE DESIRES TO SACRIFICE HIM-SELF TO ME?"*

A weaker voice answered, *"I am brother to Morthen. I come to offer you my allegiance and my service."*

* * *

Jake wasn't sure about the why of what had just happened, but he knew that something had given away their presence. He looked at Kedda.

"Our plan can still be used," Kedda replied. "I will handle this unexpected development."

They'd reached the surface and were standing inside the building looking out through a semicircle-atop-a-trapezoid portal at this planet's bizarre landscape. The air was heavy, the temperature uncomfortably warm. Mist hovered thickly near the ground but thinned and vanished a few dozen feet above it. The landscape appeared as if someone had dumped gallons of deeply hued paint upon it. Two nearly full moons, one above the other, hung just above the horizon in an indigo sky. He couldn't see the sun. The long shadows streaking the landscape put it behind them, and he wasn't sure if it was rising or setting. The ground mist suggested the former, the oppressive heat suggested that the sun had spent all day baking the air.

On their left, rounded hills streaked with burgundy and olive contrasted against the rich, black soil. To the right, the land was lower and the immediate area nearly devoid of vegetation. Tall, dark green grass bordered it. Beyond that he saw shrubs, brilliant wildflowers, and trees covered with cocoa-colored bark, the over-saturated colors on this last world in their journey antithetical to the anemic ones of the first. Jake suspected that the landscape might be volcanic in origin.

Not more than two hundred feet in front of them he saw the remains of what resembled an amphitheater. Around it he saw large holes carved out of the ground. They looked fresh. Some hills on the left had missing pieces. Several trees were split and burnt.

Jake felt the first explosion and saw Trax collapse. Two more explosions followed. Even before they heard the mental voice, Kedda had been shaking. This was the first time that Jake had seen anything affect Kedda. It scared him.

36

THE FAULT IS NOT IN OUR STARS, BUT IN THE PLANETS WE WERE BORN ON

Day Seven: Final Destination, Planet Nyallos

I smelled Pirro above me and opened my eyes. I reached my hand up and clenched it around his throat.

"Your woman is fine," quickly rolled out of his mouth.

A few feet away I saw Enelle taking quick breaths. I squeezed Pirro's neck. "She's not my woman, and this was *your* fault." I wasn't sure it was, but he needed a good scare. "You forced us to take you out of the hole you'd dug yourself into and saw this as your chance to romp and play in the sun again."

I squeezed harder, released him, then pushed myself up and let my anger build. "We told you to stay behind. You've *screwed* us! You just alerted our enemy to our presence. While we sit here alive, Jake and the others could already be dead. You'd better hope they're *not*. Because there's *no* place in this universe where you'll be able to hide from me if that's the case." I put my hand on the back of his neck and pulled him toward me. "Give me the gun."

He clamped his weapon against his chest holster. His wet-dog odor rose to choking proportions. I pried his hand loose, extracted the gun from its holster, and planted the business end above his navel. "Is this the same setting you used on Esak?" He started to nod. I fired; he choked. I got up and handed the gun to Esak. "You're in charge of Pirro. If he gives you any problems or insults you again, shoot him."

"He wants-ss his-ss pants-ss."

"They're yours now." I evil-eyed Pirro. "If he tries to take them again, shoot him in the nuts at least three times." I sniffed at Pirro. "Turn off your smell glands or I'll shoot you myself right now!" I glanced at my watch and told Enelle, "I have to leave. If anything happens, go back through the Gate."

"I'm going with you."

Her eyes told me that she'd follow me anyway. It'd be safer for all of us to go. I didn't trust Pirro to be alone with Esak even with the stun gun in Esak's possession. I tried not to think of what awaited us above.

The trail of glowing stones led us past an elevator. I wondered why they hadn't used it until I saw the access card slot. Kedda had a card, but I didn't. The trail stopped at an upward spiral of stone stairs. This entire structure was made of dark gray stone, too smooth and polished to be natural. There were no joints anywhere, not even on the stairs, as if the place had been carved from one huge block of material.

At the top of the stairs, we found everyone still alive. Jake signaled us to be quiet. He gave a knowing look to Enelle, then whispered, "What's *he* doing here?" Meaning Pirro.

"The bad boy chased Esak through the Gate. Where's Kedda?"

"He said something had alerted Vraasz and went to meet with him."

"Yeah, Pirro's fault," I said. "What's Kedda hope to accomplish except his own death?"

"He said he'd be okay."

"But Vraasz must know we're here. I heard his voice in my head."

"We all heard it. Kedda said that Vraasz knows only about him right now and that we should still carry out the plan."

Trax set the staff aside to avoid drawing on its power, which Vraasz might sense, and made Jake invisible so Jake could go outside and look around safely. As Jake left, I noted the amphitheater ruins outside across from us. I'd seen this in my dream several days ago. Had I somehow tapped into this whole scene, or had Arion or the dragons transmitted it to catch my attention? I hoped it was the latter because my future plans—assuming I got past this—didn't include putting "Psychic" on my business cards.

Pushing those unpleasant thoughts aside, I approached the doorway. The air inside was relatively cool, compared to the heat and humidity outside. Lingering wisps of mist curled along the ground. An odd combination of smells struck me: new-house basement, moist autumn leaves, onions. As hot as it felt, I knew that once I got outside, the heat would dissipate the last of my deodorizing fragrance. Invisible or not, Vraasz would smell me.

Little of this made sense. We'd spent seven days wandering in and out of danger and dicey situations just to sneak up and take the artifact? Why us? With Arion's powers, why not hire a competent thief and beam him down to snatch the goods then beam him back up? Given what touching the briquette and Trax's staff felt like, I sure as hell didn't want to touch that artifact.

A few minutes later Jake's disembodied voice startled me.

"Our target is standing on an overlook above us, two stories up. A long stairway on the left as you face him will take you there." Trax re-materialized Jake. "I saw Kedda with him," Jake said.

"Kedda's alive?" I said.

"For now. I didn't hear any heated words, but there's a lot of recent destruction out there."

Trax brought out two of his explosive spheres, did something to activate them, and gave one each to Jake and Jen-Varth. "The further you throw it, the better for you." After Trax did his invisibility spell on them, and they agreed to move slowly to avoid disturbing the mist and attracting attention, they went out to hide on opposite sides of the amphitheater. The ground was hard enough so they wouldn't leave footprints.

I took the gun from Esak, gave it to Pirro, and quietly warned him, "You're a Protector, trained to act in a mature and professional manner. I'm trusting you to protect Enelle and Esak. Kedda is out there and in danger because of you. Right now, he's all that's preventing the bad guy from detecting us. If Kedda dies before we finish what we came to do, Bad Dude will know we're here and won't hesitate to dispose of us. Remember what those earthquakes were like, stay inside, and don't count on sex to be a part of your afterlife."

"When we are invisible, my Magick will let me see you," Trax said to me.

"Is there any way I can see *you*?" I asked. He shook his head no and cast the spell.

Rivulets of sweat trickled down my sides as I stepped outside. The heat made me remember my dream again and how Vraasz had vaporized his former partner. I reached into my pocket to make sure I had Kedda's ring. When my fingers contacted it, the head-voices began and didn't stop even after I let go of it.

"*I offer you a trade.*"

"*What could you offer me to spare your life? That you are Yorben gives me reason to destroy you. Your people did not share their discoveries with those who could make better use of them. After I dispose of the Elves, I will turn my attention to your race.*"

Strangely, in my head, I could tell their voices apart.

"*Several days ago, I was with the Elf. He believes that I am on his side. You and I had brief contact until the Elf severed it.*" Kedda paused.

I thought it was me, not Kedda, that he contacted outside Arion's keep.

Kedda continued. "*My people would destroy our artifacts and waste their power. I came to help you find and use them.*"

"*Why do I require more?*" Vraasz countered. "*I have the most powerful one.*"

"*Each one not under your control allows an opportunity for rebellion against you.*"

I stopped next to the bottom of the stairs, made of the same black stone as the underground corridors, and remarkably well preserved. Looking up, I saw Vraasz, diagonally opposite where I stood, in what I assumed were the spectator seats of this amphitheater. Even with his back to me, he was far more intimidating in person than in my dream. He was half again Kedda's height.

The steps were short enough that my long legs had no trouble taking them two at a time, barely panting as I did. The thick air on this world invigorated me.

Vraasz stretched his massive arms in front of him. In the

distance two hills exploded into dust. Fuck! He wasn't even touching the artifact!

"*Are you convinced that no one can oppose me?*" Then Vraasz levitated Kedda until he was a hundred feet or more above him. "*You offer me nothing that I do not have. The knowledge you have could prove troublesome to me. I should kill you now.*"

"*I can deliver the Elf who imprisoned Orfo,*" Kedda said calmly, speaking down at Vraasz while floating in the air.

"*I do not require you for that.*"

"*But others of greater power control the Elf. I can sacrifice them to you.*"

What the hell? Kedda was referring to the dragons. Given his recent behavior, I wasn't sure whose side he was on now.

"*For the moment, you have my attention, Yorben. Though your life has no importance to me, if you have told the truth, I may let you keep it.*"

Kedda sank back to the ground. By the time he touched down, I was at the top of the stairs and fifty or sixty feet away from them, invisibly standing at one end of two long blocks of stone that I thought might be balcony seats. It was a nice view of the amphitheater. What kind of entertainment had the Yorben enjoyed here?

Vraasz stood at the far end of the front bench, which held the Tri-Lith, satin black and innocent, within his reach. Even from here it made my body tingle and my heart race. He placed his right hand on top of it and extended his left at the smaller of the two moons floating in the sky. Power rumbled inside me. The rumbling stopped and nothing happened for several seconds.

Then a chunk of the moon blew away!

Vraasz swept his arm along the landscape. As he did so,

the land rumbled. Trees uprooted, and a wall of dust arose in the distance.

Oh, shit. I could see my hands—I was visible! And as soon as Vraasz turned around, I was toast.

Something pushed me hard and knocked me to the ground behind the second row of benches. I became invisible again. Trax whispered in my ear, "I can distract him while you get the artifact."

There was no way I could get to it. I shook my head, knowing—hoping—he could see me. Even if I could grab it, I'd only have a few seconds to figure out how to tap into its power, because Vraasz didn't need it to blow me apart. I turned my eyes skyward and wondered, *If I miraculously succeed in this, will they put an ugly statue of me in the Galactic Hall of Fame?*

Vraasz's thoughts boomed again in my brain, "*When the sun sets here again, I will begin my conquest.*"

Kedda pointed down to where Jake was hiding. "*Others came with me. They hide below and believe I'm on their side against you. Show them your power.*" Half of what remained of the already crumbling amphitheater blew up. *Jake? Jen-Varth?*

I crawled forward, to the end of the front row of benches, for a better look. I didn't see any bodies, but there was a lot of dust. Vraasz stretched out his hand again. I saw Jake float up over the ruins and above the clear area between the amphitheater and us. Vraasz let him drop. He was only ten feet above the ground, and Jake managed a tuck and roll, but the fall clearly dazed him.

Pirro ran out, his stun gun pointed at Jake, and shouted up at Vraasz, "I'm not with them. They slaved me and forced me to come!"

And Pirro *shot* Jake. Jake's body twitched once then went limp.

Pirro fell to his knees, bowing onto the ground without looking up at Vraasz, "Please, spare my life!"

Vraasz turned to Kedda. "*I admire betrayal. It has saved your life. Do you wish to keep him as your slave?*"

Kedda nodded.

With a gesture that I knew was for show—because his mind did the real work—he yanked Pirro up, through the air, and dropped him beside Kedda. Pirro was still clutching his weapon. That flew out of Pirro's hand and exploded several feet above him.

Making sure I was still invisible, I scrunched down. What was I supposed to do now? We'd been betrayed, and we had no weapons of any use against him.

"Stand up," Trax whispered. He put his arm around me, pulling himself close, and made us visible. "We'll stop you!" he shouted to Vraasz. "Take the staff," he told me, "and don't release it no matter what happens."

I hesitated but complied. No jolt when I touched it.

"*Should either of these humans concern me?*" Vraasz asked Kedda.

Kedda shook his head. "*They are weakling Mages.*"

Vraasz fired an energy bolt at us. It sparked around us and dissipated. Vraasz blasted us again. No effect at all, not on us anyway. It did, however, kick up dust around us.

The staff had held out against Morthen and Adana, but they were car batteries. Vraasz was a nuclear reactor.

He looked at Kedda, "*You have lied to me.*" He flicked his hand at Kedda as if to cast him away, but . . . Kedda . . . didn't . . . move?

Surprise registered on Vraasz's face, such as it was. I

saw him focus his power at Kedda. A moment later, Kedda wasn't there. This was a Magick world, and Kedda wasn't Magick. Where the fuck had Kedda gotten the power to do that? Had he tapped into the Tri-Lith?

Meanwhile, the staff felt more comfortable in my grasp than ever before. "Does this thing have any offensive weapons in it?" I asked Trax.

"If it does, I don't know how to use them."

A beam of light hit Vraasz from down below—from Jen-Varth. Oddly, it noticeably fazed him, but he shook it off and sent his destructo-beam down. I glimpsed Jen-Varth running as a small crater formed in the ground behind him. This was all well and good, but we'd lose this laughable battle soon unless some miracle presented itself. We were no match for Vraasz. If he could damage a moon from that far away, he could blow up half this planet from under us while he lightholed himself away. And where the hell was Kedda?

"To defeat him, you must destroy his mind," popped into my head. *"Kedda?"*

Vraasz turned his head.

Who had Kedda said that to?

He pummeled Trax and me again. His energy didn't break through the staff's shield, but it shook us. How long could it hold out against this?

Wait a minute—the safety. If the staff couldn't protect us, it would transport us back to Kedda's homeworld. All was lost if that happened. I knew I'd have to relinquish it to get close to Vraasz.

That's when my eye caught the bird flying behind him in the distance. Enelle? No! He'd kill her. I sent a thought at her.

"Scott, like we did with Morthen," she answered.

441

Vraasz heard and turned his head again, but apparently he didn't see her. Looking back at us, he sent forth another blast. The shield created by the staff was now glowing with many colors. I felt intense heat being generated around us. If he couldn't penetrate it, he'd roast us alive, and it was getting *very* hot. I was sure that at any second the staff would lighthole us out of here, but I sent out a fervent prayer anyway—in case someone was listening. Something inside me hoped this might be a dream after all.

On the end of the bench, the Tri-Lith beckoned. Could I reach it? My timing would have to be perfect. I whispered in Trax's ear, "That bird is Enelle."

He nodded his understanding.

Grinning, I started to move us closer to Vraasz. Ten feet away should be enough, I figured. He continued bombarding us, firing energy blasts instead of a continuous beam. Some he fired behind us, destroying the benches and collapsing part of the balcony. Another hit our shield and increased the temperature. My hands were turning red, and a plan was turning in my head.

Perfect timing. Jake had drilled that into me during his martial arts training. Frankly, my timing still sucked, as evidenced by the welts he left on my body every time.

"Take the staff," I told Trax.

"You won't have any defense."

"Take it! Now!"

The moment he did, I said to Vraasz, "Eat *this*, asshole!" I leaped at the Tri-Lith, belly-sliding along the stone bench toward it. At the same moment, I sent my mind into his.

My hands locked around the Tri-Lith. Serious pain exploded in my head. The mind link with Vraasz severed, and my body felt like it was being turned inside out.

Suddenly, I was yanked up into the air, somersaulted multiple times, and out beyond the wall. Hanging there, beyond the balcony, gasping, eyes watering, power sparking inside me, I saw Jake's crumpled body two stories below me. I thought I was going to vomit.

I raised my head. Through fluttering eyes, I saw a pissed-off Vraasz. Then, he was in my head. "*Give me the artifact!*" My hands strained against the pull. The bones in my fingers were ready to break. Surges of hot and cold accompanied the agony.

Vraasz released me. I shut my eyes as hot air rushed past my ears. Then, I felt myself slowing down. I landed less hard than I expected. I was conscious. I could move.

The voice in my head said, "*Kill him.*"

Kill? How could I kill him?

Another voice said, "*Scott, now.*"

Enelle? I sent my mind out to her. "*No! He'll kill you!*"

"*He'll kill all of us.*" For a moment, my mind was inside hers. I saw Vraasz from behind and approaching fast. She was dive-bombing him. He turned, looked at her.

Blinding light exploded behind my eyes. She screamed inside my head.

I felt her die.

My mind flipped back into my body and there followed: Cacophony. Sounds impossible to isolate or identify. A lifeless body falling to the ground.

My hands clenched around what was in them.

Memories—

The prickliness of cut-off circulation returning, the raw dryness of winter air in my nose, the freezing hot of a young boy's frostbitten hands, a head banged hard into a low beam, violent retching, explosive headaches, the shooting pain of an arm breaking, fire burning inside me.

Nightmarish tortures became reality: knives and needles, fingers broken, hot irons deftly placed on the skin, agonies that make you beg to die.

Consciousness waning, I prayed for it to end.

"*THE END OF THIS IS DEATH.*"

Through the racking maelstrom came, "*Form his image. Focus it, and sharpen it. Then destroy it.*" This time, I obeyed.

Vraasz's image appeared against a cinematographic blue-screen, discrete and whole. Slowly, it divided into pixels. The pixels tenuously held in place for two heartbeats before silently flying apart.

I imagined a scream.

The blank blue-screen dissolved back to reality.

My right cheek lay against the ground. Normalcy and sight returned to me. I saw my hands clutching the Tri-Lith. I relaxed my fingers and watched it tumble away.

Unbidden tears from my eyes fell onto the dry earth beneath my head. The hollowness inside me made no sense. It wasn't that I'd lost my virginity to her—virginity was overrated—but back in Morthen's castle, she'd said, "I knew you were the right man when we first linked our minds." Why did it hurt so much? Why did I feel like part of me died with her? I'd known her for a few days—I didn't even like her when we met. I'd never had someone grow so important so quickly. Would I feel the same way if it had been Jen-Varth? Or Jake? Jake, maybe, but what was so different about her?

From somewhere a feather floated down. It grazed my cheek and landed in front of my face.

"You little asshole! You *shot* me!" Jake's voice, nearby.

444

"I saved you! I made him think you were dead."

I tilted my head in their direction. Jake sat on the ground a few yards away, looking down and holding his head. Pirro stood in front of him. "So you wouldn't eunuch me!"

"That might improve your temperament."

Pirro snorted. "I thought you appreciated me."

"I appreciate people who do what they're asked!" Jake winced. ". . . But thank you."

Jake looked in my direction. "Scott?" He started to get up, but he winced again and sat right back down. "Jen-Varth? Where's Jen-Varth? See if Scott's okay."

Jen-Varth knelt beside me. "Scott's fine, Jake."

I closed my eyes and tried not to flinch when his probing hands hit a few tender spots. After I let him satisfy himself about my physical condition and sit me up, I said, "Now, please leave me alone." I buried my head in my hands as he walked away.

Trax's feet appeared in my field of vision. I tried to squeeze away the tears before I looked up at him. "Thanks," I said.

He nodded as he squatted in front of me. "I'm sorry."

I sniffled.

"If I had followed my father's instruction, I could have helped you like you helped me. I could have stopped him. When I return to my world, I will study hard and learn."

I sniffled again; he handed me a cloth from the pocket of his robe.

"Did you see what happened?"

"His power hit her, and she fell to the ground." He pointed up at where it had happened.

Jake came over finally. "Good job, both of you." I wiped my face with Trax's cloth. "Everything okay?"

445

He didn't know about Enelle yet. "Sort of," I said.

"Well, my head's pounding. I'll get everyone together so we can head back to Kedda's world, and hopefully home from there. We're taking Pirro back to Earth with us—the universe and its women will be safer. Did you ever listen to him speak when you weren't wearing your translator? He sounds like a Russian with an Australian accent—or vice versa." Jake massaged his temples. "You sure you're okay? You look worse than I feel. Cheer up. We won."

I shook my head. "Not all of us won."

"What do you mean?"

Amid the sound of flapping, leathery wings, everything around me vanished. I was suspended in emptiness and confronted by Marhesse and Fezeccah. Marhesse's mental voice boomed in my head, *"Would you sacrifice another for her to live?"*

"What?"

"Who would you have let die instead of Enelle?"

"I already killed for you."

"You can change what happened. You can heed the advice that was given you and make the decision that you should have made."

What did he mean? Other words replayed in my mind, Kedda's words from earlier, *To defeat him, you must destroy his mind.* Now they made sense. Kedda had been talking to *me*, not to Vraasz.

Marhesse repeated, *"Who would you have let die instead?"*

"No one . . . Me."

Marhesse snorted. *"You don't have that option. You have a destiny beyond this. The girl is your soulmate."*

"My soulmate?"

"I ask again, which of your teammates should die in her place? Consider Kedda. He was prepared to die because he believed that he caused all this. At the end, he lied to alienate you and to convince Vraasz of his sincerity."

"Why should Kedda die? It wasn't his fault that I didn't listen. Why can't you just restore her life?"

"You make a good argument. Alive, Kedda plays a role in restoring the greatness of the Yorben civilization. Perhaps one of the others? Jen-Varth sees no future purpose for his life, yet there is the boy Esak to be cared for. What if Dayon stays with your group? He sacrifices himself for Trax and does not go on to lead the Elfaeden people to greater achievements. Pirro is linked to many outcomes. In one, he saves Jake and dies himself. In another, he fails to save Jake and both die. In two others, one in which Jake lives and one in which Jake dies, he travels back to your homeworld with you, with different consequences in each case. Trax's fate is not in your hands, however. He is linked to the Staff of Chaos and to the fate of Arion. Only if Vraasz is not stopped do they die."

"What are you talking about? We *did* stop Vraasz."

"In this event line. There are others. Free will and individual choice—everything is tied to everything else. Everything is in balance, good and evil, weal and woe. What if Kedda had not taken the Tri-Lith from his homeworld and hidden it here all those years ago? The events of these past days would not have occurred because Morthen would have delivered the Tri-Lith to Vraasz. Orfo would have been freed years before you were born. Perhaps you and the girl wouldn't have been born at all."

What were the dragons offering? *Deus ex machina,* "god from a machine?" In ancient Greek drama there came a

447

point near the end of the play when everything seemed hopeless. To resolve this, the Greeks mechanically lowered an actor onto the stage—in the role of a god—to straighten everything out. Maybe this was *dragon ex machina* or *deus ex dragon*. Whatever it was called, from what I'd seen, they had that power.

The two dragons looked at each other contemplatively. *"There is one way we can grant all you ask,"* Marhesse said. *"And more."*

"What's that?"

"You will relive it all and find out. You will remember the old events as they unfold. And when they again come full circle, it will be as it should have been—you and Enelle together. But, for now, you will forget."

"Scott?" Jake's voice.

I blinked.

"What happened? You looked like you just zoomed out," Jake said.

"Uh, I felt kinda strange for a moment."

"You mean strang-*er*?"

Jake slowly scanned the area. His head bounced as he looked at each member of the team, a head count I assumed. "Everyone's here, so I guess so. When we get back," Jake said, "I'll call Bryce and tell him all about this. I can tell him who the skeleton was—one of Kedda's ancestors."

I sidled over to Pirro. "Jake and I are taking you back to our world."

He grinned. "I'm sure your females will like me."

"Our world is populated solely by men," I said.

"H-how do you reproduce?"

"A-sexually."

His expression of horror was priceless.

Jake pointed at the ground a few yards away. "Don't forget your backpack."

Weird. I thought I'd left it in Pirro's charge on Erebor. As I picked it up and slipped it over one shoulder, I saw a bird's feather pressed underneath it.

Despite the heat, I shivered and had no idea why.

"Don't forget this," Jake said as he held out the Tri-Lith.

As much as I wanted to leave it behind, I knew we couldn't. "Slip it into my backpack. I don't want to touch it. Ever again."

The tingle of a premonition—a feeling I'd come to dislike—went through me. Something important was about to happen.

EPILOGUE

It was Saturday morning. Scott Madison, suddenly and inexplicably wide awake, lay on his bed sweating profusely and breathing heavily. He was sure that he had been dreaming something unpleasant, but he couldn't recall the dream.

He heard an insistent knocking on the door of his dorm room and a raised, muffled voice. "Madison? You in there?"

"Just a *minute*."

Three loud, deliberate knocks followed.

"Just a minute!"

Scott dragged his prematurely alert body out of bed and grabbed his favorite pair of tattered jeans, carelessly thrown across the chair last night after he came back from the late movie on campus celebrating the end of finals. "I'm coming." He struggled to put the jeans on over his sweat-dampened feet and buttoned the fly while he shuffled to the door. "Who is it?"

"Matt Graydon."

He unlocked the dead bolt and cracked the door.

"You have a visitor."

The dorm hall was semi-dark. He saw Matt walking away. A hand extended and planted itself onto the middle of the door, pushed it halfway open then lowered to shake his.

"I'm Jake Kesten. Your father told me you were looking for a job. I put an ad on the dorm bulletin board—which you ignored."

"I thought it was a prank. Besides, I'm not interested. I'm going to grad school next year."

"That's what you think."

Something familiar clicked in Scott's mind.

"You want a job." He clearly made that a statement. "Have a seat and let's get this interview over with."

Scott became conscious of being shirtless, barefooted, and disheveled before a stranger who had just invited himself into his room. While Scott grabbed his shirt and put it on, unbuttoned, the man grabbed a chair, turned it the wrong way around, and straddled it backward.

"I'm sorry, what's your name again?" Scott asked.

"Jake Kesten." He pulled a tattered spiral notebook from his front shirt pocket, flipped it open, set it on his left thigh, and stretched his arms over the chair's back.

Scott felt more alert. Words popped into his mind, *"You will relive it all and find out. You will remember the old events as they unfold."* And the voice was gone. Scott found himself, mouth agape, staring at this Jake Kesten.

"You all right? You look like you just zoomed out. You remind me of my younger brother, Alex. He's two years older than you. He spaces out like that. He graduated from Penn State and now works for the Army Corps of Engineers. You'll have to meet him sometime."

THE CARDINAL'S HEIR

JAKI DEMAREST

Cardinal Richelieu is dead, a victim of poison. His heir, niece Francoise Marguerite de Palis, arguably the most gifted Sorciere in France, takes over his powerful spy ring, The Cardinals Eyes, and sets out to find her uncle's killer.

Historical Fantasy
ISBN# 1-932815-10-4

WINTERTIDE
LINNEA SINCLAIR

For centuries the Infernal War has been waged by witches and sorcerers to control the Orb of Knowledge.

After tragedy strikes her family, Khamsin must set out on a journey, accompanied only by the enigmatic Tinker, a journey that magick omens have directed her to take.

One of them knows the truth. One of them is seeking, just as she is sought. The war for the Orb is about to end. But only love can win it.

Fantasy
ISBN# 1-932815-07-4